ORDER
OF
SWANS

JUDE DEVERAUX

ORDER OF SWANS

/||MIRA

ISBN-13: 978-0-7783-6842-7

Order of Swans

Copyright © 2025 by Deveraux, Inc.

For questions and comments about the quality of this book, please contact us at
CustomerService@Harlequin.com.

TM is a trademark of Harlequin Enterprises ULC.

Mira
22 Adelaide St. West, 41st Floor
Toronto, Ontario M5H 4E3, Canada
MIRABooks.com

Printed in U.S.A.

THE BEGINNING

PROLOGUE

Twenty-six years ago

Jobi was on the ship, going through space, and headed toward home. But before he got into the pod to sleep for the long journey, he wanted matters settled with Graceen. She was sleeping on the bed behind him, and it would be quite some time before she woke up. On the far side of the room was a shelf with small things she'd collected during her year on Earth. Beside a dried sunflower was a pretty rock that Jeff had given her. Jobi smiled at what he'd heard called a "spark plug." Common on Earth but strange on Bellis, their home planet. Half a dozen photos were in pretty frames. In one, Jeff and Graceen were sitting on the grass and laughing. Graceen's belly was already big, but then, Earth people did produce extraordinarily large babies.

He picked up a photo of all of them. Graceen, Jeff and his parents, who'd been so welcoming. At the end was Jobi. They'd taken him into their family and shared their lives with him.

Behind him, Graceen made a sound like a groan. He put the picture down and turned to her. *Please don't wake up*, he silently pleaded. When she did wake, he was going to have to tell her what he'd done.

What was that Earth saying? *For the greater good.* He had foreseen that what he'd done was the only way. Would she believe him? Maybe so, but she'd still hate him. She was here, starting the long trip back to Bellis, while her husband and child were left behind on Earth.

He thought back to Graceen's pregnancy. Every day, he'd talked to the child she carried, explaining what was to be done. He told her unborn daughter who she was, where she was from and what he'd foreseen that she was to do—not that he knew the details. He didn't know if any of his knowledge reached the unborn infant.

Jobi was glad he'd been able to foresee the exact time of the birth. It was earlier than the Earth doctor predicted. He invited Graceen to go on a walk in a forest with him, and he did his best to quiet his nerves. He'd certainly never before delivered a child! His insight made him believe it would be all right, but he wasn't *sure*.

To his great relief, as he'd hoped, the birth went well. A grassy meadow, a breeze in the trees in pretty rural Kansas, and the child popped out into his waiting hands.

She was an active baby, moving and fussing—until Jobi started telling her a story. Like the Recorder her mother was, she grew quiet and listened. Her eyes were brown like her father's. *How different from Bellis*, Jobi thought.

Graceen raised her arms to hold her daughter and he handed her over. They didn't leave until the sunlight began to fade. He knew the Earth protocol so he took them to a hospital. Papers were filled out and examinations of mother and child were performed.

When Jeff and his parents showed up at the hospital, Jobi stepped aside.

He gave them three days together.

Jeff and Graceen named the baby Kaley, not a Bellisan name, but that wouldn't matter. On the second day, Jobi embedded the chip into Kaley's left forearm. It left a tiny mark and he hoped Jeff wouldn't notice. Graceen would see it and know what it was. The chip would allow Jobi to keep track of the child. It would let him know when she was ready for what she was meant to do. That is, *if* she responded to her birthright and to all that Jobi had tried to teach her.

By the time they had to leave, Jobi had almost given up hope that his teaching had reached the child. He'd seen nothing about her that wasn't like every other earthling. But when he entered their house on that last day, he heard little Kaley crying. Jeff was holding her, looking frustrated and helpless. "She's been fed and changed. I don't know what else to do."

To Jobi's great joy, he could "hear" her, feel what her problem was. "She misses the dog," he said. Jeff opened the door, the dog entered and instantly, Kaley stopped crying.

Jobi was so pleased that he turned away to hide his smile. One of the things he'd tried to instill in the unborn baby was a connection with animals. He wasn't clear how it would be needed in the future, but it would be. He was relieved that he'd succeeded in reaching her mind.

It was an hour later that he did what he had to do.

He put the drops in a cup of water, lifted Graceen from the bed and she drank it. When it was done, he left the house, leaving her husband to find her. Jobi didn't want to hear Jeff's cries of anguish when he found his wife unresponsive, and seemingly dead.

When it was over, Jobi returned to take care of it all, meaning that he'd taken Graceen away and lied about what had happened. He'd encouraged Jeff to stay on his parents' farm and run his auto shop. He strongly suggested homeschooling for the child, as he knew she would be "different." Jeff nodded, but Jobi wasn't sure if he'd heard him or not.

It had worked out as he'd envisioned, and now Graceen, still sleeping, was on the ship headed toward home, while her grieving family was on Earth. Jobi had told Jeff that Graceen's rich, powerful relatives—whom he'd never met—had taken her body home. In a way, it was true.

On the ship, Jobi lied even harder. He told the officers that the Earth child had died. Long ago, there'd been repercussions for leaving behind half-lights, as the children of Bellisans and earthlings were called. Sometimes they had unusual abilities. In the far past, those children had not been treated well. Superstition had caused great turmoil. But now unusual children stirred the interest of earthlings. They started asking why and how. Whatever abilities Kaley had, he didn't want them to make people dig deeper to find out more. It was imperative that earthlings didn't find out too much as it could cause great distress. Jobi hoped that the chip in her arm would allow him to keep oddities about her under control.

As he lied to the officers on the ship, Jobi had to quieten the pounding of his heart. If anyone knew the truth, that the danger from this child was not to earthlings but to his world, they would destroy the child.

Again, Graceen made a sound. She was waking up—and Jobi was going to have to tell her that her family had been taken from her. She'd believed that she was going to be allowed to stay with them on Earth.

Jobi let his breath out slowly. He'd foreseen that something was going to happen on Earth in their future. His vision didn't clearly show what it was, but he knew that it would allow him to spend time alone with Kaley. That was when he'd return to Earth. She'd be a young woman by then and he'd need to start training her.

For a moment, he looked skyward. How could he train her for a task, yet tell her nothing about it? How would he get her to agree to leave her family, her home and her planet without telling her why? Suddenly, the twenty-plus years he would have to find answers seemed very short.

When Graceen opened her eyes, Jobi went to her. After he told her the truth, they would go to their pods where they would lie down and be attached to wires. Their brains and bodies would be fed, exercised and healed of any medical issues during the long time it took to go home. He hoped that the time would mellow what was sure to be her hatred directed at him.

1

January 2021
Fort Lauderdale, Florida

With her eyes still red from crying, Kaley looked like she'd lost
all hope in life.

Jobi was at the little granite-topped island that was identical
to the one in her apartment next door. His brown eyes reflected
her misery. "I'm sure you'll find a way to work this out." His
voice was as rich and dark as his skin color.

For all that Kaley was twenty-six and Jobi in his fifties—he
wouldn't confirm his age—there was no young person versus
old dynamic between them. But then, Kaley had been homeschooled by her grandparents. It was people her own age who
puzzled her. Besides, her family had known Jobi all her life.

He was mixing her a drink. "Your teacher really upset you,
didn't he?"

"If by that you mean he destroyed my life, yes." She fell back
in the chair. Her body seemed to contain no energy. Jobi's apartment had colorful art from around the world, while Kaley's held
inexpensive furniture she'd bought in one store on one visit. If
she ever, finally, at long last, got her PhD, she didn't want to

be burdened with possessions. Every aspect of her life had been in preparation for now—and it had all been taken away by one ego-mad professor. He had left her at a loss of what her future would be.

Jobi handed her the drink.

In her family, Jobi was almost a legend. He'd introduced her parents to each other and had lived with her family for a whole year. He'd even delivered her. Her grandparents loved to tell the story of how Jeff's new wife had gone for a walk with Jobi. "Then they called us from the hospital," her grandfather would say.

Years later, Kaley was in the henhouse gathering eggs when a man appeared in the doorway. She'd seen so many photos of him that she knew who he was. She couldn't help hugging him, then she took him to her dad and her grandparents.

Sometimes Kaley wasn't sure how it happened, but a few weeks later she was with Jobi, taking turns driving a rental truck, and heading toward Florida. Jobi had a job and an apartment waiting for him. The plan had been that she'd help him get settled, then fly back to Kansas. But that didn't happen.

When the world was suddenly shut down and Jobi's job was canceled, he suggested she take the apartment next to his and devote herself to writing her PhD dissertation. Kaley had protested that she couldn't do that. Her family needed her to help with the farm and her dad's car repair shop.

But to her surprise, they agreed with Jobi. "Stay there," her dad said. "You need time to concentrate on your dissertation. If you come back for a Kansas winter and thousands of chores, you'll be overwhelmed."

It was the sunshine and the January warmth of South Florida that sealed the deal. She had money saved from years of summer jobs and she was given a deal on the apartment, so she stayed. Her grandmother shipped all her research books to her.

The first night in her apartment, she and Jobi cooked burgers and he said, "Want me to train you? Get you out of academic shape?"

She'd laughed. Before she went to college, she'd been in good physical condition. Riding horses, milking cows, chasing chickens, working on cars with her dad. She'd always been active.

Leaving the farm to go to college had ruined her. She'd not had much of a social life, but had spent her time studying and researching. Mostly sitting. She'd put on several soft pounds. "That's too much," she told Jobi. "You'll want to..." She waved her hand. They couldn't go out so activity was limited.

"Catch up on my reading? I'll go crazy. There's a splendid gym downstairs. Let me practice on you."

The way he said it made her laugh. "You wouldn't like to help me with my writing, would you?"

"Writing about what?"

"Fairy tales and folklore."

His eyes widened. "They teach that in college?"

"Oh yes. Someday I plan to teach at a university. I'll live in a stone house that's strong enough that no wolf can blow it down, and I'll be very happy."

His eyes widened with every word she spoke. "I have no idea what any of that means. It's too American for me."

She'd been surprised. No one had told her Jobi wasn't from this country. Or had she forgotten? "You're not American?"

"I live on one of the islands of Bellis, and before you ask, no one has heard of us. We don't get visitors because we have no natural resources anybody wants, and no fancy hotels. What we do have are miles of beaches, a couple of mountain ranges and a few lakes with brightly colored frogs. They hop around a lot."

"It sounds heavenly," she said.

"It is."

"But you left."

"I wanted to see the world, and I still do, but..." He was quiet for a moment. "This will be over soon, I'm sure of it, then I'm going home."

The next day, Jobi began to train her. He said he liked to experiment and she was his test subject. He taught her weights, yoga and defense skills. They practiced archery outside near the dog lawn, and often went to a firing range. The pounds came off her and were replaced with muscle.

In return, Kaley told him about folklore and how important it had always been to the world. "Oral stories were used when most people couldn't read." She often read to him, and they agreed that the stories they liked best ended happily.

"Better than ending with people chained in caves or losing the fight with a hungry dragon," Kaley said. She swallowed. "Or burying heads in a flowerpot." They'd laughed in agreement.

Finally, the world opened up and Jobi said he was going home. Forever. When he'd first told her he was leaving, Kaley had been sad, but she'd thought that by the time he did leave, she'd have been awarded her PhD and she'd be on her way to fulfilling her dream.

But this morning, one meeting had changed her entire life.

Jobi gave her an intense look that she'd come to know well. "Tell me again what happened."

Outwardly, she was calmer now, but inside she was screaming, *What do I do now? Where do I go? What will I do? What can I do?*

Right after she left the professor's office, she'd flown home from her alma mater in Indiana. On the flight, she'd not allowed herself to fully comprehend what happened. Besides, if she thought about it, she might start crying. She didn't want strangers asking her what was wrong.

A car service drove her the few miles to her apartment building. As if he'd sensed that something was wrong, Jobi was standing before his open door. Without a word, she went inside, he closed the door—and Kaley let the tears flow. She told him what had happened.

While reassuring her that she'd eventually get her pig-proof stone house, he made her a gin and tonic. Then he asked her to repeat her story.

She gulped half her drink and tried to think more calmly. "As you know, I turned my paper in weeks ago." All through grad school, she'd researched for her dissertation. As she'd read and studied, she drew conclusions and put them together. She knew her field of folklore had been well researched, but there was room for original thought, and she believed she'd had some ideas that were hers alone.

But her professor had not agreed.

He'd tossed her thick paper onto the end of his desk as though it was distasteful. "I've heard it all before." There was no empathy in his voice. "Not one word is new or original or even interesting. Cinderella? Really, Kaley? The bloodiness and cruelty of fairy tales is not new. And why can't you distinguish between fairy tales and folklore?"

"Many of the great folklorists combine the two." She wasn't able to fully understand what he was saying. It was hard to comprehend that her years of work were being dismissed as if they didn't matter.

"Not for a dissertation," he snapped. "Maybe you should try the commercial world."

That insult was like a slap in the face.

"If you insist on fairy tales, then they must be new and fresh," the man said.

"How can they be new?" she'd asked. "Folklore's definition is of age."

He gave her that I-am-the-professor look of disgust, then turned away. It seemed that the loose papers on his desk were more important than her work. "That's for you to figure out." He waved his hand in an autocratic way, letting her know that he was through with her.

She wouldn't allow herself to give up. He didn't like her paper, but maybe the dissertation committee would. "I can defend it," she said. *Defending* was what the presentation she'd do before the doctorate professors was called. In this case, it was well named.

"There is no defense of this." His voice was almost a growl, and he didn't have the courtesy to look at her. "I won't offend them by showing them this tripe."

Kaley had wanted to lash out at him, yell, curse, but she managed to control herself. "I guess I should find some undiscovered country and tell *their* stories." She hoped her sarcasm sounded as venomous as she felt.

But the professor turned to her with a smile. A man notorious for never being pleased about anything was smiling at her?

"*That* is something I'd like to read. Or hear. Be sure to record it all." For a second, he seemed to be imagining a new country and new stories. But then he turned away and Kaley knew she was being discarded. Holding her head as high as she could manage, she left. A few hours later she was home—and Jobi was waiting for her.

After she'd told him the story the second time, she didn't feel any better. Her sense of hopelessness had not left her. "I don't know what to do. I can rewrite my paper, but I have nothing new to say." She grimaced. "I wonder if the people on your islands have any stories that have been passed down through generations."

In the time they'd been living next door to each other, they'd spent many hours together in the gym, but they'd also socialized. They'd shared meals and afternoons at local fairs.

During their time together, she'd asked him a lot about his home. He'd always been reluctant to tell much, but she'd not given up. *Primitive* was the word he used most often. *Isolated* was a close second. She'd learned that his island had no cars, no internet, no cell phones, not even any computers. "And certainly no airports," he said. "We don't even have a dock for ships."

He'd sounded embarrassed, so she replied with humor. "Ships have things called anchors. They can park anywhere."

He'd smiled in thanks. "Beauty," he said with a faraway look. "Pristine, perfect beauty is what we have in abundance."

Of course she did an internet search. There was a Wikipedia entry but it was short. The words *unexplored islands* made Kaley's eyes widen. "Like the Korowai in Guinea and the Vietnamese Ruc," she whispered in awe. "And the Sentinelese of India." Those people killed anyone who got near their island. Those places were proof that even in the twenty-first century there were communities that no one had been able to penetrate.

Kaley asked Jobi many questions, but he was always evasive, almost secretive. That seemed to fit what she'd read about keeping the world away from them.

But now, as she sat there, drink in hand, the professor's words echoed in her mind. He wanted to read about *an undiscovered country*. She'd asked her question as a joke, but it had ignited something inside her. She waited for Jobi to answer.

"I can't imagine that anyone would want to hear our stories."

"I would." Kaley's heart, and maybe her whole life, was in those words.

Jobi gave a small smile. "I'm not sure we're that interesting. Although, King Aramus does like a good story."

"You have a king?" He hadn't mentioned that before.

"Oh yes. He lives on the island of Eren. He used to live in a palace. It was a splendid place with marvelous mountain views. But then, to be fair, people say the Old Royals are the real rulers, so maybe he shouldn't have a palace. Of course, he did step down and now he has a splendid house, but—" Jobi waved his hand. "It was all set up long ago and far away, as they say in your stories."

Kaley's jaw dropped. All her many questions and he'd never hinted at any of this. *Old Royals? A palace? A king who may have been overthrown?* About a thousand fairy tales ran through her mind. "How long ago? How far away?" Kaley's voice was so low it could hardly be heard.

"A hundred years or so, I guess. It was Tomás's father who changed things."

"Tomás? The *king*? You sound like you know him personally."

"His family and mine are related."

Kaley gave him a hard look. "You are related to a *king*, but you never told me that?"

He smiled. "We're not exactly British royalty. Lots of islands have kings, or queens, or—"

"I want to go," she said. "For the summer. That's all."

"But your home is here. You haven't seen your family in over a year."

"We'll survive." She held her breath as she waited for his reply.

When Jobi looked at her, there was no humor in his face. "What if I told you that my country is on another planet and it takes three years of Earth time to get there?"

"I'd say, 'I'll download a lot of books.'"

Jobi didn't smile.

Kaley let out her breath. "Metaphorically, I'm sure Bellis is like being on another planet, but Wikipedia says you're real, so I'll take that."

Jobi said nothing.

Kaley stood up. "Please take me with you."

"You're upset now, and I'm sure that you'll find a better way to spend your summer than with old me."

"I know you want to protect your country and I swear that I won't betray you. I can say I collected the stories from an anonymous source." Her eyes widened. "Please tell me you aren't saying that if I go I'll never be allowed to return."

Jobi shook his head. "You could return at any time you want. We don't imprison intruders or harm them, but then we don't allow many earthlings to visit us."

Kaley smiled. "Yes, I'm an earthling. Tell me, do your people look like you or do they have eyes on antennae? And how do *you* breathe on Earth?"

Jobi reached up and popped out a couple of contact lenses. When he looked up, she saw that his eyes were ocean blue. Beautiful! She knew him well enough to understand why he'd hide the unusual coloring of his blue eyes with his dark skin. He wouldn't like to stand out, to call attention to himself.

"There are three known planets that have the same atmosphere," he said. "That's why we Bellisans can visit Earth."

Kaley started to reply, but his fantasy wasn't her concern now. "What else am I going to do? Go home and raise chickens? Or maybe I should do more coursework at another university, then try to get my doctorate there. That's years of repetitive work. To go where others haven't been is an opportunity I can't pass up."

Jobi gave what appeared to be a look of defeat. "What about your apartment?"

A bit of hope ran through Kaley. "I'll sell my furniture and send my books home." Her eyes were pleading. "One summer. Three months. That's all I ask. You can introduce me to the king, let me hear some stories, then I'll return to write a whole new dissertation."

He was quiet for a moment as he thought about what she was saying. "Are you sure your dad won't mind if you're away for the whole summer?"

Kaley knew she'd won. She hugged him before he could come up with more excuses as to why she couldn't go. She paused at the door. "How much time do I have to get ready?"

"Six days," he said quickly. "We'll take a charter plane down to Key West and board there."

"Board a ship or a plane?" she asked, teasing. When Jobi hesitated in answering, she waved her hand. "How silly of me. It's on a spaceship and it's out of Key West because those people wouldn't blink an eye if an alien craft landed in front of them. Right?"

Jobi's blue eyes were twinkling. "Exactly right."

"I have lots to do." She hurried out of the apartment.

For a moment, Jobi stood still. He was glad to have cheered her up.

Last night, yet again, he'd tried to foresee exactly how Kaley would help his country, but his vision was mostly a blur. He knew that Roal's son, Tanek, was involved but Jobi wasn't sure how. There was a young man with a dragon, which meant the king's obnoxious son. Of course, the Nevers were there. And he saw another man. He was big. Somehow, they would all become involved with Queen Olina—the woman he'd been careful not to mention to Kaley. But then, she'd probably be excited at the idea of an "evil queen."

A wave of guilt ran through him. Kaley hadn't believed him about being from another planet, but at least he'd told her the truth. He chanted, *"For the greater good. For the greater good."* That was what this was all about. It was larger than one or two people. It was his entire country!

When he'd calmed somewhat, he began to smile. He'd achieved what he set out to do. Now he needed to prepare. He had a list of things to take back to Bellis. But then, wasn't that the point of these trips? Borrowing, known on Earth as *stealing*, was what they'd been doing for centuries. And in return, they'd added a lot. One of his main pleasures was watching YouTube videos about things on Earth that no one could explain. Nazca lines. Voynich, a book they'd accidently left behind. The "disappearance" of the Russian Amber Room. Tomás enjoyed that room very much!

Still smiling, he left the apartment. He had three mating pairs of animals to pick up. Earthlings were saying they were going extinct and Jobi needed to save them.

2

Inside her apartment, Kaley leaned against the door. "Worst day of my life," she whispered.

As she remembered the smirk on the professor's face, she allowed herself to imagine returning in triumph. Her new dissertation would be declared as "Groundbreaking new material in the world of folklore." She envisioned the committee giving her an award. Or pinning a badge on her. Her work would be called "The Best of the Best" and she'd be able to choose where she wanted to teach.

She stepped away from the door and shook her head to clear it. She'd read too many fairy tales. The poor tailor might marry a princess and eventually become king, but in the world of academics, there were no awards for doing your homework correctly.

She looked around her bland apartment. She much preferred Jobi's colors and artifacts. Did any of the lovely things he owned come from his home country? As for her meager possessions, she'd talk to the building manager about the furniture and get book boxes out of the big green bin downstairs.

As she went to the kitchen, she smiled at Jobi's joke about being from another planet. "At least I'll be able to breathe without an oxygen mask." She wondered if he was writing a sci-fi novel and she was a character in it.

The first thing she needed to do was to call her family. She hoped they wouldn't be too upset that she wasn't going to be coming home soon. With her best it-doesn't-bother-me attitude, she told her grandparents about the professor rejecting her dissertation. "But it's all right. I have some new plans."

"That sounds lovely," her grandmother said. "A break will do you good."

Her grandfather wasn't so nice. "Give me the bastard's name and I'll introduce him to my shotgun."

"Stop it!" her grandmother said. "She doesn't need to hear that, even though I do agree with you."

Kaley smiled. Was there anything more pleasing than people being on your side?

"So what are you planning to do?" her grandfather asked.

"I'm going with Jobi to see his islands. I'll be gone all summer."

There was a long pause and Kaley thought they were going to protest, but then her grandfather said, "Yes, that's what you need to do."

He sounded so sad that Kaley almost changed her mind about leaving, but then her grandmother said, "What can I send you?"

Her dear, practical grandmother. "Jobi said there are mountains so send me a box of winter clothes. My UGG boots and the Canada Goose down coat you gave me would be nice."

"All the catalogs have cashmere sweaters on sale. I'll order some and have them sent to you."

Her kindness made Kaley almost start crying again. With the lockdown, she hadn't seen them in the past year, but she'd talked to them nearly every day. Surely, there was some sort of phone service on Jobi's islands. She heard a door open and close. "Is that Dad?"

"Hi, K-dell." Her father, Jeff, took the phone.

Hearing his nickname for her made Kaley swallow repeatedly. How would she deal with not hearing from them for three whole months? "I…"

He heard the tremor in her voice. "What happened?"

"Nothing important," Kaley said. "Just…" She trailed off.

In the background, she heard her grandfather say angrily, "That SOB teacher turned down Kaley's paper."

Her dad came back on the phone. "Is that correct?"

"Yes."

"And she's going with Jobi," her grandfather said.

Again, she heard the door open and close, then the sound of birds. Her dad had gone outside.

"So, Jobi wants you to go with him," Jeff said as though it was something final.

"Yes. I can learn some new stories and write a new paper and—"

"When?" Jeff asked quickly. "Where do you meet? How will you get there? I need to know the exact time you're leaving and the place."

"Dad…" He sounded so fierce that she was concerned.

"Sorry," Jeff said. "I know Jobi well. I know he'll take care of you, but I have something I want to send to you. I want to make sure it gets there at the right time and place."

She was hesitant. "He said we're taking a small plane down to Key West, then we'll get on—" She stopped herself from adding Jobi's joke about boarding a spaceship. "Then we'll fly to his country and stay—" It dawned on her that she had no idea about accommodations. Jobi said there were no "fancy" hotels, but what about small ones? "In a palace," she said. "Or the king's house. Jobi is related to the king."

"He never mentioned that." Jeff paused. "Okay, honey, you have my blessing, but I want to know when and where you are to leave. You won't forget to tell me?"

"Of course not."

"Do me a favor and don't tell Jobi I asked. Tell him I think you're a mature young woman who has the wisdom to make her own life decisions."

Kaley gave a loud laugh at that. Her father still thought of her as a child who needed constant protection. "I'll tell him that for sure."

"Call me every day," he said. "And I'll call you, too."

"Dad, it's only for three months. I'll be back in the fall."

For a moment, Jeff was silent, then he spoke in a low voice. "Sure. Just three months. Your grandmother wants to talk to you about colors and what socks she should send. And do you want your red dress? Here, you talk to her."

Kaley was so puzzled over her father's attitude that it took a moment before she could understand what her grandmother was asking about clothes and shoes.

When she got off the phone, Kaley realized she was exhausted. It had been a long, traumatic day. She fell across her bed, fully clothed, and went to sleep. When she woke, it was morning, and her mind was full of all she needed to do.

She texted Jobi.

Are we still on for the trip?

She held her breath as she waited for his reply, hoping he hadn't changed his mind.

Are you packed yet? he replied.

Kaley danced about the room for a few moments, then got busy thinking about what to take. The first item to go in her suitcase was her little photo album. It held a dozen pictures of her family. Her favorite was of her parents holding her. Their heads were together, with Kaley, just a few hours old, in her mother's arms. The happiness on their faces held no premonition that days later, her mother would die. "She just didn't wake up," her father had told her.

Unknown to her family, Kaley had joined every ancestry site there was. She'd sent her DNA sample to all of them. Oddly, on each one, her ancestry had come back partially as "unknown." There had been long, boring explanations about what that meant, but all Kaley cared about was finding a blood relative on her mother's side. There were dozens of cousins from her father, but nothing from her mother.

One of her professors used to work with her grandfather building computers. After an introduction, they became friends and she talked to him about her search for her mother. He said that if no one in her mother's family had sent in their DNA or had never been put in the system for a crime, it wouldn't be there. "Are you sure her family is in the US? Maybe they're from some secret part of Russia that no one has explored," he'd said, teasing.

They laughed together, then he talked about the "old days," meaning the 1970s, when the professor and Kaley's grandfather had worked together on the ground floor of the computer world.

She smiled at the memory and then began to choose clothes and shoes to take with her, and she downloaded as many books as possible onto her iPad.

A big part of the reason she'd accompanied Jobi on the long drive to Florida was so she could bombard him with questions about her mother. He'd been there that one year when her parents had been together.

Unfortunately, Jobi's most frequent answer was "I don't know." Back then, he'd been a destitute young man, fresh out of college, so he'd worked on the farm with her grandparents and washed cars for her dad. "Your parents didn't exactly have time for anyone but each other," he said to Kaley's questions.

"But you delivered me," she said.

"Oh yes. Now *that* was scary!" He said it all happened so fast that he could hardly remember it.

After so many of his nonanswers, she stopped asking him questions about her mother.

Just because they were leaving soon didn't mean that Jobi let up on training. In the gym, Kaley bombarded him with questions about his country's food, religion, transportation, language. She wanted to know everything. She especially wanted to know if there were any animals not known elsewhere in the world.

Jobi smiled. "I've been away for so long that I don't remember any of it." Once again, she got no real answers about anything.

On the day before they left for Key West, he told her that he'd been in contact with some friends at home and it was agreed that the best place for her to get stories would be on the second island, Selkan. "You'll have a guide who'll take you wherever you need to go. And if you don't find enough there, you can go to the third island."

"That's very kind of you." Every word he said made her more sure that she was doing the right thing.

When he told her the time and place of where they were to meet the plane to take them to Key West, she texted her father. He sent a thumbs-up emoji but no other reply.

Finally, the day came and they were to board a little wind-up puddle jumper of a plane. There was a pilot and Jobi and Kaley. No other passengers.

"This must be expensive," she said as she buckled herself in. "I think— Oh!"

"What is it?" Jobi was standing.

"I think I saw Dad. He wouldn't show up, would he? But maybe he wants to say goodbye." She unbuckled her belt. "I'm going to go look."

Jobi leaned over her. "Have you ever seen one of these?" He

was holding a little tube of steel, about the size of a wooden match. One end of it had a blue light.

"I'll look at it when I get back."

Jobi took her left hand, turned her arm, then touched the blue light to the tiny scar on her forearm.

A slight electrical charge went through her. With a dreamy smile, Kaley sat back down. In the next second, she was sound asleep.

"Sir?" the pilot said. "Some man has parked a pickup in front of us. He's blocking our takeoff."

"Of course he's here." Jobi clamped his teeth together as he threw open the plane door. "Starken-el!" he muttered when he looked outside. Jobi had an idea of what Jeff wanted—and he did *not* like it.

The pilot looked shocked at Jobi's foul language. *This must be serious.*

"I'll take care of this." With anger, Jobi went down the stairs to the tarmac.

3

Kaley was sitting on a rock. To be fair, the rock seemed to have been cut off at the top to make it into seating. In front of her were plants. Sort of tropical, sort of like a big-leaf forest. She didn't know which. But then she was so disoriented she might be asleep and dreaming. She felt dizzy and empty-headed. The light seemed to indicate it was late afternoon, but she wasn't sure *who* she was, much less *where* she was, and certainly not *when*.

A man came to stand in front of her. He wore a blue shirt and darker blue trousers. She had no idea who he was—or if he was real.

But then hands reached out to her and she managed a little smile. She'd know those hands anywhere. Jobi. They were the hands that held out dumbbells, strapped her into boxing gloves, readjusted a rifle to her shoulder and showed her how to pull back a bowstring.

In spite of the familiarity, she didn't look up.

"Feeling weak?" He sounded amused.

She gave a tiny nod.

"You slept through the whole flight so it's no wonder you're groggy. Here, let me help you." He took her left hand, turned it over, and as he did before, he put the blue light of the little tube against the scar on her arm.

Kaley felt a bit of an electrical charge, and with it, life seemed to be coming back into her. She blinked rapidly as the fog in her mind began to clear and she could remember more. "What is this thing you keep putting on my arm?" Her voice was hoarse, as though she hadn't used it in a long time.

"Magic," Jobi said. "Straight out of one of your fairy tales."

"I don't remember that being in any of them. Dad said aliens from another planet gave me that scar. We have a running joke about it."

"How clever of him." Jobi didn't sound pleased.

Her head came up. "Dad! I saw him as we were about to take off."

Jobi picked up a box from the ground and handed it to her. On the side in big letters was the word *Kansas*.

"I think you saw the name and thought it was him. It's a gift he had delivered to you."

She started to say that seeing a word on a package and seeing a person were two different things, but she didn't. She took the package Jobi was holding out.

"Mind if I take care of the baggage? Will you be all right here?"

With every second, Kaley was feeling better, but she wasn't ready to get up and go exploring. "I'll be fine."

After Jobi left, she sat still, feeling life come back to her. She had no memories since they got on the plane in Key West. She thought she'd seen her father, but then Jobi put his little light on her arm, and… That was it.

The box from her father was on her lap. Her hands were shaking as she opened it. Inside was a Leica camera, a little point-and-shoot with a retractable lens. She didn't know much about cameras but it didn't look too difficult. Besides, it was very cute. It was easy to slip in a battery and she was glad to see that her father had charged it. In the bottom of the box was a sprig of dried rosemary. She and her father loved the smell and they grew a lot of it around the farm. For a moment, she felt a wave of homesickness, but she recovered. She'd be home soon enough.

She closed the box, then looked around. In front of her was a wide dirt path that curved, with foliage hiding both ends. As a farm girl, she thought how one good rain would turn that path to mud.

With effort, she managed to stand up. She put the camera on the stone and started doing stretches that Jobi had taught her. *How long was that flight?* she wondered. Her body felt odd, as though she'd just recovered from a long illness.

She had her face against her knees when Jobi returned.

"Good girl. Now push that rock down the path."

"Ah. The nonexistent humor of a personal trainer. So how is everything?" She started to go the way he'd come, but he caught her arm.

"The bags will be taken care of." He slipped her arm into his. "Shall we go meet the king?"

"Not like this!" She had on cotton pants, a T-shirt and a denim jacket. "I'll put on a dress."

"And a tiara?"

"Of course. The emerald one should do it."

"Or the diamonds and pearls. Either one."

They laughed together as they walked.

"Really," she said, "I would like a shower. I feel like I have moss growing on my skin. How long were we on that plane?"

"Too long," he said. Before she could ask more, he said, "How about we meet the king tomorrow? Today you can explore and..." He hesitated. "You can meet Tanek."

"That sounds ominous. Is he a Gandalf?"

Jobi knew who she meant as they'd watched *Lord of the Rings* and *The Hobbit* together. "Tanek isn't an old wizard who makes fireworks." He still seemed to be laughing at her. "Tanek is— No. I think I'll let you make your own decisions about him. Now, about the bathing facilities. We have a volcanic pool of perpetually warm water. However, you'll have to share it with the villagers. We pay no attention to nudity here on Bellis."

"Ah. Right," Kaley said hesitantly. "Shaking hands and hugging while starkers? That sounds like fun."

Jobi squeezed her hand. "How about a tub hand-hewn out of stone? Or a hot shower like a waterfall? In privacy, of course."

"I do believe I'd like that better. Not to disparage local habits, but still…"

When they rounded the curve in the path, they saw a house— if it could be called that. It was one story and it extended—or rather rambled—so far along that neither end could be seen. There were turrets and sections that went up high, and long, low causeways with glass walls. Windows were everywhere: tall, short, wide, narrow. Some were made of stained glass depicting a menagerie of animals and especially birds.

The low sunlight glinted off the colors of glass. Highly polished metal on the doors gleamed. The never-ending roof was made of red tiles, but not like any she'd ever seen. These had hints of colors that sparkled.

Kaley's eyes were wide. "Is the old palace bigger than this?"

"Yes. This is barely the guesthouse." Jobi kept her arm in his and they went forward.

She was glad when they didn't enter through the main doors. They looked to be twenty feet tall and made of metal. Plus, there were two big, burly men standing in front of them. The men had on dark gray uniforms with brown vests that sparkled. Kaley nodded toward them. "Armed?"

"Oh yes. And very well trained."

In the next moment, three huge wagons went by. They were pulled by heavy horses, the kind used to advertise beer.

They stood still as the last wagon lumbered by. "That will be our transportation?"

"A smaller version, but yes." He was watching her reaction.

"Seems like fun." Her eyes widened. On the far side of the road was a little girl—and she was wearing a red cape with a hood. "Look at that! Is that normal dress for here?"

"I think it's personal taste." Jobi sounded cautious.

"I feel like I should warn her that her grandmother is actually a wolf."

"I thought you wanted new stories."

The little girl disappeared at the edge of the woods. "It's habit to see fairy tales everywhere," she said.

When Jobi put his hand on a door, it beeped and opened. "You've been given a private entrance to the king's little house."

"It's good to at last get some respect," she said, laughing. As they stepped inside, she halted. The outside had been impressive but the inside was breathtaking. The walls of the room they entered were done in enamel, with brilliant colors and designs. "It looks like ancient Persia."

"Some design ideas may have been borrowed, but I'm not saying who was first or who took from whom."

The next room was mostly marble in soft shades. The furnishings were covered in silk brocade.

Kaley stopped walking. "Jobi, I've seen little of your island but this is magnificent. Why isn't the whole world clamoring to see this?"

"We're private people," he said hastily. "Let's go to your room. We can—" He stopped and seemed to be listening. She hadn't noticed the tiny plug in his ear until that moment. "I have to go. The king calls." They were in a hallway with soft lights and walls a pale ocher color. "Your room is the second one on the right." He pointed to the end of the hall. "But through there you can go outside. I believe Tanek is out there. If you don't meet him now, you might not see him until you leave."

"I take it that's a hint for me to go."

Jobi took a step backward. "Up to you."

"All right. I'll meet him first, then I'll hit the shower. Satisfied?"

"Never, but closer. Follow that path. It leads to a lake and he's there. I'd go with you, but..." Jobi gave a shrug in the direction of the door.

"Royal commands and all that. I'm sure I'll be fine."

Jobi turned and flat out ran down the hall.

"If the king calls, one obeys," she murmured as she went to the hall door. Her room could wait. It was a heavy door, with a window showing the greenery outside. The door opened easily and she went out.

The air smelled good, clean and fresh. There was a path that gently curved around pretty plants, none of which she recognized. She stepped past a bush with pink flowers and saw a man standing at the edge of a body of water. She assumed he was the guide Jobi had spoken of. He was about Jobi's age, with sparse gray hair, and he wore a dark jumpsuit with silver snaps. He didn't appear to be in good physical condition. What if one of those heavy wagons broke down? Could he help repair a wheel?

Kaley covered her concern with a smile and went to him. "Hi. I'm Kaley Arens. You're going to be my guide?"

For a moment he stared at her blankly, then seemed to understand. "I think you're looking for Tanek."

"Yes. Jobi told me he was here."

"He is." The man nodded toward the water. "He's trying to catch those two."

She turned to see two extraordinary birds silently float into view. They were very large swans, twice the size of any she'd ever seen. But even more remarkable was their plumage. Their bodies were covered with iridescent feathers. They were both silver but one had hints of green, while the other had gold that flickered in the light. They were magnificent creatures.

There was no one near them.

Kaley was looking at them in awe. "Does he ride in on them? A foot on each one, reins around their long necks?"

The man looked at her without understanding.

"Sorry," she said. "I've read too many stories of magic. Where is this guy? Should I go back inside and wait for him?"

The man pointed at the swans. "He's there."

The water was glassy calm. She was about to turn away when a tiny ripple appeared just behind the big birds. Slowly, out of the water, a man emerged. His wet hair was very black and hung down almost to his shoulders, emphasizing his trimmed beard and thick, dark eyebrows. His movements stirred the water so little that the swans didn't seem to be aware that he was there.

Kaley watched the man rising in the water. He didn't appear to have on any clothes. Honey-colored skin that covered splendid muscles rose up, higher and higher. Only when the water reached inches below his waist did she see the line of what looked to be some kind of loincloth.

The man lifted his long, muscular arms out of the water and slid them over the bodies of the swans, pulling them close.

Kaley gasped. She knew that swans were notoriously bad-tempered and aggressive. If they attacked, the man could be seriously hurt.

To her surprise, the swans curved their long necks around him and snuggled against him in familiarity and love.

"Devils!" she heard him say. There was so much affection in his tone that she wouldn't have been surprised to hear the swans giggle.

He came toward her, an arm clasped around each swan. As he got closer to shore and the water was more shallow, more of him was exposed. He was truly glorious. Nude except for the loincloth, his legs were heavily muscled. He came out of the water slowly.

He glanced at her with one of those man-appraising-a-woman looks.

Kaley sucked in her stomach and stood up straighter—and silently thanked Jobi for all the grueling workouts he'd put her through. She was glad she no longer had an "academic body."

The man gave no indication of approval or not. His interest was in the swans. He led the huge creatures to the man in the jumpsuit, then slipped pretty leashes on their necks. *To protect the older man?* she wondered.

Once the birds were busy, he walked toward Kaley. He didn't seem the least perturbed that he was 90 percent naked. He was tall, over six feet, and every square inch of him was wet and glistening. His eyes were the color of sapphires.

"You want to go to Selkan?"

Great voice, she thought. "Yes. Jobi said…" She trailed off because he'd flung his wet hair to the side and was twisting it into a knot at the back of his head. All she could do was stare.

He slipped on a loose white shirt. When one of the swans squawked, he quickly went to them.

Kaley watched as he calmed the silver swan. His hands on the bird were caressing, and he was talking in a low, gentle, soothing voice.

"I see you've met Tanek," Jobi said from beside her.

From his tone, she knew he was teasing her. She probably looked like a preteen at a boy-band concert. She started to defend herself, but then gave a one-sided smile. "Can I keep him? I promise I'll take care of him, and I'll exercise him every day. Twice."

Jobi gave a snort of laughter, then slipped his arm into hers. "Let him get dressed and we'll meet at dinner."

"You don't think he'll need any help getting ready, do you?"

Jobi shook his head as he smiled in what appeared to be satisfaction.

She halted and squinted her eyes. "You aren't matchmaking, are you? Fixing me up with some island guy so I'll stay here?"

"Why would I do that?" he asked innocently. "Why would I want my best friend to stay with me forever?" He didn't wait for her answer. "Tomorrow, the king has a proposition for you."

"To be his two hundredth concubine? Tell him stories every night so I'm not executed?"

Jobi laughed. "Not quite, but he does plan to foot the bill for your travel. You'll have the best our country has to offer."

"That sounds good. And it's horses and wagons?"

"Yes. But the king's carriage is shiny and cushioned. And you'll have guards."

"I'm not sure Swan Boy needs them. He looks like he can handle anything on his own."

"I dare you to call him that to his face."

"No, thanks. So lead me to the shower, please. I feel like I have years of grunge to wash off."

"Three years' worth," Jobi said softly.

"What does that mean?"

"Nothing. Let's go to your room."

4

After a long, hot shower, Kaley felt better. She put on a blue robe that was hanging on the wall and wrapped her hair in a soft towel. She sat down on a stool to admire the beauty—no, the majesty—of her room. It really was out of a fairy tale. The bed was shaped like a big shell, with gauzy fabric hanging from a carved bar in the ceiling. The rug was a delicious mix of pale pinks and greens. The furniture was covered in peachy-pink silk. Someone had unpacked her suitcase. On a pretty dressing table all her cosmetics had been laid out. On the bench at the foot of the bed was her red dress. It looked like it had been freshly steamed. There was a tall, old-fashioned wardrobe filled with the clothes she'd brought—and half a dozen beautiful pieces had been added.

"No wonder wars were fought to become king," she said.

She rubbed her hair dry—she couldn't find a blow-dryer—and put on her red dress. It showed off what hard work with Jobi had done to her body. Red high heels went with it.

When she was ready, she opened the door to the hall but saw

no one. Should she wander about or wait until someone came to get her and lead her to dinner?

She was about to step out when she heard someone talking. The voice was muffled, but it sounded male and it seemed to be coming from the room next door. *It's probably Jobi*, she thought. He hadn't said so, but it made sense that he would be in a room connected to hers.

When she saw that the door was ajar, she pushed it half-open. It wasn't Jobi there, but the guide, Tanek. He had on one of the gray uniforms, his back to her, the right side of his body hidden behind a bed curtain.

Instantly, Kaley stepped back into her room. She didn't mean to invade his privacy. But then his words stopped her.

"How do I know what that island is like? I've never been off this one."

He was the guide *but he'd never been to the island?* she thought.

"You should go with us," he said. "I need a wedge between her and me. She… I'd rather not tell you how she acted toward me. It was embarrassing."

Kaley could feel her face flush. Remembering the way she'd looked at him, it was not her finest moment.

"I was in the water, chasing after Indienne, and she—" He cut off as he listened. "Yes, I had on very little clothing. Stop laughing! I can't figure out what Jobi is up to. Why her? She knows nothing. She's utterly useless. You've heard what Selkan is like. I'll have to take care of her every step of the way."

He was quiet for a moment. "What's she like? From what I've seen, she thinks she's to run the whole trip. I guess I'm supposed to carry her luggage." He gave a low laugh. "Yeah, maybe I am the useless one. Please go with us. Jobi can arrange it. It's the king and you know how much he loves to spend money. We'll have the best Selkan has to offer." His voice took on the sound of secrecy. "All right, I'll tell you the truth. After I get rid of her, I plan to go to the homestead. You and I'll get to see the old place." His voice became coaxing. "We can stay for a week. Just us. Does that sound good? Please, Mekos, I need some help with this woman, maybe even protection. I have to go. It's time for feeding. Think about this." He paused. "Yeah, me, too."

Quietly, Kaley shut the door. He was right. She had been thinking she'd run everything. And as a result, she'd been the quintessential "Ugly American." At home, she would never have so blatantly lusted after a man as she had with this man. Her excuse was that he'd caught her off guard. She hadn't been expecting… What? A half-naked man on a tropical island? Ha ha. It's exactly what she should have expected.

Obviously, the man had a family and people he loved. His girlfriend, or maybe his wife, whom he'd been talking to, was someone he wanted to be with, but he was giving up time to take Kaley to an island he'd never visited.

She sat down on the bench at the foot of her bed and looked at herself. Red dress, low-cut at the top, high-cut at the bottom. Nope. She wasn't going to wear that to dinner. She went to the wardrobe and pulled out something that was more in tune to the island. Over a plain cotton tunic and trousers, she put on a loose robe. The fabric was beautiful and its volume concealed the shape of her body.

I can't start the trip like this, she thought. *I have to set things right with this man.* She'd make sure he knew she wanted nothing from him other than being a guide. And yes, the girlfriend or wife he was talking to—on a cell phone?—was welcome to go with them.

She left the room and went back to the water. It was still and quiet, with no swans or any other animals in sight. As she'd hoped, the man was there. He was sitting on a short stool with his hands inside a canvas bag of what looked to be feed for the swans.

He glanced up at her but then looked back at the bag. He gave no greeting.

This is a very bad way to start the trip, she thought. She sat down on a stool that was a few feet away from him. She didn't know where to begin, but she needed to be honest with him. "I overheard you talking to your...friend."

He gave her a one-eyebrow-cocked look.

"I want to apologize and say that you're right. In this expedition I am the useless one. I don't know anything about your islands or your way of life." She paused, giving him time to politely contradict her, but he was silent. "I want to make it clear that I don't think it's empowering for a woman to say, 'How dare you!' then to never listen to anybody about anything. You are the leader and I will respect that."

He was looking at her intensely and he seemed about to say something, but she felt a gentle nudge on her shoulder. When she turned, it was the silver-and-gold swan. It was much larger when it was so close to her. She'd seen how tame they were but even so, she doubted if she'd have any trouble with them. To put it mildly, animals *liked* her. She lifted her arm and the swan curved its long neck, then rubbed its face on her cheek. Smiling, Kaley talked to it in that singsong baby talk people used with animals. "You are so beautiful that you take my breath away." She stroked its long neck. "When I saw you, I gasped. Surely nothing on this earth could be as lovely as you."

The swan wrapped around Kaley's neck so that its head was on the other side of her face. It was like a glorious scarf. Kaley nuzzled more, then looked back at the man. He hadn't moved, and he was staring at her in wide-eyed, stony silence.

"I'm just here to observe," she told him. "I want to hear stories, take a few photos, then I'll go home. I promised my family that I'd only stay for three months. That's all the time anyone has to put up with me."

The swan tightened its grip on her neck. "You want to show me something, don't you, sweetheart? What is it?"

Kaley looked back at the man, who hadn't moved so much

as an inch. "I've never seen swans as gentle as these. You've done a magnificent job with them." She gave a little cough when the swan tightened the grip around her neck. "All right. You have my attention. Oh! I bet you have babies. Could I see them? Please?"

As though it understood her words, the swan removed itself from her body and stepped to the side, waiting for Kaley to follow. She stood up. "Sorry, but I need to go. Is this Indienne?"

He gave a curt nod.

Kaley took a step forward. "When I get back, I'll apologize more. I really am sorry and I promise to behave myself. And please tell your girlfriend—or is she your wife?—that I'd love to meet her and I'd like to see the homestead, too. Ow!" The swan had pecked her shoulder. "All right, let's go."

She followed the swan down the path.

Tanek watched her until she was out of sight. When he turned away, he wasn't surprised to see Jobi standing there. He wore an expression of pride, but he also looked shocked.

"Did you see that?" Tanek said. "Only people in *my* order can do that. They—" He stopped as a swan ran its head against his leg. "Traitor!" he mumbled, then looked back at Jobi. "Who the starken-el is she?"

Jobi's face lost its look of surprise and went full-on pride. "She has no idea who or what she is and I'm certainly not going to tell her. As for you, find out for yourself."

He started to walk away, but Tanek stepped in front of him. "At least tell me what is *empowering* to a woman. Does she have a chip that makes her strong? Does she grow bigger? What does it mean? Power of what?"

Jobi didn't say anything.

"And she spoke of *this earth* and that she plans to be home in three months. Does she even know where she is?"

"What a lot we all need to learn," Jobi said. "As for me, I have a meeting with the king—unless you want to keep me here to ask more questions. I'm sure King Aramus will understand my tardiness."

Tanek's face showed what he thought of that, but he stepped aside. "She thinks Mekos is my wife."

"I guess she knows as little about you as you do about her. It's a perfect match." Jobi walked away at a quick pace so Tanek couldn't see his frown. At least he'd escaped for the moment!

It was late when Kaley got back to her room, and she was exhausted. She'd had to tell the swans the story of the Ugly Duckling three times. They'd sat so still, had been so attentive, it was as though they could understand her. But she was used to that. After the third telling, Indienne ran all of them off in a flurry of giant wings and angry squawks, and escorted Kaley back to the king's house.

Kaley's only thought was that she was glad she didn't see Tanek. She didn't want any more of the man's disapproving looks. Tomorrow she'd tell Jobi she was very sorry she'd messed up her first meeting with the guide. Maybe she should have ignored the fact that he was mostly naked and hugging a couple of giant swans. She should have been cool about it. But she hadn't been and now he despised her so could she please have another guide? Certainly someone who had been to the island they were going to visit would be better.

When she got back to her beautiful room, she realized that she'd forgotten about dinner. But there was a platter of cheese and olives, bread and sliced meat, and a huge glass of cold white wine. There was also a note from Jobi saying they were to meet the king tomorrow morning at nine.

"And what do I wear to meet the king?" she asked, yawning. She was too tired to make any decisions. She put on her flannel pajamas and went to bed. *Where is a telephone?* she thought as sleep overtook her.

5

When Kaley woke up, she knew it was early. She also knew she should behave by staying in her room and waiting for Jobi to come and get her to go meet the king. She'd already screwed up when she met the guide, so she shouldn't repeat her error.

On the other hand, she really, really wanted to see the place. And not with an escort who'd only show her the sites she was supposed to see.

She looked at her watch on the bedside cabinet. It wasn't quite 6:00 a.m., but she could see that it was light outside. Maybe if she just took a walk, not toward the water, but somewhere she hadn't been, it would be all right. No one had warned her not to go out, and the little she'd seen seemed safe.

The table holding last night's food was there, and she was glad to see it was untouched. She didn't like the idea of someone in her room while she was sleeping. She quickly pulled on a tunic top, the most bland she could find, leggings and light sneakers. She didn't want to draw attention to herself, but if Jobi showed up, she wanted to be able to move quickly. She grabbed a big bread roll from the basket, put a piece of cheese inside and left the room.

As she started walking in the opposite direction of the water, she told herself she'd not go far from the king's house.

The sound of voices made her quicken her step and she came to a small plaza. The houses surrounding it were low, mostly one story, light brown and pretty. There were flower boxes with bright red blossoms. In the middle was a stone-floored area with a raised wooden platform. It was like where a band would play. But now it had four short masonry towers on it and each one had a single stone in front of it. The rocks were progressively larger until the last one was almost a boulder.

The plaza was filled with men. She saw a few women, but it was mostly excited men and it looked like money was being handed back and forth. It appeared that a contest was about to begin and the men were laying bets.

She didn't want to draw attention to herself as she watched what was going on. She went up three steps of a doorway and slipped back into the deep shade. She had a good view over the heads of the many men, but then, they were too excited to notice a stranger.

A man stepped onto the platform. He had a large belly and a very loud voice—and he was speaking in a language she didn't understand. But it was easy to figure out what he was saying. He was challenging someone to come up and try his luck in a strength contest. For a fee, of course. The man was waving a large bag of jingling coins in temptation. *Wonder whose face is on those coins?* she thought. *Is it the king's? But didn't Jobi say he is no longer the real king? Is there a story in that?*

Kaley couldn't help laughing at herself. She watched as three brawny young men tried their luck at picking up the stones and putting them on top of the towers. One man made it to the second rock, but the others couldn't even pick up the first stone. When the announcer faked sadness at their failure, the crowd booed him. He laughed and rattled the bag. It was growing larger. He waved his arm, trying to get more people to try their luck, but no one did.

Kaley could feel the excitement fading. The contest was too difficult and the crowd knew it. Thinking she should go back, she went down a step, but then a hush fell over the crowd. She saw that on the far side, something was happening. She stepped back up to her hiding place and waited.

When the crowd parted, she saw a head above them. It was a man, probably in his forties, with a shiny bald head and a full black beard. When the crowd stepped aside, she saw that he was at least six foot eight and probably weighed about three hundred pounds. He wore baggy tan trousers and heavy leather boots. Above the waist, he had on a dark vest and nothing else. There was not an ounce of fat on him.

"My bet's on him," she whispered. Everyone seemed to agree as there was a flurry of money going back and forth. The announcer was frowning as he dumped coins into the bag, which grew substantially larger and heavier. *He won't like losing all that*, Kaley thought.

As the big man mounted the steps up to the stage, she saw the audience looking at each other in question. *He's a stranger*, Kaley thought. *They don't know who he is. Interesting.*

The man so easily and quickly picked up the stones and mounted them on the towers that it was almost an anticlimax. The crowd's attention was fully on the big man, their breaths held. But Kaley, from her higher stance, saw something else. The announcer had stepped to the far side and she saw him give a nod to someone in the crowd. Whoever it was began to move through the throng. The people were so intent on the man on the stage that no one noticed him.

He moved toward Kaley, then stopped not far from her. He was a small, lithe-looking man, like a runner. As she watched, he did a few stretches, as though he was about to enter some competition.

There was something suspicious about him. She went down the steps and moved closer to the man. He didn't notice her, but turned to the stage, where the announcer was handing over the purse of coins to the big man. The crowd erupted into cheering and the man went down the stairs to the plaza. As he walked forward, people slapped him on the back in congratulations.

When he got to the edge of the crowd, and closer to Kaley, the small man made a leap. He grabbed the pouch of coins out of the big man's hand and took off running. Kaley was prepared. She put out her foot, then her entire body, and the little man went down. The bag of coins flew upward and she caught it. It was similar to what she'd done so many times in the gym with Jobi when he tossed her a weighted ball. She threw the bag back to the big man and he grabbed it.

Obviously, the whole contest had been a scam. They were never going to allow anyone to win the money. She was glad she'd been able to help beat them at their own game. As she made her way through the crowd, she was pleased with her interference, but she also hoped that Jobi wouldn't find out. He didn't like her risking danger. But it was over and she'd won.

It was a full three minutes before she realized she was being followed. Uh-oh. Did the scammers think she was part of some gang? Should she run back to the king's house? But that would lead them there. This was bad!

In the next second, someone grabbed her arm and pulled her between the buildings. She prepared to fight as Jobi had taught her, with teeth, headbutts, whatever she could use. But then Kaley saw it was the big man. She followed him without question.

They ran between the buildings but unfortunately, he didn't appear to know his way around any more than she did. When they came to a dead end, he put her behind him, his arms extended in protection. The men chasing them would find them soon.

It was Kaley who saw the low roof. She couldn't get up to it by herself, but he could, and he could give her a boost. They could hear men's steps and their angry voices. They were very close.

She pointed to the roof and gestured up. He nodded, then grabbed her by the waist and practically threw her up. She landed on her stomach and skidded a few inches across the rough roof tiles. She spit out dirt and what she hoped weren't bird droppings. The heavy pouch of coins landed near her head. She hoped his aim was that good and he'd meant for it to land where it did.

When she saw the man's hands as he was pulling himself up, she tied the strings of the bag onto a loop on her trousers, and stuck what she could into her pocket.

The man was right behind her. He grabbed her shoulders and lifted her so far up that her feet were in the air, then he let her go and she hit the roof running. She followed him as best she could until they reached the edge of the building. Below them was an alleyway with a building on the other side, but in between was empty space. It was a long way down.

Kaley looked at the man and shook her head. She couldn't jump that far. He probably could, but not her. She motioned for him to go, then started to untie the bag of coins for him to take.

Instead, he walked back a few feet and motioned for her to come. She knew what he meant. She was to run and jump.

Again, she shook her head. Behind them, they could hear men shouting. They were going to be on the roof in seconds.

The man gave Kaley a look that said she either ran or he'd throw her. She ran. When her feet reached the edge, she felt a strong hand hit her in the lower back. As if she were a Ping-Pong ball, he swatted her across the empty space.

This time, Kaley landed on her feet in a one-leg squat. In the distance, she could see the king's house. Oh no! What time was it? She looked at her watch. She had eleven minutes to be on time for the king's appointment.

When she stood up, the man was beside her, and she pointed to her watch. So far, they hadn't spoken a word, but then she had no idea what language he spoke.

With a nod of understanding, he went to a door that led to a stairwell. It was locked. Wide-eyed, she watched the man pull the door off the hinge, set it aside, then motion for her to go first.

Kaley went down the stairs two at a time and reached an outside door quickly. At the bottom, they stopped, their backs against the exterior wall. For a minute, they listened, but they heard no voices or steps.

The man tapped his wrist, meaning Kaley's watch. She didn't hesitate as she ran in the direction of the king's house.

When she reached the door closest to her room, Jobi was waiting for her, and he was dressed splendidly. All blue and gold. He downright sparkled.

As he looked her up and down, she kept her shoulders straight. She knew she was a sweaty mess. Not what one would wear to make an appearance before a king.

"Do I want to know?" he asked.

"Absolutely not."

"What is that?"

He was nodding toward the fat pouch of coins tied to her trousers. "Oh no," she said. "I forgot to give it back to him."

Jobi's look softened. "You'll see him in a few minutes. Give it to him then."

"You know him? Oh. Wait. You think I mean Swan Boy. Nope. Not him."

Jobi's eyes widened. "You… With another man?"

"Give me some credit. What happened wasn't sex. It was straight out of *Aladdin*. We—" She broke off. She had no idea how to explain what happened. "Are we going to be late?"

"Hope not. There are public executions for that."

Kaley looked at him in shock.

"Come on. Whatever happened, I bet Tomás has heard about

it. He has his own Jafar." The stories of Aladdin were some of Jobi's favorites.

"Now you tell me." The main thing in her mind was how she was going to find the big man and give him back his money.

By the time she and Jobi got to the throne room, Kaley was quite nervous. She'd never dreamed of meeting a king. If she had, she would have imagined herself wearing a beautiful gown. Something à la Princess Catherine. Kaley's grandmother would probably have made it on her Bernina, but it would certainly be better than what she had on. The front of her shirt had been scraped raw when she slid across the roof. There were streaks of dirt and debris all over her. She picked off a little bird feather.

"That won't help," Jobi muttered.

"Great," she muttered. "Now I feel even worse." The heavy pouch hit her leg but she didn't tighten it. Maybe the king would know who the winner of the strength contest was. Did she dare ask?

When they entered the big room, the sheer brilliance of it so dazzled her that she forgot everything else.

She paused at the doorway, looking at the chandeliers, and the walls of what appeared to be gold and crystal. It all sparkled and shimmered. If the opulence wasn't reminder enough of who lived there, every ten feet or so stood one of the muscled guards, a long sword sheathed at his side.

She followed Jobi to the back of the room. There were several people ahead of them, all of them seeming to be waiting to speak to the king.

Kaley looked through the crowd toward the front. Sitting on a rather plain chair was a small man wearing a long robe with colors that moved even when he was sitting still. She wasn't sure, but it looked like the fabric had feathers on it. *So that is what he does with the swans,* she thought. They clothed the king. He was talking to three men and seemed unaware of the others in the room.

"Speak of the devil," she whispered to Jobi. Coming toward them was the swan herdsman, Tanek. It was hard to believe but he was dirtier than Kaley was.

"What the hell?" Jobi muttered. "What a disrespectful, lazy generation you kids are."

"*I* was saving a life," Kaley said. "I have no idea what *he* was doing. Maybe he—" She stopped talking because coming from the opposite side of the room was the big man from the morning. He was as dirty as when she'd last seen him. Everything they'd done went through Kaley's mind and she was joyous at seeing him again. Since she was hidden by Jobi, he didn't see her. She untied the pouch, stepped to one side, then yelled, "Hey!" She threw the pouch in his direction, then ran full speed toward him.

His reaction was as fast as she was. He caught the coin bag with one hand, tossed it to Jobi, then grabbed Kaley by the waist, lifted her and turned her around full circle in the air. The people around them watched in shocked silence.

"I'm Kaley," she said.

"Sojee." He set her down, then they stood beside each other and looked toward the king on his throne.

Jobi put himself beside Kaley, with Tanek on the end.

"I, uh..." Kaley began.

"Don't even try to explain," Jobi said under his breath. It was the first time she'd ever heard genuine anger in his voice.

Since they were far back in the room, Kaley thought the king probably didn't see her display with the big man. But she was wrong. He waved his hand and all the people moved to the sides of the room.

Kaley and the three men were now in direct sight of the king. Behind him was a tall, thin man, wearing all black and holding a tall staff. What appeared to be a huge emerald was on his headdress. Bending, he said something to the king.

"Jafar?" Kaley whispered, but the look Jobi gave her made her stop talking.

The thin man stepped back and the king spoke. "I see that small effort has been made in dress. Perhaps being a King of the People can be carried too far."

Kaley wanted to defend herself, but she said nothing.

The king looked at her. "It seems that you will have no objection to Sojee being your guard."

His sarcasm made Kaley smile, and it made her know he was aware of what was going on—as a good king should. Was it Jobi who'd told him there were problems between her and Tanek? Or had *he* complained about *her*?

She didn't know what the protocol was, but she dipped into a curtsy. It lost a lot considering what she was wearing, but she did go down rather low. From the look on the king's face, the movement was not something he was familiar with, but he seemed to like it. "Yes, thank you, sir." She wasn't sure what to call him. "May I say that your wisdom and insight into this matter is commendable? The replacement is very welcome."

The king looked puzzled. "Replacement?"

Again, the man in black said something only the king could hear. "Really?" The king stared at Kaley. "Is it true that you'd rather go on your journey with big, ugly Sojee than with Bellis's finest? With Tanek?"

Kaley wanted to be diplomatic. "I think Sojee and I are better suited personally. We work well together."

The king looked at Tanek. "Can it be that there exists a woman who doesn't want you above all other men? I believe the sky may be falling. Should we consult about the coming storms? Is our world in danger?"

Kaley choked on a giggle, but again, Jobi gave her a look to behave herself. "I'm sorry, sir," she said. "I don't mean to disparage Mr., uh, Tanek. He's probably a very nice man, but the swans need him. Sojee seems more one of the ordinary people. It's them I want to talk to and hear their stories."

"Ah, yes," the king said. "Our Tanek can be intimidating." He seemed highly amused by the idea that Tanek was not a woman's first choice for anything.

Jobi spoke up. "Obviously, Kaley and Sojee have been somewhere *together*." He gave her a glare of reproach. "However, I have not been told where or when or even *why*. After we have talked—"

The king waved his hand in dismissal. "Yes, I'm sure you will fix it, Jobi. You always do. But now I have something important to say." He looked at Kaley. "I have a small request of you. My youngest son is on Selkan and I want you to find him. You must tell him that Princess Aradella has agreed to marry him."

"That sounds lovely," Kaley began, but beside her, Sojee took a step forward. There was anger in his step—and he was headed toward the king. The guards around the room also felt the anger. There was the sound of steel being drawn.

Without taking time to think, Kaley pretended to trip and put herself in front of Sojee. She glared up at him in warning. Whatever he was about to do, he had to stop.

He didn't look down at her, but he gave a quick nod and stopped moving.

Kaley turned to face the king, her back to Sojee, but she didn't move away from him. "I'm sorry, sir. I'm a clumsy person. Ask Jobi. Thank goodness Sojee caught me before I fell and harmed your beautiful floor."

The king frowned, not sure what had happened. He looked at Jobi. "My son will be found and the message given?"

"Of course," Jobi said, then turned to Kaley. "Go!"

The four of them hurried through a side door, then stopped in a small room. As soon as the door closed, each person gave a sigh of relief.

"I think we all need to talk," Jobi said, but no one agreed.

Kaley looked at Tanek. "We have an excuse for the way we look, but what about you?"

Through it all, Tanek had not spoken, but he'd been the re-

cipient of the king's derision. "I was out all night searching for
a missing little girl."

Kaley's eyes widened. "She was wearing a red cloak?"

"Yes." He showed his surprise.

Her voice lowered. "Did you find the wolf?"

"We did, but how did you know what it was? You should
have told us. It would have helped." He was frowning at her.

Jobi stepped forward. "She knew but she didn't know. I think
we should prepare to leave. After today, I think the sooner you
get out of here, the better." He looked at Kaley. "*Both* men are
going with you, as well as some of the king's guards. Right now
you need to get clean and pack enough clothes for three days.
Leave the rest here." He looked at Sojee. "You will meet us at
the lake." He turned to Tanek. "You will come with me."

No one questioned his authority. They just silently obeyed.

Jobi looked across the table at Tanek. He could tell the young
man was unhappy. They were in an old restaurant that was a
common type on Bellis. Centuries ago, some bored, homesick
Bellisan guards had created one on an Earth island called Bri-
tannia. The earthlings called it a "public house" and the con-
cept stuck. They shortened the name to "pub" and they now
believed it began with them.

"I've always known I was to *do* something," Tanek said.
"Grandpapá made sure I studied and trained. I thought it was
so I could fight the tyranny that we live under. So far, we've
done—" He looked around as if he were being heard.

"You're safe here," Jobi said. "You can speak your mind."

"I'm to escort some know-nothing female from Earth to do
what? Listen to stories? I've seen that she's odd, but for all I know,
all Earth people are like her."

"They aren't. There's more to her than you can see, and much
more than she knows."

"What does that mean?"

Jobi didn't answer his question. "She's a beautiful young woman."

"Oh no, you don't," Tanek said. "I'm not interested. It's good that she dislikes me so much. I want to know what the *truth* is behind all this."

"It's as you were told. Story gathering is the cover. The true purpose of the trip is for you to find the king's youngest son."

"Right. Then I tell him he's to marry some princess of the old kingdom. I don't think King Aramus is going to give up his throne to some girl. Not that he actually has a throne any longer. *They* saw to that!"

"This marriage will help reunite the kingdoms. Put us back together." Jobi took a swig of his drink, a locally made beer that wasn't very strong. "You've been on Earth and so have your parents. You're well qualified for the job. You have any better suggestion of who to send with her?"

"I was a child when I was there and I remember very little of that time!" Tanek snapped, then calmed. "I'm willing, but you should go with us. You can distract her while I do what I need to. I have people to meet, information to gather. Go with us."

Jobi gave a shiver. "That island scares me. It's a violent place. As for Kaley, you should be grateful she's here. It's because of her that the king is paying all your expenses and hiring guards to protect you. And there's Sojee! He can break a man in half like a twig." Jobi lowered his voice. "Most important is that you get open passage to go to the island. You don't have to hide or sneak. You'll be able to do what you must under the cover of working for the king."

"What happened between her and that man? She made a fool of herself in front of the king."

"I think the king rather enjoyed it. But I don't know what Kaley and Sojee did. Whatever it was, it seems to have made them friends."

Tanek looked away for a moment. "You know that our homeland is on Selkan. I've always wanted to see it. Grandpapá told me so much about the place. There's a type of swan there that we don't have. It's pure white." He tore off a chunk of bread from the basket in the middle of the table. "What's she like? Really?"

Jobi took his time answering. "She's more independent than she knows. I spent years training her so she can do things. She's not as strong as you, but she has the advantage of speed." He gave Tanek a look of warning. "She has her entire life planned out, down to her old age. Once she gets her stories, she'll demand to return home."

"And it'll take another three years to get there." He gave Jobi a hard look. "She doesn't know where she is and when she finds out, I'm sure she'll take it out on *me*. She'll—"

He was interrupted by a Never appearing out of nowhere. The pretty little creature's wings glistened even in the low light. She said something to Tanek but Jobi couldn't understand her. It always annoyed him that, even with his abilities, he couldn't decipher the language of the Nevers. The fairylike people bonded with one person and they never shared, never betrayed, thus their name. As though she could read his thoughts, she gave Jobi an insolent little wink, then *poof!* she disappeared.

"She says the king wants you. Now."

Jobi sighed. "He is a man who can't bear to be alone."

"That's a good quality in royalty since they're always surrounded."

"I guess so." Jobi stood up. "Don't let Kaley get near The Museum of Earth. That could cause problems."

"The what?"

"You heard me. Take the ferry to the island, meet whoever you need to, get the king's youngest son, then send him back here. You can stay on the island. As for the stories, if Kaley hears two or three new ones, that's enough. Tell her some swan legends, then show her your back. That'll make her happy. I must go. That man is going to use me to death." He took a step toward the door then looked back. "Zeon is my friend. You can trust him. If you have problems, go to him and he'll help you."

"Does this person know our goal?"

Jobi gave a one-sided smile. "He started it. He's the leader." He hurried to the heavy door and left.

6

When Kaley got back to her room, she quickly packed her duffel bag, then her backpack. "'I'm going on an adventure,'" she said, quoting *The Hobbit*. "But without trolls." Wherever she went, she was glad Sojee would be with her. Not so much Tanek, who tended to look at her as though she was a duty, something he had to put up with.

There was a quick knock on the door and she opened it to two guardsmen. One thing about Bellis was that it was certainly a mix of people. When she realized that the men's eyes were dark purple, she stared. She had to make herself look away as they took her bags.

Kaley gave a last look at the beautiful room and reluctantly left. Wherever they went, she was sure it wouldn't be as luxurious as staying in the king's house.

She followed the men along a path she'd never seen, going in the opposite direction of the village where she'd met Sojee. They stopped at a carriage—or maybe it should be called a Carriage. Big, shiny, black, trimmed in gold, flamboyantly impres-

sive. Four gorgeous black horses were harnessed to it. Sojee and
Tanek were already seated. Sojee was grinning while Tanek was
frowning. Nothing unusual there, she thought.

Sojee held his hand out to help her up and she sat beside him,
facing Tanek. She ran her hand over the black leather uphol-
stery. "This is worthy of royalty. Or does all of Bellis travel this
way?" When Sojee said something incomprehensible, she realized they had never actually talked. They'd exchanged names
but no other words.

He reached into the pocket of his vest—which was now over
a shirt that covered his bare torso—and pulled out a tiny metal
pen. When she saw the blue light, she leaned away.

"Oh no, you don't! The first time I saw one of those, Jobi put
it on my arm and I went to sleep and woke up sitting on a rock.
I don't know what happened in between." *And I plan to ask Jobi
what is in my arm that makes the pen work*, she thought.

From Sojee's expression, he had no idea what she'd said. He
looked at Tanek and they exchanged a bit of dialogue in another
language. Sojee looked shocked.

She glared at Tanek. "Did you tell him something awful about
me? Like that I'm not to be trusted alone with a man?"

Tanek's eyes widened in surprise. "I told him what you said,
then added that that tool is illegal on this island. That seems to
have surprised him."

She felt like he was hiding something, but she was sure he
wouldn't tell her what it was. "Maybe the king gave it to him."

Tanek spoke to Sojee, who shook his head. "He wants you
two to be able to understand each other, and he promises that
he won't put you to sleep. I'll make sure he doesn't."

"I trust *him* more than *you!*"

Sojee seemed to have understood her as he laughed in a way
that made Tanek give him a look of disgust. She held out her
arm and Sojee touched the blue tip to the little scar. She felt a
tiny electrical shock, then a surge of energy.

When Tanek told Sojee what Kaley had asked about the carriage, she understood him.

Sojee chuckled. "What we drive is more suited for hauling the contents of the outhouses."

Kaley laughed so loudly at his joke that Sojee looked at Tanek in triumph.

It was late afternoon so the guardsmen lit the big lanterns at the sides of the carriage. It made a soft golden light. The men clucked at the horses and they began to move.

"I wish I had on a Cinderella dress," Kaley said.

"Is that one of your stories?" Tanek asked.

"It is." Her answer was curt, not rude, but certainly not friendly. She looked at Sojee. "Have *you* ever been to Selkan?"

"Only once."

"So tell me about the place."

"What I have seen is not as fine as my home island of Pithan, but good." He told of mountains and lakes and areas of flat plains.

"What about animals?" she asked. "I know there are wolves here. What about lions? Tigers?"

Sojee and Tanek looked blank.

"Wild cats? Jaguars? Mountain lions?" The men stared at her. "Cats. Like house cats, only bigger."

Both Sojee and Tanek shrugged. They had no idea what she was talking about.

"Tell her about the men," Tanek said.

"There are many men on Selkan." Sojee spoke in dismissal, as if it didn't matter.

She looked at Tanek. "Is that supposed to be bad?"

"Probably not to you." Tanek turned his head away.

Kaley glared at him. Was that a put-down? she wondered. Did he think she made a pass at every man she met? She smiled at Sojee. "Any birds on the island? What are the houses like?"

"Big, sturdy houses, and many birds." They were passing through open land, with some forest. There was no sign of habitation. "This is the king's land," Sojee said as explanation for the barrenness.

"He seems to own a lot for someone who is no longer officially the king." She cocked her head at him. "Why did you almost attack him?"

"I'd like to know that, too," Tanek said.

Sojee stiffened. He was already taller than both of them, but he seemed to grow. "We Pithans don't want to see her forced into a marriage."

Kaley stared hard at him. "Why do I get the feeling that you're telling only about ten percent of the whole story?"

He didn't answer.

When they reached the water, the carriage came to a halt. Before them was a small dock, with four rowboats tied up. Half a dozen men were working there. They wore black and they kept glancing at Kaley in a way that made her step closer to Sojee.

"These young men are from Selkan," he said. "They are a generation that has grown up without women. They look on them as mysterious creatures."

"Don't we all?" Tanek muttered.

Kaley narrowed her eyes at him but he turned away.

"Here it comes," Tanek said.

Sailing into sight was a small but majestic wooden ship with a single sail. In the front was the carved head of what could be a dragon. Kaley's eyes widened in appreciation. "It's beautiful." She stepped away from the men to go to the end of the pier to watch it arrive.

Sojee and Tanek went to the carriage to oversee the unloading of the luggage.

"She doesn't know where she is, does she?" Sojee asked.

"Not at all. I hope we can keep it secret long enough that when she finds out, it will be Jobi on the receiving end of her wrath. I don't want to be blamed!"

"I agree, so we must try to hide it. Are you good at lying?"

"I don't know," Tanek said. "I've never had to do much of it. But in this case, I'm willing to try."

The men went to stand beside Kaley as the ship was tied to the dock. A long plank was lowered and she walked up it, Sojee and Tanek behind her. Their bags were tossed on the deck. Tanek had the most and she wondered if it had anything to do with the homestead he wanted to visit.

It took only minutes before they cast off and were sailing across the calm blue water. There were several men on board, with their black hair and purple eyes, and they never stopped glancing at Kaley. It was unnerving. When she moved to stand between Sojee and Tanek, she heard the word *Nessa*. It was the name of the prince they were to find. It was annoying that the men were having this conversation without her.

"I don't think it will be difficult to find him." Sojee cut a look at Tanek. "I believe you have friends who move about rather freely."

"You have been spying on me." There was no animosity in Tanek's voice.

They were talking to each other over Kaley's head, as if she weren't there.

"I like to know who and what I'm with," Sojee said.

Me, too, Kaley thought, then spoke up. "You mean Mekos." She was pleased that both men looked down at her in surprise.

"Ah, yes. I was told that Mekos is a Lely," Sojee said, and Tanek nodded. "Tail?"

"Ears," Tanek said, and the two men gave low laughs of sharing a secret.

"What does that mean?" Kaley asked, but the men said nothing. Deeply annoyed, Kaley went to the other side of the deck and looked out at the water. She did her best to ignore the boatmen staring at her. With their every task, from coiling rope to adjusting the sail, they moved closer to her.

7

Even though she'd been told that the island of Selkan was mostly men, Kaley wasn't prepared for seeing it in reality. When they disembarked in the town of Doyen, a wagon was waiting for them. On the side was painted an outline of what she assumed was the island, with a symbol in the middle. She didn't ask, but she had an idea that meant it belonged to King Aramus. It was a far cry from the elegance and luxury of the one on Eren. This wagon was so hard and sturdy that it could probably withstand an earthquake and a hurricane at the same time.

She stood in the background as they showed the bordermen the papers the king had sent with them.

Three of the king's guards met them. They looked as strong as the horses, with their leather clothes and knives that hung on to their belts and stuck out of their tall boots. Each man had deep scars on his face. One man's face had healed in a way to make a permanent sneer. The men were talking to each other while they leered at Kaley in a vulgar way.

Instinctively, Kaley stepped closer to Sojee, and Tanek moved to her side. He looked ready to draw a weapon on the men.

Sojee picked up a heavy case and tossed it onto a pile. "The scars are from a game, not combat. They present no danger to us."

Neither Kaley nor Tanek looked like they believed that.

Another guard came forward. He was also scarred, but he didn't have the predatory look that the others did. He angrily said something to the three men in a language she didn't understand, then left.

Kaley got into the wagon.

"I can adjust you to understand," Sojee said as he sat down beside her. He put his hand on his pocket, meaning his magic blue-light pen.

"No, thanks," Kaley said. "I don't want to hear what they're saying."

Tanek nodded. "The captain's name is Garen and he's to stay with us every minute that we're here. He's never to leave us."

"Great," Kaley mumbled. "And what's second prize?"

The men looked at her, not understanding her comment.

The guards took their places on the front and back of the wagon. Unlike the men on the ship, who seemed to know they weren't supposed to stare, these men looked at Kaley like ravenous predators. She was well covered but she pulled her collar up to hide more of her face. The captain saw her movement and snapped at the men, but they gave little smirks and didn't stop stealing glances at her.

Tanek moved from the opposite side to sit beside her so Kaley was wedged tightly between him and Sojee. She scooted back so the men were farther in front of her.

In other circumstances, the two large men would be intimidating, but not to these guards. In fact, they seemed to be amused. They started talking to Tanek and Sojee.

"I don't think we're scaring them," Kaley said.

Tanek spoke. "They want us to play their sports game with them."

"The one that scarred their faces?" she asked.

"Yes," Sojee answered.

"I vote no," Kaley said, and the men nodded in agreement.

As they drove through the town, Kaley peeped out around the men and looked at the place. It was very different from Eren. There were no boxes filled with flowers, no pretty railings. The houses were all large and heavy. Doors were tall and thick and often covered with big nail heads. The fading daylight made the town look like something out of a horror film.

The only people she saw were men. They wore leather clothes and heavy boots, and when the wagon passed, the men stopped and stared. Kaley moved back farther, letting the muscular arms of Sojee and Tanek hide her.

It seemed like a long time before the wagon stopped. They were in front of a building with massive doors. Small windows were framed by stone and covered by iron bars.

"It's the inn and it's better if you stay covered." Sojee got down, held up his arms and lifted her out of the tall wagon. She stood close beside him as Tanek got down.

She looked around. "I think that just looking at this town is making hair grow on my chest."

The two men looked at her in surprise, then Sojee laughed. Tanek just stared.

The captain of the guard, Garen, said something to Sojee, then the heavy door opened.

Inside, the inn had high ceilings with huge rafters and beams. To one side were tables, each one looking like it must weigh hundreds of pounds. Several men were eating and drinking from metal plates and mugs. They halted and silently stared at the visitors. Kaley kept her face hidden.

Sojee spoke to Garen, then said, "We're to follow him." Sojee went up the stairs first, then Kaley, with Tanek close behind her.

When Garen threw open a door to a room, Kaley was happily surprised. It was quite pretty, with curtains of fabric printed with little blue flowers. The bed was a four-poster and looked soft and comfortable.

"This is lovely," she said, looking at the scarred man. "Thank you."

When Sojee translated, Garen smiled. He was pleased.

As two other guards dropped Kaley's duffel and her backpack on the floor, they looked around the room in awe. Garen snapped at them and they left. He spoke to Sojee, then he, too, left.

Kaley looked at Sojee and Tanek. "So we share this room?"

Sojee grinned. "No. It's yours alone. We're next door. They're sending supper up to you. Ah, here it is."

An older man, with scars on his face and bare arms, set a platter down on a table. It was a slab of meat that had to be about six pounds. There was nothing else with it.

"Nice appetizer," Kaley said.

The man was puzzled, not understanding her sarcasm.

"Tell him thank you," Kaley said. "It's very nice and I'm sure I'll enjoy it."

When he was told, the man grinned, showing that he was missing several teeth.

Sojee yawned. "This has been a long day. I think we should go to bed early. Tomorrow we'll look for the prince."

"Sounds good to me," Kaley said. "I can see a bathtub through that door so I'm going to have a long soak. I'll see you two early in the morning."

Sojee explained how to bolt the heavy door from the inside, and told her she was to let no one in. Kaley yawned and promised to securely lock everything.

The men hesitated but they finally left and Kaley sat down to her steak, which was delicious. If there was one thing men could do well, it was cook meat.

She ate as much as she could, then she unzipped her bag and pulled out black sweatpants, her hiking boots and her black hoodie. She tied her hair back and pulled the hood forward, all while muttering, "Do they really think I don't know what they're planning to do? If they do find the king's son, how will they persuade him to go with them? Hold a sword to his neck? But then, Sojee doesn't *want* him marrying the princess so he won't try very hard, so—" She stopped muttering and looked at herself in the mirror. She was as covered as she could get. Nothing girlie was showing.

When she opened the door and looked out, she was scared. She reminded herself that they were protected by the king. Sojee had a pouch full of papers telling who they were and— Her thoughts didn't help.

She did her best to swagger down the stairs. Since she'd spent a lot of her life in her father's car repair shop, she knew how boys walked. She stomped down the steps in a way that made the men at the tables not even look at her. It appeared that they were used to men who kept their faces covered.

She went to a far corner that was dark and had to wait only minutes before Sojee and Tanek came down the stairs. She clomped over to them. "You boys from outta town?" she said in a deep voice.

The men looked at her in shock. Tanek recovered first. "Starken-el! What are you doing here?" He grabbed her arm and pulled her back into the dark corner.

She pushed his hand away. "I'm going to help find the prince. I am *not* staying alone in that room. What if one of these men decided to break in? Who'd be there to stop them since you two are out frolicking around town and leaving me all alone, by myself, undefended?"

Tanek's face was red with anger, but before he could speak, Sojee's laugh stopped him. He put his hand on Tanek's shoulder. "Boy, have you not learned that the strength of women is in their words? She will beat you every time."

"She—" Tanek began, then stopped. "You will stay covered."

"Yes, sir," Kaley said meekly, making Sojee laugh again.

Still angry, Tanek threw open the big door to the outside. When two men, obviously drunk, came in, he pushed Kaley behind him, hiding her.

Outside, there was little light in the streets, but a whole lot of horse manure.

"Did you two have dinner?" she asked. "It was the best steak I ever had. So how do we find the prince?"

"He has a dragon," Sojee said. "We look for it."

"You mean like a Komodo? I didn't know they were tamable."

"Your woman's voice will draw attention to you," Tanek said in warning.

She knew he was right. As she walked, she heard the men talking behind her.

"She can't keep up," Tanek said.

"I know that she can," Sojee said. "But she will fear the dragon."

"Ha!" Tanek answered. "It will roll on the ground with her."

"And how do you know this?" Sojee sounded almost angry.

Kaley turned to them, walking backward. "Are you two going to fight over me? I'm a prize? I should wear a steeple hat with a veil, and toss my hankie to my chosen champion. Surely, being part of a fairy tale will get my dissertation approved."

The two men looked at her in puzzlement, but when her voice caught the attention of a passing man, she turned away, smiling broadly.

They walked over the rough cobblestones for what had to be hours, going in and out of so many places that were open that Kaley began to regret her decision to go with them. Several times, Sojee stopped men and asked if they'd seen the prince.

Each time, he was sneered at. One man spit out a glob that almost hit Kaley's boot.

"People don't seem to like the prince," she said. The men didn't reply to her observation of the obvious.

About an hour before dawn, the men went into yet another tavern, but this time, they sat down at a table in a dark corner and ordered big mugs of beer. Kaley drank half of hers in one gulp. When she looked up, the men were staring at her. "I'm thirsty. Tell me about this island. Why aren't there any women?"

"There are few women on this island," Sojee said.

"I can see that, but the men must have mothers and probably sisters. Please tell me these macho men haven't locked the women up somewhere." The beer was making her feel lightheaded.

"Male and female are separated at seven years old," Tanek said. "The under-seven boys are on Pithan." He looked at Sojee, who nodded.

She took another drink. "Why is this done?"

Sojee leaned back to let Tanek answer. He seemed to be the historian. "There was a lot of anger between the sexes, each accusing the other of causing the problems. They said it would be better to live without each other."

"I can understand that," she said. "I mean, separating people."

Anger rose in Tanek's face. "How is that understandable?"

Kaley drank more of the strong beer. "Well…when a woman is angry about something at work, instead of listening, the man tells her how to *fix* it. He can't find anything—unless it's with a rifle. Women cook three meals a day, and no one pays any attention, but if a man makes pancakes on Sunday morning he expects to be praised for the next month. Basically, women get the Second Shift. They have a job, then go home and do eight hours of housework. A man has a job, goes home, drinks beer and fiddles with his hobby. I could go on, but is that the kind of problems they had here?" She didn't wait for an answer, but finished her beer. "So how are babies made?"

"That is strictly controlled," Sojee said.

"Ah, fornicating under command of the king," she said. "I read that in a Sara Medlar book. It got abbreviated." With a sweet smile, she put her arms down on the table, rested her head on them and closed her eyes. She heard nothing else.

Sojee looked at Tanek. "Do I carry her back or do you?"

"I'm sure she would prefer you," Tanek said.

"Why does she dislike you so much? What did you do to her?"

"Nothing."

Sojee's face showed that he didn't believe him.

"She was a bit, uh, aggressive at our first meeting and I... I wasn't receptive."

"Are you saying that you let her know you weren't interested in her as a woman?"

Tanek was silent.

Sojee shook his head in disbelief. "She's beautiful, she has a superior body and she entertained the grumpy old king. And there are those eyes of the richest brown! But you turned her down?"

Tanek had no intention of talking of this. "You could wake her with your illegal pen." He ordered two more beers. That he wasn't leaving showed he had something more to say. "Where did you get that pen?"

Sojee took time to answer, as though considering whether or not to confide. "I am strongly connected to the Old Kingdom."

Tanek wanted to ask more but he didn't. He believed that trust had to be earned—and he was trying to gain Sojee's. "I have some things I need to do here," Tanek said. "They are private." He nodded to Kaley. "What are we going to do with her?"

Before Sojee could answer, a Never appeared. He'd heard of them, but hadn't seen one. She was a tiny woman with a bright light that surrounded her, and she was exquisitely beautiful. He stared in awe.

Tanek smiled in a way that showed he loved the little creature. "This is Arit," he said to Sojee, then looked back at her.

"I wondered if you could cross the water." He reached into his pocket, withdrew a leather pouch and took out a spoon that was no bigger than a straw. "Did you come for me or my beer?"

Sojee saw her reply, but he couldn't understand what she was saying. He watched Tanek tip his mug, fill the spoon with a drop of beer and hand it to her. Her wings slowed and she landed on the salt pot to sit and drink her beer.

"Prince Nessa is encased," Arit said.

"With a Selkan?"

Sojee understood only what Tanek said.

"Yes."

"That's not good," Tanek said. "He's promised to a princess, a female."

"He likes both. Or everything." She held out her spoon for a refill.

"Is he as bad as people here seem to think?" Tanek refilled the spoon and handed it to her.

"Worse." Arit looked at Kaley sleeping with her head on her arms. *"I saw her today. She is very pretty, and she has extraordinary eyes. They're like moonlight on Pithan."*

Tanek looked at Sojee. "You have brown moonlight on your island?"

He guessed what had been said. "On some nights, it's as beautiful as Kaley's eyes."

Tanek gave an eye roll, then looked back at Arit. "Too bad you can't talk to her and keep her busy today. I have to see someone and I don't want her knowing. But I dare not leave her alone."

"Do not let these men see her. They are very lonely. Do you understand me?"

"All too well."

Arit was smiling at Kaley as she held out her spoon for a third beer. *"You two would make beautiful babies."*

Tanek grimaced. "She's from Earth and wants to return there. And I have other things to do in my life."

"*You are probably right,*" Arit said. "*Besides, you're too old for her. She needs a younger man.*"

Tanek groaned. "Go home and sleep."

She fluttered her wings and rose about a foot above the table. "*Tomorrow, I will tell you where the prince is.*"

"Thank you."

She started to leave, but then turned her attention to Sojee, who was still staring at her. Suddenly, she flew directly toward his eyes.

Tanek came out of his seat, fearful that he would instinctively swat at her.

But Sojee didn't move. When she buzzed in front of his left eye, he winked his right eye in a flirtatious way.

She flew back and turned to Tanek. "*He is very controlled. He has done more than you think he has, and he is more.*" She paused in the air. "*I've heard stories that there is a white swan on this island.*"

"Is there?" Tanek said. "Where—?" But Arit was gone.

When her laugh came out of the void, even Sojee heard it. "The sweetest sound," he murmured.

Tanek stood up and nodded to Kaley. "You carry her."

Sojee touched his pen to Kaley's arm and she woke up. Or at least she woke enough to walk out of the tavern, sandwiched between the men, her hood covering her face completely. They left her in her room, then Sojee wedged the door closed. No one would enter without everyone hearing.

He and Tanek went to their room.

8

Kaley woke to a racket coming from her door. It sounded as though it had been nailed shut and a herd of elephants was trying to pry it open—and they were succeeding.

When Sojee and Tanek entered, she flopped back on the pillow. "I was right about the elephants." Behind them were two men carrying trays of food that they set on a table on the far side of the room.

Kaley felt so bad that she could only open half of one eye. She saw Sojee touch his forearm to the arm of one of the men. In addition to translating, whatever was embedded in his arm seemed to be a credit card system.

She rolled over in bed. *I must ask them to explain what has been put inside their arms. And mine. And when, where, how did I get it? I have to—* She went back to sleep.

"No, no," she heard Sojee say, then he scooped her up, blanket and all, and set her in a heavy wooden chair. "You have to wake up. We're going out."

"You boys go without me. I need sleep."

"You have to eat, then we will go," Tanek said. "You cannot stay here alone."

Kaley groaned. "Let me guess, breakfast is twelve pounds of beef. If I promise to eat every bite later, will you two let me sleep? Please?"

She felt one of them—probably Sojee—rummaging about in the blanket that was wrapped around her. She thought that she should protest, but she was so hungover she didn't care. She was only vaguely aware when he pulled her left arm out. He was holding the little blue light and he touched it to her arm. There was an electrical jolt that was a great deal stronger than what she'd felt before. "Ow! That hurts. I want to—" She broke off and blinked rapidly. "Oh. I mean, oh!"

"Better?" Sojee asked.

She threw the blanket off. "Yeah, I do feel better." She looked across the room to the bath. "I'll just, you know, then I think I'd like to have that dozen pounds of beef. I'll be right back."

Minutes later, they were seated around the table and going after the best beef she'd ever tasted. She held up a piece on a fork. "This is unfair to Kansas. You're trying to wipe out centuries of cattle drives and wranglers and…" At their looks, she quit talking.

"We must go out today," Tanek said.

"To search for the prince?" The men exchanged looks but said nothing. *More secrets?* she thought. "Sightseeing? Shopping in Selkan for pretty dresses?"

Again, the men looked at each other.

"If you two would tell me what you're hiding, it would save a great deal of time."

Sojee's eyes twinkled. "Young Tanek has private business in town. Would you like to escape our guards?"

"I would love to," she said.

"She can't—" Tanek began, but when the other two turned to him with faces like a block wall, he threw up his hands in surrender. "If we're caught, we'll find out what the prisons here are like."

"I imagine they're easier for men than for a woman alone," Kaley said sincerely. Whatever Sojee and his magic light had done, Kaley felt great. "Mind if I take a shower? I'm pretty grubby from last night's bar hopping."

Sojee stood up. "We will return in two herins." He and Tanek scurried out of the room.

"They have a different measure for time?" she murmured as she went to the bathroom. "I thought time was universal."

About thirty minutes later, they returned. Obviously, they'd not spent any time getting clean. She strapped the little camera her father had given her over her T-shirt and positioned it at her waist so it wouldn't encumber her front or back, then she pulled on a dark hoodie.

"We found a route to where Tanek needs to go," Sojee said.

"It's impossible to get there unseen," Tanek said.

"We can." Sojee looked at Kaley, grinning.

She smiled at him. "I bet roofs are involved."

He returned her smile and nodded.

From the way Tanek looked at them, he didn't appreciate being left out.

There was an old, rickety set of back stairs to the inn and Sojee went first, gingerly testing the strength of the rotting steps as he went down. At one point, he picked up Kaley by the waist and swung her down to a more solid step.

She couldn't resist turning to Tanek and saying, "Sojee will help you down, too."

Tanek narrowed his eyes at her, then made a leap that sent him sailing past Sojee and onto the ground. "Need help?" he asked as he looked up at her.

Sojee shook his head at both of them, then led them away. It wasn't easy to keep up with his long strides. Sometimes she'd give a little jump to cover the extra space between them. Tanek said nothing as he followed. They ran down an alleyway and, like before, Sojee vaulted up onto a roof. Kaley held her arms overhead and he easily pulled her up—or so she thought. When she got to the top, she saw that it was Tanek who'd lifted her. She pushed from him so hard, she almost fell backward, but he didn't move. That he caught her by the arm was quite annoying.

They were on their third roof when they heard an unusual silence. There had been the constant sounds of horses and men, even the clanking of steel, but it had abruptly become eerily silent.

"Get down," Tanek ordered, and they obeyed. The three of them flattened themselves on the rooftop and peered over the edge to the street below.

At first, Kaley wasn't sure what she was seeing, as to her it was an ordinary sight. A woman, wearing a long dress, her hair in braids, was walking on the street. Behind her were three children, then came a man who was strutting. That was the only way to describe his proud walk.

Every man on the street and in the few shops had stopped to watch them. There was such longing on their faces that it hurt to look at them. It was obvious that the sight of a family was an unusual one.

When they passed out of sight, the three rolled onto their backs and looked up at the sky.

"That was sad," Kaley said. "These men are very lonely."

"That's what Arit said." Tanek sighed.

"And who is that?" Sojee asked, amusement in his voice. "Anyone we've met? Sounds like she's the love of your life. Let's invite her for a beer."

Tanek rolled to his side, head on his hand, and looked across Kaley to him. "She's no one *you* will ever be alone with."

Sojee laughed.

"Should I be jealous?" Kaley asked.

"Yes!" Tanek said.

"No!" Sojee said.

She got up and looked down at Tanek. "We need to get to the place you want to go to because I think it's going to rain. Water might clean you two up—or melt you, I'm not sure which. Let's go somewhere quiet so you two can explain why I have something in my arm that connects me to people I've never met and to a place I have never been."

Tanek got up quickly. "Jobi. He can answer *all* your questions. But yes to needing to be someplace." He pointed. "There." He looked at Kaley. "Think you can make it?"

Where he was pointing was across a wide expanse between two buildings. "Easily," she said, but inside she wanted to run away. It was going to be difficult and dangerous.

"If you're too afraid," Tanek said, "Sojee can take you back. You'll be safe and protected."

"Drop dead." She went to the edge of the roof. There was a wide, empty place between the buildings. She looked at Sojee and he nodded in understanding. They'd do the human Ping-Pong ball act where he swatted her across.

But in the next second she saw Tanek running directly toward her. She started to step aside—as Jobi had taught her—but Tanek was too fast. As he passed, his arm went around her waist, and together they flew from one roof to the next.

When they hit, Tanek twisted and landed on his back on the hard roof—with Kaley on top of him. They were nose to nose, belly to belly.

She was trying to recover from the Tarzan act minus the jungle vine, while Tanek was smiling at her. He had nice teeth. That didn't matter as his arms were tight about her, holding her to him. "You can release me now."

"Sure? You still look scared."

"Let go of me, you jerk! It's starting to rain."

"You can shield me so I won't melt."

She jabbed her elbows into his rib cage, but it didn't seem to hurt him.

Still smiling, he let her go, rolled to the side and stood up.

Kaley stayed sitting on the roof and looked up at Sojee. "I like your way better."

"His landing onto his back seemed very practiced."

Kaley grimaced. "Probably. No doubt he's done that with Arit and Mekos and who knows how many from the other islands. I'm sure he's done it many times."

Tanek shook his head. "I catch fighting swans who weigh more than you do."

"Was there a compliment in there?" Kaley asked. "Or am I an angry swan? Even so, they're beautiful, so I accept it as a compliment."

Tanek didn't reply as he climbed down the side of a building on a ladder that didn't look very stable. The rain started coming down heavily, making everything slippery.

By the time they reached the building Tanek had pointed out, Kaley was soaked. She was blinking back water as they got to the door. From the look on Sojee's face, he planned to pick the door up and set it aside.

But she slid in front of him and turned the knob. The door opened and they walked inside. She couldn't resist a smirk at Sojee. She took off her wet sweatshirt, draped it over a chair back and looked around.

The rectangular room was obviously an old schoolhouse. One long wall was windows and the opposite wall was blank, as though it had once held chalkboards and maps. There were four rows of benches set under long tables. The place didn't appear to have been used for years.

"More sadness," Kaley said.

"There are fewer children, so many of the schools closed." Tanek's voice was hard, with anger underneath.

Sojee was looking around with as much surprise as Kaley felt.

"Where did you go to school?" she asked him.

"The one my father went to and his father before him. We had the same mean old master who liked to use a cane on us." Sojee smiled. "I broke it over my knee."

Kaley laughed. "And you?" she asked Tanek.

"I was taught by my family." He was looking out the window on the short wall, moving about as he tried to see through the rain.

There was a little light hovering under the cover of the roof overhang. "What's that?" Kaley asked.

"Whatever it is, it might get wet," Sojee said.

Tanek said nothing, just kept looking out the window.

On the other short wall were low cabinets, with seven framed portraits above them. There were four men and three women. "Who are these people?" Kaley asked. "Are they past presidents of Selkan?"

Both Tanek and Sojee were silent.

Even more secrets, she thought, and couldn't help gritting her teeth. The last portrait was of a woman with dark hair and deep blue eyes. "She's pretty." She read the name. "Vian Yrbain. She looks like someone I've met, but I can't think who. My dad is great at remembering faces. I bet he'd know who she resembles."

When the men stayed silent, she turned and saw that they were both staring at her. The little light outside was near the window by Tanek's head. Even it seemed to be watching her.

"What?" she asked. "Are these people some great secret?"

"They are the Peacekeepers," Sojee said.

"What does that mean?"

The men were silent for a long moment, then Tanek spoke. "They live on the fourth island. You won't be allowed to go there."

"Why not? Couldn't the king—?"

"No!" Tanek said. "No one can get a pass to that island." He turned back to look out the window just as the little light began to blink. "I must go. I'll be back soon." He went out into the rain and down the street.

Kaley sat down hard on a bench. "Did I stumble onto some mysterious, forbidden secret?" When Sojee said nothing, she looked up at him.

"The Peacekeepers rule all four of the islands. Years ago, they moved the Swankeepers' home from Selkan to Eren."

"Why were they moved?"

Sojee shrugged. "I don't know. It's not my Order."

"They issued orders?"

"Yes, but that's not what I mean. Everyone belongs to an Order. Tanek is of the Order of Swans."

"Of course he is. And you?"

Sojee said, "Jobi is in the Order of Sight. Aramus is from the Order of Kings."

Kaley didn't give up. "And *you*?" She could see that he was debating whether or not to tell her. "It would greatly raise my self-esteem if *I* knew a secret. Since you and Swan Man have a zillion of them that you keep from *me*, I'd like to have at least one of my own."

Sojee nodded. "You are right. I am of the Order of Royals."

Her eyes widened. "Wow. Are you a prince? A king?"

"I am related to Princess Aradella, yes."

Kaley smiled broadly. "I love this! So Tanek doesn't know?"

"No." Sojee smiled at her in conspiracy.

"I promise I won't tell him," she said. "Sometimes I think he believes you're as unnecessary as I am. Do you think Prince Nessa will recognize you as a big-shot royal?"

Smiling, Sojee held up his left arm. "Your words aren't easily translated to me. I am not a…"

"Big shot. I think you are, and Tanek can suck it."

When Sojee's laugh rang through the empty room, Kaley joined him. They were so loud they didn't hear the door open.

"You are Kaley?" a man said from the doorway.

Sojee instantly sobered and reached for his sword. He was obviously mortified that a man had entered without his knowledge.

Kaley stepped forward. "I am." She held out her hand to shake his.

He took it with both of his. "I am Collan. I live there." He pointed to a nearby house that had a blue door. "I traveled with Roal."

Her expression showed that she didn't know who that was.

"Tanek's father. Tanek was with us when he was a child." He looked at her side. "It's true. You do have a camera."

"I haven't used it, but then I'm not much of a photographer. Just some cell phone stuff. Actually, I haven't seen my phone since I got here. I'll have to ask Jobi. He—" She broke off as the men were looking at her.

Collan spoke. "I want to ask a… I believe you call it a favor. Will you take my photo with my sons? I want to get it to my wife and daughter on Pithan."

"Do you have an email address? WhatsApp?" She received blank looks. "Right. No internet towers. I don't know how to send the photos."

The men were looking at her in silence, letting her know that they had no idea, either.

"Yes, of course I'll take your picture."

Collan's voice lowered and his eyes were pleading. "I know other men. Their wives and daughters are not here. Could you…?" He waved his hand and didn't finish.

"I'll take photos as long as the batteries hold out. I'll fill the SD card. I'll—" She could see they had no idea what she was talking about. "Bring 'em on."

Looking like he was going to cry in gratitude, Collan ran back out into the rain.

She turned to Sojee. "I get the feeling that we're going to be bombarded with men. It won't be easy to remember all the names. I guess we can have them hold papers with their names on it. Kind of like criminals. What can we use for ID boards?"

Sojee had no idea what she meant but it didn't take them long to solve the problem. By the time they'd searched the old cabinets and found erasable boards and fat markers, there were half a dozen men with their sons lined up in front of the long window wall.

"Take a seat," Kaley said to Collan. He held his name board—written with symbols unknown to her. His two sons stood behind him, hands on their father's shoulders. "Smile," she said, and they did.

By the time Tanek returned, Kaley and Sojee had set up an assembly line for photos. Somehow, it had become a party. Food—meaning meat—appeared and lots of beer. The men knew each other and were laughing and catching up with news. It had turned into a happy occasion. Kaley wanted to say, "If you had women here, this socialization would happen often," but she didn't.

The rain had almost stopped when Tanek opened the door. As he looked on the scene, his scowl showed his mood.

Unfortunately, Kaley was close to the door.

"What do you think you're doing?" He was almost growling. "We're trying to keep things private."

"So you can do your secret sleuthing? Meet people to talk about...whatever?" She didn't give him time to answer. "You do realize, don't you, that if it weren't for me, you wouldn't be here? Tomorrow I want to talk to some people about old stories—which is why we're here. And oh yes, did you save the grandmother from the wolf?"

His eyes showed his shock. "How did you know that?"

"When you share your secrets with me, I'll tell you mine." She started to walk away, but turned back. She motioned to the many men in the big room. "If your purpose is to meet people, I think I've made more friends on Selkan than you have.

Funny how being *nice* works." She walked away from him and he went back outside.

Minutes later, the king's guards arrived. They were angry at having lost them.

Sojee spoke to them in their own language, then touched his forearm to theirs—to give them money, she guessed—and the men left. Except for the head guard, Garen. He seemed to be curious. He asked Sojee questions about the camera settings, who then asked Kaley, who usually answered, "I don't know." In the end, Garen was snapping the photos. He situated the men for better poses and when the food arrived, he had them include that in the pictures.

Near sunset, the camera batteries gave out. Her father had equipped the cute little camera with several SD cards, so they weren't full, but both batteries were exhausted.

Even after the photo session ended, the men didn't leave. They were enjoying themselves.

"They're going to set up a smoker soon," Kaley said. "They'll throw in some big fish and a turkey."

A few minutes later, Tanek appeared outside the window and yet again, the little light was beside his head.

"Is that light on his ear?" Kaley asked.

Sojee didn't answer. He drew himself up to his full height and spoke in a voice so loud that the windows rattled. He told them they had to leave *now.*

Kaley plastered herself against the wall to keep from being run over as the men left. Garen was last. He and Sojee exchanged some words, then Sojee held out his arm to give the man money. But Garen shook his head and didn't accept it.

Sojee went outside with Kaley close behind him.

"The prince is at a tavern," Tanek said as he looked at Kaley.

"I'm going," she said firmly.

He didn't try to argue. "You must cover yourself."

She understood that. Today she'd been with men who'd at

one time lived with women. That was different from the men
in the streets.

Kaley strapped on her camera, put her sweatshirt back on,
pulled the hood over her face and left the schoolhouse. This
time, Tanek led, with Kaley, then Sojee last. She was glad there
were no rooftop leaps involved, but they did go through some
rather dodgy alleyways. She didn't want to see what was lurk-
ing in the dark doorways.

When Tanek abruptly stopped at the corner of a building,
she almost ran into him.

"The prince is here."

"With that beast of his?" Sojee asked.

"Yes." Tanek stepped back to let Kaley go past him.

"No!" Sojee reached for his sword. "She can't face that thing.
I've heard that it's killed people. We must—"

Kaley didn't hear what else was said as she slipped past Tanek
and went around the corner. Standing there, backed by a stone
wall, the low sun hitting it, was an incredibly beautiful animal.
It was about six feet tall, with a sturdy body that curved. It
had thin horns that branched into two, and a heavy tail curled
around its strong body. It was covered in iridescent green scales
that glistened in the sunlight.

Kaley could only stare at the incredible beauty of the animal.

Behind her, Sojee started forward, but Tanek put himself in
front of the man.

Kaley took a step forward, then, as she'd done with the king,
she made a deep curtsy. She went very low in respect and ad-
miration.

The animal extended its foot, then lowered its head in an
answering bow.

In the next second, Kaley opened her arms wide and went
to the gorgeous animal. It kept its head down and let her hug it
and run her hands over its body, while she told it how beautiful
it was. She gushed praise and adoration.

Tanek stepped aside so Sojee could see what was happening.

"Dragons pledge to one person." Sojee's voice was low. "They bond even more closely than your tiny lady does." He looked at Tanek. "How did you know?"

"My swans wrapped their necks around her."

"But you are from the Order of Swans. She's an earthling. Other earthlings have been here, but none of them can…" He stopped talking as he watched Kaley with the heavy beast. She was tickling him under his jaw—a jaw that could make fire and fry people. "You think she'll ride away on him?" He was being sarcastic, but he was also in awe. "I was not prepared for this."

"Neither was I," he said. "I plan to get more information out of Jobi, whatever I have to do. Come on, we have to talk to the prince and get him to go home to his father. Why do I think the kid won't want to leave here?"

"After this, maybe his dragon will choose to follow our Kaley."

"Ours?" Tanek said. "Far from it. You have your pen? We might have to use it on the prince."

"I'm more than willing. Should we leave her here with… with that?"

"Ha! That creature might be able to create a Lely."

Sojee laughed at that but Tanek didn't. "We must go," Sojee said loudly to Kaley, and motioned toward the door to the tavern.

She gave a sigh and hugged the dragon's head. "I don't want to leave him. His name is Perus. Isn't that a pretty name?" She laid her cheek against his. "I'll be back as soon as I can." Reluctantly, she let go of him and stepped away. "Behave and don't burn anyone up. Okay?"

Tanek and Sojee were as far away as they could get. Sojee opened the heavy door. "He talks to you?"

"Sort of. I can hear things from him," Kaley said. "So where's the prince?"

Inside, Tanek went to the man behind the long bar. "The prince?"

The man jerked his head to the side. "Back there. I'll pay you to take him away. How much do you want?"

There was a crash of metal and wood against stone, followed by the clanging of steel. Sojee held out his arm to the barkeep. He meant to pay him for what was broken.

Kaley kept her face covered and stayed close behind Tanek as he went to the back of the dark tavern. The prince was at a table with half a dozen young men who didn't look like people you would trust. She absolutely did *not*, under any circumstances, want them to know that a woman was nearby.

As for the prince, he was almost as tall as Tanek, but of a slim build. He had the king's blue eyes, with black hair that stuck out around his head in a carefully arranged way. He wore a belted purple robe that was trimmed in gold piping and looked very expensive. But even the rich clothes couldn't make him handsome. That he appeared to be on multiple drugs didn't help his looks. He was brandishing a knife that flashed in the light of the wall lanterns.

Tanek stepped forward. "Your father wants to see you."

Nessa gave a laugh that told what he thought of that idea. "Oh yes. He wants me to marry Princess Bitchy."

Instinctively, Kaley stepped back against Sojee. She had an idea that hearing disparagement of his relative would make him attack. But Sojee didn't move. She looked up at him and he shrugged in a way that said the name was fair.

"She has agreed to the marriage," Tanek said. "She awaits you."

The young men laughed at that. It was as though they were saying, *Of course she has.*

"Entice him with money and power," Kaley said softly.

"Once you're married to her, you'll rule all of Pithan," Tanek said. "You'll be the king of the whole island. They have palaces and great wealth and—"

"Who is that behind you?" the prince asked, trying to see Kaley.

Sojee stepped out of the shadows. His size said everything so he didn't need to speak.

The prince looked disappointed. "I thought I heard a woman's voice."

"It's his," Tanek said. "He sounds just like a girl. We need to go now. Your father sent guards and they can take you back."

Nessa gulped one of the beers on the table. "I have all the wealth I need. I don't have to live with a princess who is old and plain-faced and has a tongue sharper than any steel."

"They do, don't they?" Tanek said. "A woman's words can cut a man in half." He glanced back at Kaley, hidden deep in the shadows, and saw her glare at him. "But I'm sure you're man enough to control her."

"Why should I try?" He looked from Tanek to Sojee, then at the drunken young men near him. It was as though he was calculating how a fight would turn out. "Tell my father I will *not* marry that old hag of a princess. I'd go with Olina before her." He smirked. "You won't be able to find me again." He gave a whistle of three tones, and a second later, his dragon appeared at the window. It bent its head and punched out the window. In a practiced leap, Nessa jumped on the dragon and in an instant, they were gone. The only thing they left behind was a hole where the window had been and six young men who cared only how much beer was left.

"Let's go," Tanek said.

Sojee led the way out of the tavern, pausing only to again touch forearms with the barman. "For the window."

With Kaley in the middle, the two men slowly walked back toward the inn. They didn't care if the guardsmen found them. They looked as dejected as they felt. They had failed their mission.

"So who is Olina?" Kaley asked. "And how old is Princess Aradella?"

Tanek had his mouth set as though he might never speak again.

"She's nineteen years old," Sojee said, "and no, she does not like fools."

"That leaves Nessa out," Kaley said so cheerfully that Sojee almost smiled. "And who is Olina?"

"Queen of Pithan," Tanek said.

"Queen of the island? And there's also a princess? Please tell me this is a stepmother story. I love those. Evil personified." She drew in a sharp breath. "Does she keep Aradella locked up in a tall tower with no door and the princess has really, really long hair?" The idea so fascinated Kaley that she stopped walking.

The men got two steps ahead, then halted and looked back at her.

"Olina is married to Aradella's uncle," Sojee said. "He was made king after his older brother, her father, died in an accident. She does not live in a tower, and her hair is not especially long."

"Oh." Kaley sounded disappointed. She started walking again. "It was just a thought."

Sojee suppressed a smile. "Her cousin did live in a tower."

"Was she rescued by a gorgeous young man?"

"He lived there, and a young woman scurried up the side to get to him. I believe she carried a key between her teeth." Sojee was looking at her in amusement.

"Great!" Kaley said. "A mix-up of the sexes. I can use that in my new dissertation." Again, she halted. "Wait a minute! If this Olina is queen, how can Nessa be crowned king if he marries a princess?"

"Order of succession. He would be king when it is time," Sojee said.

"You mean when this Olina is dead? This story is getting better," Kaley said.

Sojee looked at Tanek. "Who's going to tell the king what his son said?"

Both men looked at Kaley. "Me? Are you kidding?"

"It will be good in your dissection," Tanek said.

"Dissertation," she corrected.

"You're cutting us into pieces and examining us," he said.

Her mouth dropped open. "Did you just make a joke?" She looked at Sojee. "I have seen the light."

He laughed. Even Tanek gave a bit of a smile.

When they got back to the privacy of her room at the inn, she said, "I haven't seen any phones. How do we contact the king?"

Sojee looked at Tanek with interest. "Yes, how do you do that?"

Tanek set his jaw and made no reply.

Kaley sighed loudly. "Secrets on top of secrets. Okay, the important thing is to tell the king in a diplomatic way. You can't say, 'Your drunken, druggie son is refusing to marry the beautiful Princess Aradella.'" She looked at Sojee.

"Perhaps *beautiful* is too much."

"Powerful?"

"Very intelligent."

"Yes."

She looked at Tanek. "I'll write it down for you and you can read it to the king—or to whoever listens for him. You can—"

"I can't read that."

"Oh, sorry," she said. "I didn't know. I guess you could take some classes. You could—"

"I can't read *your* language!"

Kaley stayed serious. "What about the swans' markings in the sand?"

He looked at her like she was crazy, while Sojee suppressed laughter.

"So how do we do this?" Kaley asked. "I can write it, then read it to you while you're on the phone."

"No!" the men said in unison.

For a moment she put her head in her hands. "I'm not allowed to see you talk to the king?" She turned to Sojee. "But *you* can?" She took a breath. "All right. So the two of you can do this without me, but you have to be *nice*. *Kind*. You can't say awful things about his son."

"I'm sure he knows," Tanek said.

She glared at him. "All parents know the truth about their kids, but outsiders can't say it." When the men hesitated, she said, "So what's for dinner? Chicken?"

"I don't eat birds," Tanek said, then hesitated. "If you were to speak to the king, what would you say?"

She hid her smile as she began to tell her ideas of how to handle telling the king about his son.

Thirty minutes later, the men had secured Kaley's door and were headed down the stairs.

"I assume you mean to send the lovely Arit to relay your message to the king," Sojee said.

"Of course, just so the earthling doesn't see her. She's too close to figuring out where she is. When she does, I want Jobi to be with her. He's the one who should receive her anger."

"I have more faith in Kaley than that. I don't think she'll be hysterical."

"Not at you, but at me. Come on, we need to order beer. Arit likes it dark and strong. I truly dread telling the king that we're failing in this mission."

"You and me both," Sojee said.

9

Kaley was waiting for the men to return. Maybe they'd come back and say that the king understood. Or maybe he knew of a way to "capture" the prince. Lasso him then turn him over to the guards? But she knew that with the aid of his magnificent dragon, they would never find him. Truthfully, her main hope was that when all of this was over she would finally get to talk to some people about folktales.

When it got late and she was sleepy, she showered and started to put on the pajamas from her suitcase, but some instinct was warning her to stop. It was possible that the men would show up and tell her they needed to leave, and she wanted to prove that she could be ready in an instant.

With a bit of a smile, she decided to prepare for whatever might happen. In case she needed to move quickly, she put on her yoga clothes: black undies, black leggings and a black tank top. Over them, she put on a clean set of sweatpants and a hoodie. It was uncomfortable, but she left her shoes on. She got her backpack and filled it with her camera and dead batteries.

She zipped the pack closed and slipped it under the bedcovers. When the men showed up, she'd jump out, fully ready to leave with them. She smiled as she imagined their surprise.

In the bottom of her duffel bag was a tiny tube of nail glue that she'd bought when she'd torn her thumbnail. On impulse, she let a few drops fall over the scar on her forearm, the place that Sojee used his magic pen. Maybe the glue would block him if he used that thing on her.

Yawning, she at last climbed into bed and was asleep right away.

She was awakened by the noise of her door being opened. Yet again, her main thought was sleep. *Did those two ever sleep?* She kept her eyes closed.

As soon as they entered, she realized that this was different. It wasn't Sojee's heavy clumping feet, wasn't Tanek's lighter, quicker step. She waited for them to say something, but the people—there seemed to be two of them—were being as silent as possible.

She heard a slight noise at the foot of the bed and knew it was her duffel bag being moved. Thieves had somehow broken past the elaborate barricades on the door and were now looting her room. The last thing she wanted was for them to know she was awake and aware of what they were doing. Men who had been denied being with women for years were not something she wanted to deal with. She started sending out thoughts. *Sojee and Tanek, please wake up.*

She felt one of the men close to her. Her heart was beating hard. Would he hear it? She lay as still as death.

The man's face was near hers. She could feel his breath, smell it. He bent over her so long that she was racked with fear. Was there any way she could get her knife out of her backpack? Could she kick even though her legs were entangled in the covers?

When the man touched her arm, she had to swallow hard not to scream, and had to hold very still. Maybe the goods in the room were enough and he wouldn't attack her physically.

When she saw the tiny blue light and felt the almost familiar touch of the pen, she wanted to fight, but she lay still. Was he putting her to sleep so he could… She didn't want to think of it.

But in the next second, the men were gone. She heard the door close and felt the unmistakable silence of an empty room. Still, she didn't move. She wanted to give the men time to leave the inn with what they'd stolen. She didn't want to encounter them in the hall when she ran to Sojee and Tanek. They were going to be very angry when they found out what happened!

It was probably only a few minutes but it seemed like an eternity before she moved. She put on her backpack, the only thing left in the room, then went to the door and opened it. There was no lock on it. She peered out. The hallway was empty.

How had the men gone through the traps Sojee had set on her door without making a sound? Had the thieves broken into the men's room, too?

Silently, she went to their room next to hers. To her horror, their door was not fully closed. Inside, a wall light showed that their room wasn't like hers. It was plain and bare. There were two beds, one on each side of the room, and they looked hard and uncomfortable.

The big canvas cases they'd brought weren't in the room.

Sojee was in the closest bed. His bare feet hung past the bottom as the bed was too short for him. Tucked in beside him was his big sword and he had on his shirt. Hanging from the bedpost was his vest with its pockets. She grabbed it and felt. The pockets were empty! His little pen was gone and so was the leather packet that held the Papers of Passage signed by the king.

"Sojee," she said. He didn't move. Cautiously, she touched his shoulder. Abruptly waking a man the size of Sojee wasn't something she wanted to do, but he remained still. *The pen has been used on him*, she thought, then went to Tanek. He, too, was deeply asleep. "You have to wake up," she said. "Please wake up."

When the door to the room was thrown back loudly, she jumped and pulled her hood over her face.

A man she assumed worked at the inn was in the doorway, silhouetted by the light in the hall. Behind him were two big men.

"Out!" the first man yelled. "All of you, get out!"

"Thieves broke in." Kaley did her best to deepen her voice. She was a woman alone, with no protection. "My brothers—"

The man didn't let her finish. "Your bill wasn't honored! *You* are the thieves! You have no passage from the king! I should give you to the law." He jerked his head toward the big men behind him. One grabbed Tanek and pulled him up while the other one struggled with Sojee. With what she assumed were curses, the first man helped with Sojee. Kaley grabbed Tanek's shoes and Sojee's vest, and she was glad the men slept with their weapons. She didn't think she could hold all the steel they carried as she followed behind them. She was careful not to show her face or let the men touch her. They didn't know she was a woman and she didn't want them to find out.

The men shoved Tanek and Sojee out the big front door, and they landed facedown in the mud. It was raining again, so hard and fast she could hardly see where they were. The door to the inn slammed behind her.

Tanek was the first to move, then Sojee.

"We have to go," she said, then louder, "Please wake up. We must get out of here."

Tanek began to push himself up, and Sojee did, too. Whatever setting had been used on the pen, it was strong.

She went to Sojee. His feet may be bare, but he was fully weaponized, and far too big for her to handle. As Tanek tried to stand, she pushed him toward Sojee. The only way the men could move would be together.

The tiny bright light she'd seen around Tanek appeared. She could hardly see it for the rain, but then it flickered. "I don't know what you are, but I really need your help. Where do we go? What do we do?"

The light moved ahead, then returned. "You want us to follow you?" It flickered. Yes.

Kaley put herself between the men who were leaning on each other. "Come on, guys, let's follow the light." It was slow moving and she could barely see ahead of them, but she realized that the light was taking them back to the schoolhouse. It was easier getting there using the streets than leaping across the rooftops. "Collan's house," she said, and the light flickered again.

They stumbled through the pounding rain and when Kaley saw the blue door ahead, she wanted to weep in relief. She managed to lead Tanek and Sojee to lean against the side of a building, under the eaves, where they'd be sheltered. They were instantly asleep.

Kaley ran to the door and pounded on it. A sleepy Collan answered. "What—?" he began, then stopped when he saw who it was. He invited her in, but she pointed. The two men against the wall could hardly be seen. Collan yelled something she didn't understand and she saw his two sons come into the room. They ran out into the rain and led Tanek and Sojee into the house.

Collan shut the door behind him. "You can't stay here," he said.

"I know. I'm sorry. How do we get back to Eren?"

"Do you have the king's passage papers?"

"Not unless they're hidden on the men. Everything was stolen. They took…" She didn't know how to describe the blue pen—or if she should since she knew it was illegal.

He said something to his sons and they searched the clothing of the men, then shook their heads. Collan put his arm to Sojee's forearm then Tanek's and shook his head. "There's nothing registered. Whatever he has charged in the last day will not be paid. Creditors will be after you." He lowered his voice. "They can be cruel." He looked at her hard, letting her know what he meant. A woman would not survive them. "You can't leave Selkan without the papers. I have little credit. I—"

"No," she said. "We can't put you in danger."

"Do you have somewhere to go?"

"No. I don't know this place. I—" Behind the man was the tiny light and it started flickering frantically, as though in warning. "Swans," Kaley whispered, then louder, "Swans. I can hear the word. Is there a place, a homestead, for swans? I don't think it's inhabited now."

"Yes, there is. It's in the mountains. I've not been there, but I know where it is." Collan turned to his sons, spoke to them, and they hurried from the room. "They'll get the wagon and they'll take you there. But..." He hesitated. "We'll have to hide all of you."

She knew he meant her as well. "Of course," she said, but then looked at him. "Do you know who is after us? Who would do this to us?"

"Prince Nessa would want you out of his way. Were the thieves of your guard?"

"I don't know. There were two of them, but I kept my eyes closed and didn't see them."

One of his sons returned and nodded to his father. The wagon was ready. Sojee and Tanek had gone back to sleep.

"Will they ever wake up?" she asked.

"Not for a day. There is only one thing that can do that to a man."

Kaley knew he was asking if they had access to one of the illegal pens, but she wasn't about to tell him. "Selkan beer?" she asked.

He knew she didn't want to tell, and he smiled. "You make me miss my daughter. My sons will take you up the mountain. I'll stay here and lie about ever having met you."

"I hope you are the best at lying of any man on this island."

"Then I will have a lot of competition," he said.

She followed the sons out the back door to a covered area.

They managed to get Sojee and Tanek into the back of the wagon, then the young men climbed up to the seat.

The rain was still blasting down so Kaley went to the two horses. "I'm sorry for this," she told them. "We wouldn't go if it weren't necessary."

She went to the back of the wagon and looked inside. The two big men, one on each side of the wagon bed, took up most of the space, yet she was supposed to get between them. Collan was holding back the big canvas cover that didn't look like it would keep out the rain. "At least I won't get cold."

"I doubt you'll even live through it," he said, deadpan.

Kaley nodded. "It might be the better alternative." She took a deep breath, climbed up, then snaked her way between the two men. Tanek, sound asleep, threw an arm around her and Sojee put his leg up against hers. "I'm going to be squashed."

"Better that than what might happen if you stay here." Collan fastened the canvas down and the wagon took off.

10

Kaley was reluctant to wake up. There was something sticking in her back and her foot was so numb it seemed it may have been cut off. She kept her eyes closed as she tried to remember what happened during the night. Tanek and Sojee, heavy and rain-soaked, had been hard asleep. She couldn't imagine what she would have done if she hadn't had the little light that led her to Collan's house. He and his sons, the wagon, the horses, saved them. She remembered crawling into the back. Tanek and Sojee had acted like she was a teddy bear, but after that, she didn't remember anything.

Slowly, she opened her eyes. She was still in the wagon but she was alone. Over her head was the canvas covering. It had water on it but it wasn't leaking, and it was daylight out. There was an old blanket over her that smelled of horses, and under her head was something wadded up to use as a pillow. She pulled it out. It was Sojee's shirt.

Life was coming back into her body and she wondered where she was. Her clothes were damp as she scooted down the wagon bed and climbed out. She pulled out her backpack and Sojee's shirt and set them beside what looked like part of a wall.

She wanted to call out, but she was too cautious to do so. The horses had been unhitched and she wondered if they and Collan's sons were still there.

The first thing she saw was what had once been a village. There was a downhill road that was paved with large stones. Wagon tracks were worn into the rocks, but much of the pavement had been uprooted, leaving deep holes. There wasn't much left of the small houses that lined the road. Roofs were missing or falling in. Doors hung open. Windows were broken and bare. The place had an eerie feel, with no sounds, not of birds or animals or people.

At the top of the hill was a very large two-story house—or what was left of it. Most of the upper floor was gone, and it didn't take being a soldier to see the house had been blasted apart.

As she got closer, she saw holes in the walls and shattered windows. Doors had been torn off. She'd seen no evidence of guns since she'd been in Bellis, but only gunfire could have done this to the building. She walked along the front of the desecrated structure. Through windows and doors that had been ripped apart, she could see inside. There were uprooted mosaic floors and partial walls that had once been painted. "Swans," she whispered. Every picture showed swans.

This belongs to Tanek's family, she thought.

When she reached the end of the big house, she saw a lake in the back. For the swans. It would have been beautiful if it didn't have ruined pieces of the house in it. The upper part of a dome stuck up. Was it once a lookout tower? By the lake was part of what had been a fountain. Carved stone swans lay in pieces around the circular base. Kaley picked up a stone head and looked at the back of the house. It was worse than the front. The huge holes in the thick walls could only have come from heavy artillery.

Had Tanek's family fought the invaders with swords and daggers? she wondered. If so, there must have been a lot of deaths.

She thought back to the conversation she'd overheard. Tanek had sounded happy when he talked of going to the homestead. He spoke of seeing *the old place*. Would he have been looking forward to it if he knew he was going to see a battlefield?

If Tanek was just seeing this, how was he doing? she wondered.

She carefully put the stone head on the side of the fountain and slowly walked along the back. Under the destruction, she could see the beauty of the place. Near the water was a round gazebo. Three of the six pillars that held the roof up had been shot away. The domed roof was covered with tiles of emerald green, and on the top was a sculpture of a swan, its wings raised as if it was about to fly away. One wing was half-gone.

She stood there for a while, looking out over the water, imagining what it had once been. Iridescent swans on the blue water, Tanek's family calling to them. It must have been a magical place.

When she heard a slight sound, she turned to it. At the side of the house she saw Tanek. He was sitting on the steps of a small separate building that may have been a chapel. Since the roof was gone and the windows torn out, she couldn't tell what it was. He was sitting there staring at the side of the house in silence.

Had he been a close friend, she would have asked him to talk to her, but she didn't. She sat down beside him on the steps. She didn't have to know him well to see that his face was a study in devastation. In grief and shock.

She said nothing, just waited. If he wanted to talk, she was there.

"I was lied to my whole life," he said softly.

It didn't take much to figure out what he meant. The happiness she'd heard from him at the idea of visiting his family's old home didn't match what they were seeing. She waited for him to continue.

"My family told me they left here for the swans, that it was a voluntary move. The swans would be better off on Eren so they went there." He nodded behind him but he didn't look over his shoulder.

Kaley turned and saw that lying on the floor inside the little building was the broken statue of a man. The head had been hacked from the body; one leg was crushed.

"That's my grandpapá, Haver. He was a brilliant man. He taught me everything I know. He was the one who discovered more of what the feathers can do." When Tanek turned to her, she saw that his eyes were red from crying. "By the time he was my age, he'd learned more than all our ancestors had. His discoveries saved lives." Tanek stood up. "The feathers. Did you know that they have healing powers?"

"No," she said softly.

"They do. Crush them, blend them, make lotions, capsules, and they'll heal sickness." He took a breath. "But there's something few people know. The swans have to *give* their feathers. If you take them, they don't work."

He turned away and ran his hand over a window frame that had once been beautiful.

"I understand," she said. "They only give the feathers to people who love them. To your family, to the Order of Swans."

He leaned back against the stone wall. "Yes. My grandparents told me great stories about this place. I've dreamed of it all my life. I didn't know..." He waved his hand to indicate the destruction. "Why did no one tell me the truth of why they left?"

"They wanted to protect you," Kaley said. "My father used to sugarcoat every bad thing that happened. It's what parents do."

He closed his eyes for a moment, and his lips were tight. "When we got here last night and I saw what had been done to our family, I talked to my father."

"Did he tell you what happened?"

Tanek took a few moments to calm himself. "He did. The government said the healing powers of the swans made them belong to 'the people,' not to just one family. We had no right to keep them to ourselves, so they would take over the care of the swans. My grandpapá protested that it was more than one family, that it was an entire village. It was the industry of hundreds of people. But the government didn't agree. They took it all." He moved his hand to indicate the village. "It was a violent over-taking. The town and our homes were blown up. Many swan-herders and artisans died." He paused. "Grandpapá only gave up when his youngest son was killed. My uncle. Until today, I didn't even know he existed." Tanek looked away, not wanting her to see the tears in his eyes.

"And after they took the swans, they found out that the feath-ers they stole had no power," she said. "I can believe that. Your swans are loving creatures."

Tanek worked to get himself under control. "It took the gov-ernment two years to realize their error, then they set up a new homestead for our family. It's on the water on Eren, at the top of the island, with high walls and guards and absolute privacy. We are protected."

"Protected from the people who did this to you?" Kaley didn't conceal the bitterness in her voice.

When he looked at her, he seemed to be pleased by her under-standing. He started to say something but they heard Sojee call out. He was near them.

Tanek had a look of panic. "I…" When he rubbed his eyes, she understood. Machismo. That male creed. He didn't want Sojee to see that he'd been crying.

Kaley didn't have time to think of a lie to cover Tanek's di-lemma. Instead, she picked up a handful of sand and threw it into his face.

"What the farkel!" he said—or at least that was how the trans-lator in her arm made it sound.

When Sojee came around the corner, Tanek was spitting out sand and trying to clear his eyes, which were very red. "I stumbled and got sand in his eyes. So sorry." Kaley looked at Tanek. "Do you need any help?"

"Not from you," Tanek said with a grimace.

"Collan's boys took the horses back." Sojee was looking at Tanek hard, as though he was trying to figure out something. "Did you know this place had been destroyed?"

Kaley took a step toward him. "Where did you get those boots? I didn't see yours at the inn. Too bad as we could have used them as boats in the rain." She smiled sweetly at him.

Sojee stopped staring at Tanek. "I found them in a stone chest. They fit me."

"Stone?" Kaley said quickly. "I bet it had a heavy lid. Did you move it?"

He looked down at her with amusement. "I did."

"I'm proud of you. Why don't we go see that chest?" She was giving Tanek time to regain his composure.

Tanek was brushing sand off his face and out of his hair. "Those boots probably belonged to my grandpapá." He spit out more sand. "He was a big man."

"Then why are you so small?" Sojee asked.

Kaley knew that was a male-to-male insult and she started to protest. Tanek was anything but *small*. But then, she was glad to see that he smiled.

"He had a small wife and my mother is tall but thin," Tanek said. "Generations of women cut me down."

Sojee grinned. "They do that to all men."

"Give me a break!" Kaley said. "I saved the *lives* of you two whiners and you haven't even thanked me. It took a lot of strength to pull you two out of the mud."

"Who did you lift first?" Tanek asked.

She knew he was making fun of her, but she was so glad he was smiling that she didn't mind being the object of ridicule. "Why, Sojee, of course," she said. "Then he picked up little you. Only took one hand."

The men laughed, but their eyes lingered on her. There was gratitude in them.

"My pen," Sojee said softly. "It was taken from me. I…"

She saw that he was embarrassed at having been attacked in the room.

Tanek looked at Kaley. "Didn't they go into your room? They didn't use the pen on you?"

"They did, but I blocked them."

The men's eyes widened. "With your mind?" Sojee asked.

"No! I don't have any power like that. I used nail glue."

"What?"

"I put nail glue over that scar on my forearm. I hoped it would block the signal and it did."

"What is nail glue?" Sojee asked.

"Obviously, it's very potent stuff. I'm just glad it worked and I didn't go into a deep sleep. It would have been bad if at least one of us hadn't been awake."

The men looked at her for a long moment and she could see the puzzlement in their eyes. "Why don't we go see that chest you found? Any normal-size clothes in it?"

"There were some for children. Young Tanek here could fit them."

"If they have shirts for you," Kaley said, "we can use them as sails on your boots and float over to Eren. I have a few things I'd like to say to the king." She held up her arm. "Is there any money left on these things?"

"Very little," Tanek said. "Your king wasn't pleased when we told him we couldn't get his son. He took away all he'd given us and most of our personal credits as well."

"He's not my king!" Kaley said.

Tanek gave a sound like "Hmph!" and walked ahead. He seemed to know where he was going in the derelict house. He stepped over a fallen wall, then disappeared through an open doorway.

When Kaley hastened to follow him, Sojee moved beside her. "You stumbled and accidently threw that much sand directly into his eyes?"

Kaley didn't reply to his question.

"You're protecting him."

She stopped walking and faced him. "Yes, I am!" She was fierce. "And I'd do the same for you, so pretend you believe every word I say. Got it?"

Sojee blinked a few times, then said, "Aradella will like you." With that, he strode ahead and caught up with Tanek.

"Aradella?" Kaley said. "The young woman whose nickname is Princess Bitchy? I'm not sure I like that."

Ahead of her, Tanek stepped out of the doorway. "Can't you keep up with us?"

She wasn't fooled by his question. He didn't want her to be alone even if it appeared that no one else was there. And the truth was that Kaley didn't want to be alone. She didn't trust appearances any more than he did.

Tanek and Sojee were standing in what had once been a large room. What was left of the floor was blue-and-white tiles showing a flock of swans. The walls were frescoed with more pictures of swans. There were tall, empty spaces of what had been a wall of windows that looked out at the water. Remnants of a bathroom were to the side.

"My guess is that this was your grandfather's bedroom." Kaley looked at Tanek and he nodded. "Did he draw a floor plan for you?"

"He did." They exchanged smiles.

Sojee had gone to the corner to a beautiful stone chest that was the size of a sarcophagus and was pushing the heavy lid back.

"There isn't a...you know...inside, is there?" Kaley asked. It did look like a coffin.

"No," Tanek said. "Grandpapá didn't want the children who

ran in and out of his house to get into his weaponry, so he made it so only he could get into the chest."

"There are no weapons in here now." Sojee was leaning over so far he was half inside it.

"I'm sure that what was in there was used," Tanek said so softly only Kaley heard.

Sojee pulled out clothes from the chest and tossed them onto the lid. The shirts and trousers, even the socks, were old, but they were in excellent condition.

Kaley picked up a soft, cream-colored shirt. "This feels like cotton but it's not."

"It has swan feathers added," Tanek said. "The fabric isn't made anymore."

"Whatever it is, I like it." Sojee began to remove his dirty, torn clothes.

"Should I leave?" Kaley asked.

Tanek pulled his shirt over his head. "There's nothing you haven't seen before. Tell us what happened last night. Every word of it. Was it the king's guardsmen?"

As before, Kaley was staring at Tanek's bare chest. He was what men were supposed to look like in fantasies!

Sojee put himself in front of Tanek. He, too, was mostly nude, but he didn't have the same effect on her that Tanek did. "Was Garen involved?"

"I don't think so." She turned her back to the men and looked at the pretty blue wall. "I didn't see them but I heard their steps. They were light. It could have been two of the men who came with Garen. Do you think Garen sent them?"

"I have no idea," Sojee said. He pulled on a shirt, and when she turned around, he smiled warmly at her. "You did a good job. No soldier could have done better. We thank you." With that, he picked her up and hugged her, making her laugh.

When he set her down, she looked to Tanek for his thanks, but he said nothing, did nothing. "Do you find me so repulsive that you can't touch me?" She was half serious, half teasing. "And after last night when you wrapped yourself around me?"

Sojee gave a loud laugh. "That is the problem with ol' Tanek. He wants to wrap and wrap and wrap—"

Tanek said something in a language that didn't translate for Kaley, but she understood it. The gist of it was that if Sojee didn't shut up, Tanek would hack him into small pieces. Kaley smiled broadly, and Sojee slapped him on the back so hard he almost fell forward. He put his foot out and stayed upright. "Thank you," Tanek said to her.

"Maybe I'm not so useless after all," she said.

"We would have awakened," Tanek said.

"Boooo," Kaley said, and the men laughed. She went to the few clothes left on the stone lid and looked through them. There were two more shirts and one big pair of trousers. If she put on any of it, she'd trip. She looked down at her sweat-suit set. It was torn, dirty and all around hideous. On the other hand, the men looked clean and cool and comfortable. "No clothes for your little grandmother?" she asked Tanek.

"There was a wooden cabinet over there." He pointed to the far wall that was now empty.

That he knew so much about the place made her see even more how much the homestead meant to him. He'd waited all his life to see the place and was now standing in the ruins. "Oh, well," she said. "Maybe something will show up." She hesitated. "I don't mean to be bossy, but if we're to leave this island, we need to plan how to catch a dragon and its rider. I know a bit about training a dragon but not catching one."

They looked at her blankly. "Sorry. That's an American joke." She paused for a moment. "I want to say that I think it's right of you to keep the islands of Bellis hidden. If it were known to the world that dragons—or I guess lizards—as big as Perus existed here, people would kill each other to catch them. Do-gooders would go crazy trying to 'save' them, but the truth is that people here are taking care of them quite well." The men were staring at her. "Are there many like Perus?"

Tanek answered. "He's the only one I've ever heard of. I don't know where he came from."

"There's not a nest and breeding parents anywhere?" she asked.

"Not that I know of," Tanek said, and looked at Sojee, who shrugged.

"No Order of Dragons?"

"No." Tanek was so serious that Kaley felt she was offending him. Or, more likely, they were keeping secrets from her. Kaley was about to, yet again, tell them what she thought of that when Sojee said, "Is anyone hungry?"

"Starving," Tanek said. "But if we find any food here, it's probably ancient."

"Come with me," Sojee said. "I did find some food this morning, and it's extraordinarily delicious."

Kaley wanted to try to get the men to tell her whatever they were hiding, but her stomach won over. As filling as beef was, even it wore off after hours of struggling through the rain and being thrown about in a wagon.

Close to where Kaley had left her backpack, Sojee picked up an old bag, opened it and pulled out three really cute decorated gingerbread people. There was one girl and two boys. He held out one of each to Tanek. "Which do you want?"

With a glare, Tanek took the boy.

Kaley took the girl in her pink skirt, with her golden hair, and began to eat from the bottom up. It was the best gingerbread she'd ever had. Soft but crunchy and not too spicy. "There's nothing like an overload of sugar to lift a mood. Where did you get this? Is someone in the village selling it? It would be nice to think this place is coming back to life."

"It never will," Tanek said. "It's ensourced."

"What does that mean? Oh! That it's haunted?"

Sojee frowned. "That word doesn't translate. What do you mean?"

"Inhabited by the spirits of people who have passed on." They looked blank. "Died."

"No," Tanek said. "Tabors."

"Are they ghosts?" Again, she got blank looks. "I think Jobi is going to have to explain the words for this. Where did you get the gingerbread kids?"

Sojee seemed glad to change the subject. "While you were sleeping in the wagon and our Swan Boy was bewailing his ancestral home, I did some exploring."

Tanek looked at Kaley, but she shook her head. She hadn't told Sojee about his tears. "What did you see?" she asked.

"A house made of these cakes. Even the roof is cake." He held up the foot that was left of his gingerbread man. "There were a couple of kids there picking off pieces and filling their pockets. I joined them."

"Children?" Kaley asked. She could feel her face draining of blood. "Hansel and Gretel?"

"Never heard those names before but it was two girls. I don't know how they're on Selkan. Anyway, one called the other Sira, then they ran off."

"She prefers boys," Kaley whispered. "Did you see who was inside the house?"

"No." Sojee didn't sound interested. He looked at Tanek. "How does a house made of cake stand up to the rain?"

"Maybe you didn't see a bigger roof covering it," Tanek said.

"There wasn't anything over it. The house is in the middle of the woods, with a trail leading to it. I didn't see anybody but there were toys around it. Dolls and slingshots and—" He stopped because Kaley had stood up.

"We have to go," she said. "Now. This minute. We've got to go to that house."

The men didn't move. "I'll go hunting," Tanek said. "There's deer around here so we'll have something to eat. We can—"

"No!" Kaley said loudly. She took a breath, then looked at Tanek. "Remember how I knew about the wolf and the little girl in the red cape? The wolf was dressed as the grandmother, right?"

Sojee looked at Tanek in disbelief. "That's true?"

Tanek shrugged. "It is. We vowed to tell no one. It was too strange."

"Like I know about that, I know about this," Kaley said. "The woman who lives in the gingerbread house captures children so she can…" She didn't want to say out loud what the witch did.

Sojee didn't move and his smile seemed to say that he thought her story was amusing but there was probably no danger.

But Tanek stood up. "We'll go."

Kaley was grateful that he believed her.

They looked at Sojee and he nodded. "If there's any danger to children, I'll help."

11

Sojee didn't take the path he'd used earlier, but led them through the forest. It wasn't easy walking across the fallen branches. The ground was covered with vines that seemed to grab at Kaley's feet. When she was struggling to free herself, Tanek put a strong arm around her waist and pulled her out. He set her down and they continued walking.

When they came to a little hill, Sojee motioned for them to get down. They stretched out on their stomachs, with Kaley in the middle. Just below them, in a beautiful forest setting, was the gingerbread house. It was more enchanting and enticing than any storybook had ever pictured it. The walls were soft and warm-looking, and the roofline was edged with hundreds of dancing gingerbread figures. Their happy faces were outlined in colored icing. There were boxes made of candy that were filled with icing-covered flowers. The dirt was chocolate. The windows of the cottage were made of layers of crystallized sugar that seemed to promise even better treats inside.

What no book had been able to convey was the heavenly

scent. It was apple pie fresh out of the oven, muffins, cakes, doughnuts and the spicy gingerbread. The smells wafted up to them. Kaley closed her eyes for a moment then started to get up. Two hands, one from each man, pressed down firmly on her lower back.

"Right," she said. "Sorry."

"What do you know of the owner?" Sojee asked her.

She noticed that he didn't say "witch." Was it a forbidden word? "She has very bad eyesight. She..." The reality of the old story that she'd heard since she was a child came to her. Her voice was barely above a whisper. "There was a boy and a girl. She put the boy, Hansel, in a cage and fed him a lot. She wanted to fatten him up so she..." Kaley could hardly say what the story told. "So she could eat him. Each day, she had him hold up a finger to see how fat he was getting. But Hansel found..." Kaley swallowed. "In the back of the cage were bones from past children she'd murdered. Hansel held up a finger bone to show her he was still thin. The woman was angry that he wasn't gaining weight."

"And the girl?" Tanek asked.

"She was worked half to death," Kaley said. "And given very little to eat."

The men looked at each other and nodded in silent agreement. Sojee spoke first. "I'll draw her out, then you and Tanek can go in through the side of the house. Once I've dispensed with the woman, we'll send the children home." He was looking at her in question, waiting for her agreement.

"Yes," she said.

"Stay here until I signal you," Sojee said.

He made it sound simple and she lay beside Tanek, both of them watching as he went down the side of the hill and put himself in front of the adorable, fragrant little house. How could anything bad be in there?

"Come out!" Sojee bellowed. He looked like the giant he

was as he stood there, sword at the ready. He was a formidable opponent.

In the next second, out of the chimney came sparkling balls. They were the size of a softball and were so cute that all they could do was stare. The silvery spheres looked like they would taste good.

Sojee seemed as mesmerized as Kaley and Tanek were because he didn't move, just watched the balls slowly come down. It was very much like fireworks.

But then, one of them came within a foot of Sojee and burst into flame. Hot, red, angry flame. When Sojee's shirt caught fire, Tanek was up and running in an instant.

The sparkling fireballs doubled in number, aiming at both men. Kaley stood up. There was nothing at the sides of the house, and all attention was on the men. She knew she had to use the time the witch was focused elsewhere to get into the house.

As Tanek swatted a fireball away, he saw Kaley and nodded. It was as though he could read her mind.

She stepped into the shade of the forest and ran toward the far end of the house. The hill was steeper there and she half ran, half scooted down. When she looked around the house, she saw Tanek make a leap into the air as he redirected a ball away from Sojee. Her eyes widened as his jump was so high that his feet were level with Sojee's head. *Like a swan*, she thought. She turned back to the side of the house. In picture books, the gingerbread house had flat sides, as though giant slabs of the cake had been baked in an enormous oven. But that wasn't the case here. There was a frame to the house and the walls were six-inch square slabs of gingerbread that overlapped like roof tiles. It would be easy to pull them off. But then it had been built to trick kids into eating it.

The problem was that the witch was still inside. She needed the woman to get *out*! Kaley went to the corner of the house and waved her arms to Tanek. When he looked, she made a motion of going in. He understood.

He reached inside his boot, pulled out a thin knife and threw it at one of the sugar windows. There was a scream of outrage from inside and bursting out of the front door came a hideous old woman. She was as ugly as she was portrayed in books. Wiry gray hair stood out from her head. She had a big nose, large, crooked teeth that had probably never seen a toothbrush, and a dumpy body. She was surrounded by hundreds of the fireballs— and she was aiming for Sojee.

Kaley wanted to do something to help the men, but instead, she frantically began tearing the gingerbread slabs off the side of the house. It took only seconds to get through. Inside, it was small and warm, but that was probably from the giant oven against the wall. In the corner was the cage and inside was a very plump little boy.

When there was a movement to the side, Kaley reacted by picking up a skillet, ready to use it as a weapon. But a little girl, thin to the point of emaciation, and filthy, heaved herself off a wooden shelf and stood up. "I'm sorry," was all Kaley could say.

She went to the cage and to her horror, she saw no door, no keyhole, no way of opening it. The boy came to stand by the bars. "How do I get in?" she asked him, and saw that he didn't understand. It looked like the thing that had been planted in her arm didn't know their language. Outside, she heard yelling, and blasts of light flashed through the candy windows. "Hansel?" The boy's eyes lit up. It was a word he knew and he nodded.

She pantomimed how to get the door open, but he shook his head. She looked at Gretel. Did she know? No.

Kaley saw a slop bucket in the back of the cage. When they first arrived, the boy had been locked inside and left there. The children had probably been too frightened to pay attention to the opening and closing of a cage door, and it didn't appear to have been opened since.

She looked around the little room. There were shallow shelves with dirty bottles on them. She picked up one. It was full of eyeballs. Another seemed to contain tongues. She tossed them to the floor in disgust.

There were more shouts outside. Voices she'd come to know well were yelling something to her. A warning. In the next second, she heard a sizzling sound and half a dozen silvery balls fell inside. Gingerbread wasn't good at keeping out fire!

Gretel threw her skinny arms around Kaley's legs. *Help me,* she thought, then said loudly, "Someone please help me!" Smoke was beginning to fill the room.

On the wall with the nasty jars a light appeared. It was tiny and the smoke nearly hid it, but she saw it. It was the light that had guided her to Collan's house! It landed on something hanging on the wall. It had a string, like a necklace. At the bottom was a half-round pendant that looked like something from her father's car repair shop. Very ordinary and unremarkable.

When the light flickered, Kaley grabbed the necklace and took it to the cage. "Please," she whispered, coughing at the smoke. Gretel was holding on to her so tightly, Kaley could hardly move, but she didn't dare send the girl outside into the fireballs.

Kaley touched the pendant to the cage but it didn't open. The smoke was making her eyes water. The smell of gingerbread burning black in the fire filled the place with acrid smoke.

Her vision was blurry, but it seemed that the light that wasn't far from her face showed a tiny woman. She had wings and a dress that glistened. Kaley blinked hard. The woman was still there and she was motioning something. She was putting something over her head.

Kaley understood. She put the necklace on and it instantly felt warm against her chest. Then there was that little electric charge she'd felt from Sojee's pen. When Kaley touched the necklace, the front of the cage came open and Hansel ran out.

He grabbed his sister's hand, she didn't let go of Kaley, and the three of them got out through the hole in the side of the house.

Outside, she directed the children to run up the hill to safety. They were coughing but managed to obey. Kaley went around the corner of the house. She was going to do what she could to help the men. The air seemed filled with the blazing silver balls.

When the men saw the children run up the hill, and saw that Kaley was safely outside the burning house, they stopped jousting with the lethal balls and stood still. Kaley felt a sense of panic. The men were going to be hit!

But neither man seemed to care about that. In tandem, they walked toward the hideous old witch. She was screaming what sounded like spells, but the men didn't stop. When they were a few feet from her, Tanek took a step back. He was letting Sojee take the stage.

Kaley watched as Sojee picked up the little woman, turned her sideways, lifted her over his bent leg and broke her body in two. The sound of her bones breaking filled the air, and Kaley looked away. When the necklace she was still wearing began to feel too warm, she took it off. She wondered if she should throw it into the fire but instead, she put it in her pocket.

12

Kaley didn't ask the men what they did with the broken body of the witch—but there was black smoke pouring out of the stove's chimney in what was left of the cute little cottage. They'd been happy to see Hansel and Gretel's father come for his children. Kaley ran to tell him that he needed to watch out for his new wife, the children's stepmother.

Sojee followed her and translated. The father said quite a bit to Sojee before he took his children's hands and led them away. Kaley asked what the man said. "The woman is dead," was all Sojee replied, then he went down the hill and said no more. She thought about how the stories said the stepmother had died but not how. From the look on the faces of the father and Sojee, it wasn't a "natural" death.

As Kaley went down the hill to join the men, Tanek came around the burned cottage holding a haunch of venison. "I found this in the back." He was smiling broadly. He took his other hand from behind him and held up a bottle of wine. "There's a shed full of these bottles and they are Pithan's best."

"Ah," Sojee said, "true, but Selkan has the best beer." He looked at the big piece of meat. "Can you cook it?"

They looked at Kaley.

"Because I'm female, I should know how to cook? Do the laundry? Scrub the toilets?"

Yet again, they gave her a blank stare. They had no idea what she was talking about.

"Yeah, I can cook it," she said. "I saw a firepit over there, and there's a spit."

"You will spit on it?" Sojee asked.

"Translation error." She was laughing. "Do you guys know how to uncork the wine?"

That seemed to translate well as Tanek stuck the cork between his teeth and twisted. The bottle opened.

In jubilation, they raised their arms and gave a shout. They'd saved the children and found wine and food. It was good to be alive!

As the men wrestled the meat onto the big skewer and built a fire, Kaley rummaged in the ruins of the house and found tall mugs. She discovered a stream not far away and used it for washing the mugs and herself. She stripped down to her tank top, cleaned up as best she could, then put the dirty sweatshirt back on. Her tank top was a bit too revealing since she'd inherited her grandmother's ample bosom.

Tanek found the garden hidden behind the trees. The three of them stood there looking at it with smiles. It was beautifully kept. There were carrots, potatoes, onions, fat tomatoes, long green beans and four kinds of lettuce. Everything was ripe and ready, not bothered by seasons. "More magic," Kaley said. "The old witch certainly lived well."

"She had to have a backup for when she ran out of—" When Sojee saw the look on Kaley's face, he didn't finish.

Kaley found the skillet she'd almost used as a weapon, and with fat from the meat, she fried the potatoes with sliced onions. The men looked at her as if she were performing magic. "I learned it from camping with my dad."

Kaley insisted that the contents of the jars in the cottage be destroyed. While the meat cooked, they drank wine and cleared out the house. She didn't look to see what was in the jars as she tossed them to the men. They found a shovel, dug a hole and emptied the contents into the earth. They put the empty jars on top, like a reminder of the horror that had been.

Finally, they were able to sit down on the grass and eat. They were on the side of the cottage that was still standing and it made a pretty background.

"Such evil in such beauty," Tanek said. He had a metal plate full of meat, potatoes with onions, and chopped salad. He looked at Kaley. "You said that in this expedition, you are the useless one. You said to me, 'You are the leader and I'll always respect that.'"

Kaley wasn't sure what he was getting at but Sojee did. "We could have left *you* behind," he said to Tanek, and he nodded in agreement.

Their compliment was so sincere that Kaley felt her face turn red. It was oh, so very pleasing. "Who wants more potatoes?" She refilled the plates of both men.

"You've seen our country and our lives," Tanek said. "What about your life?"

With all the wine, his face had softened. The man she'd known until then would never have asked such a personal question. "It's not very interesting. My mother died just days after I was born, so I grew up with my grandparents and my father. He has a car repair shop. I have no idea why, but I've always been fascinated with folktales."

"Like the one of the gingerbread house?" Tanek asked.

"Yes, exactly like that. My plan is to teach. And I'll never stop researching."

"But you came to Bellis instead," Tanek said.

"I'm here so I can write a new paper," she said. "The first one was turned down so I need some new stories."

Tanek made no reply to that, just looked down at his food.

"Have you found the stories you need?" Sojee asked.

"Oh yes. One or two more and I'll be ready to go home. I miss my father and my grandparents terribly." She looked at Tanek. "We have that in common."

There was a look of question from Sojee.

"My grandpapá was Haver Beyhan."

Sojee's eyes widened, then he put his hand to his heart and bowed his head. "I salute you."

"You didn't tell me he was famous," Kaley said.

"I am wearing his boots." Sojee's voice was full of awe. "And his shirt, but it is burned." He sounded sad.

Kaley was thinking of what Tanek had told her. "You must have been miserable when he died."

There was silence from the two men.

"What am I missing?"

"He disappeared," Tanek said. "He went out and never returned. He—"

Sojee cut him off. "With wine, you can cry as easily as laugh. We've had too much happiness today to go the other way. Our young friend seems impressed with your jumping skills, so you must show her." He looked at Kaley. "Swan Men can do that. It's left over from long ago."

"It's weakening," Tanek said. "Grandpapá could soar a foot higher than me. Even my father is better than I am."

"Ridges fading?" Sojee asked.

Tanek nodded.

"Okay, you two. Let me in on this. Ridges that are fading? What does that mean?"

"Show her!" Sojee said. When Tanek didn't move, he said, "She likes the front of you well enough, so she shouldn't be shocked by the back of you."

Tanek gave an expression of disgust then shrugged. He drained his mug of wine, stood up and removed his shirt.

Kaley'd had too much wine to be able to suppress a sigh—which made Sojee laugh.

"Go on, Swan Boy. Turn around."

Tanek seemed to take a breath for courage then turned. On his splendid, muscular back were two dark brown, curved—as Sojee called them—ridges. They were about a foot long and stood out more than an inch from his skin.

It took Kaley a few seconds to understand. "They're where wings grow," she said. "We have body reconfiguration, too. Do you attach wings for a costume?"

Sojee laughed. "It's where the wings used to be when his ancestors were great soaring birds."

"They *grew* there?" she asked in astonishment.

Tanek nodded. "They were soft when I was born, then yes, they grew."

"Go on!" Sojee drained what had to be his fifth mug of wine. "Let her feel what they're like."

Tanek knelt in front of her, his bare, broad back inches from her face. She ran her hands over the ridges. They seemed to be made of horn, like on a cow—or more likely on a buffalo. Since Kaley had had three mugs full of wine—her excuse anyway—her hands wandered downward to his waist, then up to his shoulders, then out to his arms. His warm brown skin was deeply shaped by hard muscle.

"I cry for relief!" Sojee said as he refilled his mug. "I hunger for my own island where there are women. Many of them."

Kaley came out of her trance caused by touching Tanek. "Sorry," she murmured. "Inappropriate of me. I didn't ask permission. I—" She picked up her mug to hide her embarrassment.

Tanek stood up and both men were staring at her.

"You say strange things," Sojee said.

Tanek was looking at her in an odd way. "She is empowered!"

"What does that mean?" Sojee asked.

Kaley started to make an effort to explain, but she laughed. "I have no idea. I thought there was going to be a show of leaping. Or is it swan soaring? Whatever it is, I'd like to see it."

Tanek left his shirt off, stepped a few feet away, then gave a couple of spinning leaps. They weren't nearly as high as what she'd seen him do when he was fighting the witch's fire. Part of her wanted to urge him to put more effort into it, but instead, she smiled. He made her think of a warrior who would miss the target on purpose to prevent others from knowing his true skill. When it was necessary, Tanek had leaped much higher, but then maybe adrenaline had spurred him on. Actually, she liked that he wasn't a showman.

When Tanek sat down, Kaley turned to Sojee. "What about you? What are your special skills?"

He poured himself more wine. "I can pick things up and put them down. And I can break things."

"Like my grandpapá," Tanek said softly, his voice full of memory.

"Of course he could," Sojee said. "He was a big man. Like me."

His voice was so full of pride that they laughed, then the men turned to her in expectation.

"I cooked this meal," Kaley said, but the men kept staring at her. "I've been a human Ping-Pong ball and played Tarzan across roofs. That should be enough."

The men said nothing but they looked away, disappointment on their faces.

"I have a remarkable ability to remember stories. I can tell you folklore tales from Russia, China, India, the Vikings, Scotland—" She broke off because they were looking bored. "Okay, you asked for it." She stood up. "Jobi found a yoga teacher in our building and we had many sessions. I was very good at it. He wasn't."

The men had no idea what she was talking about.

She crossed her arms to remove her voluminous sweatshirt, but paused. "Do you mind?"

"I do not," Sojee said solemnly. "But our Swan Man may not survive."

Kaley removed the top and bottom so that she had on leggings and the low-cut tank top. Maybe it was the wine, but she wanted to show that she did have some physical abilities that the men probably did not. Unlike Tanek, she did want to show off.

The grass was soft and lush and she went a few feet away. She knew the men were staring at her. As Jobi had promised, he'd taken away her soft "academic body" and put some strong muscles on her. She hesitated, thinking about what poses to do, then she gave a little smile. Her first pose was "Sleeping Swan." Front leg bent, back leg extended, head on the ground.

She began a succession of poses, each one requiring more strength and flexibility. When she reached back to put her hands on her toes, making her body into a backward circle, she was pleased to hear them gasp. She did leg up, leg down, head at her knees. There were more. A bound swan. Shapely swan neck. She ended with the most difficult, a Hamsasana, a full swan pose. Her body was straight, rigid, then she lifted up on her hands, body supported by her upper arms, her feet off the ground— and held it for a full minute. It was a show of strength, balance and endurance.

She came down, put her arms into a reverse prayer pose, her eyes closed for seconds, then she opened them. The men were staring at her in awe. It was gratifying! "Sure you wouldn't rather hear a story?" she asked.

The men laughed loudly, and she felt as though she'd passed some test to be a partner with them. She started to put her concealing clothes back on, but Sojee said, "They look very dirty. You should wash them and leave them to dry."

"I see," she said, her mouth twitching in merriment. "You like the yoga clothes."

"Yes," Tanek said. "Yes."

Laughing, she picked up her sweats and turned toward the stream.

"What is this?" Tanek was holding up the necklace that had fallen out of her pocket.

She told them how she'd used it to open the cage to release the little boy.

"It doesn't look like a key," Sojee said.

"When I put it on, it got warm," Kaley said.

Sojee frowned. "I'm not sure I like that." He put the necklace on and waited, but it did nothing. He took it off and handed it to her.

Kaley put it on and Sojee said, "It's quite handsome."

The necklace turned a pale pink and got warm. "How odd. Did you lie?" she asked.

"Yes, he did," Tanek said. "It's ugly."

The necklace went back to dull gray and got cool.

"Tell me what you thought of me at yoga," Kaley said.

"Easy for anyone to do," Tanek said. "And I didn't enjoy it at all."

The necklace turned red and it was so hot that Kaley lifted it off her skin.

Sojee slapped Tanek on the back. "That was one of the greatest lies ever told."

At that, the necklace turned back to cool gray.

"How interesting," Kaley said. "I think I should start asking you two questions about everything and see what the necklace has to say."

"I think you should put it in your pocket and leave it there," Sojee said seriously.

When the necklace stayed gray, Kaley laughed. He was telling the truth. "That's the first time I've ever seen you scared. I should wear it all the time. Anyone want to help me with the washing?"

"We need to clean up here," Tanek said.

"And you wonder why men and women were separated."

Smiling, she went to the stream and washed her two pieces of clothing.

When she returned to the ruin of the gingerbread house, the fire was out, and the men looked ready to leave.

Tanek said, "We should go. It'll be safer if we stay the night inside the walls of the homestead."

"Are you afraid the king's men will find us?" Kaley asked.

"Possibly, but this woman could have friends." Sojee looked at Tanek. "I would be honored to stay in Haver's bedroom."

"So would I," Tanek said.

"You two will have to tell me about him," Kaley said. "Maybe the little light will help us find out what happened to him." She'd meant it as a joke but both men halted and stared at her.

"What light?" Tanek asked.

"Oh. Did I leave that out of my stories?" She knew very well that she had.

"You did." Tanek was serious. "What light?" he repeated, but this time with more urgency.

She told them about being directed to Collan's house.

"In that rain?" Tanek asked. "The light was in that storm?"

She didn't understand why he was getting upset. "Yes, and today it was in the house. I could hardly see for the smoke. It…" She paused. "Maybe I didn't tell you because you'll think I'm crazy. I hallucinated that I was seeing a little woman, a fairy, a pixie, something. She showed me the necklace then demonstrated that I was to put it on. I'm sure that smoke was full of toxic gases, but if she wasn't real, how did I know to touch it to the cage?" She looked at Tanek for him to answer, but he didn't reply.

Instead, he ran into the forest and was soon out of sight.

"Where's he going?"

Sojee looked at her, but said nothing. When he glanced down at her necklace, she knew he was asking for a level of trust that was difficult for her. Whatever Tanek was doing, Sojee was not going to tell her. "Will there ever come a time when you two tell me everything?"

"Yes," he said.

When the necklace stayed cool and gray, she took it off and put it in the little pocket made to hold her phone. "So where is he going?"

"Urgent call of nature," Sojee said.

It was such a blatant lie that she laughed. "I need another mug of wine."

"Me, too." Sojee filled her mug and held it out to her.

She raised it. "To lies that cover the truth. May they always be for a good purpose."

They drank to that.

13

It wasn't yet sunrise when Tanek woke. He looked through the darkness at Kaley sleeping nearby in what had been his grand-papá's bedroom. He wasn't surprised to see that Sojee was gone. That he'd been able to leave without waking Tanek made him grimace. He was slipping. What was next? A swan could move without his knowledge?

He sat up and looked at Kaley. She was on the far side of the room and she had all three of the blankets on her. She'd insisted that there was one for each of them, but during the night, Tanek had spread his over her. It looked like Sojee had done the same thing.

Silently, he stood up and walked to her. She was asleep, but frowning. His father had told him how badly earthlings reacted to alcohol and he was seeing it for the second time. If he left her, she would awaken feeling ill.

Bending, he touched his forearm to hers. For less than a second, he felt her headache, her stomach turmoil, her all-over body ache. It was enough to make him feel sick. But his energy quickly cleared away the pain from both of them. She lost the frown and settled into a deeper sleep.

For a moment he stood there watching her. She was really pretty, and her physical display yesterday was... He smiled at the new word. *Empowering*. Yes, it had given him so much "power" that it had been difficult to conceal. How Sojee had laughed at him!

As silently as Sojee had been, Tanek slipped out of the room, went through the ruined house and headed up the hill. He remembered every word his grandpapá had used to describe the house, so he knew where the Place of Peace was. It was where Haver went to think and plan. To be alone.

Tanek reached the top just as the sun came over the horizon, and he sat down on a flattened rock. Haver had chiseled the top off and planted the nearby tree. The colors of sunrise, the blues and greens, reflected off the water below. His father, Roal, told him that Earth's sunrise was different. "Another star lights their planet," he'd said. "The colors are not like ours."

Just before Kaley arrived, his father told him that Jobi wanted him to help this young woman. "Earthlings aren't like us, but Jobi has worked on this one for years. He says he trained her but I don't know how or at what."

It had made sense to Tanek, but what he'd never imagined was that the earthling wouldn't be told about her past. She had less knowledge than a child. Not only did she not know where she was, she also had no idea what she could do—nor did Tanek.

There was a tiny, familiar sound and he repressed a smile. "You let her see you!" He was frowning and sounded as though he was angry.

"I'm so sorry." Arit fluttered in front of him, her head down, looking like she might cry. "I disobeyed you. I betrayed you. I should not have done that. Can you forgive me?"

Tanek smiled. "Not bad. I almost believed you were sincere."

Arit gave a giggle, her wings going so fast they were a blur.

He held out his arm and she lit on his wrist. "You worried me."

"I'm sorry about that. I didn't come when you called because I was sleeping."

She was referring to the fact that he'd called for her yesterday but she hadn't arrived. He was upset when he heard that she'd been in a rainstorm then inside the smoky house. Nevers weren't made to withstand harsh conditions. They liked softness and sunshine. He gave her a hard look.

"I am well. I ate toris berries and healed." She flew up to his shoulder, then bent to kiss his cheek above his beard. Turning, she used his beard as a grassy wall. She yawned. "I like her."

Tanek put his hands behind his head and leaned back against the tree. It was mature now, no longer the sapling that Haver had planted. "I like her, too, but when she's told that Jobi stole her away from her home, she won't like *me*. She'll want to leave right away."

Arit didn't answer for a moment. "She's very brave, and she can see me! She rescued those children even when she was choking from the smoke. She would make a good mother."

Tanek groaned. "Don't you start on me!" He changed the subject. "What are the king and Jobi up to? They don't care about those stories she's interested in, so why?"

"He wants to unite the islands. He—"

"He told me that." Tanek's voice was growing louder. "But what does this woman have to do with it? And why did the king take everything away from us? We're going to struggle to get food, so how are we to find that rotten son of his? Without papers, how do we get home?"

Arit was calm. They'd been companions since Tanek had returned to Bellis as a child. When he'd disembarked the ship, Arit and Haver were waiting for him. From that moment, they'd represented what Tanek most wanted: a home. He'd adjusted to them and to the swans quickly. "I may be able to let you hear the king since that man has no abilities at all," she said.

"Just in ordering life or death."

Arit shrugged. "That's physical."

"Which, in your world, doesn't matter." Since she was leaning against his beard, he couldn't see her, but he could feel the vibrations of her wings. She was peering into the minds of people.

As he knew, she could see some of the past, most of the present, but none of the future. "Oh! Yesterday, Jobi's heart was beating very fast."

"Show me what caused it." His grandpapá had told him that his relationship with Arit was unusual. When they'd met, Tanek had been a very lonely boy. As for Arit, she was absolutely sick of her seven older sisters. Turning her over to a boy who'd never been on Bellis was their idea of a hilarious prank. "The fool is on them," Haver had said, laughing, then added, "You two are a 'match made on Earth.'"

Arit was trying to see into the past as to what had so excited Jobi. "My, my, my," she said, then transferred the image to his mind.

Tanek closed his eyes as he saw Jobi standing before the king.

"How are they doing?" the king asked. "Do they like the inn? Are the guards helping to find my son?" Jobi didn't reply, but, as Arit had said, his heart was beating fast and hard.

The image was gone. "Starken-el," Tanek whispered. "It's Jobi who stole everything. But why? How can we achieve anything without papers and funds?"

Abruptly, Arit stood upright on his shoulder. "She is awake and she's going to the candy house."

Tanek sat up. "How do you know that?"

Arit didn't answer.

He sighed. She'd tell only if she wanted to—or had to. "I'll go to her."

"Will you impress her with more soaring?"

He knew she was being sarcastic. Yesterday he had intentionally dampened down his display. "I don't feel worthy of matching Haver Beyhan," he said modestly, but there was an undertone of laughter. "I must go. She is insanely curious and afraid of nothing. I don't know if she's brilliant or stupid."

"Those are good mother traits," Arit said, then vanished before Tanek could reply. Her laugh rang out into the air.

When Kaley woke up, neither of the men were in the ruined bedroom. As she lifted the three blankets off her, she smiled. The men took good care of her! When she stood up, she expected to feel hungover after all the wine she'd drunk, but she didn't. In fact, she felt good. One of the men, probably Sojee, had left a chunk of meat for her and a mug of cold stream water. After a trip to the bushes, she took them both and started walking.

She thought she should explore the homestead more, but she didn't want to. Instead, she went down the trail, then through the woods. She wanted to look at what was left of the gingerbread house. Her fear was that the place had repaired itself and was ready to repeat the same story over and over.

When she reached the little cottage, she let out a sigh of relief. It was still in ruins, with only two walls standing. She couldn't resist pulling off a couple of shingles and nibbling. Whatever else was said about the witch, she knew how to bake!

Kaley sat down to the side, not far from where they'd cooked yesterday—*and where we laughed together*, she thought. It had been a nice break from pulling men out of the mud and following a tiny light through a rainstorm. This was the first quiet time she'd had since she'd found herself sitting on a rock, reeling from dizziness and wondering where she was and how she got there. As she ate, she looked at the house.

It was weird that there were fairy tales here on Jobi's islands. The truth was that everything was strange to the point of being unbelievable. She'd been so busy that it was as if she was purposely being given no time to think. Well, finding Sojee had been of her own doing, but still...

What was especially odd was that she'd been able to do everything that was required of her. She'd studied the fairy tales that were on these islands. Jumping across open spaces and scurrying up the sides of buildings were things she'd done in her training sessions with Jobi. It was almost as though he knew what was going to happen. Even if he'd hoped she'd go to his home with him, how could he have known she was going to be doing these things?

But then, he'd always had hints of premonition. "Take an umbrella," he'd say on a sunny day, and later there'd be an unexpected thunderstorm. "Take a left here." They managed to miss a traffic jam. It happened so often that she paid little attention to it.

Only once was it serious. She'd had an appointment in Miami. To get there, she had to go down the dreaded I-95. That highway was not for nervous drivers! Jobi told her she was *not* to go. He was fierce, saying he'd forcibly hold her there if he had to, but she was not to get on I-95 that day. Later, when she saw that there'd been a massive pileup and several deaths, she wasn't surprised. She asked him about it but he told her to do ten more reps of lat pulldowns and didn't answer. They never spoke of it again.

Since she'd been on the islands of Bellis, everything had been new and strange—but at the same time it was all familiar. Little Red Riding Hood? Hansel and Gretel? A witch with a magic necklace? It was what she'd been studying all her life.

But none of it made sense. Those fairy tales had been written decades ago. But here, on these isolated islands, they were happening *now*. If she did write about her experiences here, who was going to believe that there were some islands where fairy tales actually *happened*?

She thought back to how Jobi had given her little time to get ready to leave, but she'd had a massive amount to do. She wished she'd spent more time researching the islands, but she'd looked only at one site. She should have done a deep search of the whole internet.

Actually, when she thought back on it all, she should have made a protest of the hateful way her professor had tossed her dissertation aside. There had to be a way she could have filed a complaint. She should have stayed and fought, not run away as she did.

But there was Jobi, her best friend, packing to leave forever, and talking about his beautiful, unexplored islands, telling her of a king and hinting at new and different stories. She'd had a choice of going with him or facing her problems alone.

Something is wrong, Kaley thought. *Really, really wrong. What's happening here doesn't match up with reality. I need to—*

When she heard a noise, her senses came alert. Maybe she shouldn't have come out alone like this. Maybe the witch didn't live by herself. Maybe there was—

The noise came again and she recognized it as an animal sound. There was a little cry, like a puppy, then a quick bark that sounded like a warning.

She put her mug down and went closer to the house to investigate. At first, she didn't see anything, but then she saw a little creature was caught in metal fencing. It looked like a trap that had been made especially for it. She'd never seen an animal like it. It was the size of a rabbit but thin like a fox, and it had tall, narrow ears. Its fur was light brown flecked with black-and-white hairs. It was a male and the poor thing was trapped by its right front paw and its snout. It couldn't get out. When Kaley stepped toward it, the animal growled at her. "I promise I won't hurt you," she said as she went nearer.

But then she heard the little cry again. It was coming from inside a pile of burned gingerbread and charred wood. She left the animal in the cage to move pieces aside, being careful that nothing fell down on whatever was making the sound. When she had a hole in the debris, she saw that deep down there was a baby of whatever the larger animal was. It was very small and impossibly cute. "Did you come in here for the gingerbread?" she asked in a soothing voice. "Poor thing, I'll get you out."

She reached in as far as her arms could and the baby, a female, nipped at her fingers. It had sharp little teeth, and Kaley drew back. She moved another wooden beam so she could get closer, but again, when she reached for the little one, it tried to bite her.

The male gave a sharp bark and the baby closed its mouth. "Is this your daughter?" Kaley asked. "And you were trying to rescue her?" This time, when she reached out for the little one, it didn't bite. Kaley's hands closed softly around it. "See? Daddy knows I'm trying to get you free."

She could feel the little creature's heart pounding so she held it for a moment, stroking it gently. It calmed down to the point where it snuggled against Kaley's hands. "I need to get your dad out, okay? You can stay over there and eat all the gingerbread you want." She put the little creature down on the grass and went back to the father.

When she reached out her hand to the trapped male, it didn't move. "I mean you no harm," she said. She couldn't resist running her hand over its head, then down its body. "Your daughter is beautiful and so are you."

The animal didn't move as she opened the wire that was holding its foot. She pried open the latch that held its snout. "You risked your life to save your daughter. I'm impressed."

When the animal was free, it didn't run away, but turned to look at her—but that was what she was used to. All her life she'd had a close bond with animals. So close that she spent a lot of time trying to hide it. She didn't like being called a freak or the other names people came up with. She put out her hand, palm up, and the animal reached out the paw that had been trapped and touched her fingertip. "You're welcome," she said.

In the next second, the animal was gone, moving so fast and quietly it could hardly be seen.

Smiling, Kaley turned away, and in that second, she saw the tiny woman she thought she'd seen when she was in the smoky cottage. It was only a flash of light and color, then it disappeared. "I think I may be losing my mind," she whispered. "Fairy tales are one thing but real, live fairies are another." Shaking her head in disbelief, she went out of the ruins and into the sunlight, and she saw Tanek coming down the hill. "Everything all right?"

"We have no food or papers and little credit, but other than that, it's grand," he said.

She held out her mug of water to him.

He hesitated, but took it and drank, then stretched out on the grass. "We must make a plan."

"Definitely." She lay down a couple of feet away from him, and took her mug back. "It smells good here."

"It does. I like those cakes."

Kaley got up and broke off a couple of shingles, handed him one, then lay back down. It was nice to relax and not be fighting something. "Do you have any brothers or sisters?"

"No." Holding his gingerbread, he put one hand behind his head and turned his face up to the sun.

"But you have a world full of swans. You must have been a happy child. Was your school good?"

"Oh yes," he said. "I fit in well. No one said anything when birds followed me everywhere. Best was when a hawk picked up a kid's pet. I had trouble getting it back. That bird didn't understand why I was taking food from him."

Kaley was smiling at his sarcasm. "But I bet you were great at sports. You could soar over the goalposts and win every race. Did you ever go swimming with your fellow students?"

"Just once."

His tone made her stop laughing. "Did they see your ridges?"

"Yes. I was a great source of laughter to them all."

"And after that?"

"I believe you call it *homeschooled*."

"By your grandfather?"

"Yes."

"We have things in common," she said. "I was homeschooled until college, and the three adults in my life were very busy. I spent more time with animals than with humans." She smiled. "I probably should have a tail and fuzzy ears."

That joke seemed to amuse him more than it deserved, and it took him a moment to recover. "Did I hear you talking to someone?"

Even though they were acting as friends, Kaley wasn't going to betray the little animals. For all she knew, the men considered them good to eat and would go hunting for them. "Rabbits," she said. "I tend to talk to all animals. It's just a habit. Can't seem to break it. Sometimes it causes problems, but it's okay most of the time. I..." She was talking too much and too fast.

He didn't look at her, but she was sure he knew she was lying.

They were quiet for a moment, then he asked, "Does Jobi know of this house of cakes?"

She wasn't fooled by his nonchalance. "Is this question why you're being so chummy with me?"

"I don't know that word."

She could feel that his body had suddenly tensed up. "It doesn't mean that I intend to endanger your chastity. Did that translate?"

"Perfectly." He was smiling in that smug way that only men could do. "And I am relieved." He paused for a moment, then said, "You didn't answer my question."

"Yes, Jobi knows about the old fairy tales. I used to read them to him. He was always very interested. He— Wait! Do you think Jobi knew the gingerbread house was here? Did he tell the king? Were our things taken away so we'd come to your family's old home and find the house and the cannibalistic witch? Did they know that you and Sojee would destroy the place?"

"That's a lot of questions."

"And you're not answering." She raised on one arm to look at him. "If you don't tell me the truth, I'll start keeping even more secrets from you. That's fair, isn't it?"

Tanek laughed. "I am bested. Yes, I think there was a reason behind our being here. If everything was taken from us, where else could we go?" He paused when he saw Sojee approaching. "But if you hadn't blocked the men, you would have been thrown into the mud, too." He looked at her. "Or worse. I can't figure out why all three of us would be left without our senses. How were we to get here?"

"I have no idea." Kaley sat up and smiled at Sojee.

"Are you two figuring out how to find the kid with the dragon so we can get out of here?" Sojee asked as he looked down at them.

Tanek didn't move from his easy position of lying on the grass. "Kaley found rabbits so we may have to hunt food."

Sojee looked hard at her. "Rabbits?"

She didn't blink at his look of disbelief. "*Brown* rabbits," she said firmly.

For a split second, his eyes widened, acknowledging that she was lying.

Tanek made no sign that he knew what was going on between them.

Kaley stood up. "I need to see if there's a pot inside that mess." She nodded toward the house. "I can make a stew with the venison."

Sojee looked toward the trees. "Or maybe I'll find some brown rabbits to put into the pot."

"They ran off that way." She pointed in the opposite direction that the animals went.

Sojee smiled in a knowing way, then went into the forest, and Kaley went back into what was left of the gingerbread house.

Tanek stayed where he was for a while, then got up and went into the trees, keeping a good distance between him and the other two. "Arit," he said softly, and she was there instantly. "I need to talk to Jobi." He held up his arm and she brought up a little screen and there was Jobi, frowning.

"I don't have time now. The king—"

Tanek ignored his plea. "She needs to be told the truth. Anger is building in her and she's starting to keep secrets."

Jobi's face showed alarm. "About what?"

"If I knew, they wouldn't be secrets."

Jobi gave a satisfied little smile. "You like her, don't you?"

Tanek frowned. "Is that what this is about? You're trying to match me with her?"

Jobi smiled. "Would that be so bad? Tanek, you're like a son to me, so take my advice and tell Kaley the truth about where she is. Rip the bandage off."

"What does that mean?"

"It's an Earth saying. You must stop hiding the truth and tell her all of it. Just do it and be done with it."

"Then *I* will get her hatred."

"And that matters to you?"

His tone was so patronizing, so I-know-best, that Tanek felt anger rise in him. They were searching for *food* but Jobi was matchmaking. Tanek's voice was calm. "I think you're right. I should tell her the truth. I'll tell her that it was *you* who had all our goods stolen and *you* who removed our credits. If she hadn't had the foresight to block the thieves, I hate to think what could have happened to her alone in that room." His voice rose. "I'll give it to her like a blade cutting her heart out. And if you don't know, that's a Bellisan saying."

"Wait! I—"

Tanek didn't hear any more as Arit took away the connection. They smiled at each other—then Arit laughed so hard she did a somersault in the air.

"How long do you think it will take him to replenish our resources?" he asked.

"I hope it's not until after Kaley's stew is ready. She's a good cook, isn't she?"

Arit disappeared before Tanek could groan in reply.

14

After they'd eaten the stew, they talked about leaving. If they were going to find the king's son, they'd have to head out into the world of Selkan.

Sojee hadn't been able to find any *rabbits* so he was looking near the gingerbread house to see what else the witch had hidden. So far, he'd only found more bottles of wine. Tanek had also been searching the area, but at every sound, his head came up, as though he was expecting something to happen.

It was Kaley who saw the young man standing at the head of the road that led down to the gingerbread house. She ran back to the others. "It's Nessa. He's here. He's at the top of the hill. I think he's looking for us, but I didn't see Perus."

Tanek reacted instantly. He drew the sword he'd been wearing since they'd been there, his face stern, and said, "Both of you are to stay here." He started forward, his head down, as though he was ready to attack.

Sojee and Kaley stayed behind, not moving.

Kaley said, "You're right to go alone, but if the dragon is there, he'll burn you up in an instant. Too bad about that."

Tanek, his back to them, halted.

Sojee said, "That's true. He likes her, but he'll probably enjoy frying *you*."

Tanek gave a great sigh, but didn't turn around. "Then stay out of sight."

"Not so easy for me to do," Sojee said, and Kaley unsuccessfully covered a giggle.

The three of them started forward. "If he can hide a dragon, he can easily hide armed guards," Kaley whispered, and Tanek glowered at her to be quiet.

Suddenly, Tanek stood up. "It's not Nessa." He didn't explain as he jammed his sword into the ground, then took a knife out of his belt and tossed it to stand upright beside his sword. Another knife came out of his shirt cuff, then two more knives appeared.

Kaley watched in astonishment.

Sojee said, "Boot."

Tanek was looking straight ahead as he bent to quickly unfasten the hooks on his boots then stepped out of them. He was barefoot. "Stay!" he ordered, and this time, Sojee and Kaley gave him no argument.

They watched him. Kaley had never seen anyone move with such stealth. The young man standing at the top of the hill had his back to them. He was far enough away and they were concealed by the trees so he couldn't see them.

Sojee nodded to Kaley and she understood to follow him. They slipped into the forest, then went up the hill, being as quiet as they could. Whatever Tanek was doing, they wanted to see it.

It was astonishing that a man of Tanek's size could be as quiet as he was. The young man certainly didn't seem to hear him.

When Tanek was several feet from him, he leaped. No, as he called it, he soared. He sprang up from the ground and coasted through the air. He was like a ballet dancer, but one with magic powers.

Sojee and Kaley watched, mouths open in astonishment.

When Tanek was high in the air, the young man whirled to face him, then he also sprang up into the air. He was lighter so he went even higher than Tanek. As the two men soared, Tanek caught the younger man's ankle and pulled him toward him. They were two people flying so high that it wasn't humanly possible. Tanek was the strong one and he held the young man so that for a long minute, they were in the air together. Flying. Gliding.

Finally, they came down to the earth, touching lightly, then standing there looking at each other.

"They're like swans," Kaley whispered. "I'm not sure they're human."

Sojee nodded. "You're right. That's Mekos and he's a Lely."

"What's that?"

"Rare. Special." He was smiling in a way that said he'd just seen something few people ever did. "They're not easy to make. I'm impressed by our Tanek."

Kaley wasn't sure they should interrupt the two of them, but when Sojee went ahead, she was right behind him.

Tanek and the young man were talking in a language she'd never heard before. It was low and throaty. Whatever the origin, it was sultry and sexy. She held out her arm for Sojee to fix it so she could understand them.

"I don't have my pen, remember? Besides, that language isn't in the library. It's only understood by people in the Order of Swans." He paused, his eyes sparkling. "If you married into that order, you could speak it."

"Are you matchmaking young Mekos and me?"

Sojee laughed at her deliberate misunderstanding.

Finally, Tanek turned to look at them. "This is my son." His voice was low, and it held more pride and love than Kaley had ever heard anyone speak.

She didn't want them to see how that announcement struck her. *Son? As in wife?* she thought. He sure hadn't mentioned that little fact.

Mekos was a bit shorter than his father, and overall smaller, but handsome to the point of being pretty. He had a head full of black curls, and his eyes were the color of Santa Fe turquoise.

"You're beautiful," he said to her. His voice wasn't as deep or rich as Tanek's, but nice. "I've never seen eyes like yours."

Kaley smiled at him. "And I've never seen eyes like yours."

Mekos smiled back. "You're from Ear—"

"He brought food," Tanek said so loudly it was almost a shout. "A wagon full of it."

"That's great!" Sojee said so loudly a dozen birds flew out of the trees.

Kaley was so used to things being hidden from her that she just rolled her eyes. Tanek put his arm around his son's shoulders and they walked toward the old homestead. "Guess he wants to show his son where his grandfather used to live." Her voice dripped sarcasm. They both knew Tanek was taking his son away to tell him what was going on, privately.

They heard horses moving away from them. Sojee leaped onto a low wall, looked toward the sound, then got down. He gave a quiet chuckle. "Whoever came with the boy is leaving."

"I know. This place is encircled."

"Ensourced," Sojee corrected. "Too dangerous for the cowards. You ready to see what's in the wagon? Or do you want to keep feeling sorry for yourself because no one is confiding their very souls to you?"

"Hmm. Difficult choice. I'll have to think about that."

"I bet whatever is in that wagon was sent from the king's table. Eren produces a cheese so good it can replace sex."

"Not possible."

Sojee was smiling. "And there's their bread. It's made from six grains and flour from a nut found only on top of the mountains. And there's a—"

"Beat you there." She took off running. She was faster and he got to the wagon a full minute behind her. "Slowpoke."

"I'd be faster if you'd show me how to do those circles with my body."

"I can teach you how but I'd have to break a few bones." She was staring at the back of the wagon. It was loaded with crates and huge cloth-wrapped bundles. "Why is there so much? I thought we were to go back to the town to look for Nessa."

Sojee was leaning over the side. "Do you think soldiers are told why they're to risk their lives?" He reached inside. "Look what I found." He pulled out Kaley's duffel bag.

She couldn't help a squeal of delight and grabbed the handle. "Clean clothes! What a luxury!"

"Our Tanek will be disappointed about that." He was referring to the fact that the yoga clothes she was wearing showed off her every curve.

"He never looks," she said. Sojee was stretching to reach the packages in the middle of the wagon. "Put me in and I'll hand everything out."

He took her by the waist and swung her up into the wagon. It was packed so tightly she had a hard time finding a place to stand. When she did, she could see Tanek and Mekos at the far end of the ruined house. When Mekos turned and saw Kaley, he raised his hand in a wave, but then his father said something and Mekos looked back at him. "They're talking about me."

"Of course they are. A pretty girl in a place like Selkan needs protection."

She handed him a three-foot square wooden box. "Ha! We both know that Tanek is telling Mekos which secrets he's not allowed to tell me."

Sojee didn't smile; his face was serious. "There's just one secret."

Kaley looked skeptical. She pulled the necklace out of her pocket and put it on. "Now repeat that." He did and the necklace stayed cool and gray.

"Feel better now? Can we unload this? I'm hungry."

"You just ate."

"And?"

Laughing, she handed him two more packages, then he stopped and looked at her. "How does that thing work on you?"

"You mean to check if I'm lying?"

Sojee nodded.

Kaley looked at Tanek with his son. "Tanek is the ugliest man in the entire world." The necklace did nothing. "Interesting. How about this? I don't like any animals at all." The necklace didn't react. She looked at Sojee. "You try."

"I like sleeping on stone floors."

When the necklace turned pink and hot, Kaley smiled. "I like this. I can lie with impunity but you guys have to tell the truth. I think that's fair."

With a grimace, Sojee pointed at a huge bundle.

Kaley bent to pick up the big package. She expected it to be heavy so she did a dead lift as Jobi had taught her, but the package was so light it hit her in the face. "What in the world is in this?"

"I hope I know." Sojee held out a knife to her, handle first. She slit the cords and out popped fat, fluffy blankets. "Warmth and comfort," he said. "I hope those are from your swan people."

"They don't belong to me." Kaley glanced at Tanek with his son. They were still talking, heads together. "You'd think he'd hide somewhere so there's no possibility that I'd hear him."

"He can't bear to let you out of his sight. Open that little one there and pray for cheese."

She did as he asked and yes, it was cheese. It was a rich color of orangish-red and smelled very good. She dug the knife into it, carved out a chunk and got it almost to her mouth before she switched and held out the sample to Sojee. He took it, ate, then closed his eyes. "I take it that's the cheese you wanted."

"Oh yes." He held up his arms for the next package and Kaley tossed it to him.

Twenty minutes later, they'd unpacked it all. The big cases that the men had taken from the inn were on the bottom. To Sojee's great disappointment, his magic pen—at least that was how Kaley thought of it—wasn't there. "Of course they'd keep that," he muttered.

Sojee swung her down and she looked at the great pile of packages. "It's like we're to set up house here. Maybe they should have sent chickens and seeds. Maybe tomorrow they'll send a plumber to install a toilet and a tub. What's going on?"

Sojee could only shrug in answer. "They're coming." He nodded to the necklace. "Unless you want to get burned by that thing, you should take it off."

Kaley wanted to protest, but she was a guest in their country and she should respect their traditions and... "Oh hell!" she muttered, and took off the necklace. Being sure she was hearing lies would make her angry, but it wouldn't make them reveal what they were concealing. Besides, did she really and truly *want* to know?

The first thing Tanek did was pick up the edge of one of the blankets. His verdict was a grunt.

"Do they pass?" she asked.

"Not the best but good."

Mekos was looking at Kaley. "He saves the best for our family. We—"

Tanek cut him off. "There's a new plan." He didn't wait for comments. "Sojee and Kaley will stay here at the homestead. Mekos and I will go into Doyen and find Prince Nessa."

"But I want to go, too." Kaley knew she sounded like a kid begging, but she didn't want to be left behind.

Tanek didn't meet her eyes. "My son knows Nessa. We think he'll come if Mekos calls him."

"But—" Kaley began.

Tanek looked at her. "It will be safer if we don't have a woman with us. Protecting you is…" He didn't finish.

"Sure," she said. "Next time, you can get yourself out of the mud."

For a long moment, they stared at each other. Kaley was on the verge of anger and Tanek looked as though he was about to relent.

Mekos turned to Sojee with wide eyes that said he'd never seen his father like this. Sojee gave a shrug in answer.

When Tanek spoke to Kaley, it was with a soft voice. "Jobi has friends on Selkan. He'll send them here to tell you stories. And I'll go to Collan and ask him to come up here. You like him." Tanek put out his hand as though he meant to touch her, but then let it fall to his side.

Mekos waited a moment to give them time to speak but they didn't. "So?" he said loudly. "What have you three been doing up here? Watching the blue of the sunrise? Discussing philosophy? Or, knowing my dad, searching for the white swan?"

Kaley stepped back from Tanek and picked up a metal box. "We've been fighting evil and eating gingerbread."

Sojee lifted a big crate. "And we watched your father jump around fireballs while waving a sword in the air."

Tanek picked up the bundle of blankets. "It took both of us to fight that old woman off."

"They risked their lives to create a diversion to give me time to get the children out so they wouldn't be eaten." Kaley loaded another box on top of the one she had.

Mekos looked at them, piled high with the bundles. "I want to hear this story."

Tanek started walking toward Haver's bedroom. "Then you're in luck. We have the best storyteller in Bellis." Sojee followed him.

Kaley stayed by the wagon beside Mekos.

He looked at her. "Whatever has happened here, you've certainly become friends." He reached inside his shirt and drew out a key on the end of a cord. "Perhaps this will be my way to join you." He called out to the men. "Look what Grandpapá gave me." The men turned to look at him. "He sent it tied around Indienne's neck." He looked at his father. "She misses you."

Kaley said, "Don't tell him that or he'll start crying."

Tanek said, "Maybe it's not me she misses." He looked at his son, his eyes serious. "Indienne wrapped her neck around Kaley, then took her to see the fledglings."

Mekos showed his shock. "She won't let *me* see them!"

"They are soooo cute!" Kaley said. "And they like my stories. They—" She stopped since the men were staring at her.

Mekos held the key up higher. "I vote that we open the hidden cellar door and you three tell me everything. What is gingerbread?"

"You guys can do this," she said as she set her packages down and looked at Mekos. "Come with me, and we'll find the lock that key fits." She and Mekos went toward the ruined house, walking close together.

Tanek and Sojee moved everything into Haver's bedroom under the part of the roof that was still intact. It would be sheltered from the rain. They put most of the food inside the stone chest.

When they finished, Sojee said, "She needs to be told. Even if you keep her hidden here, she'll figure it out."

"I'm going to do my best to keep her busy with her stories." Tanek's tone showed that he'd been thinking about this. "Mekos and I need time to find that lazy, worthless prince. Once we have him, I plan to fly her back to Jobi on the dragon. That should make her happy."

Sojee gave a snort. "If you get near that monster, it'll cook you." Tanek was looking at him. "I see. Yes, it might fly with her, but you'll never be allowed on it." He paused, seeming to be studying Tanek's face. He wasn't worried about a dragon. Sojee lowered his voice. "If you do get her back to the king, then what? Is your job over? Do you go back to the mountains with your swans and she gets on a ship headed to Earth?"

"I have no idea. I'm not included in the overall plan—and I doubt if the king is, either. From what I can figure out, all of this is from Jobi and a man named Zeon."

"Never heard of him."

"Me neither. I'm going to ask around town and see if anyone knows who he is—and what he's involved in."

"I could ask the same of you," Sojee said. "Kaley isn't the only one who'd like to know what this trip is really about."

Tanek looked like he was debating whether or not to confide in Sojee, but Kaley's voice made him keep quiet.

"You aren't going to believe what Mekos and I found," she said. "Well, actually, it was him and his key."

"You found the door. I never would have seen it without you," Mekos said.

"I'm used to cellars. Kansas tornadoes." They were looking at her blankly. "Land hurricanes except they whirl about?" No comprehension. She looked at Tanek. "We found some clothes and I think they're made of that swan cloth that you said never deteriorates. There are beautiful things stored away in a man-made cave." Neither Tanek nor Sojee responded. "Come on! Stop looking so glum. Mekos and I are going to throw a party." She turned to the young man. "Let's go get dressed. I want that pink gown." They started walking. "Unless you want it."

That made Mekos smile. "I want my great-grandpapá's gold vest."

"You'll look great in it. I'll make a few stitches and it'll fit. Sojee can wear the shirt and—" They were out of earshot.

Tanek and Sojee hadn't moved from their place by the doorway. "She certainly does like my son."

Yet again, Sojee slapped Tanek so hard on the shoulder that he almost fell forward. "Maybe your lusty young son will be receptive to her—what did you call it?—her aggression? From

what I'm seeing, Mekos is already letting her know he's interested in her as a woman."

As was often said, if looks could kill... The one Tanek gave
Sojee would have done it. The big man would have fallen into
a mass of blood and crushed bones. Instead, as Tanek followed
his son, Sojee laughed loud and hard.

15

The contents of the cellar were a treasure trove, hidden away under a door concealed by floor tiles. They all went down the stairs together.

Tanek held up a robe of velvet. The cuffs and borders were embroidered with gold thread. "This was ceremonial. He wore it when he met with the king and ambassadors and…" There was no need to explain who *he* was. Tanek's voice was heavy with memory.

"I think it'll fit you," Kaley said.

He stepped back. "It's too big. I could never fill it."

"Look at this!" Mekos held up a robe of deep blue that looked to be silk but was probably made from swan feathers. "It's exactly my size."

"That was mine when I was your age," Tanek said. "I wore it to the first meeting with a Peacekeeper."

"How do I look?" Sojee asked. He'd removed his burned shirt and put on one of black that had silver embroidery on the cuffs and collar. "Was it Haver's?" When Tanek nodded, Sojee said, "I am honored to wear it."

Each of the men chose clothes while Kaley stood silently to the side and watched. Finally, they turned to her. "There." She pointed to a tall cabinet against the wall.

"It's Grandmamá's cabinet, the one that was against the wall." Tanek looked at Kaley. "She was about your size."

"And her husband was Sojee's size?" Kaley asked in surprise.

"Obviously, she was a woman of taste and wisdom." Sojee sounded so serious that they all laughed.

Kaley withdrew a dress of pale pink, the fabric smooth like satin. The top was low cut, but had folded panels over the upper arms. The bodice was embroidered in an intricate design in heavy silver thread. It went down the front of the skirt. "It's a princess dress," she whispered.

Tanek went to her. "Grandmamá sewed it. I used to hold the yarns for her, and when she got older, I threaded her needles."

Kaley held the dress in front of her and turned halfway around. "It is fit for a queen."

"Look at this!" Mekos said. He was holding a flute made of wood and inset with thin blue stones laid in a complex pattern. He blew the dust off, put it to his lips, then played a little tune.

"That's wonderful," Kaley said. "We can dance. We can—"

"Ow!" Sojee had hit his head on the low ceiling. "I want cheese and wine and a ceiling fit for a man."

"I agree," Kaley said. "I just need my makeup from my backpack and some privacy, then we can dance the night away."

The men were feeling her happiness. They picked up clothes and went up the stairs. Tanek tossed her pack down to her.

By the time Kaley was dressed—and the gown fit like it had been made for her—she was shy about appearing. She hid in the shadows for a moment. The men had set up a table from parts of the ruined house. It was growing dark and there were candles lit. The wide board they'd found was bowed by the weight of the food they'd unpacked. There were even pewter mugs, plates and flatware.

As for the men, they were an extraordinarily handsome trio. The fading light gleamed off the sparkle of the clothes they had on. Sojee in his black shirt, Mekos in a robe his father had worn, and Tanek... To Kaley's eyes, he was by far the best. Contrary to what he'd said, his grandfather's robe fit him perfectly.

Slowly, she walked out and was pleased when the men stopped talking and turned to look at her. Their silence was the greatest compliment she'd ever received. The dress, the bracelets she'd found, the star pins in her hair, which she'd put up, made her feel beautiful. She twirled full circle. "I've never worn anything like this."

Mekos came forward and offered his arm for her to take, and she did. He led her to a seat at the table. Even though the chair was bricks that had been stacked up, it felt like a throne.

"To our lovely princess." Sojee raised his mug of wine, and the men drank to her.

"Not a real princess," Kaley said. "Not like yours."

"Aradella would kill to look like you. Literally." Sojee wasn't laughing.

"Should I feel sorry for Nessa?" she asked.

"No."

The way Sojee said it made them laugh and they tore into the feast. Cheeses, breads, meats, pickled vegetables, dishes she'd never seen nor heard of. There were many new flavors for Kaley, all of which she liked very much.

"These are from all of the islands?" she asked.

"Only three," Tanek said. "There is nothing from Empyrea."

"The mystery island," she murmured, and kept eating.

The abundant wine made Kaley feel good. "I think I could soar in this dress."

Mekos stood up. "Shall we try?" He held out his hand to her.

"But you have to provide the music."

Sojee wiped his mouth with one of the napkins that had been sent. "I can make music. Take the girl to dance."

Kaley took Mekos's hand and he led her to the flat area in front of the table. It had once been a big room. Now there was no roof but the floor was fairly intact. "I'm not sure— Oh!"

Sojee started singing in a rich, well-trained voice. It was a fast song in a language she didn't understand. When Mekos picked her up by the waist and swung her around, she realized that it was a movement Jobi had taught her. He'd not told her it was part of a dance from his country, but she knew the moves. With her hands on his shoulders, he lifted and spun her around, then he put her down and they stepped back, then forward. The movements were repeated to the rhythm of the music.

"I am soaring." She was laughing.

"No," Mekos said. "To soar together, both people's feet must leave the ground. Only my father can do that with a person who is not of our order."

The wine was making her forget her reserve. "Then he does that with your mother?"

Mekos laughed as if she'd said something hilarious. "I'm a Lely." Sojee changed to a slower song and Mekos pulled Kaley closer to him.

"I have no idea what that is, except that it's something special."

"Strange is what we are." Reaching up, he moved his hair back on the side that wasn't facing the table. His ear was pointed and a bit hairy. When Kaley's eyes widened, he said, "You should see my mother's tail!"

"Oh no! I told your father that since I spent more time with animals than with humans, I should have a tail and fuzzy ears."

"Did he laugh at that?"

"He did. So, what do you mean your mother has a tail?"

Mekos pulled her closer, spun her around again and put his mouth by her ear. "My father is a rare man who can reproduce with a woman like my mother."

"Is something wrong with her?"

"She is an older woman, but no, nothing is *wrong* with her. Please don't tell Papá but she'll probably come here soon."

Kaley quit smiling. "Still carries a torch for her, does he?"

"A torch? Do you mean a fire big enough to burn a town down?"

"Yes, that's exactly what I mean." She felt like a balloon deflating. "He loves her that much?"

Mekos's smile turned to a frown. "I meant that he'd like to throw her into a burning building."

"Well, in that case, I love hearing good news."

His laugh echoed around the old walls.

When Sojee stopped singing, they went back to the table. Kaley picked up her wine, but Mekos took the flute and went to sit along the far wall. He began playing a quiet, haunting melody that made Kaley close her eyes to listen.

Sojee said, "He's good with that."

"There isn't much that my son can't do." Tanek sounded awed as well as proud.

"So how did you win a woman like his mother?" Sojee asked.

Kaley put down her mug and leaned forward to listen.

"I didn't. She came to me."

Sojee nodded. "That makes sense. I guess she knew you could give her a child."

"She knew but I didn't."

"And she left the child with you? How old were you?"

"Sixteen." Tanek was smiling. "It's not in her nature to keep her cub. So yes, she brought him to me when he was only minutes old. He was very small. I grew up the moment I held him."

"Maybe you grew up together," Kaley said.

"No. That wouldn't have been fair to him. He didn't need a friend. He needed a father."

"And what did *you* need?" she asked.

"Everything I have. I have a home beside my father and I have my son."

"And you have your swans," Kaley said. "Add your precious white swans and your life will be complete. You are a one-man island."

He gave her a look as though he was trying to figure out whether what she'd said was good or not.

Sojee gave a snort, and said, "It's the blue swans he needs to look after. *They* are the most valuable."

Tanek started to speak but Mekos stopped playing and Sojee stood up. "There is too much talking and not enough wine. And far too little dancing." He looked at Mekos. "Can you play 'Hana mokea'?"

"Of course." The two men looked pointedly at Tanek, still sitting and holding his wine.

"If I must." Tanek heaved himself up, then held out his hand to Kaley.

She did not like his attitude! "I don't think—" He took her hand and pulled her to him, chest to chest. She was staring into his impossibly blue eyes.

"Properly!" Mekos said as he took up his flute and played while Sojee sang.

"That's a folk song," Kaley said. "I'd know one if I heard it in any language. I bet it has a story. I need to—" She started to pull away, but Tanek held her tight.

"It's a story of love that lasts forever," he said. "Love that is unbreakable, that withstands all the trials that it's put through."

"Like Haver and his wife?"

He didn't answer but twirled her around. Her beautiful skirt spread out, seeming to pull them closer. When he stepped back, he took her with him. His eyes grew dark and she could feel a slight vibration coming from him. It enveloped her, passing from him to her. In the next second, her feet came off the ground. She thought he was lifting her up, but his arms were level with her body. She bent to the side to look down. They were three feet off the ground. She felt a moment of fear, then it left her, and pure pleasure flowed through her. She felt the joy of soaring through the air. She put her head on his shoulder, wanting to be closer to him. His hands left her waist and engulfed her body, as though he was pulling her into him, merging them completely and totally. It was as though they were one person.

She wasn't sure how long they were in the air but it wasn't long enough. Holding her, he went down to the ground slowly. Her toes touched so lightly she could hardly feel them.

For a second, they held each other, eyes locked, then Tanek abruptly released her. He turned his back on her and took his seat at the table.

Kaley stayed where she was, blinking rapidly, her body vibrating. She didn't know when the music stopped but it was silent around her. She managed to get herself under control, then, without looking at Tanek, she sat down at the table. She drained the rest of her wine and looked across the floor at Sojee and Mekos. They were staring at her. "Anybody want to do shots?"

They didn't know the literal translation of what she'd said, but they figured it out. The air filled with their laughter and they went back to the food. Suddenly, they were all ravenous.

16

As they ate and drank more, Kaley didn't consciously think about what she was doing, but she vividly remembered Sojee saying, "There's just one secret." With every minute that passed, the more she wanted to know what that secret was. Maybe she wanted to feel that she *belonged*. That she was part of the group.

She thought young Mekos might be the weak link in keeping the secret. When he emptied his cup of wine, she refilled it. Tanek frowned but Mekos made a quick grab at the cup and drained it.

"Parents protect their children." Kaley was reminding Tanek that his father hadn't told the truth about what happened at the homestead.

Tanek gave her a calculating look, as though trying to figure out what she was up to. She smiled at him as sweetly as she could manage. After Mekos had another cup, Tanek held out his hand. He wanted to connect with his son's arm to clear away the fuzziness the wine was causing. But Mekos stood up. "My father can project his abundant strength into others," he said to Kaley.

She stood up with him. "And what can you do?"

"Hear things. Smell. See. I can move quickly and squeeze through tiny places." He gave her what he seemed to believe was a lascivious look. But he was a drunken teenager who needed practice.

"Come on," she said. "Let's dance, and I'll teach you the meaning of the word *killjoy*. Then Daddy can clear your mind."

"You can teach me whatever you want." Again, he was trying to be sexy, and again, it failed.

But Kaley didn't laugh at him. She went into his young arms, and as Sojee began to sing, Mekos twirled her around the room. She let him nuzzle her neck.

"You earthlings smell good."

"No foxy scent?" She was teasing him.

"If you did, I'd think you were my relative."

She laughed. As a folklorist, she loved the myth that his mother was half fox. It's probably what was told to him to explain his misshapen ears. "But you're an earthling, too. I'm just from another country."

He pulled her closer. "You're from a whole other planet. We must thank Jobi for bringing you here."

She smiled. "Another planet? That's impossible. It would take years to get here."

"It's three years from Earth to here," he said.

Three years? With all the wine she'd had, her mind wasn't the clearest it had ever been, but she remembered Jobi saying, *What if I told you that my country is on another planet and it takes three years of Earth time to get there?* Mekos was holding her more tightly. What he was saying couldn't be true, but something about it was giving her chills. She glanced at the table. Tanek was watching them, looking as though at any minute he'd spring forward and separate them. She put her head back and laughed as though Mekos had said something funny. "I saw a woman," she whispered. "She was tiny and surrounded by light."

"That's Arit," Mekos said. "My father's Never. She thinks I'm a worthless child, but then she's in love with him."

Kaley was trying to control her breathing. "What does she do?"

"Communicates. Papá talks to people through her." Mekos twirled her around. "My father thinks I'm a virgin."

"Any woman can tell that you're not." She was lying. "A dragon, swan wings that grow on a man's back, fairy tales that are real. They're things that I've seen."

"And there are many that have been hidden. Nessa let me ride Perus once. It was almost as good as soaring."

"Who put the thing in my arm?" she whispered.

"Jobi. He told Grandpapá that he had to go back to get you when you were ready."

She pulled back to look at him. "Ready for what?"

"I don't know."

Kaley again glanced at Tanek. He looked like he was about to pull his son away. "Does Tanek know why I'm here?"

Mekos put his face on her neck and she could smell the wine on him. "No. He yells at Jobi that he must tell you where you are and that I must—" He suddenly stood up straight. "Oh no! He told me I'm not to tell you."

Kaley stepped away from him, then with a face not show-ing her emotion, she went to Tanek and held out her arm. She wanted all the effects of the alcohol removed. He touched his forearm to hers. As always, the little electrical current went through her, but this time she could feel his energy. He was worried about something.

"What did my son say?"

"Nothing of interest. You should put him to bed. I'm…" She nodded toward the darkness that surrounded them. A nature call.

When Tanek's eyes were on his son, Kaley slipped away. She wasn't sure where she was going but she couldn't stay there. She went to the bedroom where their things were stored. She care-fully took off the beautiful dress. Holding the soft fabric against her face, she thought that she should have been suspicious at hearing the gown was made from swan feathers. There was no such thing. But then, there were lots of things that should have alerted her to... What? That she'd been taken to another planet?

She changed into trousers, a T-shirt and a jacket, then stuffed her backpack with a full outfit. When she left, she saw that the men were at the table, still drinking, but Mekos looked like he was dreading telling his father what he'd done.

Kaley crept along the side of the building, but Sojee stepped in front of her. For someone so big, he could certainly move quietly. "You know," he said.

"Yes. I..." She wasn't sure what to say. None of it had sunk in yet. "I'd like to be alone for a while."

"You deserve that." He looked into the dark surrounding them. "There's no one else here or Mekos would have heard them."

"Because his mother is part fox?" Her voice was full of sarcasm.

Sojee nodded.

"Do you know *why* I'm here? It couldn't be just to help find that obnoxious prince."

Sojee's face was more serious than she'd ever seen it. "Jobi is in the Order of Sight. He sees into the future. He says you're needed, but that's all we know."

They turned at a noise. Tanek was propping his limp son upright and trying to get their forearms together.

"Don't let him follow me," Kaley said. "I need time to think. Alone."

"We owe you that."

Feeling stunned, with too much in her mind to be able to think clearly, she walked into the darkness, but there were tree branches on the ground and she stumbled. Without thinking where she was going, she turned and went toward the derelict village. The houses had been broken and blasted, with axe marks on some of them. Maybe the destroyed village was symbolic of the way she was feeling.

The gravel crunched and slid under her feet, but she kept going. The blue of the moonlight allowed her to see enough that she could walk. She went down side roads and between the crumbling houses.

It couldn't be true, she told herself. These people were insane. That had to be it. These islands were an asylum for delusional, mentally unhealthy people. Someone told them they were on another planet and they swallowed it. They...

She couldn't embellish the lie enough to make herself believe it. Mekos said Jobi returned when she was *ready*. Did that mean when she was an adult? If so, her entire life had been directed toward now, on this planet.

She began to think of odd things that had happened throughout her life. She'd been homeschooled. When she finally did integrate with people her own age, she'd learned how different she was. Animals liked her. Not a little but a great deal. She rarely fit in with other people. Later, Jobi, twice her age, was the closest friend she'd ever had.

At least that was what she'd thought. But it seemed that he'd had an ulterior motive. Was he paid to befriend her? To kidnap her? To steal her away from her family? Had those years of training been a duty to him? All their laughter, shared meals, shared... In her mind, they'd shared confidences.

What about the single entry she'd read on her computer about his islands? Did *he* put that in there? Her eyes widened. Did he have something to do with her professor turning down her dissertation? He wouldn't have done that. Couldn't have. That would be too cruel, too low-down, mean and dirty.

Her grandfather had often said, "Honey, if you want to know what a person's up to, look at the result." The result of her life was that she had suddenly found herself alone, with no future, and only one close friend. Then that *friend* had conveniently decided to leave the country. Kaley had begged and pleaded to go with him.

Everything she thought she knew about Jobi had been a lie.

She sat down on a rusty iron chair that was in front of a house that had once been pretty. A wooden shutter hung by one hinge. A flower box was on the ground and the moonlight showed little white flowers peeping out of the soil.

When she looked to the side, she saw two gleaming eyes. They were cautious, looking like they were asking her a question. It was the little creature she'd pulled out of the witch's trap. She patted her lap and he silently came forward and leaped onto her legs. She stroked his fur. "You're so quiet I bet even Mekos couldn't hear you. But then, from the look of you, maybe you're his second cousin."

She'd meant it as a joke, but the words brought tears to her eyes. Three years to get here, three to get back. Even if she left tomorrow, it would be six years that she'd been away from her family. Did that mean nothing to Jobi? Did only *his* world matter?

Her tears came harder. Would she ever see her grandparents again? They weren't young, and six years was a long time. Her father! She remembered seeing him at the airport. That was when Jobi put that pen on her arm and she blacked out. What had he done to her father? Did Jobi care about anything or anyone except his own interests? What had Sojee said he was in? The Order of Sight. That made sense. Jobi's premonitions. He saw car pileups before they happened. What else had he foreseen and prevented?

It seemed that all Jobi cared about was *his* mission. *His* goals in life. Kaley's plans and dreams, the people she loved, meant nothing to him.

The little animal seemed to feel her stress and snuggled into a ball on her lap. It would soon be daylight and she was feeling the exhaustion of what she'd learned and all that had happened during the day. The door to the house was open. She picked up the little animal and went inside. A room held an old wooden bed frame with a rusted iron lattice across the bottom. She stretched out on the bed, drew her knees up, with the soft warmth of the animal next to her, and was instantly asleep.

When she woke in the morning, she wasn't surprised to find one of the swan blankets covering her. She had no doubt that Sojee had found her and covered her as she slept. By now Tanek had been told that she at last knew the truth, but he would probably stay away from her. A wooden crate was in the front room and it contained food.

Part of her thought she should go back to the others. Maybe she should sit down and talk with them. Like an adult. She'd ask questions about how to get back home. Was there a spaceship schedule? Did anyone have enough credits to buy a ticket?

But she didn't go back to the old house. Instead, she put some food in her pockets, took a ceramic bottle of water and started walking. She didn't want to stay still, and she definitely didn't want to talk to anyone. She needed to adjust to what was impossible yet seemed to be true. And most importantly, what did she do now? Ask? Plead? Demand? If she knew what they wanted from her, she might have a card to play. Something to work with in her threats. If you don't take me home *now*, I'll... What? Not prevent any more fairy tales from coming true? None of them had seemed bothered by a witch in a house made of cake.

She left the village and followed the gravel road upward. There was a path going up the mountain, with trails wandering off to the sides. She followed two and they led to what may have been seating areas. Had Tanek's famous grandfather hiked these paths? Or did some animal that she'd never heard of live there?

She went back to the main trail and started up. It was a hard climb and she was breathless when she got close to the top of the mountain. Beside her was the little animal, scurrying in and out, sometimes pausing to listen. When she got to the top, she

gasped. Before her was a large pond. It was perfect in its still-
ness, cleanliness and the beautiful blue color. To the side was a
tall stone pavilion. It was like the one near the house but this
one was intact. It hadn't been blown away by some angry enemy.

Kaley went to it. There were four stone pillars to the roof,
with steps leading up to a wide floor. There were four chairs
made out of carved white stone. Of course the arms were in the
shape of swans. She sat down on a middle chair, the creature on
her lap, and looked out at the perfect water.

"You're going to have to tell me your name." She closed her
eyes and tried to listen. Nessa's dragon had told her right away,
but this one was silent.

When she opened her eyes, she drew in her breath. On the
water, having arrived in absolute silence, were three white swans.
She'd seen many of them at home...on her own dear Earth...
but none like these. They were as big as the iridescent swans
she'd seen on the first day with Tanek, but these were only of
the purest white. The only color was the black band that went
around their eyes, then extended back. "Like Cleopatra," she
whispered. "Are you Egyptian?"

The birds didn't seem to be afraid of her.

Kaley stood up, put the animal to the ground and walked to
the birds. They didn't move away, but then she didn't expect
them to. She sat down on the side of the pond, slipped off her
shoes and put her feet into the water. It was cool but not cold.

Slowly, the swans came forward and paused in front of her.
She bowed her head to them and they bowed in return. Then
they glided forward and bent so she could touch them.

The little animal was beside her and she turned to him.
"Aren't they beautiful?" She looked startled. "Tibby. Is that
your name?" He made a soft sound like a snuffle, then crawled
back onto her lap. "Jealous, are you?"

The swans rubbed against her shoulders then her neck and
up to her cheeks. Their feathers were as sleek as they looked.

One of them moved back, then bent its long neck to the water, picked up a white feather and held it out to Kaley.

"I am honored," she said as she took it.

The swans moved back and effortlessly slid across the still water.

Time seemed to pause. She had food and water and her thoughts, but they didn't seem to have a solution. It was as though she went through the stages of grief. She'd gone through shock, then denial. Her anger was taking longer. How could Jobi have done this? Had he really planned it for years? Did he cut her arm and put whatever it was inside there? Did his premonition tell him that her mother was going to die?

She had no answers for any of her questions.

She paced, going around the pond several times. The swans stayed close by on the water, and Tibby curled up on the grass. They were calm, not in the least upset by her movements that were sometimes fast and angry.

By sundown she was into bargaining, thinking how she'd play it to make Jobi return her to her own country. It was too far-fetched to think of Earth as "my own planet."

When it grew dark, she was exhausted. She stood at the side of the pond and stared sightlessly into the water. The swans raised their heads, went to her and seemed to want her to follow them. She went to the far end of the pond where there were tall reeds. One of the swans extended its enormous wings and flew a few feet into the thick, dense field of waist-high grasses.

Kaley knew she was to follow and she didn't hesitate. It was wet walking, but she made her way through and she saw a huge, soft, feathered nest. With gratitude, she stretched out in it, and the swan sat down close to her. It was warm and quiet, and she was soon asleep.

In the morning, Kaley didn't feel any better. She had no answers to her questions. She had no idea why she was there and certainly not how she could get away.

As before, she wasn't surprised to see that the box of food had been brought up and was under the cover of the stone pavilion. Of course Sojee had done it. For a moment she thought how she needed to go back to them, needed to talk, to ask questions. It didn't do any good to hide away in isolated silence. Her inner therapist said she needed to address her problems and figure out how to deal with them.

But Kaley couldn't make herself do any of it. If Jobi had spent years of his life to achieve his goal of hijacking her to his planet, a few words from Kaley wasn't going to make him backtrack. And any person who could keep such a monumental secret for so long wouldn't spill his guts the moment he was asked to tell all.

She ate a bit, then snuggled with the swans and Tibby. The way she felt now, she might stay there forever. *Then what will the others do?* she thought.

Tibby suddenly came alert and the swans quickly went to the far side of the pond. They looked like they might fly away at any second.

Kaley braced herself. It was probably Sojee, sent by Tanek, to try to persuade her to return and do...whatever it was that she'd been kidnapped for the purpose of doing. Save their planet? How? Her blood was needed? Her...? She couldn't think of anything she had or could do that was superior to what others had and did. *Why me?* screamed in her mind.

She was so sure she was being warned of Sojee arriving that Kaley didn't at first see the tiny light, then the wings, then the bright pink of a little skirt. She just sat there blinking as the tiny woman came into view. "You're Arit."

The little woman said, "I am."

Her voice was stronger and louder than Kaley would have guessed. "Mekos said you're called a Never."

Arit straightened her body, her wings fluttering more slowly, and proudly said, "We never betray, never share."

"Really?" Kaley said. "You know any Lost Boys?"

Arit's shock made her wings beat so fast that she shot backward in a flurry of wings and clothes. "Yes," she whispered. "Peter. How...?"

"I'm beginning to get the hang of this place. Did someone send you to try to talk some sense into me?"

"No one knows I'm here. Could we...?" She looked at the pavilion in the background.

"Sure." Kaley got up from her seat on the grass and went to one of the chairs. Arit settled on the arm of the one next to her. "All the stories left out how tiring wings must be."

"I usually lean on Tanek," she said. "His beard is very soft, and his arms are exceptionally strong."

"Et tu, Brute?" Kaley saw that she had no idea what was meant by that. "Are your clothes made from the swans?"

She gave a quick nod, indicating her lack of interest in that matter. "Tanek and Mekos left to search for Prince Nessa. If they return him to the king, you'll be given Papers of Passage and you can leave. Tanek is deeply worried about you."

Kaley could see she was upset about that. "Is he angry at Mekos?"

Arit stretched out on the stone arm, her gossamer wings folded beneath her. "That couldn't happen, but Mekos is hurt. He blames himself for having disobeyed his father, but Tanek is glad you've been told. He just hopes you aren't blaming *him*."

Kaley looked out at the water. The swans were still on the other side of the big pond, and Tibby was nowhere to be seen. "Tell him I found his white swans, and that I slept in their nest. And they gave me a white feather."

"You should tell him when he returns."

Kaley avoided replying to that. "Do you know anybody named Tinker?"

Again, Arit looked shocked. "My oldest sister. She's with King Aramus."

"Of course she is. Higher up and she gets the perks."

The two women looked at each other and exchanged girl smirks of understanding.

For a while they sat in silence, looking out at the water and the beauty of the swans.

"Why was I brought here?"

"I don't know," Arit said. "I'm not sure anyone does."

"Except that it was all done by Jobi. Was he paid to pretend to be my friend?"

"I don't think he knows why he's done things. There are only three people at a time in the Order of Sight and Jobi is the weakest one. He knows you're to help his country, but he isn't clear on how it comes about."

"What about Sojee and Tanek? Mekos? Are they being paid?"

"Not in the way you mean. The men have their own reasons for agreeing to guide you."

Kaley nodded at that. "Sojee wants to protect his princess, and Tanek is doing something in secret. He has meetings with people. I think Mekos just wants to be with his dad." She looked at Arit, but she was silent. As Mekos had said, the beautiful little woman was in love with Tanek, and she was obviously very loyal to him. "Can you read people's minds?"

Arit took her time answering. "I can see into the minds of some people."

"Tanek's?"

"Oh yes. Everything." She gave a chuckle. "He likes you."

Kaley ignored the last comment. "Sojee?"

"Less so, but I know that he will kill to protect his order. He knows that you're important."

"Mekos?"

"No," Arit said sharply. "He has a very strong mind, and he can hide what he thinks and feels. There is not a Never who will join with him."

Kaley thought she could understand that. "And what about me?"

Arit shook her head. "I can see nothing that's in your thoughts.

Someone very powerful is watching over you." She put up her hand. "No, I don't know who it is."

"Can you see into the future?"

"Not at all."

"Too bad because I'd like to know if I'll ever see my family again. My grandparents. My father." She turned to the woman. "For as long as I can remember, I've known what I wanted to do with my life. I could see the house I'd live in, my studies, what I'd write." Kaley took a breath. "All that's gone." She tightened her lips. "Do you know if Jobi made my professor turn down my dissertation?"

"Not for sure, but he probably did. I see in his mind that he's ruthless in what he wants to achieve."

"At the expense of my entire life. I'm sorry, but I don't really care about that nasty little prince getting with a princess who doesn't want to marry him. I just want to go home to my family. I want my stone house and to…" The tears were coming again. She'd kept them at bay but now they were back.

"I'm sorry this has been done to you." There was sadness in Arit's voice. "Please return."

"Not yet." Kaley gave a half smile. "I'll stay here for a while longer. Maybe I'll find some frogs to kiss."

Arit looked at her in horror.

"It's a joke. If you kiss the right frog, he turns into a handsome prince, then you get married and live happily ever after."

Arit looked serious. "A lot of men could offer you that, and just so you know, Tanek loves anyone who loves those farken birds of his." Her wings began to flutter. "I'll find Tanek, and I'll tell him all." She grimaced. "And maybe I'll find someone who can turn him into a frog. Why any woman wouldn't want him just the way he is, I do not understand." She didn't give Kaley time to answer but vanished.

She looked out at the swans. "Farken, are you? Now I see why you run away from her." Tibby came out of the grasses.

"You're afraid of a tiny creature like Arit? Wait until you see Tanek after she's made him into a two-hundred-pound frog."

There was no response from them. Kaley stretched out on the grass, hands behind her head, and looked up at the sky. *Maybe I'll stay here forever*, she thought. *If I refuse to participate, maybe they'll send me home.*

17

Tanek and Mekos had been searching for Nessa for days. At first, they'd asked in Doyen, but no one had seen him—and the townspeople would have been glad to give him up. With no success there, they went into the countryside, but no one had seen a dragon.

Tanek had contacted Jobi and told him about a drunken Mekos spilling the truth to Kaley, then how she'd run away, wanting to see none of them. Tanek said that he and Mekos had immediately set out for the town, hoping to find the prince. He added that Arit said Sojee had found Kaley, and Sojee made sure she had food, water and warmth. Jobi's only response was to nod, then rush away to see the king.

On the third day of searching, Tanek and Mekos left the countryside to go back to town. Tanek left his son at an inn on the outskirts of Doyen. Since neither of them had slept much in the past days, Mekos fell onto the bed in a stupor. Tanek looked at the bed with envy but he didn't use it. He grabbed food, then headed into town to continue his search. Maybe Nessa had returned while they were away.

To Tanek's shock, the town was a site of chaos. People were yelling and wailing in grief. Armed guards, wearing uniforms he didn't recognize, were forcing their way into houses. The men pulled young girls—who no one knew were hidden there—into the open and dragged them away. The girls were crying and their families were begging, pleading for the girls to be released.

When Tanek reached the center plaza, it was filled with people shouting. There was blood on the stones. They were looking up at a tall wooden platform with steps that were soaked in blood. At the top were six guardsmen standing by and impassively watching what two young women were doing. They were cutting themselves, slicing off parts of their left feet, then trying to jam their blood-dripping feet into what looked to be a shoe made out of glass. Why? he wondered. Was this another vicious Selkan game? It so sickened him that he turned away.

As he went through the crowd, Tanek asked some men what was going on and the answers he got were so ridiculous that he couldn't believe them. But the grief on their faces was so horrible that it was hard to remember why he was there and what he needed to do. He stepped behind a wall and brought up the screen that showed Jobi's face. The older man was in his room in the king's house, a large breakfast set before him.

Tanek didn't bother with niceties. "We can't find Nessa." He had to shout over the noise around him. "But we must get Kaley back to Eren so she can go home to her own planet. She's hiding on top of the mountain and she's crying! *You* caused all of this."

"Yes, I did!" Jobi said. "Everything bad you can say about me is true, but I know that the only way to save our country is through her."

"And how does she do that? By leading an army? Who will follow her? Selkan men? After what I've seen here today? No! The women on Pithan can't—"

"I don't know!" Jobi yelled, then lowered his voice. "I can't see the answer, but I've dedicated my life to preparing her for the future that I can see."

"One that she knows nothing about and wants nothing to do with? Why did you have to trick her?"

"Earthlings refuse to believe we exist. If I'd even hinted at the truth, she would have run from me and said I was insane."

"Right now, she's running from all of us. I don't blame her for wanting to leave here. Why should she help us? For honor? We have none. You've made us as corrupt as the Peacekeepers. We—" An abrupt sound of people screaming filled the air and he waited until the sound went to a low moan of grief. "We—"

"What's going on there?" Jobi yelled.

"It's horrible. I've never seen anything like it. There *are* women here and they're coming out of hiding, but only so they can cut off their own toes and heels. It's a bloodfest. I want Mekos and Kaley off of this island!"

"Heels? Toes?" Jobi asked.

"I want our credits restored so I can take Kaley and my son back to Eren. If I have enough I can bribe the ferrymen. I can—"

"You'll have it but only if you tell me what's happening there."

"It's some prince. He's related to Aramus. He fell in love with a girl and she ran away, but she left behind—"

"A glass slipper?"

"Yes," Tanek said. "The idiot prince is having women try the shoe on, and to make it fit, they're cutting off—"

"I know!" Jobi's voice was rising. "Don't you see? The winning woman will get to live in the king's gated compound in the south. They can have families to visit. They'd no longer have to hide. But now that they've exposed themselves, the losers will be sent to Pithan with the other women. They may never see their fathers and brothers again. So yes, they're desperate to fit into that shoe. You must get Kaley down from that mountain. Tell her a prince is searching for a woman to fit in the glass slipper."

"Not on your life!" Tanek said. "I'm not going to expose her to this horror. She might think *she* should wear the evil thing!"

Jobi was trying to stay calm. "Kaley won't fit the shoe because she's not the right girl. There is no danger to her. You have to understand that telling Kaley what's going on will get her to leave the mountain." He saw Tanek's hesitation. "I'll get the king to postpone trying on the shoe until you return, then you can stay with Kaley to make sure she's safe. That won't stop it as those girls are desperate, but it'll give you time." His voice rose. "You have to trust me! Kaley can end the violence that's going on there. I don't know how, but she will. You *must* do this!" His voice broke. "Please. For all of us. And for those poor girls."

Tanek had no reply to what he was being asked to do. He touched the disk in his arm and broke off the connection. He didn't like what Jobi had said, but he knew what he had to do.

When Tanek stepped out from behind the wall, he saw a man in a uniform pull a pretty young woman from her family's home. She had short hair and wore men's clothes. She was crying, as were her parents and a little boy. The girl's foot was bleeding.

Tanek's instinct was to grab the girl, to save her. If Sojee was with him, he would have tried, but alone, he'd end up in prison, where he'd be no help to anyone. He glanced up at the sun. It was early. His pace quickened. Mekos had had about three hours' sleep. That wasn't enough but it would have to do. Tanek pressed the right side of the disk in his arm, then blinked in surprise. Credits had been abundantly restored to his account. A guard came running and spoke to the man holding the girl, and he released her. She went running back to her mother's arms, and the screams were replaced with cheers. It looked like Jobi had persuaded the king to intervene. But how long would it last?

There was a stable behind the inn and he quickened his pace. The horses he and Mekos had rented earlier were old and worn

out, but it was all he could afford. Now it took only minutes
to hire the two best horses, with saddles. He took the stairs up
to the room two at a time. Mekos was sprawled across the bed,
boneless in that way only young people could be. He started to
wake him, but then didn't bother. He put his sleeping son over
his shoulder and carried him down the stairs.

As promised, the horses were saddled and waiting. Tanek
wasn't going to risk Mekos sitting alone on a horse, so he put
his son in front of him and tied the second horse to his. He
mounted the horse behind his son, not waking him, and quickly
left the town. With a good pace, he could be at the homestead
in a couple of hours.

Arit appeared out of nowhere and Tanek had to calm the
horses. They felt her more than saw her and were unsettled by
the strange little creature. She landed on Mekos's sleeping shoulder. "Kaley doesn't want to leave that mountain."

"How do you know that?"

"I have ways," she said cryptically. "And I think she hates Jobi."

"She is one of many." He was urging the horse to go faster.
"Do you have any real news or not?"

"She wishes you were a frog."

Tanek looked from the road to her. "Your mind-reading tal-
ents need work. That was a misunderstanding. Her humor is
not easy to grasp."

"I understood her perfectly!" Arit said, offended.

The second horse could see the bright light that surrounded
Arit and didn't like it. The animal misstepped and Tanek called
out to calm him. "I think you'd better go."

Arit flew up so she was in front of Tanek's face. "She wants
you to be a frog so she can kiss you." She flew backward, smiling. "And oh yes, she has befriended three big white swans.
They gave her a feather."

Tanek was so shocked that he almost lost his grip on his son.

With a smug little smile, Arit vanished.

★ ★ ★

Tanek halted at the homestead and untied the second horse from his saddle. Sojee reached up, took the still-sleeping Mekos and held him like a baby.

"We found no sign of that useless prince," Tanek said. "No one has seen him or his oversize lizard." He nodded toward the mountain. "She still up there?"

"Yes, and she won't come down easily. She—"

Tanek cut him off. "Maybe I can persuade her. If not, I'll…" He waved his hand as though to say he'd do what had to be done.

Before Sojee could reply, Tanek kicked the horse and raced up the mountain path. Behind him, Sojee grimaced. When he saw the little light that he knew was Arit, he glared at her. "It seems that you left out that she's guarded by a tabor."

Arit didn't answer, just made the light around her blink a few times, then she disappeared.

Sojee looked down at Mekos, his body limp in his arms, carried him to where they'd made makeshift beds and put the boy down. For a moment, Sojee looked at his young face, smoothed his hair back and smiled. "Maybe one of my daughters will suit you for a wife." Still smiling, he left the room. He had weapons to sharpen. He needed to be ready to deal with whatever had so agitated Tanek.

Kaley was lying on her back by the water, with her hands behind her head. The sky was a pale purple with a few pinkish clouds, with streaks of green. She'd told the swans that the clouds weren't nearly as silky as they were. It hadn't taken long to find out that they loved compliments. Tibby was beside her, curled into a ball and pressed against her waist. She told him that the curves of both of them were made to fit together.

It was the first day since she'd left the men that she wasn't feeling as though she was trapped and had no choices in life. "Acceptance," she said aloud. Maybe she'd reached that stage of her grief. She must accept where she was and make the best of it—which meant she had to get out of there as fast as she could. She'd lost six years of her life but that was better than spending the rest of it where she didn't belong.

She heard footsteps behind her. They were too light to be Sojee and too heavy for Mekos. Beside her, Tibby made his little snuffle sound of warning, then he vanished. He had a remarkable ability to crouch so low that he couldn't be seen even in short grass.

She looked at the swans. They had come to the edge of the water, and she could feel their excitement. If they could speak, they'd be saying, "He's here! He's here!"

Kaley didn't move. Not only did she know who was behind her, she also knew what he was going to say. She needed to return to them. For her own good. For the good of Bellis. Something like that. There'd be no mention of her family or what her life was going to be, or—

"I was told you want me to be a frog," Tanek said.

She didn't look up at him. "Only if you wear a gold crown." The swans were filled with nervous anticipation. Tanek was moving about but she didn't know what he was doing. Getting feed for them? "It's all right. You can trust him," she said to the swans, pretending that they didn't know who or what he was. Tanek gave a little laugh at the absurdity of that statement. "Oh yes. I forgot that you're related to them. But then, Arit ran from them."

"That's because Indienne tried to eat her. She thought Arit was an insect."

"Did you say, 'No, no. Don't eat the love of Daddy's life?'"

"Arit would like that title."

"You mean *Daddy*?"

He was laughing and she heard his steps. As he walked past her, he didn't look down.

He was naked. Not wearing his loincloth, but stark naked.

Kaley came up on her elbows and watched him walk into the water. Heavens above, but he had a beautiful body!

The swans, who had been Kaley's friends for days, gave all their attention to Tanek. They wrapped themselves around him, rubbed their sleek feathers against his body, their heads nuzzling his neck and arms.

"Don't blame you," Kaley murmured.

When Tanek was waist deep in the water, he turned to her. "Can you swim?"

She sat up in a way that she hoped seemed casual. "Rather well. Jobi the mercenary made sure of that."

"That word doesn't translate." Tanek lifted his chin while the swans caressed his neck with their heads.

"It means that he did it all for his own purpose. There was no actual friendship between us."

"Mmm," was all Tanek said, but then he was in some sort of ritual with the birds so he couldn't talk much. He turned and stretched out in the water, his bare behind exposed to the sun— and to Kaley. The swans went over and under him, their movements sensual. He went to his back, his arms outstretched, his body just under the water. He barely moved but he was afloat.

Of course he can swim as well as the birds, she thought.

"Did he tell you that I've been to your Earth? It's where I first saw white swans."

Her curiosity was overriding her depression. "How? Why?"

He was gliding easily in the water. "I was born on a ship. My father was very young and he knew about machines so he was hired to go on a trip to Earth. He did something with the engines." Tanek's tone expressed that he couldn't understand why anyone would want to do that. "One night a pretty officer knocked on his door and..." Tanek broke off with a smile. "I didn't see Bellis until I was ten years old."

She sat up straighter. "What did you think of my planet?"

"I only remember the swans. Papá said the long sleep of the

return erased my memory of the early part of my life. Whatever the cause, all that is a blur."

They were quiet for a few moments, then he said, "Our credits have been restored. We can return to Eren, but I don't know how long it'll be before you can go back to your family." He paddled a bit, twirled in the water, then lowered his voice. "Would you like to join us?"

She'd never heard him use that tone. It was sultry, enticing and inviting her to something she couldn't refuse. It made her remember the king saying, "Can it be that there exists a woman who doesn't want you above all other men?" Right now she couldn't remember why she'd thought Tanek was celibate, that he stayed away from women. *This* man knew his way around women quite well. And, unfortunately, his enticement was working on her.

Kaley stood up. "A swim might be nice." She wasn't going to remove all her clothes, but taking off the top layer would be all right.

He was treading water, with the swans close by watching the two of them with interest.

"You are better," he said in that inviting way. "I told Jobi you wouldn't need some silly glass slipper. I said you were stronger than that and—"

She halted with her pants at her knees. "What glass slipper?"

He frowned, but quickly recovered his expression of seduction. "It's for a contest. Ridiculous, really. The woman who fits the shoe has to marry a prince, but she does get to stay on Selkan near her family."

Kaley pulled up her pants. "We have to go. Now."

His face of seduction disappeared and he frowned. "There's blood! I don't want you to see—"

The anger she thought she'd suppressed came forward. "So help me, if you try to stop me from going, I'll…I'll disappear into the next fairy tale and you'll never find me again!" With her hands on her hips, she glared at him in challenge.

The swans backed up on the water, looking from one to the other.

Tanek got out of the water. He seemed oblivious to his nudity—or, Kaley thought, maybe he was using his gleaming body to distract her. Either way, she didn't relent.

He pulled on his gray pants, no underwear, and looked at her. "You don't understand. It's a bloody mess down there. The girls are—"

"I know! They're cutting off parts of their feet to fit into the shoe. Don't you see? We have to find the real Cinderella, and I think I may be the only one on this planet who can do it."

As he put his shirt on, she saw the pain on his face. She reminded herself that he didn't know what she did. Her voice softened. "I promise that I won't cut any of *my* body parts, but I think I can help the girls who are doing that."

"Jobi said he would halt the search until you got there. He said you're the only one who can stop the bloodshed."

"For once that traitor is right about something. Are you ready to go?"

"More so than you." He nodded toward her shirt that was unbuttoned to her waist.

She looked at him while she fastened it. "Was all this...this seduction meant to make me do what you wanted?"

His half smile was her answer.

"Something else in my life that wasn't real." She was frowning. "Do you have a horse?"

"Have you ever ridden one?"

Considering that she had so easily fallen into his trap of seduction, she wasn't feeling good about him. "Yes. Can you drive a pickup with four on the floor?"

He had a blank look, then he gave a low whistle and the horse came from behind the stone pavilion.

As Tanek checked the saddle cinch, Kaley saw Tibby's eyes peeping through the grass. "I'm going to town to save Cinderella," she whispered, then hurried to the horse.

She mounted first, then Tanek got on behind her. His arms were around her, her back to his chest. He took the reins and they headed down a wide, steep path that was the opposite direction from the homestead.

When she looked back at the water, with the swans watching them in curiosity, she thought of how he'd enticed her into going with him. His nude body, his caressing of the swans, all done before he casually mentioned the carnage going on in the town. His actions were meant to get her to do what he wanted her to. She held on to her anger for only about a minute. She reminded herself that men the world over, no matter where that world was, tried to seduce women into giving them what they wanted. Whether a woman fell for it made the difference. "Where is Mekos?"

"With Sojee. Sleeping."

"Are you sure?"

She watched as he held out his left arm, then touched the scar and pressed. To her amazement, a small screen appeared. It showed Mekos in Haver's bedroom, sleeping soundly. "Steve Jobs would be jealous," she said. "But then, I guess people who travel through space can do that. Where are the ships that go to Earth?"

"On Empyrea."

"Ah yes. The forbidden island that no one has seen."

"My father's been there. He says I was, too, but I was a child and they put me to sleep."

"To keep you from remembering?"

"Probably."

She was quiet for a moment as they rode. It was nice being snuggled against him. "I assume you and Mekos were looking for Nessa but you didn't find him."

"Mekos tried to summon him and we asked, but no one had seen him. They very much want to get rid of him since his dragon set fire to some crops."

"No doubt under Nessa's orders. Did you offer any bribes?"

Tanek urged the horse to go faster. "I barely had enough credits to pay for the inn!"

It sounded like he'd been as angry at Jobi as she was. In the distance they could see a farmer. He had no tractor but a wooden plow pulled by a huge black bull. "How does your planet have spaceships but no cars?"

"You have asked the fundamental question. We all want to know the answer to that. Can one of your folktales explain it to us?"

The bitterness in his voice made her remember his secret meetings on the island. Are they why he'd agreed to escort her? "You're a revolutionary, aren't you?" She lifted her hand to her Truth Necklace and waited for his reply.

"I want to help change things, yes."

The necklace stayed cold. "Does Sojee know what you're doing?"

"I believe he's starting to guess."

"What about Mekos?"

"His only concern is if girls like him."

"They do."

"Too farken much! Last year he— Never mind."

"Did he impregnate a girl when he was sixteen?" she asked innocently.

"Only I have that honor," he said, then urged the horse forward and they stopped talking.

As they rode, she felt him relax against her. They fit together comfortably. *Like Tibby and me*, she thought. Or like him and his swans. It crossed her mind that it was too bad she was going to leave soon, but she quickly wiped that thought away.

When she tipped her head back to rest against his chest, she felt his body slacken. He seemed to be relaxing to the point of sleep, but the instant she tried to take the reins, he became alert. She knew that falling asleep in a saddle could lead to accidents. When the horse slowed, she began talking again. "Tell me a secret about your planet."

"How do I know what's different from my world and yours? Tell me of your world."

"We have cars. They're—"

"I do remember them."

She wanted to ask questions about his time there, but she was more curious about his planet. She thought of the ridges on his back. "Do you have some genetic memory of your wings?"

"I dream about them. There's a legend that I have relatives who still have wings." His voice was growing heavier.

"When did you last sleep?"

He gave a half shrug as his nonanswer.

"Give me the reins and you can sleep against me."

That made him chuckle. "You couldn't hold me up and I'm sure I'd bash my head if I fell off. We'll be there in an hour, then you can…" He had nothing to say about what she was to do because he didn't know.

Kaley would have answered him, but she didn't know, either.

18

Tanek took them to the stables in Doyen. When he ducked his head to get through the double doors, Kaley felt the energy leave his body. Maybe he was relieved that his part of the job of getting her there was over. The spotlight was now on her. *If only I knew what to do*, she thought.

She swung her right leg around, glad there was no high pommel to get past. But then she sat still in the saddle. Tanek appeared to be asleep. If she got down off the horse, he might fall. "Tanek!" she said. "I need help here. Could you—?"

Her body came alert when she saw a man step out of the shadows. Since they were on Selkan, a place where there were few women, she felt the hairs on her neck rise. But in the next second, she recognized him. It was Garen, the man who'd been the head of the king's guard. Her body tightened. She wasn't sure, but she thought it was men from that guard who'd drugged them and stolen their possessions.

Garen came into the light. There was a large, new gash on his face. It was deep and had been sewn together with thick black threads. It was quite hideous-looking.

"I'm sorry," he said, looking up at her on the horse.

She was surprised that she could understand him.

He held up his arm that held the chip. "Adjustment." His eyes were pleading. "I tried to stop the men when they robbed you, but I couldn't control them." He made a motion to his cheek and the ugly wound. "They told me you were dead, but then I saw you and him..." He didn't finish, but glanced at Tanek, then back at her. "Would you like some help?"

"Please," she said. "I need to go to where the women are..." She waved her hand, not wanting to say what she was envisioning.

"It's bad," he said. "The women have been hiding for years but now they've come out. They're taking knives to themselves. I didn't like seeing that. I had to leave." He reached up and helped Tanek down, but he couldn't hold him and had to let him fall into a pile of straw. "He must not have slept in a while."

"For days." She didn't want to tell the reason for that. "Which way is it?"

"You shouldn't go."

"I must. I think I can stop it. I'm not sure how, but I have to try."

Garen looked serious. He withdrew his sword and held the blade before his face. "Then I will help you. I failed before so I swear my life to you now. But I fear that if you try to stop them, when it strikes, the women will go after you with their knives."

"What strikes?"

"The clock at four. The women will start again in one herin."

Kaley gasped. "Fifteen minutes?" She started running out the door before he could reply. Unfortunately, there was a dense crowd surrounding the platform that she could see in the distance.

Garen pushed and shoved to clear a path for her.

"Can you hold off the crowd so I can talk to the girls?"

"I'll try, but will they listen?" He gave a mighty shove to a big man who looked like he might hit back, but then he saw Garen's scarred face and moved aside. It seemed that the men who were in the cutting games were respected—or maybe feared.

"No," Kaley said, "but maybe if I yell enough, I can get the cowardly prince to talk to them. They'll listen to *him*."

When they reached the stairs to the platform, Kaley's stomach heaved. There was blood everywhere. She nearly lost it when she saw what looked like a severed toe.

On the platform stood six armed, uniformed guards. They were stoically watching Kaley and Garen as they climbed the stairs. At the top, each guard gave Garen a nod of respect and didn't try to stop them from stepping onto the blood-soaked boards.

When she got to the back of the platform, she looked down to the ground and saw a line of young women. They were waiting for when they could start again in trying on the slipper. Waiting for a chance to stop spending their lives in hiding. Their faces were hopeful and afraid.

Kaley looked up. Above them, on the wall of a brick building, was a clock that looked like it was straight out of Pinocchio. It had a carved roof and a little door that would probably open to reveal a cuckoo bird. She had just minutes.

Kaley looked down from the clock. There, on a gold-trimmed stand, sitting on a purple velvet pillow, was the shoe. It was for the left foot and it was indeed glass, with a short heel and a rounded toe. For a moment Kaley forgot about the women. Here was a real fairy tale in all its blood and enchantment. Silk tassels mixed with self-mutilation; magic with evil.

A uniformed guard picked up the little shoe and held it out to her.

Kaley couldn't help herself as she took a half step forward. *What did it feel like?* "No," she said. "That shoe is no more than a size four. Too small for me."

Above her head, the door on the clock clicked, the bird came out and made the "cuckoo" call.

"You're sure?" Garen asked.

"I..." Kaley began. The clock sang out a second time. Without another thought, she found herself removing her shoe. Her sock came off with it. By the third bird call, her foot was bare. She picked up the slipper. It didn't feel like hard glass, was almost soft. It had become a common joke that Cinderella's glass slippers were the most uncomfortable shoes ever made, but not this one. Bending, Kaley lifted her foot and touched the beautiful slipper to her toes.

In the next instant, the shoe was on her foot. It fit like it had been custom-made for her.

Her first reaction was of pleasure, the joy of living out a fantasy that she'd read about all her life, then of surprise. How could that little shoe fit her foot?

She glanced at Garen and saw that he seemed to be as surprised as she was.

The clock gave the fourth call. It was time!

Kaley grabbed the shoe to take it off. It wouldn't move. "Help me!" she said to Garen.

He went to one knee and pulled, but the shoe was stuck.

At the other end of the platform, the young, hopeful women were stampeding up the stairs. Curfew was over. It was time to start again in trying to win the prince and earn the privilege of staying on their home island with the families they loved.

When the women saw Kaley standing there with the glass slipper on, with scarred, armored Garen kneeling before her, they halted. It took them a full three seconds to realize that this woman they'd never seen before, who had to be from someplace else, had the shoe on and it fit her foot.

"It's a mistake!" Kaley said, but then she drew back. She was seeing the hate, anger and absolute rage of a pack of young women. And it was all directed at *her*! The women bared their teeth, made their hands into claws and started running straight for her.

Garen threw himself in front of Kaley in protection, but the guards on the platform had been prepared for what might happen if someone fit the shoe. Garen was dragged away and Kaley saw a man hit him on the head with the hilt of a sword. He collapsed.

Four guards stood shoulder to shoulder, forming a wall in front of Kaley, blocking the screaming women who were trying to get to her. Kaley frantically pulled the shoe, trying to get it off, but it had become part of her body. She could no more remove it than she could peel off a tattoo.

It was when she saw the tiny blue light of the pen in the hand of a guard that she panicked. "No!" she yelled. "Not that! Tanek! Sojee! Someone help me. I—" When the pen touched the scar on her arm, she felt the electric current run through her body. It was strong! She blacked out.

Kaley was dreaming. She was up to her neck in warm water. A hot spring? Her eyes were closed but she could feel other people nearby. Was it Tanek? Sojee? Maybe Mekos. Were the white swans close? Maybe they had more feathers to give her.

As she felt herself waking up, she began to hear voices, but none that she recognized. They were women's voices. *Too bad*, she thought. She was getting used to being surrounded by beautiful men. It was just her and Arit and… Her thoughts began to fade.

"I thought she'd be smaller," a woman said.

"She's much too big on top. He might not like that."

A woman gave a grunt. "She has thighs like a man. She must be kept away from riding horses."

Kaley frowned. She didn't want to have a bad dream. She opened her eyes to a blurry vision. There were three women, not young, all of them dressed in flowing gowns of Easter-egg colors. Nothing too bright. To Kaley's shock, the "hot spring" she was in was a big stone bathtub set in the middle of a tiled room. She was naked and the women were washing her. She did *not* like that!

She pushed their hands away. "I want my clothes, and where am I?" Her head was aching.

The women were unperturbed by her anger. "You're here to marry the prince."

Her mind wasn't clear but then she remembered the shoe. "No. I'm not the right one. I can't marry a stranger."

The woman in blue gave a little laugh. "He won't be a stranger after the wedding night." Kaley started to get out of the tub.

The woman in pink nodded to someone she couldn't see, then put her hand at Kaley's throat. It was a soft touch, but it threatened to be more. "You should be grateful. You'll get to live with the king's family in a beautiful house. You can go outside. You'll have children." When Kaley settled down, the woman removed her hand, lifted Kaley's leg and began to wash it.

The smallest woman, in yellow, looked sad. "The other poor girls have shown themselves, so they're being sent away. But you get to stay here."

The blue woman said, "You won't have to live with all those men and their cutting games, and the way they butcher animals. You'll be with us."

The yellow woman lifted Kaley's left arm and she felt the little electrical charge. The magical pen had been used on her. "There'll be no Pithan for you."

Kaley could feel herself going to sleep. "Pithan bad?"

"Yes, it's bad. Very, very bad." The pink woman lifted Kaley's other foot and there was the glass slipper, still on her foot. It was the only clothing she was wearing.

"Pretty," she whispered, then went back to sleep.

Arit got Sojee's attention by blinking so brightly that he had to put down his weapon and shield his eyes. He'd found a sharpening stone on a foot-powered frame and had moved it outside so he could see the trailhead. If Tanek returned with Kaley, he wanted to be the first to see them. But as the hours went by and they didn't return from the mountaintop, he smiled. Maybe they were involved in some adult play. He didn't dare go up there to see. Instead, when he saw that his credits had been lavishly restored, he made a journey down the road. He'd seen a farmer with a horse that was big enough to haul a freight wagon. He hired the horse and rode it back to the homestead. If he did have to leave, he'd be ready.

Sojee was beginning to grow concerned when tiny Arit started her blinking. He covered his eyes and sheathed his weapon. He didn't know what her signaling meant, but he knew he had to *do* something.

He went to Haver's bedroom to wake up young Mekos, but the boy wasn't there. Sojee frowned at his lack of awareness. How had the boy escaped his notice? But then he remembered that he was a Lely, and in Mekos's case, he was one quarter fox.

Sojee said, "Where is he?" meaning to bring back Arit, but she didn't appear. He listened. It was very quiet where they were, but he heard a quick swish sound that he recognized. Keeping his head down, he stepped through the ruins. He'd been trained to move soundlessly, something that at times could save a man's life. At the top of a small hill, near the ruins of a storehouse, was Mekos. In his hands was a long bow and arrow, and he was shooting at a target that was too far away for Sojee to see. Curious, and staying hidden, he went toward whatever Mekos was aiming at. Yards away, almost to the village, Sojee saw that it was a small, round ball of straw, no bigger than a man's hand. It was on a rope so it was a moving target. There were four arrows in it.

Sojee's eyes widened. He'd never seen such perfect marksmanship. That Tanek hadn't mentioned this talent of his son's made Sojee suspicious. Did Tanek know Mekos could do this?

Quietly, Sojee went back to where Mekos was and watched how quickly he slipped another arrow in place. The ease of his movements showed that he'd had years of training. Sojee stepped back, then called out for Mekos. As he'd thought, the boy hid the bow and arrow from sight, then yelled, "I'm here."

As Sojee went up the hill, he murmured, "I'm so glad my daughters never hide anything from *me*." That absurd thought made him laugh.

"What amuses you?" Mekos asked.

"That I'm alive yet another day." He paused. "That woman your father loves is here."

"Is that Arit, Indienne or Kaley?"

Sojee gave a laugh that came from his belly.

"My father doesn't hide much from you, does he?"

Sojee's eyes twinkled. "Unlike you." He glanced at the pile of rocks where Mekos had hidden his weapons.

Instantly, there was fear on his young face.

"I don't betray," Sojee said seriously. "It's Arit. She was blinking fiercely, and she was so close to my face that I think her toes touched my nose."

Mekos became alert. "We must go. It's Papá. He's in trouble." He looked Sojee up and down. "We need a horse that can hold you."

Sojee's look of amusement returned. "I have one. Can you talk through Arit?"

"Only if she allows it—which is rare." Mekos pulled back his hair to expose his tall, pointed ears, and Sojee was fascinated to see them move about.

Mekos had a look of concentration. "Kaley is in trouble. It has something to do with women being cut." His head came up. "Maybe it's that game the men play."

Sojee's face fell. "You mean women are playing it for the enjoyment of the men?" He was startled when suddenly Mekos bent and pulled his bow and arrow from its hiding place. Sojee was impressed at how fast the boy drew it, but he couldn't see what Mekos was aiming at. When he did see it, he cried out, "No!"

Frowning, Mekos turned to him. "It's a tabor. Even my family stays away from them."

"This one is here for Kaley. It sleeps near her and protects her." Sojee kept his distance from the little animal as he looked at it. "We need to find her."

The animal turned, his head pointed south, then looked back at the men as though in impatience. The animal seemed to be showing them which direction they should go.

"First, we must find my father," Mekos said. "He'll know where Kaley is." He turned to the tabor, which was fully in the open. "You may follow us, but do not be seen." It was almost imperceptible, but the tabor seemed to give a nod.

Minutes later, the two men were riding hard and fast down the old road into Doyen. Their horses were fresh and the men were determined. They got there in what had to be record time. It was the tabor, disappearing in and out of doorways and alleys, that led them to the stables.

A burly man greeted them and their foam-slicked horses. "I bet you're looking for somebody." He didn't wait for a reply, just nodded toward the stall at the end.

They found Tanek half-buried in straw and sound asleep. Mekos took one of the illegal pens out of a pocket in his vest and looked at Sojee. "Don't tell Papá."

"You have so many secrets from your father that I don't know if I'll be able to remember which ones to keep."

Mekos gave a smile that looked exactly like his father's. "What you know of my doings is the size of Arit." At that somewhat disparaging remark, she appeared and gave three flashes of light so bright that it made Mekos close his eyes. It took a moment before he could see again.

Sojee grinned. "That'll teach you to not insult a lady no matter her size, her looks or her intelligence."

Still blinking, Mekos put the pen to his father's forearm. Nothing happened. Tanek was still sleeping.

Sojee held out his hand for the pen. "You're too gentle. Your father is tougher than you think." When Sojee put the pen to the scar, Tanek jolted as the charge went through him. As his eyes opened, Sojee gave the pen back to Mekos, who put it in his pocket. "Where is Kaley?" Sojee asked.

Tanek was having trouble waking up. Sojee looked across him to Mekos and their eyes agreed. This was not a normal sleep.

Tanek had to make an effort to sit up and he was rubbing his eyes. "She is…" He didn't seem to have an answer, but then his head came up. "That shoe. The glass one. She must have gone after it, but I told her not to."

"Odd," Sojee said. "Women are usually so obedient."

That Tanek didn't give Sojee a look in reaction made the big man frown. Something was very wrong with him.

When Mekos offered to help his father get up, Tanek didn't push him away. "Come on, old man," Mekos said. "We'll get you a cane."

"Who did this to you?" Sojee asked.

"I don't know. When I rode through the door with Kaley, I nearly fell off the horse. I didn't see much after that. Where is she now?"

Sojee and Mekos stared at him. That was their question to ask him, not the other way around.

"Blood," Tanek murmured, then stood up straight. "She's in the square, where the blood is."

Sojee grimaced. "Of course that's where our Kaley is. Right in the middle of whatever horror is going on. What's her story this time?"

"Some prince wants to marry a girl who left a glass shoe behind."

"That doesn't seem like a reason for blood," Mekos said. "Wait! I bet it's Prince Bront." The two men looked at him. "He's King Aramus's nephew. Lives in the south on a massive estate that's walled off. You don't know about that family?"

"How do *you* know of them?" Tanek was tightening his sword strap and checking that he had his other weapons on him.

"Mamá and I—" Mekos began, then stopped. "I'll find out where Kaley is. I'm sure people will know." He left the stables as quickly as his ancestry allowed him to do, which meant that the two humans hardly saw him move.

19

Kaley was sitting in what a fairy tale would describe as a *dungeon*. The room was dark, dank and made of stone. The walls, the floor and the tall ceiling were constructed of huge rocks. Even the bed had been chiseled out of a boulder. She knew she was belowground because she could see grass at the one window that was high up on the wall. The window had bars on it. At least they appeared to be made of iron and not rock.

Another thing that was iron was the thick cuff locked onto her right ankle. It was attached to a chain that was welded onto a hook embedded in the stone wall. Something had made the cuff rust. Blood? She didn't try to see what was smeared on it, but then her movements were hindered by a dress of about two hundred yards of what appeared to be silk. Was there a silk factory on Selkan? But no, she couldn't imagine the men who loved games that scarred them fiddling with butterfly cocoons.

She was sitting on a little stool—made of stone, of course—and the massive garment she had on was a white wedding dress. She knew that Queen Victoria had pioneered the idea of a bride wearing white for her wedding. Had the planet of Bellis seen that and adopted the idea? Or was it the other way around?

She'd have to add that to the list of questions she planned to ask her new husband, the prince she was expected to marry in about three hours. Before they sent her to the dungeon and had her shackled to the wall, she'd asked the Easter-colored ladies about him. They'd just laughed. They said she knew what he was like because she'd danced all night with him at the ball. No amount of saying "That wasn't me" had any impact on them.

Kaley held up her unchained left foot. The glass slipper was still there. Every time she wasn't being scrubbed or squeezed into a corset or enveloped in a dress that could have clothed every woman left on Selkan, she tried to get the shoe off her foot. It wouldn't budge. She'd even slammed her foot against the stone walls, hoping to shatter the thing. All that did was make her leg hurt.

At least the attempted destruction of the thing gave her the satisfaction of seeing surprise on the women's faces. But then their surprise turned to a look of fear. They seemed to think she'd done some sort of enchantment to make the shoe fit her so she could get the prince—who was thought to be the dream boy of the planet.

By the time Kaley was put into the enormous dress with its yards of skirt and a bodice that showed way too much of her upper half, they were glad to get rid of her. They couldn't hide their little smiles when her ungrateful self was escorted to the dungeon.

Of course she wasn't left alone. No telling what she could do if she had some privacy. Rip off the dress and run screaming around the chamber? From the look of the place, not even the devil would be able to hear her.

Standing in the far corner was a man in full war regalia. He had a sword, knives and a thin rope hanging over his shoulder. He planned to tie her up if she...? Kaley wasn't sure what she

could do since she was chained to a wall, but the man was prepared to stop whatever she tried.

Kaley was beginning to rethink her entire life's work—she'd
give up fairy tales and become an accountant—when she saw
a face at the window. It was Mekos. Dear, darling, beautiful
young Mekos.

When the guard, who was standing against the wall below
the window, moved, Kaley looked away. She didn't want him
seeing that there was a possibility of someone rescuing her from
something that most of the women on the island wanted.

She put her hand to her throat. An hour earlier, she'd been
allowed some privacy to use the toilet. Not that she was going
to write a new dissertation after this, but she now knew for
sure that dungeon toilets were not nice places. She gave her
best sad-faced, miserable look to the guard. "I'm so thirsty.
Could I please have some water?" In hope that he'd leave, she
crossed her fingers and one set of toes. Toes stuck in glass slippers couldn't be crossed.

The man gave a quick nod. When he turned away, she had
to work to keep from smiling. He went out the door—which
may have been wood, but if it was, it was so thick and large that
it must have taken half a forest to build it.

When the door closed and she heard the lock being turned,
she ran toward the window as far as her chain allowed. "Mekos,"
she said. It was impossible to keep the tears out of her voice or
off her face.

"You look beautiful," he said.

Tears trickled down while she smiled weakly at him. Then
Sojee's face appeared. "Best horse-riding dress I've ever seen."

Kaley's throat closed as tears choked her. A hand pushed the
others away and Tanek appeared. He was *not* smiling.

"You left me in the stables! I told you not to go alone," he
snapped at her.

"No, you didn't!" Her tears instantly dried up. "And what

was I supposed to do when you were sleeping like a baby? Are you going to get me the hell out of here or not?"

Tanek gave a one-sided smile. "That's better. Can you reach this window?"

She raised about twenty yards of skirt to show the cuff on her ankle, picked up her leg and rattled the chain all the way to the wall.

Tanek's face lost color. "Only one guard?"

She nodded.

"We'll have to get rid of him. We'll open this window and get you out."

"Open it how?" she asked. She saw Sojee's hand wave in front of Tanek. Right, the man who could break people over his knee. Iron would be easy for him. "I hope you don't hurt the guard. He's only doing his job."

Tanek's eyes widened. "Is that Earth humor?"

"This whole thing is a fairy tale. It's not real. It's—" They heard the lock; the door was being opened. Kaley hurried back to the hard stool, sat down and tried to look thirsty. The guard handed her a cup of water and she drank it in one gulp. It was only when she put the cup down that she realized it was half-full of some tasteless alcoholic beverage. Vodka? Did they make that on Selkan? When she looked up at the guard, she gave a crooked smile. Booze on an empty stomach worked quickly.

He smiled down at her in a way that every woman recognized.

"No," she whispered, then stood up. But she wasn't steady on her feet. She backed against the wall. "No," she repeated.

The guard stepped closer to her. He began unfastening his uniform.

Before Kaley could react, there was a flash of something brown. It came in through the window, then leaped across the room. Kaley wasn't sober enough to know what it was. Was Tanek soaring? Or had Mekos turned into a fox?

Her back was against the cold, damp wall when she saw something attach itself to the guard's neck. In less than a second, there was a wide, deep hole where the man's throat had been.

The guard looked surprised; Kaley had the horror of watching his shock as he fell. He collapsed at her feet.

She was still holding on to the wall, braced against it, her mind whirling from drink and shock. She saw sweet little Tibby sitting on the man's chest and rubbing his soft face against the cloth of the guard's shirt. Was Tibby sad at the man's passing? Was he trying to revive him?

It took her moments to understand that Tibby was wiping blood off his snout. He had torn the man's throat out.

Once Tibby was clean, he looked at Kaley, his eyes asking if she still wanted him, or would she hate him now? She stumbled forward to sit down on the stone stool, then patted her lap. Tibby was on it instantly. She didn't say anything to him, but she knew he hadn't liked doing what he'd done.

Tibby curled up on the voluminous skirt and closed his eyes while Kaley stroked and comforted him. She watched what was happening at the window. Sojee put his big hands on the iron of the window and pulled out the bars. To be fair, they looked like they'd been there for a couple of hundred years and corrosion was destroying them.

Mekos tried to go down first but Tanek grabbed his son's shoulder and pretty much lifted him away from the window. Kaley put both her hands on Tibby. Maybe he was what Tanek feared about letting his son go in ahead of him.

Tanek came through, feet first, and lightly soared down to the stone floor. Mekos came next. His soaring wasn't as delicate as his father's but it was good.

Sojee hit the floor hard and the other two men glared at the noise. "I'm not part bird," he said. He sounded as though it was something he was proud of.

Kaley was very glad to see them, and her inebriated state made her even more happy. While Sojee moved the guard's body away,

Tanek made sure she kept her eyes focused on him. "It's nice to see you with your clothes on," she said. "Or maybe it's *not* nice." She grinned happily as Tanek touched her forearm with his and instantly, she was sober. "What did I just say?"

"Nothing we didn't know," Sojee said as he bunched up a wad of her skirt to reveal the chain. He put his hands on it and pulled them in opposite directions. The chain broke. He looked at Tanek. "I can't get the cuff off without breaking her ankle."

That he seemed to be asking for Tanek's advice made Kaley doubly sober. "I'll keep it on," she said quickly. "Maybe I'll glam it. Put sparkles on it. But no bones are to be broken!"

Tanek was glaring at the glass shoe on her foot. "Do you know how profoundly stupid what you did is? And all of it just so you could try on a shoe! Why?"

With Tibby draped over her arm, she stood up and glared back at him. "If you were an Earth female, you'd understand completely. Can we get out of here?"

Mekos had already gone up through the window. Sojee went next, then stretched out on the grass on his stomach and put his arms down to pull Kaley up. Tibby jumped away, and like a fly, he latched onto the wall, his clawed feet digging into the rough spaces between the stones. As soon as Kaley was outside in the sunlight and on the precious grassy ground, Tibby came out behind her. He stood well away from them. She said, "Tibby is afraid of the lot of you." She meant it as a chastisement.

Sojee said, "Rightfully so." He sounded as though he was a threat to the little animal.

When Tibby made a sound, Kaley's eyes widened. "He just laughed at your giant ego." With a start, she said, "Garen! I forgot about him."

"The king's guard?" Sojee asked. "We saw him at the gate. He distracted the soldiers while we came here."

Kaley smiled. "He helped me when I couldn't get Tanek to

wake up. He—" She stopped talking when Tanek came out of the window. He wasn't smiling.

"Go!" he ordered all of them. "They'll discover us soon." He looked at Kaley. "Unless you want to stay here to get into more trouble."

"This is enough for today, but there is tomorrow."

Sojee and Mekos turned away to hide smiles, but Tanek looked like he was about to erupt in anger. They started to run, but between the skirt and the shoe, Kaley tripped. Tanek's hand on her arm kept her from falling. He took out a knife from his pocket. "What do you have on under that?" he asked. Obviously, he meant to cut the dress off her.

"Not a stitch. Very Jane Austen. No undies at all."

"And one shoe," he muttered as he put his knife away. Before she could speak, he bent and put his shoulder into her stomach, stood up with her, then began jogging across the grass. In minutes, they reached the three horses that were waiting for them. One was the size of a rhino.

"You can ride with me," Mekos said cheerfully. "I'm the lightest."

Tanek didn't bother to answer his son, but practically tossed Kaley up into the saddle on his own horse. "If this were America," she said, "I'd say something about *toxic masculinity* but actually, being rescued doesn't feel that bad." Tanek mounted behind her, his arms surrounding her as he took the reins. "I could do worse," she said softly.

When Sojee winked at her, she laughed.

"There is nothing funny about any of this," Tanek said.

She snuggled back against his chest. "I've been rescued by Shrek," she murmured. "Do you like my dress?"

"I like that you have your necklace," he said seriously.

"It was a fight to keep it. The Easter ladies said it was ugly and that I had to wear proper jewels. Then one of them said she thought it was pretty, and it turned red-hot. That scared them so much they backed off. Are you even a little bit glad to see me?"

Tanek didn't answer her question. Instead, he urged the horse forward so abruptly that Kaley struggled to hold on.

The soldiers caught up with them when they were just a few miles from the dungeon. Sojee and Tanek knew they were being followed and so they slowed. It was better if they picked their battle spot than if they were ambushed.

"How many?" Tanek asked Mekos. The young man's keen eyesight and hearing let him know more than they could.

"Six," Mekos said.

"We can take them." Sojee reined his big horse around, ready to face whatever was coming.

"Not with these two," Tanek replied.

"I can hold my own," Mekos said.

"Me, too," Kaley added.

Tanek's reply was to lift her from the horse, then lower her with one arm to stand on the ground. "Get on with Mekos."

It was an order that she obeyed. She swung up into the saddle behind Mekos. Tanek and Sojee put their horses together, effectively barricading them as they waited for the men to arrive.

Kaley whispered to Mekos, "In all the stories, one of the guards is actually the prince. What do you know about him?"

"Never met him but he's my age and said to be very handsome."

"Then he's just like you?"

Mekos smiled. "You are my favorite of my father's girlfriends."

Kaley put her hand on her necklace. It was quite warm. He wasn't telling the truth.

"Well, technically, my mother was one of them, so I guess you're the second favorite." The necklace cooled.

"Wait!" Kaley said. "I'm not your father's girlfriend. I'm—"

"Quiet!" Tanek ordered.

The faces of the royal guards were angry. They were in two rows of three each. Without a word spoken, one of the men in the back shot an arrow at Tanek, but he dodged it. Neither he nor Sojee moved, but stayed in place, protecting the two on the horse behind them. But their hands were ready at their weapons. From the tension in the air, it was soon going to turn into a battle.

Before she could be stopped, Kaley gathered the big dress and slid down off the horse. Mekos reached out to catch her, but she twisted out of reach. "It's me they want and I have to fix this." He knew she was right and he drew back.

Tanek moved the horse to block her from getting past him.

She looked up at him. "You know that I'm the only one who can change this." She put her hand on his leg. "They won't hurt me. Please."

Reluctantly, Tanek let her pass.

As she went to the first row of guards, she tried not to show any fear. They were big men. They had on helmets but she could see that they'd participated in the cutting games. She stood her ground, saying nothing, but the men knew what she wanted. After what seemed to be a very long time, one of the men in the second row said, "Let her pass." That was when she was sure he was the prince.

The horses stepped aside to make a path and she went to the man in the middle. When he removed his helmet, she saw that he was as beautiful as a fairy-tale prince was supposed to be. This was the young man the women wanted. She looked up at him. "Could we talk?"

He gave a nod, then dismounted and stood beside her. He was tall and looked quite magnificent in his guard uniform. He motioned toward the trees. If they went there, they could have some privacy.

It wasn't easy for Kaley to walk. On one bare foot she had an iron cuff attached to a piece of chain, and the other foot had on a shoe made of glass. When she stumbled, he gallantly held out his arm to her and she took it.

"You do not want to marry me?"

His voice was silky smooth, garnished with education and manners. Kaley was tempted to say, "Yes, I do want to!" Wouldn't that be a great ending for a dissertation on folklore? Marrying Cinderella's prince. "I am tempted," she said honestly, "but I'm not the one you fell in love with."

He gave a sigh, then looked away. "I have six sisters. They have a choice of men from all of Selkan. They get the best, then they live on my father's walled estate. We have houses and gardens. I already have four nieces and three nephews." He looked back at her, his eyes sad.

"I understand. There are few women on Selkan, at least ones in the open, so you put on a ball."

"They could wear a mask and for one night they could show themselves with no fear of persecution."

"And it gave you a choice," she said. "It worked. You fell in love."

"But she ran from me!"

Kaley wasn't going to explain about fairy godmothers and mice as coachmen and a fierce midnight curfew. "She left her shoe behind and you tried to find her."

"I didn't mean for there to be any...any blood."

She looked into his eyes. "She's here on Selkan. Since this place is full of men, you should look for a widower. He used to be rich but he lost it all. He has three adult children, but one is the daughter of his late spouse. She's treated badly, not like part of the family. Look for ashes on her face. Her jealous stepfamily will do all that's possible to keep you from finding her, but keep looking. She wants you as much as you want her."

He took her hand in his. "Are you sure you won't come with me? I can give you riches and love."

His words, and the fact that her necklace showed he was telling the truth, made her a bit weak in the knees. "I, uh…" She couldn't think of what to say.

He looked over her head. "There are three men glowering at us. Which one of them will take you away from me?"

"We're just friends. We're looking for Prince Nessa. He's to marry Princess Aradella."

The prince gave a sound of disbelief. "She will destroy him." He leaned forward. "She was offered to me but she frightened me."

"That's what we've heard. You don't know where Nessa is, do you?"

"On the open end of a beer bottle, as usual." He was serious. "I will get my men to find him and send him to you."

"We'd appreciate that."

He kissed her hand. "You're sure you won't stay with me?"

"Yes," she said, but her voice wasn't strong. When she took a step back, she nearly fell. He caught her arm and she lifted her skirt to show her feet. "I'm hindered by…you know."

The prince reached into his vest pocket and withdrew a key. "I imagined using this under other circumstances."

When he knelt before her, Kaley put her hand on his shoulder. He unlocked the heavy cuff on her ankle, and it fell to the ground. Then he held out his hand and she put her foot with the glass slipper into his palm. Gently, slowly, he removed the beautiful little shoe. He stood up, held out the slipper and looked into her eyes. "I have been well trained in the acts of love."

"Oh," Kaley said. "Oh." His eyes were asking if she was really and truly *sure* she didn't want to stay with him. "I, uh…"

Suddenly, Tanek rode his horse between them. Kaley had to jump back to keep from being trampled.

She looked around the horse to the prince. "Guess not. Sorry. But I sure do envy Cinderella."

"Who?" the prince asked.

"It's her nickname. She—" Tanek reached down, took her

arm and pulled her onto the horse behind him. Once she was on, he reined the horse to step backward, away from the prince.

"You are welcome at my house at any time," the prince called to her.

"Invite me to the wedding. Send the invitation care of King Aramus. He owes me big-time for putting up with his kid."

The prince laughed in a way that made Kaley again think about staying, but Tanek quickened the pace. Seconds later, they were on the road. Behind them, Sojee and Mekos were snickering like schoolboys.

20

As they rode, heading toward the homestead, they knew they weren't going to miss Doyen. "If I never see that place again…" Tanek muttered.

Kaley was behind him on the horse, her head against his shoulder. She was also glad it was over, and she was pleased that they were going "home." She was confident that the prince would find Nessa, send him to them—under lock and key?— then they could return him to his father.

She refused to think past that. All she knew was that soon, she'd be able to go to her real home, to her real family.

With her cheek pressed against Tanek's broad back, snuggled between the ridges, she looked around. *This planet is certainly beautiful*, she thought. *And I've made some good friends here.* Sojee and Mekos were riding beside them, one on each side, as though they were protecting them. *Me*, Kaley thought. *They are protecting me.*

When she tried to readjust the yards of her dress, she saw that there was blood on it. It was fresh blood and there was rather a lot of it.

"Halt!" she said loudly, and the men did. She held out a handful of fabric for them to see. "Whose is this?" All of them looked at Tanek.

"It's nothing," he said. "We must go on."

Kaley looked at Mekos. "Can you do something with him? He's been hurt and I'm sure he needs to be treated. Is there a doctor's office near here?"

The men gave her a blank look.

"Medical?" She leaned back and looked at Tanek. There was no sign of injury on him, but when she ran her hand over his arm, it came away bloody. "Let me guess. Your shirt is made of swan feathers and it magically hides great, gaping wounds." She was being sarcastic.

He gave a slight smile that let her know she was right.

"Daln's place is near here," Mekos said.

"How do you know that?" Tanek snapped.

"Who cares?" Kaley said. "Maybe his mother told him. Will you lead us there?"

Mekos looked at his father.

Tanek nodded in agreement, but they could see that he didn't like turning over leadership to his son.

"Who is Daln?" Kaley asked as they followed Mekos.

"He was the head swansman for my grandfather. They were friends."

She felt the rigidity in his body. They were the people who'd been run out when the homestead was attacked. An entire village full of workers was uprooted.

If it hadn't been for Mekos, they would never have found where Daln lived. It was like a survivalist compound, hidden and private. A twelve-foot fence with an enormous double gate was so well camouflaged that it looked like an impenetrable forest. There didn't appear to be a human in the area.

Mekos gave a whistle of four notes and out of what looked like a tree stepped a man wearing a vest of dark metal. He was holding a sort of crossbow, but one that could bring down an army tank.

The man saw Mekos, raised his hand in welcome, and the gate opened.

Kaley could feel the tension in Tanek's body.

"How does he know you?" he asked his son.

"From his fox cousins," Kaley answered. She didn't care who or how. "Your arm is covered in blood. Why didn't you say something?"

Sojee moved his big horse beside them. "Do we go in or do you two want to stay here and bicker?"

"Don't ask him that," Kaley said, "or we might be here all night. I wonder if they have any girl-size shoes here."

They went through the gate and entered a very pretty settlement. The dozen or so houses were a mix of American farmhouse and the subdued Victorian style of Australian homes. They all had deep porches furnished with wide wooden chairs. There were barns and storage sheds. To the side was a long, open building with a green roof. Inside were tables and troughs and hand-cranked machines. At the end was what appeared to be a giant stove with burners and an oven. In the opposite direction, she could see the sparkle of water. She didn't see any swans but she had an idea they were there. Nearly a dozen men came toward them.

An older man, probably the age of her grandfather, came out of the largest house. He glanced at Mekos, nodded in familiar welcome, then turned to Tanek. "You look just like Haver," he said as he came toward them.

Sojee got off his big horse, then reached up to lift Kaley down. Tanek swung his leg around and when his feet touched the ground, he swayed a bit.

The older man's face lost its smile. "Come with me." It was the tone used with a child, loving but firm.

But Tanek hesitated and turned to Kaley. "You were given a white feather?"

The men, all former swansmen, drew in their breaths sharply.

"It's..." Kaley turned her back to the men. She'd managed to save the white feather by tucking it inside her bodice. She pulled it out and handed it to Tanek. "Is it magic?"

He gave a half smile. "It's rare and it's powerful, but it's not a blue feather."

It was the first she'd heard of that. "Like Indienne?"

"No. Pure blue. It's—" When he swayed on his feet again, Daln led him into the house. More men came out of the buildings and followed them.

"They haven't seen him since he was a boy," Mekos said. "They'll have a lot to talk about."

Kaley looked at him. "*You* are going to have to do some talking. Why doesn't your father know you've been here before?" She clasped the necklace to let him know she wanted the truth.

"Because I never told him," Mekos said cheerfully, then walked away.

Sojee laughed. "I don't think you're going to get anything out of him that he doesn't want to tell. Here." He was holding out Kaley's backpack. "I thought you might need this."

Kaley thought maybe she'd never felt such happiness. Inside her bag was a change of clothes and even some shoes. "You are a saint." She looked around for a place to change and saw that a couple of men were staring at her. But she didn't blame them since she was wearing a flamboyantly gaudy dress that left a lot of her top exposed.

Daln returned and she asked, "How is Tanek?"

"He's being sewn back together and questioned within an inch of his life. The men want to know about the swans and about his father. I sent word to Noba—he's Prince Nessa's uncle—that we're looking for the boy."

Kaley was curious. "You sent it via Arit?"

Daln looked puzzled. "I don't know that Earth term. We sent a man on a fast horse. Would you like to see the home we've built here?"

"I would love that." She held up the backpack. "But first I'd like to…" She stuck out a bare foot.

He led her to a small building that had a bathroom attached, and she made use of all its facilities. "Flush toilets but no computers," she said to herself. "Crossbows but no guns. Spaceships but no cars." She didn't think she would live long enough to understand the planet.

When she was dressed in trousers and a T-shirt, she stepped out. Daln was waiting for her. In her hand were the dead camera batteries. "You wouldn't know how to recharge these, would you?"

He took them. "We have someone who can do it." He handed the batteries to a man and a nod was all he needed to tell the man what to do. She and Daln started walking. "You used to work with Haver?" she asked.

He was obviously pleased by her question. "So you know of him?"

"Tanek speaks of him often." She lowered her voice. "He was very upset when he saw the old homestead. No one told him of the battle. He thought his family left voluntarily."

Daln nodded, but didn't explain.

"I saw the empty village," she said. "Are all the swansmen who lived there here?"

"Some are, but they spread out as much as was allowed." He hesitated, as though considering what to say. "The attack was unexpected and…violent. Fire was shot from above, out of small ships. The deaths were instant for people and swans. Haver led us to fight all that we could but…" He shrugged in helplessness.

"A surprise attack wouldn't leave you time to plan. Tanek didn't know he had an uncle who was killed in the battle."

"Wellan. He was Roal's twin brother. They looked alike but they were opposites. Wellan was the swansman. Roal was the planner. Wellan was bigger and he could soar like no one else. The ridges on his back were even bigger than Haver's." Daln stopped talking and looked away, probably to calm himself, then turned back to Kaley. "Sorry. We all loved the boy, but I understand why Roal never speaks of his brother. He blamed himself because he wasn't here when we were attacked. Roal was on one of the big ships."

"Right. The ones that go back and forth to Earth. I think Tanek was with his father." They were by a long white fence and she stopped. "Can you explain to me what's going on? Why was the place attacked? Tanek just tells me pieces and it's hard to understand."

"It's called The Rightings, meaning the Righting of Ancient Wrongs. The Yuzans—"

"Who?"

She watched Daln swallow in a way that told her that what he was telling was difficult for him. "The Yuzans come from the third planet."

"Yes, the three that are alike in atmosphere," she said.

He nodded. "They are a very advanced civilization and they said they wanted to help us. They believed we were too war-like and it was because we had no uniform language or habits or even holidays. To them, we had a caste system. They said that certain groups couldn't achieve because of other groups. They wanted to make us more equal, so they put matching people on different islands. The idea was that everyone would be comfortable and at ease. After a lot of exploration, it came down to separating women from men."

Kaley was thinking about what he'd said. "But it hasn't worked. You should have seen those poor young women in town. They were cutting off parts of their feet so they could stay with their families."

"We heard they were trying to win a prince."

"That's what the story says, but that's not true. Or not all of it, anyway." She paused. "I assume the people told the... What is their name?"

"Yuzans."

"Have they been told that this separation isn't working? That the people are miserable?"

"Of course, but they say it's going very well because the people are quieter now, less angry."

"*Less angry?* They're *depressed*! They're miserable. You should have seen the men wanting me to photograph them and send messages to the women they love." She halted. "Didn't anyone protest when this was first done?"

His eyes showed that he agreed with her. "Yes. The majority of people didn't want the separation, but the ones who did want it, mainly people without families, were loud and violent. There were burnings and threats. It was all stopped when we, the entire Order of Swans, were broken apart. Our homes and families, our way of life, were wiped out in one day. When people heard what was done to us, they gave up. But by then, we all wanted peace so much that any solution seemed good."

Kaley shook her head. "And my guess is that it was all financed by the Yuzans." She looked at him. "What made them think they had a right to rule Bellis?"

"That's a question we don't know how to answer. We have some minerals they use, but we think there's more to it. We just don't know what it is."

"Because no one is allowed on Empyrea to find out."

"Right." He was pleased at her understanding.

"And now people believe that the only way it can be changed is through a revolution."

Daln grimaced. "That's what Haver said, and look what happened to him." He paused, staring hard at her. "A revolution needs a leader."

She understood. "You mean someone like Haver." She glanced back the way they'd come, toward Tanek.

"He's like his grandfather. Haver Beyhan was a man with a deep sense of fairness—and a great sense of what was right and wrong."

"And he loved the swans as much as Tanek does."

"More," Daln said.

Kaley smiled. "Were the ridges on his back bigger?"

Daln smiled. "They were. They were great, thick things that we expected to sprout wings at any moment." Daln's eyes twinkled. "His wife loved those ridges."

She could tell he was teasing her. Was it considered an intimacy that she knew about Tanek's ridged back? "I've heard little about her, but her clothes fit me."

"They would. She was beautiful. Tanek went to her when he had problems. When tiny Mekos was handed over to him, Tanek was so scared. He ran to his grandmother, asking her what he needed to do."

Like me, she thought, *he didn't have a mother.*

"Tanek takes care of the feathers now, but Mekos isn't as attached to the swans as he is."

He seemed to be trying to tell her something, but she didn't know what.

"Perhaps Mekos will have children." Daln smiled suggestively. "Or perhaps there will be another child of Tanek's. He's a young, healthy man."

Kaley took a step back. What he was thinking was clear—and it made anger rise in her. "Quit looking at me like that. You know I'm from Earth. But then, everyone knew—except me. I didn't think, *Everything here is so weird that I must be on another planet.* Nope. That never crossed my mind. What I did think was that Jobi *liked* me. Instead, he was training me to… I don't know for what, nor does anyone else seem to know why I was brought here. I haven't done one thing that's special or important." She took a breath. "Sorry. All this is new to me."

Daln was calm. "I hear you saved some children from being murdered. And you stopped girls from mutilating themselves."

"Those poor girls. They exposed themselves from their hiding places and now they're being sent away from their families."

"Did you cause that?"

"No!" She looked into the distance. "But I should have shown up earlier and stopped it. I was on a mountaintop feeling sorry for myself and…" She trailed off.

Sojee walked past them carrying a bow and arrow, and said something to Daln in a language that wasn't translated by the chip in her arm. Smiling, Daln turned to Kaley. "He said that when you get agitated, I'm to give you an animal and that will calm you down."

"That's a terrible thing to say. I'm not such a simple person as that. I— Wait! What animals do you have? Do you know what a tabor is? Have you seen Nessa's dragon? Why does no one know what a cat is?"

Grinning, Daln answered her questions, then added, "We have a two-day-old elephant."

"Nice," she said, but she was a bit disappointed. After you've seen a dragon with glistening green scales, an elephant seemed rather ordinary. "Do you have a herd? It must take a lot to feed them."

"Since none of them are taller than this, it doesn't take much." He held his hand down to about three feet off the ground.

Kaley's eyes widened. "Show me."

He glanced over his shoulder and she knew he wanted to get back to the others, probably to see how Tanek was doing.

"Go," she said. "I'll be fine. Just point me in the right direction."

"Follow the fence," Daln said, then hurried back toward his house.

She went just a few yards, then, inside the fence, to her utter

disbelief, she saw two elephants, one about three feet tall. Nuzzling it was a baby that couldn't be more than twenty pounds.
She stood by the fence, eyes wide and staring.

"He was just born," said someone close to her.

She turned to see a man. He appeared to be older than the
others but that might have been because his face was scarred and
half his left leg was missing. He had a clumsy wooden peg on it,
and a cane in his hand. She wanted to tell him about Earth tech
for such injuries but she didn't. "They're beautiful," she whispered. She was half over the fence before he could speak.

"The mother is very protective," he called in warning. "She
won't let even me touch her baby."

Kaley heard him so she was cautious. She stood a few feet
away and watched the little creatures. The calf looked at her
curiously, then at its mother in question.

Kaley said nothing, but sat down on the ground and waited.
The little elephant awkwardly ambled over to her and seconds
later, they were hugging and rolling in the grass, with Kaley's
laughter spilling out. She looked up to see the man standing
over them.

"I'm Carn." He was shaking his head in disbelief.

"I'm Kaley and I'm from Earth."

"We know. You're all anyone talks about. Now I'll have a
story to add to theirs." When he reached out to touch the calf
Kaley was holding, the mother made a sound of protest.

Kaley stood up. "I bet you'd like to have a scratch." With the
elephant calf by her side, she walked to a tree by the fence, then
rubbed her back on the bark. The little elephant did the same
thing and gave a look of ecstasy. Kaley plucked some weeds and
knelt to rub them on the calf's skin.

Carn leaned against another tree and watched them. "My
daughter went to Earth."

"Did she? I hope she liked it."

"She did." He paused for a moment. "Do you mind if I ask

you something about Earth? My daughter told me something before she was…taken away."

"She was sent to Pithan?"

He nodded, as though it was too painful for him to answer aloud. "She said the young Yuzan trainees used to practice driving in the small ships. They carved designs in the mountains and in cornfields. But she said that one time they made big cone-shaped stone structures and they're still there. Are they?"

"I don't know what you mean."

"The kids made a lot of them on your planet but the three that won the contest were in a place called Eglin."

"I've never heard of it."

"She said it's near a large river that flows backward."

"The Nile?" Kaley was shocked. "Are you talking about the pyramids?"

"Yes! That's what she called them. Are they still there?"

"They are. The outer covering is gone and no one is sure what they were built for, but they're there."

"It was a graduation contest. The winner was made a high commander."

"That was a *very* long time ago. What do you mean about carving designs on mountains?"

"She said—" He was cut off by a half scream from Kaley. She was looking across the big pasture at what was walking toward them. "Is that a…a…?"

"I think your people named them dodo birds."

"They're extinct."

"In your world, they might be. My daughter's job was to collect animals and eggs of Earth creatures that were about to die out and bring them home. Bellis has done this for centuries."

"Do you have dinosaurs?" She was half joking, half serious.

"I don't know what they are so I guess not. There are many rules about what they can and cannot bring back with them. Bird species are highly favored."

"How about cats?"

"I've heard of them, but if they're predators, they wouldn't be allowed on any of the islands."

"I know they wiped out the birds on New Zealand so…" She looked at him. "I want to see every critter you have on these islands. Do you have unicorns?"

He raised his eyebrows in question.

"Horses with a horn in the middle of their foreheads. They're usually white."

"I think Prince Bront has some of those."

Kaley groaned. "Of course he does. Mind if I…?" She nodded toward the big dodo coming toward them.

"He is very friendly and loves attention. You can—" Kaley had already reached the large bird and was stroking its frilly, hairy feathers. Beside her was the little elephant and at her feet was… Carn had to blink. By the earthling's feet was a tabor. "No one will believe this," he said softly, then left them. He was dying to tell what he'd just seen. A tabor!

It wasn't long afterward that Kaley was led to a bedroom in Daln's house. The pretty room with its flowered wallpaper and canopied bed was a young girl's dream. "Your daughter's room?" she asked, and Daln nodded. She wondered how long it had been since they'd seen each other. Years?

"Help yourself," he said, motioning to the closet and the chest of drawers.

On the walls were beautiful paintings of flowers and animals. When she got closer, she saw that they weren't paintings but needlework of exquisite beauty and precision. On the little desk was a sign, also sewn, that had what appeared to be words, but not in an alphabet she'd ever seen. "Yet something else I know nothing about," she said softly.

She showered, put on a nightshirt she found in a drawer and got into bed. The moment she relaxed, her body gave up all its energy, but she struggled to open her eyes. Her lids were so heavy that she only half succeeded. "Arit," she whispered. Instantly, a pale circle of light appeared.

The tiny woman knew what Kaley wanted to know. "He's well and sleeping. He asked about you. He worries."

"I can take care of myself," Kaley managed to say before sleep overtook her.

"I know," Arit said. "Neither of you need help from anyone." When Kaley's necklace turned dark pink, Arit said, "I guess I lied." Her laughter filled the little room.

21

When Kaley woke the next morning, she knew it was very early, yet she could feel excitement in the air. What was going on? There was a sound at the window and she wasn't entirely surprised to see the little elephant and the dodo peering at her through the glass. They hadn't yet told her their names. Nestled in the feathers of the big bird, she saw eyes peeping out. Tibby was hitching a ride. She pushed the window up, stroked all three, then went back to the room to get dressed. She found clean cotton trousers and a green T-shirt in the closet.

She tiptoed out of the house in case people were asleep. It wasn't fully daylight but she could see several men in the big open pavilion. It looked like they were starting the ovens and cleaning the tables. With Tanek there, would they soon have feathers to process? Daln raised his hand to say hello but he didn't stop working.

She turned away and started walking toward the water. Behind her was the little entourage of baby elephant and giant bird, with Tibby staying hidden. They'd been joined by some other animals that Kaley knew were extinct on Earth or about to be. The little elephant gave a ride to a pangolin.

As she knew he would be, Tanek was in the water with his beloved swans. He smiled when he saw her and swam toward the bank.

"You've been making friends," he said. The calf got closer to Kaley and the others watched. But the dodo seemed to be hypnotized by Tanek. "Can he swim?"

"I have no idea. Do you have on any clothes?"

He laughed. "Enough. The water is very warm." He was teasing, flirting, and she laughed. Behind him, three swans swam forward, looking at the dodo in curiosity.

Kaley very much wanted to join them in the water. She glanced around, making sure there were no men nearby, then she pulled off her T-shirt and trousers. She had on her matching set of blue bra and boy-cut undies. It would have to do as a swimsuit. She walked into the water.

He frowned at her clothes. "What is that word you were teaching Mekos? Killboy?"

"Killjoy." She was treading water and looking back at the animals. The dodo stepped forward and went straight into the water. His big webbed feet were good paddles. However, Tibby was not happy. He leaped off the bird's back, hit the water, went under, then came up, struggling. "Catch him!" Kaley said to Tanek as he was the closest.

"Not on your life," he replied.

Kaley went under water, scooped Tibby up and put him on dry land. "Coward," she said to Tanek.

"It's my second order. I am the ruler of it." He was floating on his back, three swans behind him.

"How's your arm?"

He turned so she could see the place that yesterday had been a deep gash. There was nothing there now, just lots of his tanned skin.

"Let me guess," she said. "The white feather healed it."

"Clever girl. Just so you know, they only work this well on me."

"You and your birds are kindred souls." She swam toward him. "Are you gathering feathers? The men are cleaning the equipment."

His face changed to serious. "I can't find many feathers. It's been years since they've been collected by one of us, so where are they?"

"*One of us,*" she quoted. "Wouldn't the feathers deteriorate?"

"No. They—" He stopped because the swans went behind him, then surrounded Kaley. Suddenly, they pulled her under the water. Shocked, Tanek went down after them. He made a lunge for her but the largest male blocked him. Kaley was paddling her feet hard, her arms struggling to take her up to the surface.

Tanek went deeper into the water, trying to come up under her but he couldn't get to her. In the next second, the water went dark. Nothing could be seen, not the glistening feathers of the birds, not the people. It was a void.

Tanek's lungs were beginning to hurt, then just as suddenly as the light disappeared, it came back. He could see that the swans had surfaced and they'd lifted Kaley onto a rock. She lay there, unmoving. When Tanek broke through, he started shouting in anger at the birds. They backed away from him, their long necks hanging down in shame.

Kaley struggled to sit up. "Stop it," she managed to choke out. "They didn't hurt me." She didn't understand the language Tanek was using but she heard his anger.

Tanek lifted himself out of the water, went to her and pressed his hand on her upper chest in a way that relieved the pressure inside her. Kaley started coughing and spit out water.

He sat down beside her, watching her.

"I'm okay. It was just the surprise." She wrung out her hair. "What is this place?"

They were in a cave. It was shallow, with a wide front that was open to the light and the water beyond. "Is that...?" She was nodding toward the back of the cave where it was dry. There was what appeared to be a mass of feathers, great mounds of them.

Tanek barely glanced at them, but kept his eyes on Kaley.

She smiled at him. "I'm all right. Honestly." When he kept staring at her, looking like he was afraid she was going to faint, she said, "Stop worrying about me. Go look at those feathers. Are there enough to be processed?"

"More than enough. Come on, let's go into the light." He stood up, held out his hand to her and didn't let go until they got to the mouth of the cave. They could see why no one had discovered the place. Forming a wall on both sides were steep, tall rocks. It would be dangerous, if not impossible, for a human to get over or around them to reach the cave. The only entrance was under water.

They sat down at one side and looked out at the water. It was a peaceful and beautiful sight.

"They were waiting for *you* to get in with us." Tanek's voice told of his wonder at that. "They didn't show this cave when it was just me."

"Maybe they were waiting for the other critters." She was trying to make a joke but he didn't smile.

He spoke first. "A cave and seeing the swans are what I remember of your Earth."

"Tell me about it."

"I was rarely allowed off the ship, but my father took me to see white swans." He smiled in memory. "He said that after that, my nature and ancestry took over. I had no interest in the ship that so fascinated my father, but Papá is Order of Swans so he understood. He supplied me with a massive amount of information, and I devoured it all."

"I like that you first saw swans on my planet. Is that why you value them so much?"

"Probably." He smiled at her. "It seems that I like a lot of Earth things."

For a moment, their eyes locked.

Kaley was the first to look away. "That trip made you lose three whole years of your childhood." She was saddened by the thought.

Tanek gave a half smile. "True, but when I got back, I made up for lost time."

She didn't know what he meant, but the mischievous look in his eyes made her understand. "You had a teenage, uh…adventure with a foxy lady and created Mekos." She looked at him. "You had to grow up quickly, but having met Mekos, I think it was worth it. You've done a brilliant job with him."

He smiled at her compliment. "Are you still set on returning to Earth?"

"Of course. My family is there. And I hope my job will be— if I can get my degree."

He turned to her. "If you stayed here, I would ask you to help me with the swans. Now many of the feathers are sent to Empyrea, but they don't know how to properly process them. Some uses have been lost." He took a deep breath, as though he was about to reveal something private. "I would like to rebuild my grandfather's home. The men say that they want to return to the village."

She nodded. "Rebuild Haver's estate, reopen the village and restart production on a big scale. Is that what's in your mind?"

"It is. But I can't do it alone." He looked at her. "I've never found anyone who could live and work with me."

"You mean to live with you and your women?" When he gave a puzzled look, she said, "Indienne, Arit, and I hear that Mekos's mother is a handful."

He laughed. "Yes, all of them." He was quiet for a moment. "What about you? Are you promised to anyone?"

"No," she answered.

"Why?"

His tone of disbelief made her smile, but she shrugged. "The animals."

"Have you always been connected to them?"

"Yes." She wasn't going to say more, but he was looking at her, silently asking her to continue. A lifetime of being told to tell no one made her hesitate.

"You can talk to them?" he asked.

"Not like you mean, but I can feel…vibrations, I guess you'd call them." She took a breath. She'd never told anyone about her oddity. "When I was very young, about four, a sheep got caught under some rocks. I could *hear* her cry for help. I told Dad and Gramps and they went out with flashlights and they found her."

"Is that unusual in earthlings?"

"Very!" she said. "After that, Dad had a talk with me. He said I could tell them what I felt but it would be better not to tell other people."

"That couldn't have been easy."

"No, it wasn't, and I slipped up too often. One Sunday after church, I told Mr. Johnson that his mule had a tummyache because he'd eaten a poison weed. I told a neighbor where his lost cow was. And I told Bobby Callow that if he didn't return the pigs he stole, I'd tell on him." Kaley took a breath. "There were more slipups, but you get the idea. People knew I was *different*."

"So you stayed out of school."

"Yes. I was homeschooled until I went to university."

"What happened there?"

Kaley shook her head. "Mostly, I studied, but then, I didn't quite fit in. I never knew how to join in girl groups, but if there was a spider, a snake, or even a frog, I was the one they called to get rid of it."

"And the men…?"

"I had some dates, but none of them lasted. One time when my date's car died, I blew out the fuel line. I wasn't asked out by him again."

Tanek tried to repress a smile but it didn't work. "And there were the animals."

Kaley groaned. "Oh yes! They followed me everywhere. It might have been all right if they hadn't included an angry bull and animals coming in from the wild." She smiled. "One day I went to the zoo with a group of kids. Let's just say that we were asked to leave and told to never come back." When Tanek laughed, she said, "It's not funny! You're followed by birds and everyone understands. It's not like that on Earth."

"Then I'm glad I live here."

Kaley didn't smile. "We have things that I miss."

"And they are?"

"Cell phones, the internet, a car at my disposal, hamburger places and—" She looked at him. "That's not true. I like Arit better than my phone, and I like finding out information from people rather than the internet. And I like food that was growing an hour ago. Best of all, I like not being *weird*." She turned to him. "What about you?"

"I'm Order of Swans," he said quickly. "We're very different."

She waited for him to say more.

"The first years of my life when I was on the ship, I had tutors— all of them women because they wanted my papá. But when I got home, I was taught by my grandpapá." He smiled. "But only birds follow me. Not elephants and certainly not tabors."

"Tibby is a sweetheart! Well, he did sort of..." She shrugged.

"Tear out a man's throat?"

"He saved me. I owe him for that."

Tanek took a deep breath, as though he was considering what he was about to say. "You're at ease with the workmen here. If you stayed, you would have a home with us." He paused. "With me."

He was looking at her seriously. She knew about the loneliness of being different from other people. His offer was kind and generous—and tempting. The little stone house she'd imagined living in was nothing beside the memory of Haver's beautiful estate. She could certainly find her stone house there! But she wasn't going to make a decision like that now. She wanted to lighten the mood. "The prince also offered me a place to live."

"Ah, yes, that overly pretty boy. Will he mind that a tabor protects you? That you cuddle swans? Nevers do not live on this island. Will Arit's visits bother him?"

"Well played," she said, and they smiled at each other.

They sat in silence for a while, neither of them wanting to return to the bustle of the compound. "What about your life?" she asked. "Haven't you wanted to get married and have more children?"

"Yes, but my *women* as you call them have caused problems." She saw that he was suppressing laughter. "How bad was it?"

"Arit made blindingly bright lights and whispers in the dark."

"I hate to ask what Indienne did."

"Made deposits in their shoes, and there were bugs in the women's food. I never did figure out how that was done."

"Long necks and an unbreakable determination." She looked at him. "I'm sorry you went through that." Her sympathy was ruined by the way she was trying to cover her laughter.

Tanek was laughing, too. "There were bugs and swan crap in their clothes and hair. It was everywhere!"

"Add that to the flashing lights and ghostly whispers! Poor girls must have been miserable. By the way, how many women are we talking about?"

His face turned serious. "If any of them had seen a house made of cake and a screeching old woman throwing fireballs, she would still be running away. And she certainly wouldn't have risked her life to save some girls who were cutting their own feet."

Kaley looked away. "I don't think I knew enough to realize the danger any of us were in."

"It's just the opposite. You know more than we do, but you

still walked straight into it." He stood up and looked down at her. "Are you ready to go back?"

Maybe it was the light from behind him, but when she looked up, it was almost as though she could see the wings that were once on his ancestors' backs. It was just a flash, but the wings appeared to be an extraordinarily beautiful shade of blue.

"If we don't show up soon, Sojee will send soldiers to find us," he said.

She stood up.

"But they would still be better than those princes of yours. How many of them are in your stories?"

"Thousands. They're the only ones who have any *fun*. The rest of us have to work twelve-hour days."

"Isn't that the truth."

Laughing, they went back into the cave.

22

Kaley was lying on soft, sweet grass with dappled sunlight coming through the trees. The days seemed longer on Bellis than on Earth. She knew she should probably ask about that, but right now she was too comfortable to care.

Tibby was in the crook of her arm and Arnot, the little elephant, was by her legs. On her right side, sitting in the grass, was Otto, the dodo. The poor guy was torn between her and Tanek, as though he couldn't figure out if he was a mammal or a bird. Stretched out on the grass on the other side was Tanek, his head resting on a five-hundred-pound tortoise as it crunched the grass. Three swans, looking like they were about to start nesting, were close by on his far side.

She thought of the picture they made, two humans nearly smothered by animals. But after the day they'd had, her only desire was to be quiet and still.

When she and Tanek returned to the compound with as many feathers as they could carry, they'd been greeted with loud, energetic enthusiasm. "If they had cannons, they'd set them off," she said, but no one understood her joke.

Tanek was soon leading young men carrying big bags under water to the cave. It took hours and multiple trips to clear out the cave—and Tanek went with every team. He wasn't going to risk injuries to unsupervised kids. Mekos wanted to help with the diving, but Sojee said he was needed at the processing area.

"Papá has made some new discoveries," Tanek explained to Kaley. "He showed them to Mekos."

"Not to you?" she asked.

Tanek scoffed. "Not my job." He started to say more, but someone called him and he had to go.

Kaley, followed by her animal entourage, went with Mekos and helped with the feathers. They were cleaned, then the barbules were carefully sliced off. She was told that every bit was valuable, including the quills and the fluff.

The pieces were collected, then boiled in a carefully measured amount of sterile water. Hours later, they were removed and laid out on trays that were put into the big ovens. Daln explained that they would be ground into powder and pressed into different sizes of pills. The water used for boiling would be made into a salve and put into tubes. "It's good for skin ailments," she was told.

While the men worked quickly and efficiently, she managed to get some information from them. Internal health problems were solved by the chips in their arms. "Sound waves," Sojee said as he emptied another bag of feathers onto the slick stone table. From the look of them, they'd been used as nesting material. Cleaning them without injuring the barbules wasn't easy or pleasant.

"You mean cancer?" she asked. "Meningitis? Lupus? Parkinson's?"

Only the oldest men had heard any of those words, but they didn't remember what they meant.

Kaley asked more questions and found out that the absence of disease meant that there were no doctors or medical clinics. That sounded good until she was told that a broken bone often meant permanent injury or even death.

"There needs to be a happy medium between our worlds," she said, but no one asked what she meant.

In the afternoon, she had an interesting talk with Sojee and Mekos. The three of them—the most inexperienced, or, as Sojee called them, the most *useless*—were together and gently washing swan debris off the feathers.

Sojee said, "I had a report this morning that the Pithan Reaver was busy last night."

Kaley didn't ask who had sent him the report. Someone from the royal family? But then, Sojee was staring at Mekos so hard that he probably wouldn't have heard her question. If Mekos heard, he didn't react. "What's a Reaver?" she asked.

Sojee, his hands on the feathers, was still staring at Mekos. "A Reaver plunders, loots and steals. And he uses a bow and arrow rather well."

Kaley looked from one man to the other, then lowered her voice. "You think Mekos might be...?" She didn't finish but joined Sojee in staring at the young man.

Mekos smiled at them. "You thought it was *me*? Based solely on the fact that I can handle a bow?"

Sojee didn't answer, just kept staring.

Kaley had a thought. "What does this Reaver do with the goods he steals?"

Mekos said, "The word is that he helps the less fortunate. I've heard that some of the women on Pithan need help."

Kaley gasped. "Robin Hood."

"I hope this isn't one of your stories," Sojee said. "People in your stories end up dead."

Mekos nodded in agreement. "Or chained to walls, or cutting off their toes, or—"

"No, no," she said. "This one is about love. For Marian. Well, there is the Sheriff of Nottingham. He's a pain but Robin deftly eludes him." She looked at Mekos. "Robin was young, talented, smart and great with a bow and arrow. The legend is that he took from the rich and gave to the poor."

"I like him already," Mekos said. "If you meet him, please introduce us. Maybe I can learn from him. As for *me*, I've been here for days. Even my mother can't travel fast enough to go between islands that quickly."

"Mother?" Kaley's eyes widened. "A female. Everything here is backward so maybe Robin Hood is a girl."

The two men looked at each other in shock. Then, in the next second, they disappeared. *Poof.* Gone.

Kaley looked at Tibby when he stuck his head up from the grass. He seemed as puzzled as she felt. "Was it something I said? Or do the two of them know who the female Robin Hood might be?"

Minutes later, the men returned and the Reaver was not mentioned again.

That was hours ago. The workers had been fed pounds of beef; all the feathers were cleared out of the cave and were being processed. At last, everyone slipped away, wanting to rest and enjoy the feeling of having done a good day's work.

Kaley stretched out on the grass, away from the others, and Tanek joined her. "How do your lungs feel?"

"Stretched," he said.

"Did you have any problems?"

"I had to help a couple of boys but they didn't give up. Heard anything from your latest prince about where Nessa is hiding?"

She looked at the tree leaves and sighed. "Nothing. He probably found his true love and forgot all about me." When Tanek made a sound as though that was impossible, she smiled.

"My concern is that the king might execute us for returning his son to him," he said.

Kaley laughed, then mimicked a male voice. "'I forgot how bad my son is. Off with their heads!'" She paused. "*Do* you execute people? No! Don't tell me that. Did you see the photos of the men on my camera? Daln got the camera batteries recharged and set up a little photo area."

"Yeah, I saw them. They were studies in grief."

"My thoughts, too," she said sadly.

"You did well today," he said.

"Thank you. It seemed almost natural to me."

"Are you sure your mother didn't have feathers? Maybe you and I are distant relatives."

He was joking, but she didn't laugh. She knew so very little about her mother.

He was quiet for a moment. "Do you mind if I ask how your parents met?"

"Through..." She hesitated. "Through Jobi. He and my mother attended the same university in the east. Jobi had a job in the west and was going to drive there, but he needed co-drivers to share expenses. My mother was the only one who answered his ad. His car broke down near my father's garage." She shrugged. "Dad said he took one look at my mother and was in love. It was mutual."

"Then Jobi left her there?"

Knowing what she did now made Kaley hesitate. *Was it as coincidental as they'd thought?* "No. Jobi called the place where he had the job to tell them he'd be two weeks late, but they said they couldn't wait, that they had to give the job to someone else. Jobi was broke and he had no car, so my family let him stay in the room over the garage. It was supposed to be just until his car was repaired, but my grandfather had broken his arm and was having a hard time working. They hired Jobi to help on the farm."

Tanek turned onto his side, his head propped on his hand. "How long did he stay?"

"Until I was born. Actually, he delivered me." When he

looked at her, she waved her hand. "It used to be a beautiful thought, but now I know he had ulterior motives."

He considered what she'd told him. "Jobi was there for months but your family didn't see any oddities in him? Your mother didn't see them?"

"If they did, they were quiet." Her voice was rising. "People in Kansas are very polite. We wouldn't say, 'Hey! You're weird. Did you come from another planet?' We'd just offer him more beef and beer, then everything would be fine. Besides, my parents were in love, and newlyweds, and I was on the way. I doubt if they saw much else."

Tanek lay back down. "Jobi didn't have anything to do with…?"

"My mother's death?" she asked. "No. It was a brain aneurysm. But maybe the stress of having me…" She didn't want to continue.

"I'm sorry that happened to you and your family."

"Me, too." His sincere words calmed her. "Jobi had been on Earth for a long time. He'd learned how to pretend to be one of us." But there had been clues, she thought. Her grandfather said that it was odd that Jobi drove so far off the interstate and that when his car broke down he was less than a mile from her dad's garage. Did Jobi foresee that the young woman he'd met at university would meet the man she was to marry? Foresee that the couple would produce Kaley—who was to do something on his planet?

Kaley didn't like to think what the truth might be. The idea of her life being predetermined and manipulated was not something she wanted to consider. Most of all, she didn't want to question what she knew about her mother. If a human could be a saint, that was how Kaley thought of her mother—and she wanted to keep it that way.

She didn't want to think about any of that. She turned to Tanek. "I bet Tibby would let you pet him if you were really, really careful."

"I'm not going to get near that creature. It's bad enough that this giant bird you found is sitting on my arm."

"Let me explain what the word *dodo* has come to mean."

"I bet I already know," he said, but Kaley told him anyway.

Mekos was deeply annoyed. Every boy his age had spent the day with Tanek diving deep under water to an unknown cave. Afterward, the boys had strutted around bragging about what they'd done, how dangerous it was and how heroic Tanek had been. "A swansman saved my life!" one of them said. "My dad says I am honored." They'd all looked at Mekos.

"You cleaned feathers?" one asked, smirking.

Mekos was about to hit the boy when Sojee grabbed him by the collar and picked him up off the ground. He didn't let him down until they were out of the sight of the boys.

"I could have won," Mekos said sulkily.

"Won what?" Sojee asked.

Mekos didn't answer. "Why didn't my father take me with him? He could have—"

"Spare me," Sojee said as they started walking. "You have other things to do than go swimming."

"It was more than that. It was..." When he saw what Sojee meant for him to see, he quit talking. In the distance, lying on the grass, buried under a pile of animals and birds, were Kaley and his father. They looked half-asleep—and old. Mekos's anger rose. "I know my father doesn't want Kaley to leave, but that's no way to win her. He should take her soaring, create songs to her beauty. *Show* his feelings. I'm going to wake them up."

Sojee clamped his big hand on Mekos's shoulder. "When you take on responsibility instead of whining that you didn't get to go swimming, and..." He glared at Mekos. "When you understand what's going on *there*, it'll show me that you're an adult." With that, Sojee turned and left Mekos alone.

23

Mekos knew that Sojee was right—not about the dull, boring way his father was courting Kaley. That was pathetic! Mekos had seen the way his father looked at her when she was turned away. It was embarrassing!

What Sojee was right about was that Mekos shouldn't be upset at not being allowed to swim to the cave to get the feathers. Those boys went because they had no other use. All day, Mekos had been questioned by Daln and the other men about the processing.

Actually, the way the men looked at him with such hope was heartbreaking. His father's dream of restoring the old homestead was what they wanted. To go back to their village, to have their wives and children and grandchildren near them. It was what gave them a reason to continue.

Mekos knew that dream was why his father was involved in the secrecy of trying to unite men to overthrow the Yuzans. They all wanted to put their country back together.

What his father didn't know was that Mekos had been working toward the same goal. In his case, it was good that parents often had no idea what their children were doing. Today, when Sojee started talking about the Pithan Reaver, Mekos had nearly collapsed. But he'd managed to stay calm—until Kaley came up with one of her stories about the Reaver being female. *Who the hell was that?* He took off running. He needed to contact Lorcan to find out what was going on.

Lorcan said yes, there had been two raids by the Reaver.

"Who is it?" Mekos demanded.

"Not me," Lorcan said. "I wouldn't fit in the costume."

Mekos rolled his eyes. Swan humor. "Find out what you can."

"Yes, sir!"

Lorcan was twice Mekos's age, twice his size. "I'll be back when I can. Papá is still searching for Nessa. I don't know if he'll ever be found." He pressed the chip in his arm and the screen disappeared.

Mekos knew the compound well and there was a door hidden behind an overgrowth of vines. It was narrow and short, too small for an adult, but thanks to his mother's genetics, Mekos could easily slide through it. A memory of his big, solid father trying to catch his son when he was a child made Mekos smile. As a toddler, he could slide through windows that were barely open.

Because he was so lost in his memories, he wasn't at first aware of the distant sounds and smells. He stepped behind a tree, put his hair back and exposed his ears. He was hearing something unusual, and smelling it.

It took him only seconds to remember what it was. Perus. The beautiful dragon that had bonded with Nessa was nearby.

Mekos left the tree and put his head back. Yes, he could also smell Nessa. His stench was as vile as his character. Mekos started to turn back. He'd tell the others that Nessa was near. Maybe that prince who'd lusted after Kaley had sent him. Maybe Nessa was under guard.

But no, Mekos smelled no other people.

Silently, he went across the grass and leaves in the way his mother had taught him. His toes barely touched the ground.

The dragon, so large and beautiful, saw Mekos but gave no alarm. It was as though he didn't care who approached his master.

Nessa was seated against a tree and sound asleep.

Mekos stepped on a few twigs. They broke loudly, but Nessa didn't stir.

Perus, head on his forearms, gave a look of *Can you believe that?* Mekos kicked some rocks together.

Nessa woke, fumbled for a weapon and said, "Who goes there?"

"It's just me," Mekos said.

"Oh." Nessa leaned back. He looked exhausted.

"Tough night?" Mekos asked. Cautiously, he approached Perus. The dragon lowered its head a bit, giving permission, and Mekos stroked the soft skin of his neck.

"He won't let me do that," Nessa said sulkily as he got up and yawned. He was wearing a long black velvet robe that had a border of gold embroidery. Jewels twinkled among the gold. When he saw Mekos's eyes widen, Nessa gave a smug smile and looked Mekos up and down. "Been cleaning the stables?"

"Feathers," Mekos said.

"Same difference. I'm glad I wasn't born into the Order of Swans. Royalty suits me better." When a hawk flew over and gave a screech, Nessa clung to Perus, looking like he was ready to fly away.

"If you're afraid of being here alone," Mekos said, "my father can take you to safety."

Nessa gave him a look of disgust. "He wants to take me back to my father. *Everyone* wants me. I can't escape. They pursue me endlessly."

Mekos stopped stroking. "Who is after you?"

"Them!" He pointed to the sky.

Mekos didn't hear or smell anyone. "Your father wants to find you. He—"

"Not him!" Nessa said. "Them! The Yuzans! They're after me. They want to take me to that evil place."

"To Empyrea?"

"Yes! The Yuzans are monsters. They want me to teach them things."

"Teach them what?" Mekos asked. As boys, they'd spent a lot of time together. To his knowledge, there wasn't anything Nessa had a talent for or that he'd bothered to learn.

"You have *never* understood. I'm royalty. I inherited the power of my grandfather."

Mekos didn't say, *The man's brutality? The greed that made him kill to get what he wanted?* "Tell me what's going on," he said kindly.

"Perus can stay in the air only so long and wherever we come down, they're there. Watching. Waiting for me."

"They know where you are from your chip."

"I disabled it." He held out his arm to show a bracelet with orange stones.

Mekos knew the stones could be found in streams on Pithan—and they were worthless. They certainly had no power to disable the chips the Yuzans had inserted into every child at birth. *Wonder how much he paid for that.* Mekos was trying to think of a reply when he heard a sound he'd never heard before. He looked up. It was late and beginning to grow dark. Whatever was making the noise wasn't yet visible. His ears twitched.

"It's them!" Nessa fell to the ground and got under the protection of Perus's heavy legs. The dragon showed no interest.

Mekos kept looking up. Two huge animals with riders flew into view. He'd never seen the creatures before. They had the head and wings of an eagle and the body of something like a deer, but with short, thick legs. The men were muscular and heavy, their faces deeply scarred. It was well-known that the winners of the cutting games were rewarded by being taken to Empyrea—and never seen again.

The men hovered above, looking down at them for minutes. Their eyesight wasn't as good as Mekos's and they struggled in the dim light. Finally, they reined their animals away and flew out of sight.

"See what I mean?" Nessa said. "They've been after me for days."

As Mekos looked at Nessa cowering in fear, he began to form a plan. His father wanted to take Nessa back to the king, but it was impossible to catch him on a dragon. If Mekos could separate Nessa from Perus, he could be captured. Right now, pleasing and impressing his father was all Mekos thought of.

He gave a longing look at Nessa's bejeweled coat. "When they first saw me, they thought I was you. Even my father couldn't tell me from you."

"That's ridiculous," Nessa said. He took Perus's reins. "I must get out of here."

"They'll follow you. Can you send Perus alone to lead them away?"

Nessa looked at him as though he was stupid. "They want *me*, not a dragon. They know he can set them on fire—but not with *me* on him. I could be injured."

Mekos sighed. "Maybe you could make a straw man and they'd follow that. A decoy. If it wore your gown, you'd fool them."

"They could tell straw from *me*," Nessa said. "And only I know how to control him. I—" He broke off as he finally got the idea that Mekos was trying to send to him. "You."

"Me, what?" Mekos asked, his eyes wide.

"You can lead them away, get close to them, then let Perus char them. When they're dead, you can return for me."

"Kill them?" Mekos said weakly. "I'm not sure I could—"

"Don't be a coward." Nessa was removing his robe. "Just keep your face hidden and they'll think you're me."

"How do I control him?" Mekos had to work to keep the excitement out of his voice and replace it with what he hoped sounded like fear.

Nessa gave a whistle of four notes and Perus tiredly looked at him. "That calls him to you. Can you remember that?"

Mekos perfectly imitated the sound. Nessa whistled six more commands and Mekos repeated them. Compared to the exercises his music master used to give him, they were easy.

Annoyed at how easily Mekos learned the notes, Nessa said, "Keep working at it and you'll get it." He held out his robe. "Be careful of that. It wasn't made for the likes of you."

"I'll try." Mekos mounted Perus. He had to control his face at the jubilation that ran through him.

Nessa looked up at him. "Keep a firm grip. He doesn't like to obey. Lead those men away then—"

Perus lifted in a swoosh of air. It seemed that the dragon wanted to get away from Nessa as much as Mekos did.

As soon as they were in the air, they went out of sight of Nessa on the ground. Perus seemed to feel Mekos's happiness and he went fast, then slow. He rolled over. For all that Mekos was part fox, he was also half swansman. Perus's flying antics suited him well. The stars sparkled in the dark sky and Mekos wanted to try to touch one.

He never wanted to stop, but he had a job to do. "We must find my father and tell him where Nessa is," he said, and Perus straightened. Mekos ran his hand over the scales of Perus's neck. "You don't need stupid whistles, do you?" The prince would be easy to find when he had no dragon to whisk him away. "This should put those boys in place," he said, and Perus gave a shiver of what seemed to be agreement.

In the next second, the big, scarred men on the strange flying animals appeared. "Starken-el!" Mekos muttered. He should have gone straight to his father instead of tumbling around in the air.

"We can outrun them," he told Perus, but he doubted if they could. The head and wings of that creature were an eagle. They were fast and relentless in a pursuit. As beautiful as the dragon was, he wasn't made for speed.

"Arit!" Mekos yelled. "Arit!" He was riding so fast he wasn't sure if the light he was seeing was the little woman. She wouldn't like being near Perus. Such animals tended to eat Nevers. "Tell Papá!" he shouted, and the light went away.

The strange creatures were gaining on them and Mekos knew he was going to have to reveal himself. They wanted a prince, not a worthless Lely. If they caught him, he didn't think they'd be happy about being tricked.

He stood up, his feet in the stirrups, and raised his arms. "I am Mekos," he called out.

To his shock, the men went faster. One held a big net and he unfurled it and tossed one handle to the other man. In the next second, they were flanking the dragon, with the extended net aimed at Mekos. "Not me!" he called out, looking at the men.

But their eyes were cold and determined. The net went over Mekos and he was pulled from the dragon, entangled in the ropes. Within seconds, he was drowsy. He knew there was some drug embedded in the fibers.

He quit struggling and looked up. Yes, the heads of the two creatures were eagles. Birds. He spoke to them in the language only the Order of Swans knew. "Take me down."

Immediately, the creatures started down. The men fought them but centuries of the language of birds overrode them.

Before they got to the ground, Mekos was in a deep, drugged sleep.

When he woke up, it was early dawn and he was in a shallow cave. It took him a moment to be able to look around. He was still wearing Nessa's jeweled robe, but there was no sign of Perus. There was a fire smoldering near him, and he could tell that the smoke had something in it. When he heard the two men approaching, he closed his eyes, instinctively knowing not to let them see he was awake. One of them threw more branches on the fire. As the smoke thickened, the men held cloths over their faces.

"You're sure that's him?"

"Yeah. I've seen him before." He gave a snort. "I thought

they were wrong when they said he'd show up with that nasty little prince. At least we got him."

The first man kicked the fire to make more smoke. "But because of him, now we have to *walk* up. I hope he gives out. I want to drag him."

"I hope his father and that big guy show up. I'd like to take them on."

Chuckling, they went outside.

Mekos opened his eyes. They wanted him, not Nessa. But why? He wasn't important. Or was this about luring his father to them?

The smoke had filled the cave and Mekos couldn't keep his eyes open. All he knew for sure was that he was really and truly deeply afraid.

24

Something buzzing around her face woke Kaley. She was in deep sleep and didn't want to leave it. Her side was on the cold ground but her back was deliciously warm.

The buzzing got louder, then came a light so bright she could see it through her closed eyelids. "I'll feed the chickens later," she murmured, and turned over to her other side. When a warm arm pulled her closer, she smiled. It was Tanek's arm, and his big, warm body was against her face.

The vibrating thing landed on her ear. It was so annoying that she swatted at it.

"Ow! You hurt me!"

"Sorry," Kaley said, but she still didn't open her eyes.

Suddenly, a cacophony of animal noises rose. The baby elephant cried out, the dodo squawked, the swans honked and Tibby gave his high-pitched cry.

Kaley moved one hand over her ear. Her other hand was under something and she hoped it wasn't the giant tortoise. A hand smoothed her hair back.

"You all right?" Tanek asked over the noise.

"Fine." She snuggled closer to the warmth of his body. "Perfectly fine."

It was his laugh that made her open her eyes. They were on the ground, wrapped around each other, her face buried in his chest, his arms around her—and between them was something called "morning wood."

She pushed away and sat up. "Sorry. I..." She didn't know what to say.

Tanek didn't seem to be bothered. "Anytime." He raised his heavy brows at the noise. "What have you done to set them off?"

"Me? I didn't do anything." She kept her face turned away to give him privacy.

"What's causing this chaos?" Sojee was glaring down at them. He noted Tanek's condition but made no remark.

Kaley held her arms out to Tibby and he leaped into them. "Something was buzzing in my ear, then there was a light and—" She looked at Tanek, eyes wide. "Arit!"

"Arit!" he echoed.

"I'm awake," Kaley called out as she tried to soothe the animals. "Arit, I didn't mean to hurt you. I was—"

"She knows not to startle sleeping people," Tanek said.

"Please come back," Kaley said loudly. The animals were calming down from whatever had upset them. She held out her hand. "Please?" When Arit landed on her hand, she saw the looks of shock on the men's faces. This was clearly unusual for a Never to do. "Has something happened?"

The light that surrounded Arit was so bright it was hard to see her. It looked as though Kaley was holding one of the witch's fireballs. "They took Mekos."

"She said—" Tanek began.

"I heard her," Kaley said. "Who took him? Where?"

"I don't know." Arit was about to cry. "I followed as best I could but they were so big."

"*Who* was big?" Tanek asked.

"Do not snap at her!" Kaley said. "She's upset, and she needs something soft to sit on."

Without turning, Tanek held out his hand to the dodo. The bird removed a few of its soft, curly feathers. Tanek took them, but he didn't give them to Kaley. He made a nest of them in his hand and Arit went to him. "Where is my son?" he asked.

"Above the Mist."

Kaley and Tanek exchanged looks, then explained to Sojee. They had no idea what that meant.

"I'll ask Daln," Sojee said. "I can't understand her anyway." He hurried off.

Kaley was too interested in what Arit was saying to question Sojee's meaning.

Arit tried to calm down enough to tell what happened. When she described the flying animals that chased Mekos, Tanek looked at Kaley.

"Sounds like griffins. Half eagle, half lion," she said.

"What is a leon?"

"Lion. Cat family," she said. "I guess the eagle head makes them acceptable here."

Sojee returned with a mug of beer. Tanek took the leather pouch out of his pocket and opened it to withdraw the tiny spoon. After Arit had had four spoonfuls, she was able to calm down enough to finish the story. When she told them Mekos had been riding Nessa's dragon, the others exchanged looks. "I tried to follow but I couldn't." Tears rolled down Arit's cheeks. "The Mist stopped *me* but it let *them* go through. How can that be? Now Mekos is gone forever."

Tanek wanted to reassure her. "My son does many things in secret," Tanek said. "Riding that dragon is proof that he's up to something. He—"

Kaley cut him off. "She said a net was thrown over him."

"Sometimes boys do things in secret. He—" Sojee began but stopped as he looked at the tabor on Kaley's lap.

Tibby was looking toward the woods, his teeth bared in threat. "Someone's here." Tanek reached for the knife at his side.

When Kaley looked at the trees, she saw something, but it moved away quickly. "It's an animal, one that I didn't see yesterday." She looked back at the men. "We have to find Mekos." She looked up at Sojee. "What is this Mist?"

The men were staring at her.

"What kind of animal?" Tanek asked.

"I don't know. They're all tame so there's no danger." They still stared at her. "A sort of bear but not very big. Okay! A reddish-brown bear with a long tail. It's probably some creature that's extinct on Earth and it—"

"By all that's holy," Sojee whispered, and looked at Tanek. "You are a dead man. Say hello to my cousin. He died over twenty years ago."

Arit stood up in her feathered nest, gave a hiccup, then flew away so fast she almost ran into Sojee's eye. He ducked to the side and she whizzed past.

"What's going on?" Kaley asked.

Tanek stood up quickly, put his shoulders back and seemed to brace himself. He looked like a soldier about to go into battle.

When Kaley stroked Tibby's fur, she found that it was standing on end. "I think he's afraid of something."

"And well he should be," Sojee said cheerfully.

"Stand by me," Tanek said to him.

"I value my own life too much." Sojee was grinning.

"*What* is this about?" Kaley asked. "If you're afraid of the animals, I'll protect you." She was half-serious but when she stood up, Tanek caught her arm.

"Go to Daln. This isn't your fight."

"Fight? I—" She didn't say more because out of the woods ran a... Kaley wasn't sure what it was. It seemed to be on all fours but it had a woman's face, then it stood up on legs as straight as a human's. She was beautiful, with lots of flowing

red-brown hair. She wore loose trousers and a jacket of colors
that perfectly blended with the forest. When she halted in front
of Tanek, Kaley could see the long, beautiful tail that stuck out
of her jacket. It was easy to guess who she was: Mekos's mother.

"What have you done with my son?" she demanded. Her
nose was rather sharp and it was pointed at Tanek as though she
meant to pierce his face.

"He ran off on Prince Nessa's dragon." Tanek was standing
rigid, unmoving—as were all the animals. Not one of them was
making a sound. Tibby was by Kaley's feet and was as stiff as
though he'd turned to stone.

The woman stepped closer to Tanek, almost touching him.
"My son is *afraid*. I can feel it."

Tanek's face changed from calm to alarmed. "Where is he?"

In an instant the woman was attacking Tanek. She was in a
rage! It was anger and fear combined. She tried to bite, claw, kick.

In what looked to be a much-practiced movement, Tanek
pulled her to him, pinning her flailing arms down to her sides.
She struggled hard against him.

The animals went back to screeching at full volume.

Sojee backed away, watching them in curiosity and with some
amusement.

When the woman dug her nails into Tanek's thighs and he
grunted in pain, Kaley stepped forward. She didn't know about
half humans but she knew about animals. Reaching out, she
stroked the woman's long hair. "It's all right," she said softly.
"We'll find him. Daln knows all about the Mist, and Arit knows
where Mekos went. All we have to do is go get him."

She could feel the woman begin to relax. Kaley tapped Tanek's
shoulder, meaning that he was to release his hold on her. He was
reluctant, but he did so.

The woman turned to Kaley and let her hold her. She was
smaller and more fragile than she'd first appeared. "We'll find
him. Did you know that Mekos made those big eagles obey him?

That's how smart your beautiful son is. And he called Arit to him. He's the cleverest kit there ever was, and we'll bring him back to you." When the animals stopped their noise, Kaley said, "Do you have friends who might have seen what happened?"

She nodded against Kaley's shoulder.

"We need to go now because we have to find Nessa and rip him into tiny little pieces." Kaley spoke so calmly that the woman almost laughed.

She lifted her head to look at Kaley. "Who are you?"

"An earthling. I'm visiting your beautiful planet."

She pulled away, stared at Kaley for a moment, then turned to Tanek. "She is too good for you."

Sojee laughed and Tanek grinned. "At last we fully agree on something."

"I am Tokala. Toki."

"Kaley Grace Arens."

Toki stepped back and looked down at Tibby, who seemed ready to attack if necessary. "He is related to my father." With that, she ran back into the woods, her tail held high, and disappeared.

Tanek turned to Kaley. "No one can tame her. You are an odd woman."

"You have horns growing out of your back from when you used to be a *bird*, but *I* am weird?"

Sojee's laugh rang out. "She has bested you. Again."

Tanek gave a bit of a smile. "Let's go find that sniveling, worthless little prince and see what price he charged my son for riding his dragon."

Tanek took off across the grounds so fast that even Sojee had trouble keeping up with him. Kaley was running behind them— and behind her was a parade of animals.

It didn't take long to find Nessa. Daln had a network of men who reported where the prince was.

"It's worse than we thought." Daln looked at Kaley, silently asking if he should tell in front of her.

Sojee said, "She can withstand it. Tell us."

"There were two of them, both former cutting champions. They were ruthless in the ring and bad-tempered out of it. About a year ago, their violence was rewarded by being taken away to Empyrea."

"But they came back," Tanek said.

Daln nodded. "We think they were sent here to get the prince."

"And take him to his father," Tanek said. "Since we failed at the job."

"But they got Mekos instead," Kaley said. "When they find out their mistake, surely they'll release him."

The men looked at her, but she didn't meet their eyes. She knew what they were thinking. Ruthless people weren't kind. "We'll..." She didn't know what to say. "Do you think they'll take money?"

"Perhaps," Daln said. "Or issue a challenge."

"I would like that," Sojee said.

Tanek's face looked hard, formed by some emotion that was past anger. "We were told they went above the Mist."

Daln looked at them in shock. "They can't— You can't—"

Sojee stepped forward. "We need to talk to that little pile of dung."

Daln nodded. "We prepared for that." There were horses saddled and waiting, one of them Sojee's heavy horse. A man was holding Kaley's hooded sweatshirt. She'd nearly forgotten that outside the compound she had to hide the fact that she was a woman.

Minutes later, they halted at a tavern. Tanek dismounted and started toward the door, his steps pounding. Sojee caught his arm. "Listen first."

Tanek nodded.

Nessa was in a private room in the back, seated at a table covered with plates and bowls full of food. He looked up at Tanek and Sojee, smiling, his mouth full. "I've been expecting you. Help yourselves." He sounded pleased at his generosity.

Kaley pushed her hood back.

"I knew you had a woman with you!" He looked at Tanek. "You lied to me! My father won't like that."

"Where is my son?"

Kaley had never heard that tone from Tanek.

Nessa grimaced. "It's always Mekos. Do you know how many times I've heard about the wonders of him? My own father said Mekos was so very handsome and so very smart. But he isn't royal, and he doesn't have a dragon. So I showed him what he was missing."

Tanek grabbed the front of Nessa's shirt and lifted him out of the seat.

"You can't do that to me. You can't touch me or—"

Sojee stepped forward. "Talk or I'll let him kill you," he said calmly.

Tanek dropped Nessa to the seat, but didn't move away.

"They've been after me for weeks. I had no peace." He was whining. "Those men were going to—"

Kaley spoke up. "If you don't tell us about Mekos, I'll help them remove your head."

"I don't know why you're angry. I'm safe. My father will reward you well."

Kaley took a step closer to him.

Nessa leaned back as far as he could. "Mekos always wanted to ride Perus, so I let him. You know that we look alike so the stupid men followed him. I had to *walk* away. On the road!" He stuck out his lower lip. "He took my dragon and hasn't returned it."

"They went through the Mist?" Kaley asked.

Nessa lifted his hand in dismissal. "You mean that old fog? I heard that it's to keep out wolves and evil people. One time I tried to get Perus to fly into it, but he wouldn't." He sighed.

"When those men see that it isn't me who they hold, they'll let him go. And he can return my robe. There are forty-two jewels on it! If he loses it, I will prosecute."

Tanek grabbed Nessa's shirtfront, then pulled back his fist to strike him.

Sojee said, "If he's dead, we can't exchange him for Mekos."

Tanek halted, considering the words.

Nessa, still held by Tanek, yelped. "Exchange? Me? A prince for the son of a swanherder and a fox? He's a freak. Worthless to anyone."

Tanek put the sharp tip of a knife to Nessa's cheek. "I swear to you that if my son is harmed, I will make you uglier than any of the men from their cutting games. Do I make myself clear?"

Nessa's eyes widened, but he didn't seem to believe that anyone would dare hurt a prince.

Kaley stepped forward and her voice was calm. "If you don't go with us, I will call Perus to me. He will be mine forever."

All the males looked at her in shock.

"Can she do that?" Nessa whispered in horror.

"Yes," Tanek said. "She can."

Sojee looked at the prince. "You are going with us and you'll stand by us no matter what we have to do or where we have to go. Do you understand?"

Nessa nodded and when Tanek released him, he jerked away. "I warn you that my father will—"

Sojee leaned forward. "Are you sure your father cares enough about you to risk anything? Or even to pay a ransom?"

Nessa made no reply to that, but they could see that he was considering the matter.

"Get up," Sojee said, and they left the tavern.

Daln and half a dozen men were waiting for them on the other side of the road. Big leather packs were tied onto their horses. "We have supplies," Daln said. "Did you find out where to go? Do we take this one with us?" He was looking at Nessa as though he'd love to be put in charge of him.

"He's going with us. He'll need a horse," Tanek said.

Nessa let out a whine. "No one cares about my dragon, and I haven't been on a horse in years. I'll be very uncomfortable."

Sojee picked up the skinny boy by the shoulders, then set him down again. It demonstrated what could be done to him. Nessa shut his mouth.

While the men outfitted the horses, Daln told them what he'd found out. "The men headed toward the top of the mountain. People used to climb up there until..." He didn't finish but they knew what he meant. *Until the Yuzans, the so-called Peacekeepers, took over.* "The horses won't go up there. We've tried. They turn away at the Mist."

"No one can get through?" Kaley asked.

"Some have but no one has ever returned. It's said that a curse was put on the place to keep people out."

Tanek looked at Kaley. "Which of your stories fits this?"

She shook her head. "A mountaintop that has a curse on it? There are too many tales to count. Is the mountain made of glass or does it float in the air? Is there a castle full of sleeping people? There's probably a princess inside, or on this planet, it might be a prince in there. Sorry," she said to Daln, who was looking at her in shock. "Please tell us what you know about this Mist."

"Nothing of any use," he said. "Animals disappear if they go through the Mist. A few men went in after their sheep but none of them returned. But it's rare that anything can get through it, and then only by accident. Most of the time it's solid."

Kaley nodded. "I don't know which story this is, but I know that there *is* a way to get past the barrier and stay alive. It could take true love or a hundred years has to pass. A virgin might be needed. Anyone?" The men kept staring at her. "I don't *know* what story this is." She thought. "I wonder if something that's not alive could get through? A truck? Or a car? I bet they have cars on Empyrea. They probably park them next to their spaceships."

They were silent, then Sojee spoke. "There are cars on this island. They're kept at The Museum of Earth."

"The what?" she asked.

Tanek said, "Jobi told me not to..." He paused, then said, "Yes. We'll do whatever it takes to get my son back. Where is this place?" he asked Daln.

25

Daln led them to the base of the mountain and they looked up in awe. An old road gently sloped up for a few hundred feet, then abruptly went upward. They couldn't see where it led because there was a thick ring of fog, the Mist, that surrounded the lower half of the mountain.

A building labeled The Museum of Earth was only a few feet in front of the Mist. "Do many people visit it?" Kaley asked.

"They used to," Daln said. "They had sweets and drinks. We'd stop there before climbing up. There are caves in that mountain. My family and I used to—" He broke off. "But then everything was changed and the Mist was put here."

For a moment they were quiet. He meant the time before families were broken up and separated.

As always, Sojee didn't allow misery. "Are we going to stand here all day?" he said. "Or are we going to steal something from Earth?"

"Besides *me*?" Kaley shot back at him.

Sojee's eyes twinkled. "Let's hope this time works out as well." He rode ahead of them.

"Was that a compliment?" Kaley called after him. "That makes two of them. If I get three I turn into a princess."

Daln looked at Tanek in question.

"Earth humor," Tanek murmured, and urged his horse forward.

The museum looked like a two-story American house from the fifties. In fact, it very much resembled the house Kaley had grown up in. In the back was a small replica of their barn.

Tanek reined in beside her. "Feeling like you've been here before?"

"Yes. How did you know?"

"I have the same feeling. I imagine black-and-white birds all around."

"Wyandotte chickens. My family raised them. They are good layers."

Sojee rode his big horse beside them. "What now?" he asked impatiently.

"I'll go in and talk to the curator." Kaley dismounted and got her backpack. When she saw Tanek staring at the Mist that was just a few feet away, she said to Sojee, "Please keep him from running straight into that."

"I plan to help him try," Sojee said.

"Of course you do," Kaley muttered. The front door of the museum was unlocked and she went inside. To the left was the usual countertop and a tiny shop. She saw framed drawings of the house for sale, some old copies of *Where the Wild Things Are* and lots of maps.

"Hello?" she called, but no one answered.

She went through a doorway and entered a big room that had been partitioned off into several three-sided rooms. The first one looked to be a kitchen in Italy. It had walls of varicolored plaster, old iron tools and a VHS player. Kaley stood blinking

at the scene. It was the most mixed-up set of time period artifacts she'd ever seen.

With wide eyes, she walked past the other rooms. There were
cavemen with a rotary dial phone, and a scene like a glamor-
ous party. Some of the mannequins were dressed in Jane Austen style, some as 1920s flappers. South American and African
artifacts were combined, with a Tahitian dancer in the corner.

"Creative history," she said. At the end was a doorway to another room. It looked like the contents of a thrift shop had been
purchased and transported to Bellis. An eighteenth-century sam-
pler hung above a 1940s typewriter. Old paperbacks by Louis
L'Amour and Mickey Spillane were displayed as reverently as a
Gutenberg Bible. She walked along, marveling at the items that
included a CD player, ballpoint pens, a potato peeler, a juice box.

At the last shelf, she paused. There was a printer and beside it
was a pile of ink cartridges. If she wasn't in such a hurry, she'd
like to set that printer up. She had no idea how she'd plug it in,
but maybe Daln's men could figure it out. She would print all
the photos that had been taken of the Selkan men.

She took off her backpack and removed the SD card that contained the photos. She had no idea what was ahead of them—
would the Mist devour them?—but maybe she could leave
behind the pictures. As she put the card on top of the printer,
she wondered if anyone would see it, or know how to use it.

"Maybe when we return..." She didn't let herself think about
that. If whatever was beyond the Mist was part of a fairy tale,
she knew from experience that it could be deadly. Was Jack and
the Beanstalk actually Tanek and the Mist? Would huge creatures be waiting to eat them?

She turned away before she let herself conjure more ugly
possibilities.

Outside, Tanek and Sojee were at the Mist, touching it, watching their hands disappear as they put them through. They tossed

rocks, listening to hear if they fell. They tried to get through in multiple places but couldn't.

Sitting nearby in a sulky pose was Nessa. He was showing his displeasure at being there.

She went to Daln, who was standing away from them and watching. "Have they discovered anything?" she asked.

"Nothing new," he answered. "But then, over the years, we've tried everything. When a boy is sent to us, the first thing he does is try to figure out about the Mist."

"Boys are sent here when they're seven. I meant to ask about that. If women are on another island, how do they have young boys to send to you?"

Daln gave a little smile. "We have the best swimmers on this island. Other men cut, we swim."

"In more ways than one," Kaley said, and he laughed at her joke.

Tanek heard them and turned, raising his brows.

"No cars," she said, then looked toward the barn.

Sojee glanced up at the house. "Was anyone there?"

"I called out but no one answered. Have you seen anyone?"

"No." Sojee had an expression on his face that made her suspicious.

"What do you know about this place?"

"I bet there are cars in that building." Sojee strode ahead.

"Secrets," Kaley muttered.

"What does your necklace say?" Tanek asked.

"It's as cool as ice. I guess secrets don't count as lies."

"Ah, more Earth wisdom." He hurried after Sojee.

Kaley ran after the two men, with Daln pulling Nessa behind him.

When she saw that the big chain lock on the double barn doors was open, she got a strong feeling that they were expected—and being watched. She whipped around to look at the house and saw a curtain move. She turned to Daln. "Did you let anyone know we were coming?"

He seemed puzzled by her question. "No."

Sojee and Tanek each took a door handle and opened them.

In front of them was one of the most beautiful sights Kaley had ever seen. A stream of sunlight came in through the loft like it was sent by angels. Stars seemed to form.

It was a Jeep Wrangler, probably late-nineties model. It was white with red interior and had four-wheel drive.

"Is this what you want?" Sojee asked.

"Oh yes!" She put her hand on the hood. That the car had recently been washed again gave her the feeling that they were expected. She went to the driver's side and looked in. "Five-speed manual. Perfect!" She thought about the strange assortment of old goods inside the museum. "I doubt if the battery is charged, and the tank is probably empty and—" She saw the keys dangling from the ignition. A little round globe of Earth was on the ring.

She looked at the men who were watching her, and her heart seemed to leap into her throat. She had no idea if this was going to work. As she tossed her pack inside and took her seat, she whispered, "Please, please," over and over.

With her feet on the pedals and her eyes closed, she turned the key.

The engine started immediately, sounding very loud in the little barn, and the men jumped back. Kaley yelled out, "Hooray! And there's gas in it!" Not much, she thought, but some. She was ready to go but when she looked at them, she thought about what they were about to do—and she didn't like it. It was a great risk! Sounding as conversational as she could, she said, "I'll go ahead, then if everything is okay, I'll come back to get you." She pushed the clutch down, put the gear into first and rolled forward.

She had only moved two feet before Tanek and Sojee put

themselves in front of the car. Nessa tried to leave, but Sojee grabbed the back of his shirt and held him. Daln stayed far to the side.

"But—" Kaley began, then stopped. She knew it was no use taking the time to argue. She lifted a hand in surrender.

There was a bit of confusion as to how to get into the vehicle but none about who went where. Tanek took the seat next to Kaley, while Sojee and Nessa got in the back. They turned to look at Daln. He didn't speak, just shook his head. He had an expression that suggested he believed he'd never see them again.

Only Nessa paid attention to it. "I will remain here. You can send Perus back to me and I'll fly everyone to safety."

"Ow!" Kaley's necklace had turned hot.

"Do you want to stay with Daln?" Tanek asked.

"Yes!" Nessa answered, and the necklace cooled.

"Thanks," she told Tanek, grateful a lie could be canceled with a truth.

He held on to the padded armrest with one hand, the console with the other, and braced himself against the seat. When she adjusted the rearview mirror, she saw that the other two were in the same position. "You guys look like my grandmother when Dad drives. He goes too fast, and she always thinks she's facing death."

Tanek kept his eyes straight ahead. "Are you more grandmother or father?"

She smiled. "Sorry, but Dad and I used to race. By the time I was eighteen, I could beat him." She let up on the clutch.

"Wait!" Sojee said. "I'm sitting on something." He held out a book to her.

Kaley took it. *"The Hobbit,"* she said. "It's my father's favorite." She gasped when a sprig of rosemary fell out. Her father often left one for her. Suddenly, a wave of homesickness hit her so strongly that she wanted to scream. Instead, she pushed hard on the horn and the sound echoed around them, seeming to bounce off the mountain then back. She let up and for a moment she put her head down on the steering wheel.

Tanek reached out and placed his hand on the back of her neck.

She lifted her head and turned so his palm was against her cheek. She knew he understood about losing loved ones.

"Can you make that sound again?" Nessa asked excitedly. "I like it!"

His words broke the mood. Kaley reached over, opened the glove box and put the book inside.

Tanek picked up the rosemary, broke off two strands, gave one to Sojee, kept one, then handed the rest to Kaley.

"What about me?" Nessa wailed.

"You don't deserve—" Tanek began, but Kaley handed Nessa a piece.

"For our son," she said to Tanek. "I mean, *your* son. Our mission." He had an annoyingly smug little smile. "If you don't stop smirking like that, I'll tell Toki on you."

Instantly, Tanek sobered.

"Coward," Kaley murmured. Again, she checked the mirrors. She saw the flash of a tail that showed her Tibby had found a crevice to hide in. She watched as Tanek took a little bag from his pocket, gave it a twist and it ballooned out. He held it up and the light that was Arit disappeared inside.

"I'm not going to leave her here alone." He didn't have to explain the dangers to something as small as Arit. He put the pouch inside his shirt, protected by his body.

With everyone settled, Kaley let up on the clutch and slowly moved forward. Since the men were holding on tightly, she crept downhill on the rutted road. She knew she was going to need momentum to get through the Mist. She'd seen that the men had encountered a solid interior. Whatever was there, she didn't think that moving slowly was going to get them through anything. She stopped at the bottom of the hill and looked at the road. The way up was very steep. It was going to take speed and torque. "I need to go fast, so you'll have to—"

"Go!" Sojee said. "Don't mind us, just *go*!"

The long, unused road was full of potholes. As she tried to gain speed, she had to jerk right and left to avoid them. She knew the passengers were being thrown about but she couldn't concern herself with that.

She downshifted, gained speed, then upshifted. By the time she reached the Mist, she was in third. When the Mist was at her headlights, she said, "May God watch over us," then floored it.

Instantly, they were inside, and cool white air engulfed them. She slowed to a crawl. She couldn't see the road or what was in front of them. It was absolutely silent. She wanted to yell, to blow the horn, anything to create noise, but it would take too much effort and she had to concentrate.

The Mist grew more dense. When she could no longer see Tanek next to her, she knew it was all or nothing. She clutched, pressed down on the gas and was glad to go faster. She just wanted to get out of that bleak nothingness!

When the Jeep burst through the Mist into sunlight, all she could think was *No wall*. They hadn't hit a wall, hadn't been crushed. They were alive.

She downshifted, braked, then sat there in idle. She could see the Mist behind them. Turning in the seat, she looked at them. "Everyone okay?"

Sojee and Tanek looked pale, but Nessa's eyes were excited. "This beats my dragon," he said.

"It can't fly or—" Kaley began, but Tanek said, "We'll trade."

She knew what he meant. When—not if—they got Mekos back, his father would give him the dragon he so wanted. "I don't think this machine can fly," Kaley said to Nessa, "but I'm not of royal blood so maybe it won't do it for me."

Nessa looked triumphant.

Sojee was looking around. "What is this place?"

She cut the engine, glanced at Tanek, and they got out of the Jeep. They were on the side of the mountain; the road ahead was steep and seemed to spiral around. The landscape was storybook pretty. There were fields of perfectly trimmed crops. Cows and goats that looked like they'd been to a salon were grazing. In the distance were cute houses with flowers in front and smoke coming out of the chimneys. They could see a few people walking. Their stride was jaunty, as though they were whistling a happy tune. It was ethereally beautiful, but at the same time, it was kind of creepy.

Tanek and Sojee came to stand on each side of her.

"I've never seen anything like this," Sojee said.

"Not in real life," Kaley said. "Just in illustrations. Do you think those people are *real*?"

"I don't know," Tanek said, "but this place scares me more than that cake house."

"Me, too," Sojee said.

"And me," Kaley said.

"What about your stories?" Tanek asked.

"My guess is that an evil witch stole the souls of everything that came through the Mist."

The men nodded that it sounded possible. Tibby was at her feet and he jumped into her arms and hid his face. He seemed as afraid as they were.

They were concentrating so hard on the view that a man's voice made them jump.

"Hello! Do you need help? What can I give you? Food? A place to stay? Credits?"

Sojee put his hand on the sword that was at his back. Kaley clung to Tibby. The man was in his thirties, handsome but not overwhelmingly so. He wasn't fat or thin. He had nice teeth, good hair, and he was smiling.

Kaley had never seen anything so scary. She hid behind Tanek's big body and Sojee stepped toward her to form a protective sandwich.

"We need directions," Tanek said.

"You're brave," Kaley whispered.

Tanek put his arm back, protecting her even more. "There were two men flying on part eagles and a boy on a dragon. Have you seen them?"

"Why, no, I haven't. Would you like some food?"

"No," Tanek said with exaggerated patience. "I want to find my son. He—"

"Ah, yes. Children. My partner and I have six children. They are good and true, all of them."

Tanek spoke louder. "The men have scarred faces and the boy is—"

"As beautiful as the sun," Kaley said loudly.

The man's face brightened. "Could they be walking?"

"Yes!" the three said in unison.

"Then they are ahead of you. We offered them food and drink but they were too busy to stop." He looked puzzled. "They weren't very polite." When he reached into his pocket, the three took a step back. Tanek drew his sword half out.

"The young man gave me this and told me to stay by the road."

"And you obeyed him?" Sojee asked.

"Of course. Why would I not?" He handed Tanek a blue stone. It was a sapphire.

"I bet it's from that robe," Kaley said.

They turned to look at Nessa, but he wasn't in the backseat. They looked at the Mist and there was the prince, trying to go back through it, but it wouldn't let him. He was kicking it and hitting it with his fists. It looked soft but it was rock-solid.

"How odd," the man said. "Why would he want to leave?"

"He likes gingerbread," Sojee said.

"We have that." The man was smiling. "You are welcome to—"

Sojee took the sapphire from Tanek and held it before the man's face. "Where did they go? How long ago? Where the frack is this place?"

The man looked serious. "They went up the mountain. I've not been there but I've heard that it is beautiful. I do not know what *how long ago* means. This is Selkan island on the planet of Bellis. Can I help you more?"

"No." Tanek sounded kind and understanding. "You may go home now."

"Thank you," the man said, and began walking along a grassy path toward the fields and houses.

Kaley fell back against the car. "Well, that was, uh..."

"Scariest thing I've ever seen," Tanek said. "I'd rather face men in a cutting game." He looked up the steep road. "You ready to go? If they're on foot, we might catch them."

Sojee went to the Mist, grabbed Nessa by the arm and pulled him back to the Jeep. Of course he yelled in protest, but they ignored him. They got in the Jeep and Kaley started the engine. "We don't have much gas left."

"Then we'll climb when we must," Tanek said.

It wasn't easy going up the mountain. Years of lack of use made the road almost impassable. Worse was that to one side was an edge to the mountain that fell straight down. One wrong turn of the wheel could send them into oblivion. Three times they stopped for the men to get out and move fallen trees. Sojee took charge of Nessa and made him help lift. He complained, but by the third one he said nothing, just grabbed an end and pulled. Sojee slapped him on the back in praise, but Nessa scowled.

At times, the Jeep struggled. Parts of the road were filled with scree and the vehicle seemed to go back as much as forward. Once, Tanek and Sojee got out and pushed the Jeep until they were on more solid ground. When they got back inside, Kaley asked Tanek, "Do you know why we were allowed through the Mist?"

"Just luck, I guess."

Her necklace grew warm. "Keep lying and you'll burn a hole in me."

Tanek took time in answering. "My guess is that we were given special permission by someone who probably cares about my son."

"Who? Toki? Your father?"

"No," Tanek said, and she could tell that he wasn't going to say more.

Kaley put her attention back on driving and watching the gas gauge get lower. She knew they were soon going to be on foot. Suddenly, Nessa let out a yell that startled them.

"It's Perus," Nessa screeched. "He's come for me."

Before Kaley could stop, Nessa flung the back door open and leaped out. He hit the ground running and disappeared into the woods. Sojee, muttering curses, untangled his long body and went after the boy.

Kaley stopped the car and looked at Tanek. She knew he didn't want any delay in finding Mekos. "I didn't see the dragon. Did you?"

He opened the car door. "I saw the tail as it flew past. I—" He broke off and listened. "I don't know that birdcall. Maybe Toki…" He didn't finish.

She knew what he meant. Maybe Mekos's mother or one of her furry relatives was signaling him. He could move faster without Kaley. "Go! I'll be fine. Tibby is with me."

"Do not leave this truck," he ordered.

"It's not a—" Kaley began, but then repeated, "Go!" He moved so fast she could hardly see him. She got out of the Jeep, Tibby with her, and they stretched. She listened but heard nothing, no birds, no sound that might be a dragon and no men yelling at anyone. Under different circumstances, it would have been nice.

She left the road for some privacy, and when she stood up, Tibby looked at her with wide eyes. She could feel that he was hearing something. "What is it?" In the next second, she felt his uncontrollable, impossible-to-disobey urge to go to whatever he was hearing. He took off running. "Great!" Kaley muttered. "It's probably a singing Siren in the woods. Maybe I should tie myself to a tree." With a sigh, she ran after Tibby.

She hadn't gone but a few yards when she saw a stone cottage. Past experience made her look around to see if three little pigs appeared. "Or a wolf," she said aloud.

When the door opened, she stepped back, ready to run away. But to her surprise, it was Garen, the man who'd helped her with photos and Cinderella's slipper. His handsome face was freshly bruised—and she felt guilty. *Did he get that from helping me?* she wondered. Tibby ran across the man's feet as he went inside the house.

"We meet again," Garen said, and he stepped back to open the door wider. "Would you like a cup of tea?" His eyes sparkled. "Or some Selkan beer?"

"I would," she said, "but the men will be searching for me." He didn't say anything but his eyes conveyed his thoughts. He'd helped her with the shoe but she wouldn't have a drink with him. "I'd love one." She followed him inside. The interior of the cottage gave *cute* a deeper meaning. She gazed at the stone walls, big fireplace, hand-hewn wooden furniture painted with folk art scenes, deep-set windows open to the cool breeze. "This is beautiful."

"Just a simple place," he said humbly as he put a copper kettle on the iron woodstove.

Tibby was stretched out on the worn stone hearth, sleepy and content, not at all as he usually was. She wondered how Garen got past the Mist but it seemed impolite to ask. She was looking around the cottage. "This place is adorable."

"Is it as nice as my aunt's house?"

She didn't know what he meant.

"My aunt Uella? The woman you killed? She lived in the gingerbread house."

All the hairs on Kaley's body stood on end and she looked

toward the door. She needed to get out *now!* "The woman was murdering children!" Kaley said as she backed toward the door.

"My aunt did have unusual dietary needs."

"For children?" she gasped. "That was her diet?"

Garen filled a pretty teapot with hot water. "Truthfully, I never liked the woman. My mother—her younger sister—put some protection spells on me when I was a child. I think my aunt saw me as an especially tasty tidbit."

Kaley stopped moving. Her insatiable curiosity and her fear for her life were pulling her in opposite directions. She watched him set the table for tea, adding a plateful of cookies. "Did your aunt bake those?" she managed to say.

Garen smiled. "It is her recipe, yes. You may leave, but please stay. I will tell you that as long as you're here, your friends won't find the dragon or that worthless prince."

She blinked as fairy tales of magic ran through her mind. "Is Perus really here?"

"Of course not." He glanced around the little cottage. "And by the way, you see this house as it is. Your friends would see it as a stone fortress. Impenetrable."

Kaley swallowed. It appeared that she was alone with a real live warlock. She should run out the door. Unfortunately, her curiosity was winning the struggle. Besides, she remembered this man helping her on that blood-covered platform, and how kind he was when taking the photos. Whatever he was, he'd taken some hard blows because of her. Cautiously, she sat down at the table.

Garen sat across from her and filled the two cups. It was loose tea. It appeared that genuine warlocks didn't use tea bags. "My grandfather made your necklace."

She put her hand on it. It didn't change temperature.

"It won't work on me," he said. "And I don't think it works on you, does it?"

"No." She'd read too many stories not to be afraid of the tea. She didn't move.

He understood her hesitation. "Remember when I swore my life to you? I meant it. You'll always be safe with me." His blue eyes lit up. "Besides, *I* don't need to use poison."

She understood what he was saying. She took a sip. "You mean you have other ways of accomplishing what you want?" Her head came up. "Did you put Tanek to sleep in the stables?"

He looked pleased that she'd figured that out. "Yes, I did. I wanted to get to know you better. I knew about my aunt and that you'd tamed a tabor." He glanced at Tibby sleeping peacefully. "You got those two men out of the tavern and that shoe fit *you*. No one else, just *you*. How could you do those things?"

His astonishment was flattering. She held up her arm. "I blocked the chip, and I knew the stories about the gingerbread house and the glass slipper." She shrugged. "It all fell into place."

"And you found the necklace my father made. It was not meant to be noticed."

She wasn't about to tell him that Arit showed it to her. "You just said your grandfather made it."

"Same man." The humor left his face.

"But—" she began, then said, "Oh." Fairy tales often told of incest. "Sorry," she murmured, and he went back to smiling. In spite of the bruises and scars on his face, he was a very good-looking man.

"I don't have time to go slow," he said, "so I'll say it all quickly. Your abilities intrigue me." He paused for a moment. "I would like to offer you a kind of employment. If you accept, I can give you great riches, and a palace to live in."

Kaley had read too many fairy tales to be enticed by his offer. "Would the palace be real or an illusion? Would you create some fake house so you could watch me every moment? You can see me but I can't see you? That kind of thing?"

He looked genuinely astonished—but pleased. "Yes. But now I won't do that."

She couldn't help smiling at his honesty. "Everything I know is in books from my planet."

"Stay with me and you can record those stories for the people on my planet. My guess is that there are more of those...events happening here."

"That's what I'm afraid of."

"I'll help you find them, then we'll work together to destroy all of them." He sounded eager. "We'll be a team. A joint partnership."

Kaley shook her head in disbelief. "On Earth I can't get a boyfriend, but here I have offers in abundance."

Garen made a sound of derision. "The others are worthless. Prince Bront believes people should give everything to him, and Tanek will place you after every bird on the planet. You'll never be first in his life."

"But you can do better?" There was no missing the sarcasm in her voice.

"I'll give you your heart's desire—whatever that is. I know of your connection to animals. If you want a thousand creatures to care for, I'll give them to you. We have animals that haven't been seen on your Earth for thousands of years."

Kaley knew she should run out the door, but what he was saying interested her. "I have friends here."

"I understand. I, too, have friends." He took a breath. "Give me one year, then, if you choose, you can return to them, and I will step aside. By then, you'll have found out what you can do on this planet. You'll know what your strengths are."

Kaley narrowed her eyes. "What do you get out of it?"

"For one year, I wouldn't be alone. I'd have a true friend and a student. And you'd be my teacher as well. I want to know more about Earth. I'd like to hear these stories that you know."

His offer was more tempting than she wanted to admit. Tibby

felt her agitation. He lifted his head and looked at her. "Maybe Jobi has a book. You could read it and—"

Abruptly, Garen got up and went to a tall cabinet that was painted with folk art. He opened a door, withdrew a small wooden box and held it out to her. When she hesitated, he opened the lid. "What do you see?"

The first thing she saw was an oil lamp the size of her palm. It was the kind from an Aladdin story and she didn't dare touch it. There was a little wooden toy of a man, its arms and legs attached with pins. A leather bag with pebbles falling out of it was in a corner. "These are things you found?" she asked kindly.

He looked amused. "If you were from here, each of those items would be fascinating. Your earthliness makes you unable to see the enchantment of them." When she didn't reply, he said, "The little man dances. He fascinates people so much that they see nothing else. The bag contains an endless supply of wealth. I think you have an idea of what the lamp does."

"Magic lamps always cause trouble," she said.

He closed the box and set it on the cabinet. "Your hesitation is Tanek, isn't it? Fertility and soaring are irresistible to women." He leaned forward. "Tanek is interested in you because you're different. If you stay with him, your powers will be wasted on cleaning swan feathers. Meanwhile, your stories will be happening. Are more children being killed? Is there suffering and torture that only you know how to stop?"

She didn't answer because it was something she'd thought about.

"If you stay with me," he continued, "even if it's only for one year, I will dedicate my life to helping you. Together, we'll search out these evils and destroy them. I have abilities that I inherited from my odious family. I'd like to use them for good." He took a breath. "Can Tanek not wait a year for you to go to school? Do women on Earth not ask such a thing of a man?"

His offer was making her head spin. He was saying things that had been in the back of her mind. Maybe the reason Jobi brought her here was to find fairy tales and destroy them. She looked down at her empty cup. Tanek had also made her an offer. But she knew Garen was right. Accepting Tanek would mean she'd live with *his* family. Share *his* life. If she sought out horrors, like *Cinderella* and the gingerbread house, she might have to do it on her own.

On the other hand, there was the promise that she could go home to her own family. But then what? Her father and grand-parents could live with her, but someday, she'd be alone. On Earth there were no real fairy tales to abolish. But she could write about them. Fictionalize them, maybe? Would a man who didn't think she was strange come into her life? She had a vision of boring her students with stories of what she'd seen and done while on another planet. Of course no one would believe her.

She looked across the table at Garen. *Just one year.*

"If..." he said softly, "at the end of the year you want to con-tinue your work, I can give you whatever you need. You can have a home, a garden. You can train others to help you. You can do what you're meant to do. You can fulfill your life's purpose."

As befitted the drama of his statement, Garen got up and went to the woodstove. The second his back turned, a tiny light ap-peared by the far wall. It was no bigger than a gnat but Kaley knew it was Arit—and she felt a sense of relief, glad that some-one knew where she was.

When Garen reached for a tin of tea, Arit's light flashed brighter, then went out. It had only been for a second but it was long enough to show an old key hanging beside a pretty little bouquet of dried flowers. *You do the same as your aunt,* she thought. *You hide your valuables in plain sight.*

When Garen looked back at her, Kaley had composed herself. She was thinking of how to get that key then leave graciously. Suddenly, a flaming arrow flew through the open window. It was so unexpected that for a moment, all she could do was stare.

The arrow hit Garen in the shoulder. For a man so scarred, so used to pain, she didn't expect the scream of fear that came from him. It echoed off the stone walls and nearly pierced her ears.

Witches fear fire!

Tibby, suddenly no longer under some magic spell, got up and seemed ready to attack.

But Kaley was faster. As a farm girl, she was used to emergencies. She grabbed the tablecloth, dishes crashing to the floor, and slammed the cloth onto the flaming arrow. The fire went out.

Even with the fire gone, Garen's face was distorted in terror. His eyes were like an animal caught in a trap. In the next second, he ran through a door that looked like a cabinet, but she saw that it led outside. He fled into the woods.

Behind Kaley was a pounding on the front door. As Garen had said, it wasn't locked, not from the inside anyway. When she flung it open, she wasn't surprised to see Tanek there, a bow slung across his shoulder, and looking terrified. He didn't say anything, just opened his arms to her.

Kaley didn't realize how frightened she'd been until she felt his strong body holding her.

He smoothed her hair back. "It's all right. He's gone now. You're safe."

Kaley nodded, her face hidden in his shoulder. She would have stayed there longer, but Arit's flashing light had brought her to her senses. "I have to get some things." Before Tanek could say no, she ran back into the house. She grabbed the box on the cabinet, then snatched the key off the wall. Tanek put his strong arm around her shoulders and they walked in the direction of the car.

When he stopped, she looked at him. "We should go. We need to look for Mekos."

But Tanek led them deeper into the forest. There were rocks and he sat on one, then looked at Kaley. "What happened?"

"I'll tell you in the car." She started to turn away, but he caught her arm.

"I don't want Sojee to know about this. It would upset him too much."

She sat down beside him. "Yes, you're right. Sojee is very protective, and he seems to think I can do anything."

"Such as jump across roofs?"

"And rescue two big men in a storm and melt candy houses and—" She knew he was waiting to hear about what happened. "It was Garen, the man from…"

Tanek nodded impatiently. He knew who he was.

"At first, I was afraid of him, but he kept talking and explaining things to me. He's as lonely as a lost sheep and my heart went out to him. He—"

"What did he say?" Tanek snapped.

"He offered me a job."

"To work with him? To be his apprentice? To learn but also to teach?"

"Yes!" She looked at him. "How do you know that?"

"A guess. What are you holding?"

She looked at the box that she was clasping so tightly it might crack. With her eyes on Tanek, she opened the lid. "What do you see?"

His eyes widened, then he smiled in delight. "The little man dances. He says his name is Clee."

To Kaley, the wooden figure wasn't moving, but she saw the hypnotized way Tanek was staring at it. She had an idea that she could walk away and he wouldn't notice. She picked up the figure, covering it with her hand, and the spell was broken. "What about the bag?"

He picked it up and poured out some pebbles, but the bag didn't get smaller. "These are very valuable as well as beautiful. Indienne would love them." He put the bag down and started to reach for the lamp.

But Kaley pulled the box away. "Don't touch that!" She put the little man inside and closed the lid. "What was the house where you found me like?"

"A stone fortress. I couldn't get inside by myself but Arit showed me the window. When Garen moved, I shot. I'm not as good with a bow as my son, so I missed his heart."

"I'm glad you didn't kill him," she said. "His life hasn't been easy." She didn't explain. "He is terrified of fire." *Like all witches,* she thought but didn't say. She pulled the big, rusty key from her pocket. "Arit showed me this."

Tanek took it and looked at it. "What the starken-el do you think this thing opens?"

His tone made her laugh. "The gates to a place we don't dare enter!"

Tanek groaned. "What are those animals that eat birds?"

She took a second to know what he meant. "Cats. Maybe it's a key to a whole island full of cats. Lions, Persians, jaguars, leopards." Tanek's look of horror made her laugh harder. "Bet they'd love those blue swans you want to see."

Tanek's horror increased. "Blue swans are *me*. *I* am a blue swan! Humans who are of swan lineage are called blue."

The image of a cute little kitty chasing Tanek made Kaley laugh harder. When she described the scene, Tanek caught her laughter so they were both in tears.

They were laughing so hard that they didn't see Sojee until he was standing inches away and glowering down at them. "Did you two forget why we're here? Did you forget your son?"

His anger sobered them.

"It's my fault," Kaley began, but Sojee had turned his back on them and they followed him to the car.

A sulking, pouting Nessa was in the backseat waiting for them. "I couldn't find my dragon." He sounded pitiful.

Kaley and Tanek exchanged looks. They now shared a secret.

26

The sun was high in the sky when the Jeep sputtered. They were out of gas. Kaley rolled to a clearing at the side of the road and turned the engine off. "That's it."

Before them was a lot more mountain. As soon as they got out, they realized it was colder than it had been.

"Look," Sojee said. Through the trees could be seen the snow-covered peak. It looked to be very far away.

"What could be up there?" Kaley asked. "A Swiss chalet? Why would they take Mekos to the top of a mountain?"

"You mean take *me*," Nessa said. "They wanted me, not him. They're using him to draw me to them."

"Never would anyone think that *you* would follow them," Tanek said softly.

Sojee and Kaley looked at him. He was saying that maybe Mekos was the real object of the kidnapping.

Sojee started removing the supply cases from the back. "Looks like Mekos has wisely kept his mouth shut. They still think he's the prince."

"We do look alike," Nessa said.

They turned to him. Mekos was beautiful; the prince was not.

Sojee tossed a pack at Nessa so hard that he nearly fell. "Put it on."

"I can't wear that. My father will—" He saw their glares and shut up.

Once they had the packs on, they started the hike up. Between the altitude and the exertion, breathing was not easy.

It was Nessa who found another jewel. And it was Sojee who saw him slide it into his pocket. The big man didn't bother asking questions. He said nothing, just picked Nessa up by the ankles and shook him. His pack fell off, then his pockets emptied. There were three jewels in there, six coins and what looked like the foot of a bird. It had red ribbons on it and appeared to be some talisman. Against evil?

Disgusted at the sight, Tanek grabbed the foot, removed the ribbons and buried it.

Sojee asked Nessa where he'd found the stones. "On the trail. They're from *my* robe. He shouldn't have torn them off. They're valuable and he—"

They turned their backs on him.

"Mekos knows we're coming after him and he's leaving a trail." Tanek pulled the pouch out of his shirt, opened it and Arit came out. She looked tired. "Can you find him? Is Mekos near?" he asked her.

Arit struggled to speak, but nothing came out.

"The altitude is getting to her," Kaley said.

"I don't know," Arit whispered. "My head doesn't work."

"See if you can sleep," Kaley said.

Arit nodded, went back into the bag, and Tanek replaced it inside his shirt.

"We need to find a place to rest for the night," Tanek said. "The men are lowlanders. They won't be able to travel in the dark. Besides, there must be predatory animals here."

Kaley's eyebrows lifted.

Sojee frowned. "You're not to adopt any animals from this place no matter how *cute* they are."

The way he said it made her nod in agreement.

They hadn't gone far when the temperature suddenly dropped from cool to freezing. When the first flecks of snow came down, Tanek and Sojee looked at each other over Kaley's head and seemed to make an agreement.

Nessa said nothing, just turned and headed back down the mountain.

Sojee caught him and started to say something but the snow began falling harder. In the next second, a wind coming down from the top of the mountain blasted them so violently that Kaley was lifted off her feet. Tanek grabbed her arm to keep her anchored to the ground. The noise of the rising wind made it impossible to hear each other.

None of the trees around them were large enough to use as a windbreak. When Kaley was again blown off her feet, Tanek put his arm around her and turned her head into his shoulder. Sojee reached behind him, pulled a rope from his pack and tied Nessa to him. He made sure the knots were strong as Nessa was struggling to go with the wind that was trying to send them back down the mountain.

Kaley, her face hidden against Tanek, couldn't see much, but when he halted, she heard him shout to Sojee. She wasn't sure what he said, but he started walking again, his body fighting against the wind. When he turned, she saw a broken sign on the ground. It was anchored by rocks that wobbled in the fierce wind. She couldn't read the sign as it was in a language she didn't know, but it seemed to give Tanek new energy and he turned off the main road.

On the smaller trail, the trees gave enough shelter from the wind that Sojee came forward. Kaley saw him shaking his head, then he pointed upward. Tanek nodded.

When they left the side path, Kaley saw where the men were leading. They were to climb up what had to be a goat path. It would be steep and dangerous on any day, but in the fierce wind and thick snow, it seemed impossible.

Tanek looked at Kaley, silently asking if she could do it. *What's the alternative?* she wanted to ask, but the wind and the noise were too much for her to do anything but nod.

The path was too narrow for them to go side by side. Tanek stopped behind a tree, removed a thin piece of rope from inside his shirt and tied it around Kaley's waist. He looked at her in question and when she again nodded, he gave her a quick smile of encouragement.

She smiled back at him, he turned and they started up the slippery, rocky path.

Twice, Kaley nearly fell, but both times, Tanek caught her. Behind them, Sojee half dragged Nessa upward. Kaley couldn't see much but at one time it looked like Sojee was piggybacking the prince.

After what seemed like hours, Tanek pulled Kaley through an opening of some kind. Sojee and Nessa were close behind them.

It was a cave. The quiet and the lack of wind felt glorious.

Tanek untied Kaley, then opened the pouch to Arit. She flew out and went to Kaley to bury herself in the warmth of her hair.

Sojee released Nessa then directed him toward the far side of the cave. He was scowling in rage and trembling with exertion.

Sojee went to the back of the cave and disappeared into what looked like a second room. They waited in silence. Were animals hiding back there?

Sojee returned quickly, holding an armload of dry wood. Best was his smile. "All clear. How about some dinner?"

Kaley looked at him in gratitude. "Sounds great." She sat down, leaned back against the stone wall and closed her eyes. Outside, the wind howled, but right now she was safe and almost warm.

Sojee pulled a blue pen from deep in his pocket and held it up to Tanek, who nodded in understanding. He touched the pen to the chip in Tanek's forearm. "This way, she won't be able to understand us." He spoke in a language he knew wasn't covered by the chip in Kaley's arm.

"Are you sure? She understands Arit."

"Recorders can talk to all the Nevers," Sojee said quickly.

Tanek said, "But she isn't—" He stopped as that didn't matter now.

"I'm going to follow them." Sojee was shoving items that Daln had given them into his pack.

"I should go," Tanek said. "I'm younger. You can take care of both of them here."

"I can cover more ground faster. Give me your arm so I can connect us."

Tanek grunted at the electrical shock that went through him. "Where did you get that pen? I thought yours was stolen."

Sojee didn't answer. "I'll climb until dawn, then I'll send you the coordinates of where I am. I'll sleep until you get to me, then we can go to the top together."

"And what if you find them before that? Will you wait for me for the fight?"

"No," Sojee said. "I can handle the two cutters."

"And their eagles?"

"I think maybe your son got rid of them."

An expression of pride mixed with fear crossed Tanek's face. "I wish I could go with you."

"You can't," Sojee said. "You cannot leave them here alone, unprotected. Put that animal near the opening. It'll raise an alarm if anything gets near." He meant Tibby, who was curled next to Kaley.

Sojee put his hand on Tanek's shoulder and looked outside. It was dark and the wind was howling. Already, several inches of snow covered the ground. He looked back at Tanek. "What are your intentions toward her? Can I trust you with her?"

Tanek looked offended, but then his expression changed to

a look of helplessness. "I asked her to live with me, to help me with the swans and to rebuild the old homestead. She gave no answer."

"She's an earthling. She probably thinks you want her to clean the ponds and sweep the floor."

Tanek laughed at that, but stopped when he saw that Sojee was serious. "She couldn't possibly think that I—" he began, but Sojee put his head down and went out into the cold.

Tanek stood there for a moment, trying to see into the dark, but there was nothing. Turning, he looked back into the cave. It wasn't very big and it was obvious that others had been there before. Was it families enjoying their time together?

He went through the opening at the back. It wasn't that he didn't trust Sojee, but he wanted to see it for himself. It was a small room that looked like it may have been man-made. Made during the time when men did something besides cut each other? he wondered.

He touched the chip in his arm, rotating it to turn on a light. The room was about as tall as Sojee was. There was writing on the walls, all of it vulgar, and he was glad that Kaley wouldn't be able to read it.

The good thing was that there was a large pile of dry wood against the far wall. He gathered an armload and took it to the front. There was enough to keep a fire going all night. Like he knew what to do, Tibby left Kaley and went to the cave entrance. He sniffed the air, then stretched out by the fire. He'd sensed nothing threatening.

Tanek opened the packs that had been dumped on the ground when they'd entered the cave. He could find only two of the swan blankets. Surely, Daln had put in four of them.

An image came to him. When Sojee had repacked his gear, he'd stuffed in one of the blankets. Filled with swan feathers, they were thin, light and magnificently warm. Daln had packed the best quality.

Tanek sat back on his heels. It looked like Sojee had taken two of them—which meant that two of the people left behind would have to share. *Matchmaking*, he thought, and looked at Kaley.

She was awake and watching him.

"Nice language you two had." She was being sarcastic as she knew the men hadn't wanted her to understand them. "I'm female so I'm not allowed in the decision-making?"

Tanek was unperturbed. "I'm male and I'm not allowed in Sojee's decision-making."

"Touché." She became serious. "What's the plan?"

He told her what Sojee wanted to do.

"Great. He's to meet those monsters alone."

"He can do it." Tanek opened a bag of dried beef and held it out to her.

She held a piece of beef up to the light. "Oh, for a bar of chocolate."

"What's that?"

"There are so many things you guys should have brought back from Earth. We have—"

Suddenly, Nessa sat up. "I saw eyes! Four of them. What's out there? If I'm hurt, my father will have you killed."

Kaley thought Tanek would snap at the prince, but he didn't.

"We put you on the far side," he said gently, "so you're in the safest place. Kaley and I will be by the entry, and the fierce little tabor is right by the fire. If anything comes in, it will have to go through us first."

When Tanek turned back to her, he rolled his eyes, letting her know what he really felt about Nessa. She watched the young man stretch out on the cold stone floor. Tanek handed him a blanket, then had to listen to how inadequate it was and how uncomfortable everything was. He returned to Kaley.

"My turn," she said. "He needs to settle down."

"Want to borrow my blade?" Tanek muttered.

Kaley opened her backpack and withdrew *The Hobbit*. Between the rosemary and it being her father's favorite book, it made her sad. She sat down by Nessa—he didn't offer to share his blanket—and began to read to him.

Tanek sat down beside her and spread one of the swan blankets over them. Arit went from Kaley to Tanek, and Kaley kept reading.

She read the entire long first chapter before Nessa fell asleep.

"That was grand," Tanek said softly.

"What are books in Bellis like?"

"We used to have stories on pages but they were deemed too excitable."

"The people must be kept calm no matter what. Is that it?"

"Yes."

"But they have the cutting games."

His face told her that he didn't understand, either.

When Nessa stirred, Tanek tossed the blanket aside, stood up and held out his hand to Kaley. He nodded toward the other side of the cave, where he'd told Nessa they'd be. Kaley followed him.

"Sojee took two of the blankets, so you and I will have to share."

Kaley looked solemn. "I promise I won't molest you."

Tanek didn't smile. He swept his hand toward the flattest place and Kaley sat down. He sat by her and put the blanket over them.

To their right, at the edge of the wide opening, was the fire, warm and inviting. Beside it, Tibby was sleeping. Outside, the wind and snow whirled and clashed. In other circumstances, it would have been a cozy scene.

"Sojee told me something strange," Tanek said. "He said that when I asked you to stay on the homestead with the swans and me, that you had no idea what I meant."

"You were offering me a place to live and a job. It's very kind of you."

He looked surprised. "That is our way of speaking of the future, of forever."

"Forever? Oh, you mean if I don't book a ride home and I stay here on Bellis? Something like Garen offered?" When he didn't answer, she looked at him. His face was serious—and hurt. Her eyes widened. "Are you saying that you were asking me something more personal? Like...?" She hesitated. "Like marriage? As Nessa to the princess?" He was silent. "You mean with a big ceremony where we invite friends and family and vow to be together forever?"

"I don't know what any of that means."

"I'd wear a white dress and walk down the aisle holding my father's arm?"

"I've never heard of that. We would clasp hands before witnesses. Or on our own. Either way."

"That's a dud. Handshakes. Then what? You do have sex here, don't you? Or is there some transfer with the illegal blue pen?"

"Do you mean the act that creates children?"

"That's the one."

"We have that."

"You're laughing at me!"

"I am. Your world seems to have many rules."

"I guess we do." She looked at him. "Are you saying that there can't be sex between you and me because you want to *marry* me?"

"Yes."

She paused. "Have you asked other women to do this hand clasping?"

"No!" He sounded shocked that she'd ask that.

"But what about Toki? And the girls Indienne didn't like?"

He smiled. "I didn't ask any of them to *live* with me. There are things that must be considered. I cannot live separate from swans. From any birds."

She remembered Garen's words. "It's about them, isn't it?"

Her voice was rising. "They like me so you want to mate with me. I fulfill some checklist, don't I?"

"I don't understand your anger, but I see that you're displeased with our ways."

"I apologize. Your offer is kind and generous." She sighed. "It's just that I always imagined some grand gesture. Like a prince who loves me so much that he searches the entire kingdom for me. All because of a slipper."

"An act that causes women to cut their bodies?"

"No, of course not, but yes, I guess so." She paused. "It's my fault. I've read too many fairy tales. Thank you for your…uh… proposal." She stretched out on the cold floor. "I think we should get some sleep now." *What an odd place this is*, she thought. No romance but lots of fairy tales.

After what they'd been through that day, Kaley fell asleep instantly. She woke when she felt Tibby's nose on her face. As before, she was snuggled against Tanek. She thought about their talk about marriage and cohabitation. "Likes me for the birds," she muttered.

She reached out to pat Tibby, but he pulled back. Arit flew to hover above him. Her light was dim and she was motioning for Kaley to follow them.

The moment Kaley moved, Tanek woke up, and his arm tightened around her protectively. Arit turned off her light and Tibby seemed to blend into the rocks. Obviously, they wanted to see Kaley alone.

"Nature," she said.

Tanek nodded, then turned over.

Kaley stood up, glanced at Nessa, sound asleep, and followed Arit and Tibby to the back of the cave to the second room. She watched as Arit flitted about and seemed to deposit little nuggets of light on the walls.

"You are very smart and of great use," Kaley said, and Arit flashed a pretty pink light at her. "What do you want me to see?"

Tibby was standing in front of the far wall, staring at it. It was solid rock and she saw nothing of any interest. There was what looked like graffiti on it but she couldn't read it. She yawned. "That's a nice wall but—" She broke off because Arit's light turned a soft shade of lavender, then the color began to grow darker. To Kaley's astonishment, the light seemed to show a hole in the rock, then it spread in a perfect horizontal line. It stopped, then went down on both sides. It was like water filling a narrow canal. It stopped at the floor.

"Is that a door?" Kaley asked. "Can we open it?"

Arit didn't speak, but went to the side. There was a flash of red light that showed a small circle. A tiny puff of smoke came out, and the door opened slightly.

"Okay," Kaley said. "Let's see what's in there." It took both hands to pull the heavy door open.

It took a moment for Arit to light the room and Kaley stared in astonishment. It was a computer room. On Earth it wasn't unusual, but on Bellis, it was extraordinary.

There were two long wooden tables and a single chair. The tables were loaded with computer equipment, old and obsolete by Earth standards, but at least they existed. There was a radio, an early cell phone, screens, keyboards with an unknown alphabet and piles of old square disks.

What was truly astonishing, even sickening, was that every piece of equipment had been destroyed. It looked like someone had hit each piece with a sledgehammer. Screens were cracked, keyboards smashed. Cords that led to what may have been a generator had been severed.

"An undercover, secret war room," Kaley said. "They were fighting against the invader of their country. This is horrible."

Tibby was at the end of the table and looking at something on the floor. He turned to Kaley with wide eyes.

"What is it?"

Arit flew to the end, then hovered there, her tiny face in shock.

Kaley made her way around a disk tower, something she'd seen in her grandfather's garage, then halted.

Between the table and the wall, slumped on the floor, was a skeleton. It had on the remains of one of the gray jumpsuits that Tanek wore when he was with the swans.

A lifetime on a farm had made Kaley used to life and death so the sight didn't frighten her. She knelt to look at the poor man. He had on a gold necklace with a round disk on the end. She lifted it and rubbed her thumb across it to see the word engraved on the front. "What does it say?" she whispered, but she thought maybe she knew.

"Haver," Arit said.

Tears came to Kaley's eyes. "Tanek's dear grandfather."

Arit sat on Kaley's shoulder. "He loved him."

"Yes, he did." She turned the pendant over. A symbol that she'd seen on one of Tanek's shirts was engraved on the back. "Tanek gave this to him."

"Yes," Arit said.

Tibby moved forward, his small body slipping under the skeleton.

"What did you find?" Kaley asked.

Tibby backed out with a little metal case in his mouth and held it out to Kaley.

Inside was a miniature painting of an older woman with a young boy. Kaley held it up to the light. The boy was Tanek and she guessed the woman was Haver's beloved wife. The two people Haver loved most in the world.

"We have to tell Tanek." Kaley ran her hand over her face. "His son, the homestead and now this. It's too much for one person."

Tibby had moved a few feet away and he was scratching at the floor.

"What is it?" Kaley went to where he was. The floor appeared to be solid stone but she saw a gap in it.

Arit made a bright blue light. Kaley picked up a piece of metal that had once been on a screen, stuck it into the hole and pulled up the flat piece of rock. Her mouth dropped open in shock.

"What is that?" Arit asked.

"A nine millimeter Ruger and four boxes of ammo."

"I don't think that's allowed here."

"I'm sure it isn't." Kaley removed the pistol from the hole. Between the men in her family and Jobi, she'd had experience with firearms. She took it out and checked if it was loaded. No. It seemed to be in good shape. She stood up and put the pistol and bullets in the big front pocket of her sweatshirt.

She looked about the room, then went to the skeleton and gently removed the necklace. When she stood up, she'd reached a decision. "Come on, let's go. We have to meet Sojee in the morning, then we'll find Mekos." She patted the gun in her pocket. "I think this will decide who wins the fight. After Mekos is safe, we'll tell the men about this and let them handle it."

Arit nodded. "Tanek will be hurt."

"Yes, he will be, but at least he'll have Mekos." *I hope*, she thought. After Arit flew out, Kaley started to leave the room, but a shadow by the skeleton drew her attention. She knew what it was: Haver's ridges. She picked up the hornlike curves, hid them under her shirt, left the cave room and closed the heavy door. Arit extinguished the lights and the three of them went back to the big room.

Kaley put the ridges, the necklace and the little painting deep into her backpack. Nessa was soundly asleep and Tanek opened his eyes as Kaley lay down beside him.

"Better?" he murmured.

She didn't answer, just moved his hand away from what she had concealed in her pocket. Minutes later, she was in a restless sleep.

27

An hour before dawn, three pine cones, skewered on arrows, flew into the mouth of the cave and landed on the fire. There were a few sparks from the pitch and Tanek looked up, saw that the tabor didn't sense danger, so he put his head down and went back to sleep.

The cones began to smolder. Swirls of blue-gray smoke filled the cave, and as the sleeping inhabitants breathed it in, they smiled. It was a pleasant smell. They went deeper into sleep. Then even deeper.

When the people, in clothes that blended with the snow and trees, arrived, those in the cave didn't wake up. The largest man grunted as he picked up Tanek and put him over his shoulder. The second man carefully removed the sleeping Never from Kaley's hair and handed the little woman to the next person. Nessa was easy, as was Tibby.

The last person, the smallest but obviously the leader, went to the back. He made an inspection, seeing what he knew to be there, then he pulled a pot from his pocket. He used the con-

tents to reseal the door that led into Haver's Solace, then he disabled the latch that opened the door. Next time, it could only
be opened under his supervision.

Once that was done, he went back into the larger room. The
people had been cleared out, and the man looked about the cave.
Their belongings were spread out, as though they'd made a home.
He closed his eyes in remembered pain. It was so like the way
Haver used to live.

Others would remove the packs, but there was one thing that
Zeon wanted. He picked up the copy of *The Hobbit*, put it inside his shirt, kicked out the fire and left.

When Kaley woke, her first thought was that she'd died and
was now in Heaven. She remembered the snow, the howling
wind, the hard, cold stone floor—and finding Haver.

In spite of what she knew to be true, her body felt clean sheets,
a soft mattress, warmth—and the deliciousness of Tanek holding her. She snuggled against him.

It was minutes before she realized he was awake, but she didn't
want to open her eyes. She was afraid that reality would make
the dream go away.

He smoothed her hair away from her face.

It took her a moment to realize that he was bare chested and
he was *clean*! "Did you take a snow bath?" she murmured.

"No. I had a tub full of hot water, warm towels, and scented
soap."

"That's my dream, too."

"It's not a dream," he said softly. "We were kidnapped during
the night and we now seem to be inside a castle."

She smiled against his bare skin. "You've been reading my
fairy tales."

"I think we're living in one of your stories, and this part is real."

Kaley finally opened her eyes, turned over and looked around.
They were in bed together in a room even more lavish and beau-

tiful than in King Aramus's house. "I don't understand. We were in a cave and—" She looked at him. "Why aren't you upset? How did we get here? Who did this?"

Tanek reached out to a table beside the big bed, picked up a card and handed it to her. It was printed in two languages.

Welcome to my home. When you are ready, please join me for a meal. My life and my resources are at your disposal to help you find your son.
Zeon

"Do you know who this is?" she asked.

"Never met him but Jobi told me of him. He said we can trust him. There are clothes in that cabinet."

"Clean ones?" She nearly leaped out of bed, but then felt the pocket of her sweatshirt. It was empty.

"It's over there on the table."

Kaley went to the beautiful table, inlaid with mother of pearl, and there was the Ruger. It had been cleaned. She turned to Tanek. How did she explain where she got it? She tried to think of a story to tell. Whatever she concocted, it would be a lie through omission.

He got out of bed. He had on loose cotton trousers that hung low on his hips. "Tell me when you want to."

She couldn't think of a reply but she was glad not to be interrogated. If she started, she'd never be able to keep from telling him the truth about his grandfather. Right now he didn't need to be distracted from finding Mekos.

"Do you know how to use it?" he asked.

"Very well."

He smiled at her, glad of her answer. "I don't know about you, but the promise of a meal makes me want to find it."

She started toward the door that she assumed led to the bathroom, but turned back. Tanek had opened a curtain and was standing in front of the window. Outside, snow whirled around a stone pillar topped with a sculpture of a bird in flight. The wind seemed to have calmed but it was still bad. She looked at the ridges on his muscular back.

On impulse, she went to him and put her arms around his waist, her head nestled between the ridges. "Thank you," she said. "Thank you for respecting me and not asking questions. I'll tell you everything when I can." She hesitated. "And thank you for offering to share your life with me."

He put his hands over hers, raised them and kissed her palms. "Go now or I'll not be able to withhold myself."

"Yeah?" She sounded so eager that he laughed.

He removed her arms from around him and she headed toward the bathroom. "I think your ridges are getting bigger. If they sprout wings, I want a ride."

He laughed again, then said, "Go!"

Kaley took a shower so hot her skin turned red. When she got out, she found clean clothes lying on a bench by the door. It looked like Tanek had come in while she was in the shower. *Like Cupid and Psyche*, she thought. She towel-dried her hair, used her makeup that had been laid out for her and left the room.

Tanek was waiting for her. He was dressed all in black. With his black beard and hair, he looked divine. She stared at him.

He turned his back to her. "There isn't room for my wings."

"Then I guess you'll have to take your shirt off," she said solemnly.

Smiling, he crooked his arm for her, she took it, he opened the door and they went into a magnificent hallway. A pretty young woman wearing a long blue dress and a short embroidered jacket was waiting for them. Smiling, she silently led them down the hall, then halted before a window. When Kaley and Tanek looked out, they could see part of the building they were in. It really was a huge castle, complete with pointed caps on towers and narrow windows, all of it made of stone.

Tanek was watching her. "Like it?"

"A fairy-tale castle? Oh yes."

The young woman led them to wide double doors, two guards opened them, and Kaley and Tanek stared in awe. *Magnificent* didn't come close to describing the room. Gold-embossed carvings and green stone made up the walls. The ceilings were painted with glorious landscapes with half-dressed men and women in gauzy gowns. There were pictures of animals that hadn't been seen on Earth in centuries.

One long wall was floor-to-ceiling windows showing the glistening snow outside. Around the room were men and women in uniforms that looked like something from the Ottoman Empire. They wore big, ballooning trousers with short, colorful jackets.

"Do you think they stole the design from Earth or the other way around?" she asked.

Tanek gave her a look that was becoming familiar: Earth humor.

To the left were two long tables. One was loaded with a buffet of beautiful porcelain dishes filled with steaming hot food. The second one had four place settings.

To the right, at the far end of the room, was a smaller table, and sitting at it was Nessa. He had two guards behind him and a young woman on each side of him, serving him. He didn't look up when Tanek and Kaley entered.

"Personal protection and private service," Kaley said. "We have princes on Earth who demand that." She looked around. "Where's Sojee?"

A man entered from a side door. He wasn't tall or big, but there was no doubt that he was in charge. Kaley and Tanek stood up straighter.

Kaley wanted to ask about Sojee but before she could get the words out, the big man entered. She ran to him and threw her arms around his waist.

Sojee was smiling and hugging her back. "Had I known this

would be my reception, I would have come to you last night."
Tanek and Sojee exchanged smiles, glad to see each other.

Sojee glanced behind him. "This monster has scared everyone."

Looking very small, Tibby entered. He had an expression
that he'd decimate anyone who came near him, but when he
saw Kaley, he nearly melted. He ran to her and leaped into her
arms. As she clutched him to her, she looked at the man. "Arit?"

Stepping to the side, he extended his arm.

A young woman, holding a pillow with tassels, entered. On
it were half a dozen colorful tiny pillows. In the center of them
was Arit. She looked like she'd had a bath, her long hair was
coiffed and she had on a pretty dress of pink and silver. She was
smiling broadly.

"You've spoiled her forever." Tanek was frowning.

"Their beer is so good!" Arit said, but only Tanek and Kaley
understood her.

After the pillow holding Arit was gently set on the table,
Kaley turned to the man. His eyes were twinkling. He was a
handsome man, probably in his fifties and very fit, like he could
defeat a dozen men the size of Sojee.

"Now that your family is here, may we eat?" That his words
were directed to Kaley seemed to say that she was the boss.

"You got that right." Sojee gave the smaller man a hard slap
on the back. He didn't flinch or lose his balance.

"I am Zeon," he said, "and you are welcome to my home."

"We need to find my son," Tanek said.

"I am of the Order of Sight and I am here to help you."

"Like Jobi," Kaley said.

Zeon gave a gracious smile. "There are only three of us. I am
the second in our order."

"Isn't the strength of power related to the hierarchy?" Tanek
asked.

"Yes," Zeon said modestly.

Sojee was at the table of food, his plate and mouth full. "Who's at the top of the heap?"

"No idea," Zeon said cheerfully. "That's kept a secret even from Jobi and me."

"This planet should be renamed *Secrets*," Kaley said.

"And your Earth is so open with information?" Zeon asked.

Sojee laughed while Kaley grimaced. Tanek was waiting through this talk for information about his son.

Zeon turned to him. "I have arranged for you to leave at sundown on horses that know the way to the top of the mountain. You'll find the men and your son at dawn, and you'll catch them by surprise."

Kaley said, "If the griffins are still with them, Tanek will charm them."

"They are not." Zeon's face was serious. "The men are waiting for other birds. They can't leave until they arrive. My vision isn't clear, but one bird has huge wings."

"Could be something prehistoric from Earth," Kaley said.

"Perhaps," Zeon said. "Please help yourself to the food. Packs are being prepared for you, and warmer clothes."

They filled their plates then sat down at the table. Zeon's portion was sparse, while the others ate heartily.

"If you have sight, how is my son doing now?" Tanek asked.

"I have kept up with him through all this," Zeon said. "He is hungry, cold and very angry, but that's good. His anger keeps him warm." Zeon looked startled as a sight seemed to come to him. "He meant to do this! But something is wrong. It isn't going as he planned. He—"

A shout from Nessa cut him off. He stood up and the two guardsmen stepped forward. "*I* planned it," he said in anger. "Not him. It was my plan and I'm given no credit for it."

They all stared at him. It was as though Nessa was saying that the kidnapping was *good*.

Both Tanek and Sojee started to get up, but Zeon gave a slight head nod and the guards escorted Nessa from the room.

Once he was gone, they looked at Zeon, waiting for his explanation.

"My vision isn't clear." He gave a little smile. "More clear than what Jobi can see, but still..."

Sojee was tearing a bread roll in half. "He has less power than you, but you have less than number one."

Zeon gave a small laugh in agreement. He'd been put in his place. "What I see is that Mekos wanted to be the savior, but the men knew who he was. They never wanted that nasty little prince, but Mekos didn't know that. They want to take Mekos to Empyrea. Why?"

They all looked at Tanek. Only he might know the answer. "I have no idea why they would want him."

Kaley let out a cry of pain. Her necklace had turned red-hot. She grabbed a napkin and put it between her skin and the metal. Instantly, it burned a hole in the napkin.

Sojee jumped up and tried to take the necklace off her neck, but it wouldn't budge.

"Tell a truth!" she said to Tanek, her teeth clenched in anger and pain.

Tanek spoke loudly. "No one on Empyrea will hurt him, but I don't want him to go."

Instantly, the necklace went cold.

Sojee and Kaley glared at Tanek, who looked guilty.

Zeon appeared to be fascinated. "You have a necklace of truth."

"More like a fireball of lies." Kaley gave a side-glance at Tanek.

"Fireballs," Sojee said, grinning. "I have a scar from one of those."

"Put white feathers on it." Kaley looked at Tanek sitting next to her. "You could have killed me! Look at this!" She held up the napkin with a hole burned in it.

Tanek kept his head down.

"No wonder you're willing to forgive me about any secrets I have." Her voice was rising. "You're holding in some really big ones." She looked around him to Sojee. "You said there was only *one* secret. I found that one out but there's this." She waved the napkin.

Sojee wasn't the least bothered by Kaley's anger. He got up to get more food. "I only know one. Looks like Swan Boy has a few more."

Kaley turned to Tanek. "You—"

Zeon's laugh cut her off. "I feel great friendship here. Tell me where you found that necklace."

Tanek had his head down and Kaley was still angry at him.

"It was in a house made of cake," Sojee said.

Kaley smiled. "That's where I met Arit, only I didn't know who or what she was."

"And later you found the tabor," Tanek said.

"Who killed that guard," Sojee added. "Wish I could have done that."

"I want to hear the story," Zeon said.

The three of them talked over each other as they told part of what they had been through. Tanek described how Kaley had run into a burning building to save two children. Sojee told that she knew what was going on in the house before she even saw the place. Kaley talked about the men fighting the fireballs. "And Tanek can soar," she ended with.

Zeon was quiet for a moment. "That was Uella's house. She's the second of four sisters. She was always very unhealthy."

Garen's family, Kaley thought. She wanted to know more about them. "Four sisters?" she asked. "Are they all like that one?"

Sojee said, "Urah, the mother of Olina, is the oldest of the four."

"Yes, that's right," Zeon said, while Kaley and Tanek looked at Sojee in surprise.

"The third one was Winel," Zeon said. "That poor girl. That ended badly for everyone, but she did have a son."

"Garen," Kaley said, and was pleased that Zeon looked surprised.

"Garen is Kaley's friend," Tanek said, but didn't explain further.

"What happened to his mother?" she asked.

Zeon grimaced. "Her father murdered her, then Garen took the man's life."

Kaley didn't feel the need to tell who Garen's father was. "What about the fourth sister?"

Zeon was looking at her in speculation, as though he knew she wasn't telling all she knew. "Reena is the youngest and she's a beauty." He looked at Tanek. "Wellan was so in love with her that it hurt to look at them. Haver—" Abruptly, he cut off and glanced at Kaley.

He knows that I found the body! she thought.

"Haver was my friend and I miss him every day," Zeon said.

"So do I," Tanek said softly. "I've only just learned of my uncle Wellan."

Zeon looked at Kaley. "There's another half to your necklace. If they're put together, they can force people to tell the truth. Ask a question and a person cannot resist telling all they know." He smiled. "Except those of us from the Order of Sight. We control our own minds."

"I'd like to have the other half," Kaley said. "There are some truths that I very much want to hear."

"I want to know more about the safety of my son," Tanek said.

Zeon became solemn. "I wish I could say that you'll be fully successful tomorrow, but there is a hindrance. These men are angry at Mekos for sending their birds away and making them walk." He took a breath. "They are men of impulse, not logic or loyalty." He looked at Tanek. "Someone wants your son very much. I can see that all of this was planned a long time ago, and it has to do with *you*."

Tanek made no answer.

Zeon shook his head, then his eyes lit up. "Ah! Your son is involved in something on Pithan. He—"

When Kaley pushed over a chair, the room echoed with the noise. She glared pointedly at Zeon. "What were you saying?"

"Nothing of any importance." He was smiling, understanding that he was not to tell this particular secret.

Now that they were fed, bathed and rested, it was as though some interior force made them turn toward the tall windows. By the look of the sunlight, it was hours before they were supposed to leave.

They looked at each other. In silent communication, they were agreeing to leave now. They'd save Mekos from more hours spent with his captors.

Sojee was the first to stand up. He stretched his shoulders. "I might take a nap."

Kaley put her hand over her necklace to cover its pink glow. He was telling a small lie.

"Good idea." Tanek stood up.

Zeon knew what they were planning. He made a motion toward one of the guardsmen. "Jobi told me of something on Earth called a magic show. Perhaps you'd like to see one."

Kaley stood up. "Oh no! I've had enough magic to last my whole life. I couldn't even get Cinderella's shoe off my foot! Too much magic." She faked a yawn. "A nap sounds good."

The door opened and three guards entered. Two were carrying a tall mirror on a wooden stand. The third one held a pretty metal box.

Zeon opened the box and removed what looked to be a Mardi Gras half mask, except that since it was transparent, it was useless.

"We'll see it later." Tanek put his hand on the back of Kaley's waist, but she didn't move.

"What does it do?" she asked.

Tanek and Sojee gave groans but she ignored them.

"It can change people," Zeon said.

"Make them invisible?" Kaley asked. "That happens often in fairy tales."

"In a way." Zeon held it out to her. "Want to try it?"

She glanced at Tanek and Sojee, who were wearing identical expressions of *Let's go!* She looked back at Zeon and took the mask. It felt fluid, like a bag filled with water. "I'm not sure it will work on me."

"Put it on and try," he said. "Perhaps it's enchantments that don't work with you, but objects do."

"Necklace doesn't work with her," Sojee said impatiently.

Zeon ignored him. As much as they wanted to leave, Zeon seemed determined that they stay. He looked at Kaley. "Put it on, then envision a different look for someone and they will change."

"Will it put me in a princess gown?" Her joke didn't make Tanek or Sojee smile. When she put the mask up to her face, it slid on like it was part of her skin. "Can you see it?"

"No," Zeon said. "Now look at someone and imagine them being different." His hand indicated anyone in the big room.

Sojee was scowling at her, impatient, ready to leave. "Maybe I should imagine the true look of a person." In her mind he was like a giant Viking warrior about to head into battle.

Seconds later, Tanek gasped.

Sojee had changed to having a gray beard and tied-back gray hair. He was shirtless, but had a heavy, fur-lined leather strap over one shoulder. The other shoulder was heavily tattooed. There was a thick leather belt about his waist that held several knives. Big wool trousers went to his knees, stopping at tall leather boots with thick soles. In both hands were axes with curved blades.

Sojee looked down at himself in shock and Zeon motioned to the mirror. Sojee stared at himself, then turned to Kaley. "Is this the way you see me?"

"More or less." She wasn't sure if that was good or bad.

Sojee bent and kissed her forehead. "I am pleased."

They all laughed, then turned to look at Tanek. It was his turn to be transformed.

He took a step back. "No. I'm fine the way I am."

"Try with a stranger," Zeon said to Kaley. "Perhaps change him into an Earth costume that is less…" He looked at Sojee, and was unable to describe his look of fierce warrior.

Kaley turned to a very handsome guard. "I'll try a tuxedo." She imagined the garment but nothing happened. Then Sojee let out a loud laugh and she turned.

Tanek had on the outfit of a seventeenth-century Highlander. He wore a green-and-brown kilt, tall wool socks and brogues. A dark green jacket with brass buttons was crisscrossed with a full armory of weapons.

Tanek looked down at the kilt in disgust. "You have dressed me as a woman."

Four of the guards about the room were female. Kaley looked at them. "Does he look like a woman to you?"

The women repressed smiles as they shook their heads. He was far, far from appearing to be female.

Sojee pushed Tanek toward the mirror.

As Tanek stared at his reflection, he shrugged. "Perhaps it has some merit. The buttons have swans on them." He looked at Zeon. "Who can use that mask?"

"Whoever possesses it. Would you like to try?"

"He'll change us all into swans," Kaley said.

"All right," Zeon said, "let's see if you two are connected."

"Do you need proof?" Sojee said. "They can't bear to be apart."

"Not true." Tanek held out his hand.

The mask was easy to remove and she put it in Tanek's hand but he didn't put it on. They turned at Sojee's growl of disappointment. He was back to his normal clothes. "I liked it," he muttered.

"Kaley," Zeon said, "imagine yourself wearing something beautiful. The favorite garment you've ever seen."

"That's easy. Something from a Jane Austen movie. Very romantic."

"Good," Zeon said, "now put it into the mind of Tanek and see if the information transfers."

As Tanek slipped on the mask, Kaley brought up images of a long, loose, white cotton gown embroidered with snowdrops. Very ladylike and genteel.

Tanek was looking at her. The mask had blended so well on his face that she couldn't see it, but then she hadn't been able to feel it on her own face.

She waited but nothing happened. It looked like there was no thought transfer or that Tanek couldn't make the mask work. It was only when she looked at the men's silent, wide-eyed expressions that she went to the mirror.

She *was* wearing the Jane Austen dress she'd imagined—only it was less than half sized. The bodice was cut so low most of her breasts were exposed. The skirt barely covered her crotch. The fabric clung like it had been spray-painted on—and she had on nothing underneath.

She whirled on Tanek. "You bastard!"

"Is...uh..." Zeon started. "Is that the dress you imagined?"

"It has little flowers on it. I sensed those clearly." Tanek was grinning broadly.

"Fix this!" she said.

He gave a sigh of sadness, then suddenly, she was back in her cotton trousers and long-sleeve T-shirt.

"Give me that mask! I'm going to put you in fishnets and heels."

Smiling, Tanek removed the mask and held it out to her.

But Zeon took it. "I believe you both need practice. The mask is my gift to you." He paused. "There may come a time when a disguise will be useful."

Tanek and Sojee nodded in understanding.

"My turn first," Kaley said, and took the mask.

The big doors opened and the woman in the hall escorted them to a beautiful room with couches and chairs. One wall was covered with mirrors. She turned to Tanek. "I'm going to change you into Mr. Darcy. Or maybe into Frankenstein's monster."

"Can you?" he taunted, an eyebrow raised.

She slipped on the mask and put him in the tiny trunks of an Olympic swimmer.

Behind them, just outside in the hallway, Sojee and Zeon watched. "They're practicing *un*dressing rather than dressing." Sojee looked at Zeon seriously. "What do you foresee if we go to Pithan?"

"Someone is blocking me from seeing much. There is a young woman. She's angry and bitter. She believes she was cheated out of what is rightfully hers."

"That would be Aradella."

"Beware of her. She will cause problems." He looked into the room. "Tanek is quite handsome, isn't he? Power and vast riches tempt even the strongest of men."

"And women."

"Yes, but not Kaley. She is—" Zeon's eyes widened as he looked up at Sojee. They'd already seen that it was his *I have a vision* look. "Does she know about you?"

"She has no idea and I don't want her to be told."

"I think she'll be pleased," Zeon said.

"I hope so." Sojee glanced into the room. "I'd like to try my hand with that mask. Do you think I can connect with my—? With Kaley?"

"I would imagine so." Smiling, Zeon stepped back. "The horses will be ready at sundown."

Sojee snorted. "And you have given the children a toy to occupy them until the time that *you* have chosen."

Zeon's laugh could be heard echoing as he walked away.

28

The climb up the steepest part of the mountain wasn't easy. They didn't go far before they were above the tree line. Surrounding them was rock covered in snow and ice. Making their way through it with only moonlight was scary and dangerous.

The horses—sturdy, hairy creatures—plodded along, heads down against the wind. When Kaley looked back, she saw Sojee walking, his hands holding the reins of his horse and the one carrying Nessa. The prince looked so miserable, she almost felt sorry for him.

Just as Sojee took care of Nessa, Tanek looked after Kaley. When her horse struggled on a narrow, crumbling piece of the old path, Tanek dismounted and guided the horses through.

As Zeon had foreseen, they reached the top just as the sun was rising.

They halted near a stone overhang that blocked the worst of the wind, and Tanek motioned for Kaley to dismount. Sojee handed her the reins to the horses, including the one holding Nessa. The men didn't speak but she knew she was to wait.

She led the animals back against the stone as far as she could. When Nessa began to complain, she gave him a look to shut up. He got down and they stood under the rock formation. Kaley kept the animals calm. Arit was in a specially made pouch on Tanek's saddle, while Tibby was at Kaley's feet. The snow had stopped coming down but the air was thick with fog. They waited in silence.

Within minutes, the sound of steel against steel rang out. She tried not to remember the deep scars on the men's faces. The men Tanek and Sojee were facing were victors in the cutting games. They were ruthless and practiced at combat.

When the battle seemed to go on and on, she pulled the Ruger out of her pocket and loaded it. "Stay here!" she ordered Nessa, then she scurried up the hill, rocks falling down behind her. When she got to the top, through the haze, she was surprised to see a wide, flat surface. It was as though someone had blasted away the tip of the mountain.

The four men were still fighting, and in the background, she saw Mekos chained to a stake embedded in the ground.

The men were in close combat and moving about rapidly. There was no way she could shoot without the risk of hitting the wrong person.

A movement caught her eye. In the sky, still far away, she saw six griffins with riders. It was a backup army and they were approaching fast!

Kaley knew she couldn't hit a person but she could cause a distraction. She shot three rounds into the air. The kidnappers were so startled at the sound that they dropped their defense. In a flash, Sojee and Tanek took them out. Kaley looked away as heads rolled across the ground.

Sojee broke the chains holding Mekos and he threw himself onto his father. Their feet left the ground, soaring in relief and happiness.

"I wanted to help you get Nessa," Mekos was saying. "I wanted to do something good."

Kaley pointed to the sky to show Sojee the big animals approaching. They needed to leave *now!*

When a strong gust of wind blew the last of the fog away, Kaley gasped. She was standing on a huge *X*. To the side, she saw an old rubber wheel. "This is a helicopter pad," she whispered, then screamed, "We have to go!"

Sojee didn't move. He stood there watching the griffins and riders get closer. "We can't outrun them," he said. "It's Queen Olina."

Tanek and Mekos came forward to stand by Sojee and Kaley. They stood close together as they watched the griffins land.

On the largest animal sat a woman. She was at least six feet tall, and she looked like she could fight any three men. She had on a golden breastplate and loose trousers that appeared to be reinforced with chain mail. There was no doubt she was the queen Kaley had heard spoken of with dread.

"Where is the prince?" she demanded. Her voice was easily heard through the cold air.

Sojee stepped forward. "He is with us."

Olina looked at the man on the griffin next to her. "Take them." The five guardsmen slid to the ground.

"No," Sojee said.

Olina gave him a look of disgust, then spoke to the guard. "Leave that one." She meant Sojee. "I have enough trouble with relatives."

Sojee took a step closer, with a look of threat. None of them were harmed.

She looked exasperated. "They killed two of my men and they've caused me a lot of trouble. They're just a swansman and a boy. They don't matter." When Sojee didn't relent, the queen looked at Kaley and sneered. "And what are *you?*"

Kaley was thinking, *A real live Evil Queen.* Obviously, they were better on a printed page than in life. She straightened her shoulders. "I am a storyteller."

When everyone looked blank, Sojee spoke up. "She's from Earth. She doesn't belong to any order."

"Then of what use is she?" Queen Olina asked them.

Kaley didn't know if her idea would work, but she figured that between her and Tanek, it might. She looked at the eagle head of the closest griffin. "Help us!" she said.

Tanek understood. He and Mekos began to talk to the animals in their swan language.

The griffins reacted quickly. Screaming loud enough to injure eardrums, they reared up on their powerful lion legs and opened their giant wings. The majestic animals flew away, leaving their mounts behind.

Queen Olina's griffin also reacted. She struggled to control the animal and to hang on. It took minutes but she got it to stop trying to throw her off.

Everyone had been watching the griffins so intently that no one had seen a guard go down the mountainside. He returned with the whimpering, terrified Nessa tied with a rope around his neck. The guard pushed him to land at the foot of Olina's griffin.

Nessa looked up in fear at being so near to one of the crushingly big feet. The claws were by his head.

Queen Olina gave Sojee a look of triumph. "I'll take him with me." She turned to her guard. "Dispose of all of them." Sojee stepped forward, sword raised.

Suddenly, Kaley heard a sound that she knew well. They all looked up. "That's a helicopter," she said. The gun was inside her pocket, her hand on it, ready to use if the queen's orders were acted on. She withdrew the pistol. "If I hit the blades, I may be able to bring it down."

Sojee shook his head. "No! Whatever that thing is, it's from

Empyrea." His tone said that meant it was untouchable. No shooting was allowed.

The chopper was quieter than an Earth one, and it produced less wind. Kaley glanced at the others. Tanek, Sojee and Mekos didn't appear to have ever seen one, but Queen Olina, her five guards and Prince Nessa weren't shocked. *What kind of world is this?* Kaley again wondered. Part primitive and part space travel.

They were silent as the helicopter landed precisely on the X painted on the flat surface. The engine was cut off and two people got out. The pilot stayed in the cockpit.

The first person to get down was a woman. She was tall and slim and had extraordinary blue eyes. She wore a long dark robe that seemed to glisten in the early light. She wasn't young but she looked fit and intelligent—and in charge. Kaley wouldn't be surprised to be told the woman was the ruler of the whole planet. Whoever she was, Kaley felt that she'd seen her before. In a book of fairy tales?

Behind her was a…a person. Its delicate-looking skin was a dark cream color and it wore a sort of tunic over leggings. It had a pleasant face, not pretty or ugly, with straight brown hair to its ears. It didn't so much as glance at Queen Olina and her guards, or at Nessa. Instead, it was staring at the four as though seeing something that wasn't real.

It was Queen Olina who spoke first, her tone sweet. "Greetings, Vian. It's good to see you again, but there's no need for you to get involved in this."

Kaley looked at the others. Everyone was looking at this woman in awe, as though awaiting an order. Except for Tanek. He was staring at her as though he might draw his sword. "She outranks a *queen*?" she asked Sojee, but he didn't reply.

Queen Olina continued. "I came to get Prince Nessa to take him to the lovely Princess Aradella, but they tried to trade him for a swanherder's son." She gave a sneer at Tanek. "They thought their disguise would allow them to steal all the riches of Pithan."

Flat-out lies, Kaley thought. Oddly, the truth necklace didn't get hot. But then, it hadn't worked on Garen, and Queen Olina was related to him.

The woman, Vian, looked at Sojee. "Why was this done?"

"It was a mix-up in identity," he said. "Young Mekos was riding Prince Nessa's dragon, and the guards mistook them, as the boys do look alike."

The woman didn't so much as glance at Nessa but instead, looked at Mekos. Her eyes went up and down him, as though evaluating him. "I can see how that would happen."

Kaley coughed to cover a laugh. It looked like the woman was a true diplomat. It's a wonder the truth necklace didn't get hot.

Vian looked at the queen. "So take the prince and leave."

Anger filled Queen Olina's face. "They killed my guards. They must be punished."

"I would imagine that it was a fair fight of a man rescuing his son." Vian looked at Sojee. "Is this true?"

"Yes, it is. The guards refused to release the boy." As he spoke, Sojee kept his head slightly bowed.

Kaley had never seen such reverence before. Did this Empyrean woman have the power of life and death?

Sojee stood up straighter. "We must take Prince Nessa to his father. Princess Aradella can't see him looking like this. And I'm sure the king will want to send a gift of appreciation to Queen Olina for having found the prince."

Vian looked at the queen. "The prince will return bearing gifts for you and for the woman he is to marry. Is that satisfactory?"

Olina visibly gritted her teeth. There was only one answer she could give. "Yes."

Obviously, the queen was lying. She wasn't happy at not being allowed to have people killed.

Vian turned to Queen Olina. "Now that it is settled, you may leave."

The queen looked like she was repressing rage. "He will not move. Nor for my men."

Kaley didn't know what she meant, but then realized she was referring to the griffins. The one the queen was on seemed to be immobile and the other five were in the distance, perched on a protruding rock. They seemed to be waiting for something.

For the first time, Vian looked directly at Tanek. It was a look so intense that it made Kaley's hair stand on end. She took a step toward him, as though in protection, but Sojee gave a slight shake of his head. No. She was to stay where she was.

After a long moment, Vian said to Tanek, "Release them."

Kaley was surprised. Could Tanek control the half-bird creatures with his mind? She hadn't seen that before!

Tanek gave a curt nod, then looked at the griffins in the distance. Immediately, they flew forward and landed beside the queen. When he walked to them, the queen's griffin bowed its head to him.

"I'm impressed," Kaley said under her breath.

Tanek turned to her and motioned his head for her to join him.

"Hug a griffin? Oh yeah." She hurried to it and snuggled the big head in her arms. The growl of disgust from the queen, sitting high above, didn't bother Kaley.

Everyone was silent while Kaley went from one animal to the next, saying soothing, loving words to each one. When she finally stepped back, the queen and her guards were staring at her, but Kaley was used to being considered odd and strange.

Vian gave a nod to Queen Olina, then she and her guards flew away.

"Now what?" Kaley whispered to Sojee, but he didn't answer. The four of them were together on one side, Vian and the androgynous Empyrean standing in front of the silent helicopter. As always, Nessa kept himself separate.

Vian looked at Sojee. "Take them away." It was the quiet command of someone who was used to being obeyed.

Sojee gave a quick nod and they headed to the path down the mountain, toward the horses.

But Tanek didn't move.

"He isn't going to fight her, is he?" Kaley asked.

"No," Sojee said. "Far from it."

"What gift is my father to give to that odious woman?" Nessa whined. "*I* should be given a gift. *I* am making the sacrifice. *I*—"

Kaley didn't listen, but turned back to see Tanek and the woman staring at each other.

"I like her," Mekos said.

"Who is she?" Kaley asked.

"One of the Seven." Mekos seemed shocked that Kaley didn't know that.

"That's where I've seen her before. Her picture was in the schoolroom."

"Come on!" Sojee said impatiently. "Let's get down this blasted mountain before it starts snowing again."

"We can't leave Tanek!" Kaley said.

Sojee smiled. "He'll be here soon. What food was packed for us?"

Tanek knew he should have felt curiosity at seeing this woman so close, but he didn't. She had dark hair like his, eyes like his. But he felt only anger. "You with your machine could have taken my son to safety at any time." When he saw that she showed no emotion, he drew in his breath. "You *wanted* my son to be kidnapped so he was brought *here*?" His voice told of his disgust and shock. When she made no reply, he softened. "You allowed it so you could see him?" He hesitated. "Or me?"

"I would not be so frivolous." When he returned to anger, she seemed to relent. Her voice lowered and he knew she was trust-

ing him with information that she didn't want known. "I needed
to interfere in Olina's plan and I knew Mekos would be safe."

"You could not have been *sure* and you changed nothing! That
worthless prince is still to marry the princess."

"Perhaps." She put out her hand as though she was going to
touch him, but abruptly withdrew it. "You look like Wellan."
Her sentimentality left her quickly. "You three *must* go to Pithan and take Mekos with you." She hesitated. "But you should
know that he's involved in something there."

"I do know. He hides his bow and thinks I see nothing. I
won't let him—"

"No! Do not stop him." She took a breath. "It's *you* who is
causing concern. You're watched closely. You—" She cut off as
though she was afraid to say more.

"Do you spy on me? On *us*?" When she made no reply, Tanek
turned away. He could see that it was no use trying to get information from her. But he halted and looked back. "What part
does Kaley have in this? She knows nothing."

"She knows more than you think." Vian smiled. "When she
looks at you, she makes me remember the night your father and
I made you. Has he told you of that night?"

"Certainly not!" Tanek was waiting for her to answer his
question.

She stopped smiling. "Try to remember. You will understand
more if you remember. You can now."

"Remember what?" he asked, but the Empyrean standing
behind her said something and she turned away. The person's
voice was neither high nor low, and Tanek had never heard the
language it used. He'd not seen many of them as they rarely
left Empyrea.

Vian looked back at Tanek. "You are to touch arms." When
he hesitated, she said, "It will be to your advantage."

Tentatively, he held out his arm and the creature put a long,
thin finger on the chip that was under Tanek's skin. There was

a slight electrical charge and for a moment he felt a sense of awe flowing through him—and Tanek was the object of that feeling. The Empyrean walked away, smiling, seeming to be happy. For the first time, Tanek looked at Vian without hostility. "Why do you not look like them?"

Her answer was a smile. "They cannot reproduce. Only a few of us can."

He looked at her in surprise. "Do I have siblings?"

"No." She looked toward the path that led down the mountain. "The others will have questions for you."

"And I'll have no answers. Not ones that I can tell."

"You sound like your father. He always wanted to know *more*." She paused as though remembering something good. "I must go now." She took a moment to look at him, then turned and went to the helicopter.

He stood there watching the big machine take off. Vian looked straight ahead, but the pale face of the Empyrean smiled at Tanek, then lifted a hand as though to say goodbye.

When it was quiet, Tanek started to go down. Out of the rocks came Kaley's tabor. It had been hiding and watching. "Did you stay here to protect me?" he asked in the swan language that animals loved. "Can you protect me from all the questions Kaley is going to ask? Can you keep that farken necklace of hers from telling on me when I do answer?"

Tibby just looked up at him.

"You're on her side, aren't you?" Tanek took a breath. "I guess I could tell her the truth." He smiled. "Would the truth make her stay or send her running? Will she go to my mother and shout, 'Take me home!'?" Tanek sighed. "Can either of us live without Kaley? No, I think not."

He continued down the mountainside.

29

Kaley was anxiously waiting for Tanek to join them. Nessa was berating Mekos. "Where's my dragon? What have you done with him? I'll have my father put you to death." In between his demands and threats, he was whistling for his dragon but Perus didn't appear.

"That creature saw his chance to get away and took it," Sojee said. Both his and Mekos's only concern was eating the delicious food Zeon had packed for them. When Tanek appeared at the top of the path, Sojee snorted. "Now you can quit worrying. Have some of this food."

Kaley and Tanek exchanged looks and he nodded at her silent question. Yes, he was all right.

He went to Kaley and held out his hand. She knew what he wanted. She put the Ruger into his hand. He checked to see if it was loaded, then wrapped it in a shirt and put it inside his own pack.

"Let's go," Tanek said to them.

Unfortunately, there were more people than there were horses, so Sojee and Tanek took turns walking down the steep slope. The temperature began to drop and the horses wanting to get home to their warm stalls made them speed up.

At the discomfort of it all, Nessa wailed, "Where's my dragon to fly me away?" in such a pitiful tone that they agreed with him.

"I bet he could carry us all," Sojee said over the wind that was starting to rise. They were below the tree line and dense forest surrounded them. The jackets Zeon had given them weren't enough against the growing cold.

It was hours before they reached the site where they'd left Zeon's castle. The tired, hungry horses pulled on the reins, refusing to go any farther. The riders dismounted, looking up at the sky. It was growing dark; a storm was approaching.

Tanek held up his arms to help Kaley down.

"We should stay with Zeon tonight," she said. "We're too tired to go on."

Tanek motioned for her to follow him into the trees. There was the pillar with the flying bird on top. It looked like the one they'd seen from their bedroom window, but there was no castle nearby.

"He must have several of them," Kaley said.

"No," Tanek said. "That's the same bird." He motioned around the wooded area. "His castle has vanished, or can't be seen. Is this like your stories?"

She thought of the illusion Garen had created. Was Zeon a witch as well as a predictor of the future?

"I'm afraid so. *Brigadoon* comes to mind. We—" The sound of a car horn made her stop talking. She and Tanek hurried toward the sound.

A little way down the path stood Sojee, grinning broadly. Behind him was the Jeep they'd left on the trail coming up. Mekos was walking around the vehicle while Nessa was blasting the horn. "Looks like Zeon brought it here."

"A truly wonderful man," Kaley said. "I hope he filled the

tank. I'll get it started and you'll experience the joy of an American car heater." She got in the front and started the engine. It did have a full tank. "Thank you," she whispered, then put the heater on. She looked in the mirror as the men freed the horses of the packs and put everything in the back. The horses ran into the forest, seeming to know where they were going.

Sojee opened the back door for Mekos; Sojee got in and pulled Nessa beside him. The boys nestled on each side of the big man like chicks in a nest.

Tanek opened the driver's door. "I'll drive," he said to Kaley.

"You don't know how."

"I watched you do it. If I see a hole, I'm to put a wheel in it."

"I'm on another planet but I have to put up with woman driver jokes?"

Tanek just looked at her.

Kaley moved across the console to get in the passenger seat. As Tanek had said, he'd watched her enough that he could drive.

"I remember doing this." He seemed to be puzzled by the memory. He glanced in the rearview mirror. The boys and Sojee were already asleep. Arit had been released from her pouch and was now asleep and nestled in Sojee's beard. Tibby was flattened on the floorboard at Kaley's feet. "She said I would remember."

The car was warm and Kaley wanted to put her head down and sleep, but she knew from experience that a tired driver in a car full of sleeping people was dangerous. "Have you ever done anything like that before? I mean with the two guards."

"No. Sojee seemed quite experienced, but my grandfather made sure I knew certain skills."

"That makes sense. Haver's son had been killed and his home destroyed. He wanted to be sure you could protect yourself." Kaley was quiet, looking out the windshield and remembering what she'd seen in the cave. Now wasn't the time to tell him of that. There were snowflakes and the heater was working hard.

"You aren't going to ask me who the woman on the mountain is?" he asked.

"I figure you'll tell me if you want me to know." She felt quite virtuous saying that.

"Then I'll wait."

"You'll what?" she half yelled, then lowered her voice. "That woman looked at you and Mekos like she wanted to carry you off to Rapunzel's tower. Why did a woman who is higher ranking than a *queen* show up for *you*?"

"That's better." He was repressing laughter. "Sure you don't want to wait until I decide I want you to know?"

"I'm going to get Zeon's mask and turn you into a frog."

"Arit told me you like to kiss frogs."

"Stop it! Who is she?"

"She is my mother." He easily missed a deep pothole in the road. "And before you ask, today is the first time I've ever spoken to her. I've seen her riding past, but I've never been so close to her."

"That's who she looks like! It's *you*. When I saw her picture in the schoolhouse I knew she looked like someone. So your father and she...?"

"Yes. It's just as I said. She came to his quarters one night." Tanek shrugged as though it meant nothing.

"You just left out that she is one of the Seven!"

Again, he shrugged.

"So the very high-ranking woman seduced your father just like Toki seduced you? Looks like you swansmen just have to exist and women come to you."

Tanek laughed. "Men in the Order of Swans are known to be fertile."

She looked at him. "You men do make good children." She was speaking of Tanek as well as Mekos.

"Thank you," he said. "Any more questions?"

"Did she show up to rescue us or did she have some other

reason?" Kaley held up the pendant of her necklace, letting him know he couldn't lie.

"She wants us—you, me, Sojee and Mekos—to take the prince to Pithan." His face grew serious. "She didn't say so, but I think that if you do this, she'll see that you get passage home."

Kaley didn't say anything, just looked out the window. The snow had stopped falling and the trees were greener. She turned down the heater. "Why is the marriage important?"

"There's unrest on Pithan. The queen probably thinks that uniting the Old and New Royals will calm them down."

"But you don't believe that. *Your* goal is to get to Empyrea."

"Yes." All humor was gone from him.

"Do you think there are more fairy tales on Pithan?"

"I have no idea. I didn't know there were any on this island." He glanced at her. "I'm sure you already have enough to write a good story for your teacher."

"A dissertation," she said softly. *Going home*, she thought. Right now Earth seemed far away. Should she go to another island and risk dangers such as being chained in a dungeon? Or should she sit down in the king's luxurious house and say she wasn't leaving until she had a ticket home?

"Tell me a story," he said. "I'd like to hear one about a young man who runs around a village with a bow and arrow and constantly risks being killed."

Kaley laughed too loud, then looked back at the sleeping people. "You know!"

"I do. So tell me *that* story."

"Once upon a time," she began, then told of the love between Robin and Marian, and the sheriff who was determined to kill the young man.

Kaley was on her third story—Tanek loved *Peter Pan*, and Arit woke up to listen—when they reached the Mist. She braced herself to go through it. It was possible that it had become the solid wall that they'd first seen.

Tanek checked the mirror, saw that everyone was still asleep, then went down a side road and turned off the engine. When he got out, Kaley did, too. He opened the back doors to the Jeep. "It's time they woke up." He started walking up a hill and Kaley followed him. At the top, out of sight of the car, he sat down and she sat beside him.

The landscape was beautiful, really and truly like a fairy tale. The sun was low in the sky and the colors of pink and purple, blue and green, were gorgeous. Below them, right up to the Mist wall, people were walking about. Men carried old-fashioned scythes over their shoulders, and women were carrying baskets laden with perfect produce.

"It's beautiful," Kaley said. When Tanek didn't reply, she looked at him. His face was serious.

He nodded to the Mist. "My guess is that they'll be waiting for us on the other side. Daln will be there for sure and maybe the king's guards. They'll want to take the prince back."

"Think your mother told them?"

He looked startled at her words. "*My mother.* It's hard to think of her as that. But yes, between her and Zeon and Jobi, I think that now everyone knows where we are."

"If they do, maybe they know what you've been talking to men about. About how you want to go to Empyrea. On my planet, we call it an insurrection."

"Here, we call it *probable death.*"

She couldn't think of anything to say. The thought of him in some to-the-death battle made her feel sick.

He took a breath as though he had something important to say. "What if you're offered a passage to Earth?"

She thought of her home, of her father and grandparents, of the little stone cottage she'd imagined as being in her future. But she also thought of Tanek's family's homestead, and swans and a dodo and a baby elephant. And she remembered Garen's offer of one year of training.

"Will you go with us to Pithan?" he asked, then said, "Will you stay with *us*?"

She didn't have an answer to that and she wanted to lighten the mood. "You mean stay with *you*? To help with the swans and the feathers?" She was teasing.

Tanek didn't smile. "What is it that angers you about my offer?"

"It doesn't. It's just that... Well, *love*! That's what. There was no mention of that. What we've been through together is like a lifetime. We've come to know each other. I need more than just a roof over my head. It's not— Oh hell! I don't know what I mean. We'd better go back. They'll wonder where we are." She started to get up, but he didn't move.

"I offer to share my life with you, to give you a home and protection, but you want *words*? Is this common on Earth?"

"Yes, but it's different. We want it *all*. Love is very important to us."

"By *love* do you mean that when I think of rebuilding my grandfather's home that I imagine you with me? That when I think of my future children, they have your brown eyes? That I see all of us surrounded by animals because you attract them? Do these things have to do with your *love*?"

"Yes," she whispered.

"I don't want part of you. I want all of you. Forever. I'm asking you to choose me over everyone and everything else. In my order, we mate for life. If he dies, she remates, but if she dies, he remains alone."

She didn't know how to explain to him what she felt. Everything was strange to her. "What if I asked you to return to Earth with me?"

He didn't hesitate. "Yes. I will go."

She didn't need the necklace to know he was telling the truth.

He'd leave his son, his family, his plans for the future, Arit, all of it, to stay with her. But was she willing to do the same? "I don't know," she said honestly.

He gave a nod, then stood up, held his hand out to her, and she took it. She started to turn away, but he didn't release her hand. Instead, he drew her into his arms and kissed her.

It wasn't a kiss between two separate beings, but a union. A blending. It was a transfer of emotions, of feelings—and of lust. Kaley felt herself melting into his big body, becoming one with him. Touching him so intimately let her see deep into him. She felt his fear of what was to come, but it was overridden by his determination to go ahead no matter what the risks were. She felt his deep love for his son—and for her. *Soulmate* was a weak term to describe what he sent to her. She felt his loneliness, his years of belief that he would always be alone, that he'd never find someone who could fulfill what he needed.

In turn, Kaley knew she was sending him her longing for her home planet, for her family, for a life that she understood, a place where she belonged. She sent him her fears of committing to a man who was so different from her. His ability to command animals with his mind, his determination to change his entire world, excited her, but it also frightened her. She was terrified that if she agreed to stay with him that she'd come to regret it. Would her longing for her home overtake her?

She wasn't aware of when they began to soar higher and higher into the air, but the bonding and the lightness of her body, of his lips on hers, made her body relax in a way she'd never felt before.

At last, he broke the kiss but held her tightly. She looked over his shoulder. They were several feet in the air and hovering.

"Do you understand now?" he asked.

Nodding, she buried her face against his neck.

"And I understand you," he said. "We will wait."

She kept her eyes closed, his skin against her face, and they slowly went back to the ground.

Abruptly, he stepped away from her, his eyes twinkling. "Yes, I'm sure Pithan has your fairy tales, and it's an island full of women. How dangerous could it be?"

She looked at him in astonishment. "Thousands of women alone and I'm with a bunch of fertile men? They'll be worse than those Cinderella girls. *I* will be the one to lose body parts. And I want to say that I do *not* like you reading my mind."

He smiled. "But you are all right that I reveal myself to you?"

"Well, yes. But that's different."

He laughed. "Let's go through the Mist and face them. After we deliver the prince to that poor girl, we can talk again."

He took her hand and they went down the hill.

30

When they were back in the Jeep and approached the Mist, not only was it soft, but it parted for them to drive through.

"Like the Red Sea," Kaley said.

"Is that one of your fairy tales?"

"Not quite. It's—" She broke off because ahead of them was an extravaganza. In the background was The Museum of Earth, but they could hardly see it for the strings of glowing lanterns and the pots of colored fire that blazed up and down. There were a lot of people, all of them wearing robes of dazzling colors with sparkling jewels.

When they got through the Mist in the Jeep, the people stepped aside. On a big, shiny throne sat little King Aramus. Behind him was the tall, thin man with the bejeweled headdress. He held a long staff topped with a jewel the size of a doorknob.

Nessa leaned forward. "It's my father. He's come here to kill the lot of you." He said it with no emotion, but as fact. The prince sat back in the seat, a satisfied smile on his face.

"Do you think he's right?" Kaley asked Tanek.

"No idea," Tanek said.

"I don't like this," Sojee said. "Drive past them."

Tanek looked tempted to do that, but the Jeep sputtered. They were out of gas.

"Zeon did this!" Kaley said. "He calculated every ounce versus every mile!"

The car rolled to a stop and people came forward to open the doors. There was a delay as they didn't know how to operate the handles.

Tanek took Kaley's hand and held it until they got out of the car. The king's guards closely surrounded them, and Tanek and Sojee began to remove their weapons.

While they were busy, Kaley looked around, and she saw Garen. He was to the right of the king and wearing a long, dark green robe. When Kaley saw him, he opened it. His left arm was in a sling. He smiled at her in a way that let her know that he didn't blame her for what happened.

She couldn't help feeling glad to see someone she knew. She looked away, but she clearly remembered what he'd offered her.

Nessa, with his head high, arrogantly walked through the crowd to his father. He bent to kiss him, but the king brushed his son away and told him to go to the side.

The three men and Kaley were escorted to stand before the king.

"You are dressed as before," King Aramus said, meaning their dirty, worn clothing. He seemed to think he'd made a great joke, but when no one laughed, the man behind him waved his hand. Everyone gave a polite chuckle.

Satisfied at his humor, the king looked at Tanek. "You were successful."

Tanek gave a nod, but said nothing.

The king looked excited, and his eyes didn't leave Tanek. "Since you've been away, things have changed. I have very good news for you." He waited for Tanek to speak but when he didn't, the king gave a slight frown.

He motioned to the tall man. "Fahir has been meeting with Queen Olina and finalizing the marriage for Princess Aradella."

Nessa leaned forward. "That princess is so ugly and I don't want—"

King Aramus put his hand up for silence, then he spoke loudly. "It has been revealed that Tanek Beyhan is the son of one of the Seven."

The crowd gasped.

"How do you know that?" Tanek spat out in anger.

Three guards drew swords.

The king was unperturbed. "It doesn't matter. Queen Olina has decided she'd rather have that attachment." He looked at Tanek, his eyes showing his great happiness. "You, Tanek, are to marry Princess Aradella. Someday, you will be the King of Pithan."

With a gasp of shock, Kaley turned to Tanek.

"No," Tanek said. "I will not do that."

The king looked confused. "You'll be *king*! Did you not understand me?"

"No," Tanek repeated.

"*I* am to marry that ugly girl," Nessa said. "*I* am to be the king."

Aramus sneered. "You would bankrupt the place."

When Tanek turned away, as though he was going to leave, things happened quickly. Three guards grabbed him. Fahir left the king's side. He stood before Tanek and locked eyes with him. In seconds, Tanek quit moving. He stood still while his arms were pulled behind him and a rope tied just above his elbows. Tanek looked as though he was in a trance.

"What are you doing?" Kaley yelled. She made a lunge but Mekos caught her. He pulled her away while Sojee stayed beside Tanek.

"Let me go!" Kaley said to Mekos, and struggled against him. He led them to a covered pavilion at the side.

"Let Sojee talk to them."

"I can talk, too. I can—" She cut off as she looked at Mekos. There were tears in his eyes. He was as upset as she was. Kaley calmed down. "What does this mean?"

"My father will be king." He said it as though he was speaking of an execution.

"Did his mother arrange this?"

"I don't know," Mekos said. "I don't know her. Grandpapá told me of her. She is very powerful. She…" He couldn't speak.

Kaley put her arms around him as he tried to hold back tears. "How can we stop this?"

"We can't. The wedding will be tomorrow. Papá is under a spell. He can't see or hear us. He won't even know he's being married." Mekos took a breath. "This is very bad. He is the Order of Swans. Once he is mated, it can never be broken. He won't—" Mekos looked at her with sympathy. "He will not love this woman but he will never betray her."

Kaley knew what he was saying. Tanek would not be allowed to marry a woman he loved, not even if the marriage ended by death. "In fairy tales, arranged marriages always end in true love."

Behind them came shouts and a clash of swords. "Sojee!" Kaley said. "What's happening?"

Mekos lifted his head and she could see his pointed ears twitch. "The king is saying that Nessa is to marry *two* of Sojee's beautiful daughters. It's compensation for losing Princess Aradella and not becoming king."

Kaley didn't react to the news of daughters. "Sojee will kill Nessa and maybe the king."

Mekos listened. "No. Sojee has been subdued. He is tied up." Mekos drew in his breath. "Fahir is coming for us."

Kaley felt panic. Mekos was the grandson of a Seven. Was something planned for him? "Go!" she ordered. "Find your relatives in the forest and stay with them. Out of sight."

Mekos barely gave a nod before silently slipping away.

Kaley turned and braced herself to face a man who could cast spells on people. The guards parted to let him through.

He was much taller than Kaley and close-up, he was older than he appeared. His eyes were small and very dark, and he homed in on her like a lighthouse beam.

Kaley looked back at him, but she felt nothing.

He stopped glaring and looked surprised, then he gave what passed for a smile. "Earthling," he said in his deep voice.

"I am. Tanek doesn't want to be king. He'd be very bad at it. He just wants to be with his birds."

This idea seemed to amuse him. "If he is put in power, he'll be able to reunite the islands. It's what he wants to do, is it not?"

She wasn't going to answer that. She'd always been concerned that people would find out what Tanek was trying to do.

Suddenly, hundreds, maybe thousands, of birds started screeching. It was obvious that they were protesting Tanek's capture.

With a frown, Fahir hit his staff on the ground. The jewel on the top sent out a bright ray of light, but the birds continued their deafening noise. Kaley blinked at the light, but she didn't look away from the man. He raised an eyebrow at her, as though considering how to overcome her.

Softly, Kaley said, "Be quiet." Instantly, the birds stopped squawking, which created an eerie silence.

For a brief second, Fahir showed shock, then he genuinely smiled. He gave a slight bow to her, as though in tribute. "Who has trained you?"

She wasn't going to give him any information. "I want you to release Tanek."

"No," he said. "I cannot. The order comes from higher than me, higher than Aramus." He cocked his head at her. "You want him for yourself, don't you? Do you choose your own pleasure over the peace and prosperity of thousands? Queen Olina is an evil woman. She rules by torture and cruelty. I think you've seen that young Tanek has goodness in his heart. He has been willing to risk his life with his attempts to reunite the islands. He will be a good king and he will benefit everyone."

Fahir paused, his face softening. "If Tanek continues what he's doing in secret, with no royal backing, he'll be charged and executed. But if he marries the princess, he can continue his work in safety—and he will succeed. He'll bring peace to many people. Which do you choose for him?"

Kaley stepped back from the man, feeling like her blood was draining from her body. "This isn't how fairy tales are supposed to end."

"I don't know your meaning. King Aramus will send you back to your planet, if that's what you want. Or..." He hesitated. "I believe you've been offered something else. An apprenticeship? That vision is not clear to me. If that does not appeal to you, I can offer you employment as a maid to Princess Aradella. You will see Tanek every day. Perhaps that will be enough for you."

He raised his eyebrows. "Tell me what your choice is and I will make it happen. You have until the sun sets." With another nod, he turned and walked away.

Garen was standing there. "You controlled the birds." His eyes were wide in awe. "You have greater power than I thought. Let me teach you how to use it." He held out his hand to her.

After a moment's hesitation, she took it.

★ ★ ★ ★ ★